Out West

OUT

Books by
Jack Schaefer

WEST

AN ANTHOLOGY OF STORIES

edited by JACK SCHAEFER

BOSTON

HOUGHTON MIFFLIN COMPANY

19 The Riverside Press Cambridge 5 5

"An Indian Divorce," and "Tricks in All Trades," from *Native Tales of New Mexico* by Frank Applegate. Copyright, 1932, by J. B. Lippincott Company.

"The Vengeance of Padre Arroyo," from *The Splendid Idle Forties* by Gertrude Atherton. Copyright, 1902, 1930, by Gertrude Atherton, published by J. B. Lippincott Company.

"The Walking Woman," from *Lost Borders* by Mary Austin. Copyright, 1909, by Harper & Brothers. Copyright, 1937, by Kenneth Chapman, Harry E. Mera, and Mary C. Wheelwright.

"Stewed Beans," and "Papago Wedding," from *One-Smoke Stories* by Mary Austin. Copyright, 1934, by Mary Austin, published by Houghton Mifflin Company.

"The Buck in the Hills," by Walter Van Tilburg Clark. Copyright, 1943, by Walter Van Tilburg Clark. Used by permission of Random House, Inc.

"Bank Holiday," from *Mojave* by Edwin Corle, published by Liveright Publishing Corporation. Copyright, 1934, by Edwin Corle.

"The Bride Comes to Yellow Sky," by Stephen Crane. From *Stephen Crane: An Omnibus* edited by Robert Wooster Stallman, by permission of Alfred A. Knopf, Inc.

"The Cloud Puncher," by William Cunningham. Copyright, 1934, by William Cunningham.

"Old Man Isbell's Wife," by H. L. Davis. Copyright, 1929, by H. L. Davis. Reprinted from *Team Bells Woke Me, and Other Stories* by H. L. Davis, by permission of William Morrow and Company, Inc.

"Death in October," from *The Happy Man*. Copyright, 1943, by Robert Easton, by permission of The Viking Press, Inc.

"Mister Death and the Redheaded Woman," by Helen Eustis. Copyright, 1950, by the Curtis Publishing Company under the title "The Rider on the Pale Horse."

"Spoil the Child," by Howard Fast. Copyright, 1938, by the Curtis Publishing Company.

"The Scarecrow," by Vardis Fisher. Copyright, 1934, by Harold G. Merriam.

"Lone Wolf's Old Guard," by Hamlin Garland. Copyright, 1923, by Isabel Garland Lord and Constance Garland Doyle.

"A Question of Blood," from *By Rope and Lead* by Ernest Haycox. Copyright, 1937, by Ernest Haycox, by permission of Little, Brown and Company.

The Riverside Press
CAMBRIDGE • MASSACHUSETTS
PRINTED IN THE U.S.A.

Editor's Note

The western story is one of the oldest staples of American publishing. For nearly a century almost every major house handling general fiction lists has regularly carried westerns. The reprint trade and now the paper-back original lean heavily on them. For generations Americans have read western stories, have liked western stories. Past performance, underlined by present, suggests they will continue to do the same as long as the nuclear-fissionists let them.

Well, of course, so runs the usual explanation, western stories are escape fiction and escape fiction is always popular. . . .

True enough, while not all western stories are escape fiction, the overpowering majority of them are. But there are many kinds of escape fiction and these rise and fall in favor while western stories continue undisturbed. There are endless other areas of time and place — all of history and all of geography and with the advent of science fiction the farthest imagined past and future and the infinite stretches of celestial galaxies — into which readers can escape through the printed word. And yet, with a consistency that would be astonishing if it were not long since a commonplace, Americans like to escape into the American West, into the West of the western story.

Perhaps that is because the western story, in its most usual forms, represents the American version of the ever appealing oldest of man's legends about himself, that of the sun-god hero, the all-conquering valiant who strides through dangers undaunted, righting wrongs, defeating villains, rescuing the fair and the weak and the helpless — and the western story does this in terms of the common man, in simple symbols close to natural experience, the derring-do of democracy, depicting ordinary everyday men, not armored knights or plumed fancy-sword gentlemen, the products of aristocratic caste systems, but ordinary men who might be you and me or

vii

our next-door neighbors gone a-pioneering, doing with shovel or axe
or gun in hand their feats of courage and hardihood.

But why worry too much about a reason or reasons. Let the
scholars and critics do that. No American need, in a sense, justify
himself by giving a reason for "escaping" through the printed word
into the West of the western story. After all, the desire to "escape"
into the West is an old ingrained American motive. . . .

As a matter of fact, escape into the West in actual physical terms
of expansion and opportunity and the freeing of men's energies was
for nearly three centuries a major part of the American dream-being-
made-reality as the waves of migration lapped ever westward from
the Atlantic coast until they met the backwash from the Pacific in
the Rocky Mountains. And the West of the western story caught
that dream, that social process, that historical movement, at its full
and final peak.

In the perspective of history all of America has been the West.
Once the West was the region just past the first sprinkling of settlements along the eastern seaboard. Again it was the upward slopes
of the Appalachians, then the valleys spilling down beyond, then
the borderland of the Mississippi. These were the Wests of their
times, so known and so calling to the people facing toward them.
You can argue, with cause, that the James Fenimore Coopers and
the William Gilmore Simmses, writing of them, were writing westerns. But the true West of the western story leaps past them. The
West of the western story is the trans-Mississippi West.

Think of this in terms of the popular symbol of the western story,
the hired-man-on-horseback who has galloped around the globe to
become a part of the national and the world folklore — the cowboy. In origin, even in name, he was a product of the earlier Wests,
of what is now the East. The first cattle ranches of America, marked
by the distinguishing features of open-range grazing, horseback
herding, annual roundups and drives to market, were developed in
Georgia and the Carolinas before cotton became king there and
somewhat later in Pennsylvania and Ohio and Kentucky and on
into Indiana and Illinois. The cowboy, so named, the man on horseback working cattle, was once well known in those areas. Cattle
drives, often with large herds traveling hundreds of miles over difficult terrain, were a regular practice. Yet few people other than spe-
cializing historians know that now. The cowboy did not come into
his own until he crossed the Mississippi.

What did he find there? . . . he and the others, the explorers, the trappers, the mountain men, the traders, the miners, the freighters, the homesteaders, the town settlers . . . .

First, and the basic conditioning quality: space, bigness, open bigness.

There was bigness east of the Mississippi, unsettled bigness too in its time. But the bigness east of the Mississippi was primarily forested bigness and forested bigness is a bigness that loses itself in many smallnesses, that closes in around those who challenge it. They must fight for space against the forest. Movement is slow and difficult. Until roads are cleared men must follow the twisting water courses instead of striking straight across country. They grow accustomed to small holdings, to close horizons, to relative narrowness in daily living. The bigness of vast rolling treeless plains and of mountains that rise sheer above the timberline is a bigness that opens outward, that beckons onward, that feeds the imagination with visions of unlimited possibilities.

The bigness beyond the Mississippi was primarily open bigness, beckoning bigness — and also a violent, raw, capricious bigness: extremes of topography and climate beyond those of the east, the highest and lowest areas of the entire nation, the hottest and the coldest, the flattest and the ruggedest, the driest and the wettest; sudden extremes of change, mountains rising abruptly out of level plains, flash floods in the midst of desert, rivers impassable one month and dry beds the next, plagues, rockslides, droughts, earthquakes . . . a huge, almost continental expanse wrought of distance, always distance, and rock and sand and sagebrush and buffalo sod and not enough water and too much water that would be subdued in part and in places but not wholly tamed.

Bigness, open bigness, violent bigness — and the right moment in history.

This West, in the nineteenth century, the favored but not the exclusive years of the western story, was acquired and held without serious opposition by the new United States, by a growing, sprawling, careless, laissez-faire democracy that had as yet no thought of immigration quotas, that made only sporadic and feeble efforts at orderly development of its public lands, and whose people regarded those lands as wide open to exploitation. Across the Atlantic in Europe population pressures were increasing, revolutions were making in men's minds and in actual fact. The machine age, with its accelerating advances in transportation, communication, tools,

weapons, was struggling into birth. . . . When the waves of settlement broke past the Mississippi, slow at first, then faster and after
the Civil War with driving impetus, they took with them people
from all the eastern states, people from all the European countries,
people of many diverse cultures, people of many diverse social and
economic classes and backgrounds. These people were not primi-
tives developing slowly with a land. They were people of assorted
civilized traditions swarming into a new land to be developed —
into a land in which settlement constantly outran law and the only
major restraints upon them were self-imposed or forced by physical
fact. They were an amazingly various people pushing forward into
a wide arena of freedom of action, confronted with conditions that
drew upon their full personal resources, that compelled them again
and again to act as independent individuals. They were repeating
the familiar American pioneering pattern of the previous Wests —
on a vaster scale, at a faster pace, at a further remove from old ties
and old traditions, matching themselves against the open and violent bigness of the West of the western story. And the effect was to
unleash human energies, to throw into sharp focus human strengths
and weaknesses, as rarely before in any period or place and never
before on any comparable scale.

The cowboy and those before him and with him and after him
were taking part in one of the great movements of human history. . . .

The record of that movement is certainly not one of sustained
achievement and success. It carried with it not only the strong, the
adventurous, the capable, but also the weak, the misfits, the outcasts, the forever restless, the hope-ridden incompetents. Death and
frustration and defeat are written often and large across it. Eastern
ideas collided with hard natural fact: for example, the idea that
one hundred sixty acres of land should support a homesteading
family — land that in much of this West, high and arid, should
never have known the crop-farmer's plow. The very lavishness of
the seeming unlimited possibilities encouraged wasteful exploitation, constant migration: the beaver are inexhaustible, so trap out
this region and move on; the buffalo are inexhaustible, so slaughter
this herd for the hides alone and move on; rip up the sod with no
thought of future dust bowls and hope for a few bumper crops and
after a few failures try again just over the horizon; tear out the gold
here and move on to the next creek. . . . And this West itself was

not merely indifferent, difficult, imposing hardship conditions; it was often actively hostile. It sometimes yielded rewards — and more often denied them. It is littered with the remains of towns that boomed and busted, others that busted without ever booming, and with the remnants of ranches and mines and homesteads where hopes were blasted. It tested and tempered its people more rigorously than did the earlier Wests except in rare and beginning and isolated instances — and it often continued to do so long after the initial fact of settlement was accomplished. Those who became its own, who stood up to the tempering and accepted the imprint, developed a toughness and resiliency of mind, an ability to face success or failure with the same essential vitality of spirit.

That is a point not to be missed. . . . If there is any one distinctive quality of the western story in its many variations, that quality is a pervasive vitality — a vitality not of action alone but of spirit behind the action. Even the hurried hack writer of quickie cowboy yarns, however unashamed and stereotyped and escapist, catches something of that spirit, for it is implicit in the material. It is the unmistakable reflection of what emerges from the authentic records of the people of the West of the western story — a healthy, forward-facing attitude toward life.

Yes, the opening up of the West of the western story was one of the great movements of human history. Those who chronicle it, even only in escape fiction, even not knowing or caring just what they are doing, even interested only in the stock cardboard characters and the same repetitious situations, are dealing with material of inherent and immediate appeal.

That appeal has been both an asset and a liability.

It has been an asset in that it has given the western story a solid and enduring popularity. It has been a liability in that it has discouraged good work, serious work, with that material. Western stories need not be well done to be reasonably safe publishing risks. A surprising number of readers who cherish high standards in regard to other types of writing are willing to condone, even to welcome, western stories of minimum average competence. There probably has been more poor writing, more cheap commercial writing, more surface-skimming escapist writing, in the field of the western story than in any other definable field of American fiction. Mediocre output has so dominated the field that the general impression, in a critical sense, has been that the whole merits little attention. Many a writer who might have brought distinction to it has deliberately shied away under the influence of that prevalent attitude.

All things change and perhaps this in time too. A check of the fiction lists of the last few years will suggest that gradually more and more writers of serious and artistic as opposed to straight commercial intent are turning to the western story. Their instinct is sound.

For there in the records of that great westward movement is vital and stimulating material whose scope and variety compass almost every human problem, almost every aspect of human experience. Despite the long past of the western story and the millions upon millions of words that have been written in the field, the dramatic and significant possibilities of that material have as yet scarcely been touched. Except in instances rare in proportion to the tremendous output, the surface only has been scratched. The rich and rewarding subsoil is there for deeper cultivation. The writer who has anything of value to say to his fellow men can say it as effectively in the western story as in any other form of fiction — and with a vitality and a directness of appeal that nowadays is missing from most.

These serious writers who are turning to the western story are, in sum, following anew an old American custom. They are "escaping" into the West . . . into a realm that still holds the old magic of beckoning opportunity and the unleashing of creative energies.

And as they look back through the multitudinous western stories already written, they discover that a few discerning pioneers have been there before them . . . that always, through the years, a few good writers, sometimes standing out, sometimes obscured in the crowded crush of the mediocre, have done good work in the field.

The foregoing is not offered as a shock-proof discussion of the western story. It represents merely the recurrent thoughts of a reader and writer of western stories pinned down with some attempt at cohesion in the process of assembling this anthology. And the stories here collected are not offered as the "best" in any critical sense whatever. They are simply stories encountered through many years of leisurely reading in the western field that, for one reason and another, have remained fixed in my memory. There are other stories I would have liked to include but could not for reasons of length, difficulty of obtaining releases. . . . No doubt there are many more which ought to be here and are not because they have not yet come my reading way.

These are arranged by authors, alphabetically, for convenience of reference. The purpose in assembling them is to present some good reading — good reading that will give a reasonably representative cross section of good work that has been done and is being done in short story form in the field — and to point the path for those interested to more of the same. Judgments that creep into the comments are strictly my own.

JACK SCHAEFER

Watertown, Connecticut

Contents

Out West

An Indian Divorce

FRANK G. APPLEGATE

I know very little about Frank Applegate except that he was associated with Mary Austin and others in reviving and preserving the old Spanish colonial arts and crafts of the Southwest and that he had a deep understanding of the Spanish and Indian cultures there. He may have written more, but I am acquainted with only two of his books, written in the early 1930's and illustrated with some of his own paintings: Indian Stories from the Pueblos and Native Tales of New Mexico The two brief stories here, in which the vital chuckle predominates, are from the Native Tales.

THE HOPI INDIAN FAMILY is matriarchal in its descent, and the children and the house and all it contains belong to the woman. It is the Hopi wife's prerogative to divorce her husband at any time if she happens to take a dislike to him, or a fancy for another; but a man, according to Hopi custom, cannot so easily abandon his wife. Thus a Hopi man remains his wife's husband solely on her sufferance, and his married life is to all intents and purposes a continuous probation in his wife's home. Coming there at any time and finding his other pair of moccasins on the doorstep outside the locked door is, to a Hopi, tantamount to a decree of divorce, in which case the dismissed husband returns to his mother's house, which remains his home throughout life, even though his mother may be dead and his sister living there with her husband. A divorce, however, takes place rarely among the Hopis from the fact that the Hopi maidens choose their husbands and, as long as the men are adequate to the marital perquisites expected of them, the wives are usually contented.

In the Hopi town of Sichumopovi, sky high on its rocky mesa, a Hopi man called George Cloud-mountain and his wife, Betty Thistledown (given names donated by school teachers), sat in Betty's house airing marital grievances. George started things by accusing Betty of having appropriated the tidbits of fat from the mutton stew which she had set before him. This accusation would not seem unreasonable, if the size of Betty's girth were taken into consideration. But he added to the insult by insinuation that her piki corn-bread was not as thin as that his mother used to make. Now this was a radical move on George's part, for it brought his mother-in-law into the affair, and soon things were so lively for George that he was compelled to make a hasty exit, in which his other pair of shoes passed him on the way out, which, it must be admitted, is a record in speed for a decree of divorce to be granted.

George gathered up his moccasins and betook himself to his mother's house, not at all displeased with himself when he contemplated the outcome of his recent bit of strategy. Up to this time George had been the most docile and complaisant of husbands, but recently he had come under the influence of a pair of dark eyes, much enlarged, peering through the thick lenses of large, celluloid-rimmed glasses. This person of the third party who completed the domestic triangle and constituted the cause of George's defection from marital constancy was Geraldine Dawn Light (name Geraldine contributed by sentimental schoolteacher), twenty years old, and recently returned from the Government Indian finishing school at Riverside, California, and now living at her mother's house near that of George's mother. There George saw a good deal of her as she sat indolently before the house watching her mother model beautiful pottery and, at the same time, giving her mother a great deal of concern, for she disdained to soil her fingers with the potter's clay or to manipulate the family mealing stones, thus driving her mother to distraction over the question of acquiring a suitable son-in-law. Geraldine, while at school, had been allowed to do some housework for one of the teachers at Riverside, and had been rewarded with part of the cast-off wardrobe of the teacher and a little money which she had judiciously laid out for the finer touches of her toilet. But Geraldine had kept her eyes open in California and had found out that there were ways of acquiring a husband beside breaking a back grinding corn with a small hand-mealing stone to please an overcritical, prospective mother-in-law, which is the usual Hopi custom for procuring a husband. Geraldine's mother was a fundamentalist, as far as Hopi customs were concerned, and was terribly scandalized by her daughter's modern scientific method. George, however, was somewhat of an artist, and the exotic always attracted him, so that he was easily fascinated. The aggressive perfume Geraldine unsparingly used met him while he was still a hundred feet away and as he ostentatiously busied himself before his mother's door, he marveled at Geraldine's frizzed bob, her large black-rimmed glasses, her thin, pink, silk waist, and the extremely short, checkered sports skirt which she wore, but most of all he marveled at the sheer silk hose, that, as far as he could tell, with all of his peeking and peering and craning of neck, covered Geraldine's whole body, except her hands and face, with a silken skin. Added to all this lure, Geraldine had acquired an interesting pallor and a thin, flat chest by living in the much lower altitude of California and in a manner different from that for which many ages of heredity had fitted her body, so that compared to her, George's full-bosomed, overplump wife, in her extremely modest calico and with her unalluring ways, appeared to him quite unattractive. Thus deeply entangled, George had teased his wife Betty into giving him a Hopi divorce, so that he might be on his way to eventually solve the tantalizing mystery of the silken hose. But George having in mind a decree recently issued by the Indian Agent, that Indians must be more legal in dealing with the marital relations, knew that he could not remarry solely on the strength of a Hopi divorce, so the next week he persuaded his recent wife, Betty Thistledown, to accompany him to the agency at Keams to see about securing a white man's divorce.

When the couple appeared before the agent and told him what they desired, he asked them if they had ever been married white man's way by the Sunday preacher, and on their answering, "No, Indian way," he told them that to be able to get a white man's divorce they must also be married his way. This seemed logical to the Indian couple, so with their consent the agent called in the missionary and the marriage ceremony was forthwith performed. When that was over, the agent turned to the newly wed pair and said, "Now, if you two still want a divorce, you must go down to Winslow and give a white lawyer two hundred dollars to get it for you, since only a white lawyer knows how. Then if he can show the court that there are good reasons why you two should have a divorce, you may get it in six months, or two years, or so, in which case you will be free to go your separate ways and remarry whom you please." George, however, who had inherited his racial forbears' urge for economy, had ceased listening to the agent after he had made mention of the two hundred dollars, and before the agent had entirely left off speaking, he had seized Betty firmly and possessively by one arm and was pushing her toward the waiting wagon. As he hurried her along he remarked, apparently to no one in particular, that it was not at all surprising to him that so many white men continued to live with such women who were unattractive.

As the rewedded Hopi couple rode the long way across the desert to the sky city, Betty Thistledown said to George Cloud-mountain very contritely, "I know I eat much of the mutton fat when I cook, also much corn-bread so I get fat, but I do not do it to make you lean, but to make you proud of me, George, so jealous Hopis won't say you are a no good Indian and starve your wife all the time." George pondered this wisdom for an hour or more as they rode along through the hot sun, and then remarked that as for him he never did like mutton fat and also that he liked his piki corn-bread a little thicker than his mother used to make it, anyway.

Tricks in All Trades

FRANK G. APPLEGATE

In the little villages of the Rio Arriba country of Spanish-Colonial New Mexico, there are still current many tales of Padre Martinez and some of the cunning means he used in providing for himself a fat living in places where other, less wordly and less self-seeking, priests had languished in emaciation.

There can be no doubt but that Padre Martinez regarded his parish and its *visitas* more in the light of sources of revenue than as spiritual responsibilities, and, being himself a native of the land, he was exceedingly and intimately acquainted with all the little failings, prejudices, likes and dislikes of his charges and could turn them all to his own account.

However, there was one village, a *visita*, under his ministration that baffled all his efforts, as it had those of his predecessors, to wring from it a revenue commensurate with its manifest prosperity. In fact, San José was a problem to the rather covetous padre and seemingly an insoluble one. It was like a thorn in his side, for although this *placita* of San José was situated at the edge of Las Angosturas, the most fertile strip of land along the Rio Grande, and had just above it mesas covered with some of the richest pasturage in New Mexico for the large flocks of the villagers, yet with all his most diligent efforts, the padre could extract from the inhabitants of this village not one *centavo* beyond the absolutely lowest

minimum fees for marriages and christenings and, for the dead,
barely sufficient masses that they might but get one foot through
the door leading from purgatory to paradise; the living leaving it to
their heaven-bound relatives to push the balance of their way
through.

Whenever the padre partook of a meal in the village, which happened whenever he made a visit there, he was served only the ordinary fare of the people, *frijoles*, chilli, *tortillos* and stewed mutton,
and never a single fowl in the whole *placita* lost even a feather
because of his coming. There was never a question of freewill
giving and even when the padre delivered one of his most eloquent
and carefully prepared sermons, the people merely appeared unin-
terested, bored, and a little sullen.

Now, Padre Martinez didn't like this situation, for although he
was full of energy and did not mind laboring in the vineyard of
the Lord, yet he felt that since he labored so diligently, there should
be at least a little harvest to gather in. However, he was not one
to give up and call a field infertile merely because the methods he
had employed heretofore had failed of results; yet try as he would,
he could, by himself, discover no solution to his difficulty. Finally,
in his perplexity, he sought out the sacristan of the church, who
was also the village storekeeper, to see whether that one could give
him any worth-while advice on how to loosen the pursestrings of
his communicants. At the same time he laid his problem frankly
and openly before the sacristan. The latter listened carefully to
the priest's tale of frustration and then, considering seriously for
a moment, said: "Padre, if you will allow me the privilege of
speaking to you as one business man to another and not like a
penitent to his confessor, I can tell you exactly what the trouble
is. The people of San José don't like your sermons."

"They don't like my sermons!" exclaimed the padre excitedly.
"Why, I preach the very best sermons I can think of to make them
turn out their pockets."

"Perhaps so," returned the sacristan, "but you don't get any
results, do you? Well, I'll tell you why you don't, and you can
see for yourself if I'm not right. Now you stand up there in the
pulpit with your back to San José, who stands there on the altar,
and do you ever mention the name of San José? No, you don't.
You stand up there and preach a lot of stuff about the Virgin and
what she can do, and all about Jesus and what he can do, and
talk about confessions and sins. Then you tell us that San Antonio

let women alone and San Francisco preached to the birds and fish and God knows what other nonsense, because none of us ever listen to a bit of it. Now what about San José? He just stands there behind you neglected while you preach away and he is the only saint any one of us here knows well or cares about. He's our *santo* and he's the only one of them all who ever takes the least trouble to do anything for us. We think he is the best saint that ever lived, for he never even got mad when his wife had a child that wasn't his. All the other saints are just wasted, as far as we are concerned, and it only makes us angry to hear their names mentioned. We want to hear only about San José."

A hint was sufficient to a man with the perspicacity of Padre Martinez and, since his next visit to the village of San José would coincide with the fiesta of San José, he took measures accordingly. On that day, as was always customary, all the people flocked to the church, but it could be plainly seen that they did so haltingly and reluctantly and from a sense of duty, rather than from any desire on their part to be there. Padre Martinez, however, was getting ready for a harvest and when the time for the sermon arrived, he made preparations accordingly. Taking the sacristan aside and giving him a box of ample size, he told him to circulate it through the congregation while the preaching was going on so that if any felt touched by his sermon, they could give then and there, while in the mood. Then in place of mounting into the pulpit himself, he turned briskly, and seizing the image of San José, placed it there in his stead. At this action, his congregation began to appear interested for the first time since he had begun to minister to them. Standing beside the pulpit, Padre Martinez began to speak. "Perhaps all of you wonder why I have placed San José in the pulpit. It is because San José, without speaking, can preach a better sermon than I. This is the fiesta of that greatest of saints, San José. San José is the best saint of them all, for San José is ready to help everyone. This San José here is the best San José in New Mexico to work miracles. San Antonio is not so good as San José. San Francisco is not so good as San José. San José didn't bother to preach to birds and fish. San José does things for you people. You men should pray to San José. San José will give you more sheep. You women should pray to San José. San José will keep your husbands safe. You girls should pray to San José. San José will find you a good man. You boys should pray to San José. San José will give you a beautiful wife. San José will help you all through purgatory. San José will help you all into heaven. San José—" Just at this point the sacristan, who up to this time had been very much occupied, came running up to the padre and, pulling him by the sleeve, whispered in his ear: "For God's sake, padre, the box is full of money now, so don't say San José again or tomorrow there won't be a single cent left in the whole *placita*, and remember, I'm the storekeeper here."

The Vengeance of Padre Arroyo

GERTRUDE ATHERTON

Gertrude Atherton breezed on to write more novels than perhaps any one person should and to take most of America and much of Europe as her province, though she did show some favoritism for her native California. But back at the beginning she took time out from novel-writing to do a series of western stories, tales of old California, published in 1902 as The Splendid Idle Forties. There are some flashes of gold in the pages. This piece is the one solid nugget. O. Henry never turned a neater trick. And this, unlike most of his, has more than a trick.

PILAR, from her little window just above the high wall surrounding the big adobe house set apart for the women neophytes of the Mission of Santa Ines, watched, morning and evening, for Andreo, as he came and went from the rancheria. The old women kept the girls busy, spinning, weaving, sewing; but age nods and youth is crafty. The tall young Indian who was renowned as the best hunts- man of all the neophytes, and who supplied Padre Arroyo's table with deer and quail, never failed to keep his ardent eyes fixed upon the grating so long as it lay within the line of his vision. One day he went to Padre Arroyo and told him that Pilar was the prettiest girl behind the wall — the prettiest girl in all the Californias — and that she should be his wife. But the kind stern old padre shook his head.

"You are both too young. Wait another year, my son, and if thou art still in the same mind, thou shalt have her."

Andreo dared to make no protest, but he asked permission to prepare a home for his bride. The padre gave it willingly, and the young Indian began to make the big adobes, the bright red tiles. At the end of a month he had built him a cabin among the willows of the rancheria, a little apart from the others; he was in love, and association with his fellows was distasteful. When the cabin was builded his impatience slipped from its curb, and once more he besought the priest to allow him to marry.

Padre Arroyo was sunning himself on the corridor of the mission, shivering in his heavy brown robes, for the day was cold.

"Orion," he said sternly — he called all his neophytes after the celebrities of earlier days, regardless of the names given them at the font — "have I not told thee thou must wait a year? Do not be impatient, my son. She will keep. Women are like apples: when they are too young, they set the teeth on edge; when ripe and mellow, they please every sense; when they wither and turn brown, it is time to fall from the tree into a hole. Now go and shoot a deer for Sunday: the good padres from San Luis Obispo and Santa Barbara are coming to dine with me."

Andreo, dejected, left the padre. As he passed Pilar's window and saw a pair of wistful black eyes behind the grating, his heart took fire. No one was within sight. By a series of signs he made his lady understand that he would place a note beneath a certain adobe in the wall.

Pilar, as she went to and fro under the fruit trees in the garden, or sat on the long corridor weaving baskets, watched that adobe with fascinated eyes. She knew that Andreo was tunnelling it, and one day a tiny hole proclaimed that his work was accomplished. But how to get the note? The old women's eyes were very sharp when the girls were in front of the gratings. Then the civilizing development of Christianity upon the heathen intellect triumphantly asserted itself. Pilar, too, conceived a brilliant scheme. That night the padre, who encouraged any evidence of industry, no matter how eccentric, gave her a little garden of her own — a patch where she could raise sweet peas and Castilian roses.

"That is well, that is well, my Nausicaa," he said, stroking her smoky braids. "Go cut the slips and plant them where thou wilt. I will send thee a package of sweet pea seeds."

Pilar spent every spare hour bending over her "patch"; and the hole, at first no bigger than a pin's point, was larger at each setting of the sun behind the mountain. The old women, scolding on the corridor, called to her not to forget vespers.

On the third evening, kneeling on the damp ground, she drew from the little tunnel in the adobe a thin slip of wood covered with the labour of sleepless nights. She hid it in her smock — that first of California's love-letters — then ran with shaking knees and prostrated herself before the altar. That night the moon streamed through her grating, and she deciphered the fact that Andreo had loosened eight adobes above her garden, and would await her every midnight.

Pilar sat up in bed and glanced about the room with terrified delight. It took her but a moment to decide the question; love had kept her awake too many nights. The neophytes were asleep; as they turned now and again, their narrow beds of hide, suspended from the ceiling, swung too gently to awaken them. The old women snored loudly. Pilar slipped from her bed and looked through the grating. Andreo was there, the dignity and repose of primeval man in his bearing. She waved her hand and pointed downward to the wall; then, throwing on the long coarse gray smock that was her only garment, crept from the room and down the stair. The door was protected against hostile tribes by a heavy iron bar, but Pilar's small hands were hard and strong, and in a moment she stood over the adobes which had crushed her roses and sweet peas.

As she crawled through the opening, Andreo took her hand bashfully, for they had never spoken. "Come," he said; "we must be far away before dawn."

They stole past the long mission, crossing themselves as they glanced askance at the ghostly row of pillars; past the guard-house, where the sentries slept at their post; past the rancheria; then, springing upon a waiting mustang, dashed down the valley. Pilar had never been on a horse before, and she clung in terror to Andreo, who bestrode the unsaddled beast as easily as a cloud rides the wind. His arm held her closely, fear vanished, and she enjoyed the novel sensation. Glancing over Andreo's shoulder she watched the mass of brown and white buildings, the winding river, fade into the mountain. Then they began to ascend an almost perpendicular steep. The horse followed a narrow trail; the crowding trees and shrubs clutched the blankets and smocks of the riders; after a time trail and scene grew white; the snow lay on the heights.

"Where do we go?" she asked.

"To Zaca Lake, on the very top of the mountain, miles above us. No one has ever been there but myself. Often I have shot deer and birds beside it. They never will find us there."

The red sun rose over the mountains of the east. The crystal moon sank in the west. Andreo sprang from the weary mustang and carried Pilar to the lake.

A sheet of water, round as a whirlpool but calm and silver, lay amidst the sweeping willows and pine-forested peaks. The snow glittered beneath the trees, but a canoe was on the lake, a hut on the marge.

II

Padre Arroyo tramped up and down the corridor, smiting his hands together. The Indians bowed lower than usual, as they passed, and hastened their steps. The soldiers scoured the country for the bold violators of mission law. No one asked Padre Arroyo what he would do with the sinners, but all knew that punishment would be sharp and summary: the men hoped that Andreo's mustang had carried him beyond its reach; the girls, horrified as they were, wept and prayed in secret for Pilar.

A week later, in the early morning, Padre Arroyo sat on the corridor. The mission stood on a plateau overlooking a long valley forked and sparkled by the broad river. The valley was planted thick with olive trees, and their silver leaves glittered in the rising sun. The mountain peaks about and beyond were white with snow, but the great red poppies blossomed at their feet. The padre, exiled from the luxury and society of his dear Spain, never tired of the prospect: he loved his mission children, but he loved Nature more.

Suddenly he leaned forward on his staff and lifted the heavy brown hood of his habit from his ear. Down the road winding from the eastern mountains came the echo of galloping footfalls. He rose expectantly and waddled out upon the plaza, shading his eyes with his hand. A half-dozen soldiers, riding closely about a horse bestridden by a stalwart young Indian supporting a woman, were rapidly approaching the mission. The padre returned to his seat and awaited their coming.

The soldiers escorted the culprits to the corridor; two held the horse while they descended, then led it away, and Andreo and Pilar were alone with the priest. The bridegroom placed his arm about the bride and looked defiantly at Padre Arroyo, but Pilar drew her long hair about her face and locked her hands together.

Padre Arroyo folded his arms and regarded them with lowered brows, a sneer on his mouth.

"I have new names for you both," he said, in his thickest voice. "Antony, I hope thou hast enjoyed thy honeymoon. Cleopatra, I hope thy little toes did not get frost-bitten. You both look as if food had been scarce. And your garments have gone in good part to clothe the brambles, I infer. It is too bad you could not wait a year and love in your cabin at the rancheria, by a good fire, and with plenty of frijoles and tortillas in your stomachs." He dropped his sarcastic tone, and, rising to his feet, extended his right arm with a gesture of malediction. "Do you comprehend the enormity of your sin?" he shouted. "Have you not learned on your knees that the fires of hell are the rewards of unlawful love? Do you not know that even the year of sackcloth and ashes I shall impose here on earth will not save you from those flames a million times hotter than the mountain fire, than the roaring pits in which evil Indians torture one another? A hundred years of their scorching breath, of roasting flesh, for a week of love! Oh, God of my soul!"

Andreo looked somewhat staggered, but unrepentant. Pilar burst into loud sobs of terror.

The padre stared long and gloomily at the flags of the corridor. Then he raised his head and looked sadly at his lost sheep.

"My children," he said solemnly, "my heart is wrung for you. You have broken the laws of God and of the Holy Catholic Church, and the punishments thereof are awful. Can I do anything for you, excepting to pray? You shall have my prayers, my children. But that is not enough; I cannot — ay! I cannot endure the thought that you shall be damned. Perhaps" — again he stared meditatively at the stones, then, after an impressive silence, raised his eyes. "Heaven vouchsafes me an idea, my children. I will make your punishment here so bitter that Almighty God in His mercy will give you but a few years of purgatory after death. Come with me."

He turned and led the way slowly to the rear of the mission buildings. Andreo shuddered for the first time, and tightened his arm about Pilar's shaking body. He knew that they were to be locked in the dungeons. Pilar, almost fainting, shrank back as they reached the narrow spiral stair which led downward to the cells. "Ay! I shall die, my Andreo!" she cried. "Ay! my father, have mercy!"

"I cannot, my children," said the padre, sadly. "It is for the salvation of your souls."

"Mother of God! When shall I see thee again, my Pilar?" whispered Andreo. "But, ay! the memory of that week on the mountain will keep us both alive."

Padre Arroyo descended the stair and awaited them at its foot. Separating them, and taking each by the hand, he pushed Andreo ahead and dragged Pilar down the narrow passage. At its end he took a great bunch of keys from his pocket, and raising both hands commanded them to kneel. He said a long prayer in a loud monotonous voice which echoed and reëchoed down the dark hall and made Pilar shriek with terror. Then he fairly hurled the marriage ceremony at them, and made the couple repeat after him the responses. When it was over, "Arise," he said.

The poor things stumbled to their feet, and Andreo caught Pilar in a last embrace.

"Now bear your incarceration with fortitude, my children; and if you do not beat the air with your groans, I will let you out in a week. Do not hate your old father, for love alone makes him severe, but pray, pray, pray."

And then he locked them both in the same cell.

The Walking Woman

MARY AUSTIN

*E*verybody who talked with Mary Austin knew at once that there was greatness in her." That is the opening sentence of Carl Van Doren's introduction to a beautifully illustrated edition (1950) of her first book, first published in 1903, The Land of Little Rain. You can talk to Mary Austin now only through her books. But that talking too tells the same thing. It is impossible to read any book by Mary Austin and not know at once that there was greatness in her.

The Walking Woman is the last piece in a book called Lost Borders, published in 1909. That is not a book of stories, though it has stories in it. Like many things she wrote, it defies classification. Like everything she wrote, it is the work of the most original, the most stimulating writer the American Southwest has yet produced. The other two stories are from a little volume called One-Smoke Stories, published in 1934.

T HE FIRST TIME of my hearing of her was at Temblor. We had come all one day between blunt, whitish cliffs rising from mirage water, with a thick, pale wake of dust billowing from the wheels, all the dead wall of the foothills sliding and shimmering with heat, to learn that the Walking Woman had passed us somewhere in the dizzying dimness, going down to the Tulares on her own feet. We heard of her again in the Carrisal, and again at Adobe Station, where she had passed a week before the shearing, and at last I had a glimpse of her at the Eighteen-Mile House as I went hurriedly northward on the Mojave stage; and afterward sheep-herders at whose camps she slept, and cowboys at rodeos, told me as much of her way of life as they could understand. Like enough they told her as much of mine. That was very little. She was the Walking Woman, and no one knew her name, but because she was a sort of whom men speak respectfully, they called her to her face Mrs. Walker, and she answered to it if she was so inclined. She came and went about our western world on no discoverable errand, and whether she had some place of refuge where she lay by in the interim, or whether between her seldom, unaccountable appearances in our quarter she went on steadily walking, was never learned. She came and went, oftenest in a kind of muse of travel which the untrammeled space begets, or at rare intervals flooding wondrously with talk, never of herself, but of things she had known and seen. She must have seen some rare happenings, too — by report. She was at Maverick the time of the Big Snow, and at Tres Piños when they brought home the body of Morena; and if anybody could have told whether De Borba killed Mariana for spite or defence, it would have been she, only she could not be found when most wanted. She was at Tunawai at the time of the cloud-burst, and if she had cared for it could have known most desirable things of the ways of trail-making, burrow-habiting small things.

All of which should have made her worth meeting, though it was not, in fact, for such things I was wishful to meet her; and as it turned out, it was not of these things we talked when at last we came together. For one thing, she was a woman, not old, who had gone about alone in a country where the number of women is as one in fifteen. She had eaten and slept at the herders' camps, and laid by for days at one-man stations whose masters had no other touch of human kind than the passing of chance prospectors, or the halting of the tri-weekly stage. She had been set on her way by teamsters who lifted her out of white, hot desertness and put her down at the crossing of unnamed ways, days distant from any-where. And through all this she passed unarmed and unoffended. I had the best testimony to this, the witness of the men them-selves. I think they talked of it because they were so much surprised at it. It was not, on the whole, what they expected of themselves.

Well I understand that nature which wastes its borders with too eager burning, beyond which rim of desolation it flares forever quick and white, and have had some inkling of the isolating calm of a desire too high to stoop to satisfaction. But you could not think of these things pertaining to the Walking Woman; and if there were ever any truth in the exemption from offense residing in a frame of behavior called ladylike, it should have been inoperative here. What this really means is that you get no affront so long as your behavior in the estimate of the particular audience invites none. In the estimate of the particular audience — conduct which affords protection in Mayfair gets you no consideration in Maverick. And by no canon could it be considered ladylike to go about on your own feet, with a blanket and a black bag and almost no money in your purse, in and about the haunts of rude and solitary men.

There were other things that pointed the wish for a personal encounter with the Walking Woman. One of them was the contradiction of reports of her — as to whether she was comely, for example. Report said yes, and again, plain to the point of deformity. She had a twist to her face, some said; a hitch to one shoulder; they averred she limped as she walked. But by the distance she covered she should have been straight and young. As to sanity, equal incertitude. On the mere evidence of her way of life she was cracked; not quite broken, but unserviceable. Yet in her talk there was both wisdom and information, and the word she brought about trails and water-holes was as reliable as an Indian's.

By her own account she had begun by walking off an illness. There had been an invalid to be taken care of for years, leaving her at last broken in body, and with no recourse but her own feet to carry her out of that predicament. It seemed there had been, besides the death of her invalid, some other worrying affairs, upon which, and the nature of her illness, she was never quite clear, so that it might well have been an unsoundness of mind which drove her to the open, sobered and healed at last by the large soundness of nature. It must have been about that time that she lost her name. I am convinced that she never told it because she did not know it herself. She was the Walking Woman, and the country people called her Mrs. Walker. At the time I knew her, though she wore short hair and a man's boots, and had a fine down over all her face from exposure to the weather, she was perfectly sweet and sane.

I had met her occasionally at ranch-houses and road-stations, and had got as much acquaintance as the place allowed; but for the things I wished to know there wanted a time of leisure and isolation. And when the occasion came we talked altogether of other things.

It was at Warm Springs in the Little Antelope I came upon her in the heart of a clear forenoon. The spring lies off a mile from the main trail, and has the only trees about it known in that country. First you come upon a pool of waste full of weeds of a poisonous dark green, every reed ringed about the water-level with a muddy white incrustation. Then the three oaks appear staggering on the slope, and the spring sobs and blubbers below them in ashy-colored mud. All the hills of that country have the down plunge toward the desert and back abruptly toward the Sierra. The grass is thick and brittle and bleached straw-color toward the end of the season. As I rode up the swale of the spring I saw the Walking Woman sitting where the grass was deepest, with her black bag and blanket, which she carried on a stick, beside her. It was one of those days when the genius of talk flows as smoothly as the rivers of mirage through the blue hot desert morning.

You are not to suppose that in my report of a Borderer I give you the words only, but the full meaning of the speech. Very often the words are merely the punctuation of thought; rather, the crests of the long waves of inter-communicative silences. Yet the speech of the Walking Woman was fuller than most.

The best of our talk that day began in some dropped word of hers from which I inferred that she had had a child. I was surprised at that, and then wondered why I should have been surprised, for it is the most natural of all experiences to have children. I said something of that purport, and also that it was one of the perquisites of living I should be least willing to do without. And that led to the Walking Woman saying that there were three things which if you had known you could cut out all the rest, and they were good any way you got them, but best if, as in her case, they were related to and grew each one out of the others. It was while she talked that I decided that she really did have a twist to her face, a sort of natural warp or skew into which it fell when it was worn merely as a countenance, but which disappeared the moment it became the vehicle of thought or feeling.

The first of the experiences the Walking Woman had found most worth while had come to her in a sand-storm on the south slope of Tehachapi in a dateless spring. I judged it should have been about the time she began to find herself, after the period of worry and loss in which her wandering began. She had come, in a day pricked full of intimations of a storm, to the camp of Filon Geraud, whose companion shepherd had gone a three days' pasear to Mojave for supplies. Geraud was of great hardihood, red-blooded, of a full laughing eye, and an indubitable spark for women. It was the season of the year when there is a soft bloom on the days, but the nights are cowering cold and the lambs tender, not yet flockwise. At such times a sand-storm works incalculable disaster. The lift of the wind is so great that the whole surface of the ground appears to travel upon it slantwise, thinning out miles high in air. In the intolerable smother the lambs are lost from the ewes; neither dogs nor man make headway against it.

The morning flared through a horizon of yellow smudge, and by mid-forenoon the flock broke.

"There were but the two of us to deal with the trouble," said the Walking Woman. "Until that time I had not known how strong I was, nor how good it is to run when running is worth while. The flock travelled down the wind, the sand bit our faces; we called, and after a time heard the words broken and beaten small by the wind. But after a while we had not to call. All the time of our running in the yellow dusk of day and the black dark of night, I knew where Filon was. A flock-length away, I knew him. Feel? What should I feel? I knew. I ran with the flock and turned it this way and that as Filon would have.

"Such was the force of the wind that when we came together we held by one another and talked a little between pantings. We snatched and ate what we could as we ran. All that day and night until the next afternoon the camp kit was not out of the cayaques. But we held the flock. We herded them under a butte when the wind fell off a little, and the lambs sucked; when the storm rose they broke, but we kept upon their track and brought them to-gether again. At night the wind quieted, and we slept by turns; at least Filon slept. I lay on the ground when my turn was and beat with the storm. I was no more tired than the earth was. The sand filled in the creases of the blanket, and where I turned, dripped back upon the ground. But we saved the sheep. Some ewes there were that would not give down their milk because of the worry of the storm, and the lambs died. But we kept the flock together. And I was not tired."

The Walking Woman stretched out her arms and clasped herself, rocking in them as if she would have hugged the recollection to her breast.

"For you see," said she, "I worked with a man, without excusing, without any burden on me of looking or seeming. Not fiddling or fumbling as women work, and hoping it will all turn out for the best. It was not for Filon to ask, Can you, or Will you. He said, Do, and I did. And my work was good. We held the flock. And that," said the Walking Woman, the twist coming in her face again, "is one of the things that make you able to do without the others."

"Yes," I said; and then, "What others?"

"Oh," she said, as if it pricked her, "the looking and the seeming."

And I had not thought until that time that one who had the courage to be the Walking Woman would have cared! We sat and looked at the pattern of the thick crushed grass on the slope, wavering in the fierce noon like the waterings in the coat of a tranquil beast; the ache of a world-old bitterness sobbed and whispered in the spring. At last —

"It is by the looking and the seeming," said I, "that the opportunity finds you out."

"Filon found out," said the Walking Woman. She smiled; and went on from that to tell me how, when the wind went down about four o'clock and left the afternoon clear and tender, the flock began to feed, and they had out the kit from the cayaques, and cooked a meal. When it was over, and Filon had his pipe between his teeth, he came over from his side of the fire, of his own notion, and stretched himself on the ground beside her. Of his own notion. There was that in the way she said it that made it seem as if nothing of that sort had happened before to the Walking Woman, and for a moment I thought she was about to tell me of the things I wished to know; but she went on to say what Filon had said to her of her work with the flock. Obvious, kindly things, such as any man in sheer decency would have said, so that there must have something more gone with the words to make them so treasured of the Walking Woman.

"We were very comfortable," said she, "and not so tired as we expected to be. Filon leaned upon his elbow. I had not noticed until then how broad he was in the shoulders, and how strong in the arms. And we had saved the flock together. We felt that. There was something that said together, in the slope of his shoulders toward me. It was around his mouth and on the cheek high up under the shine of his eyes. And under the shine the look — the look that said, 'We are of one sort and one mind' — his eyes that were the color of the flat water in the toulares — do you know the look?"

"I know it."

"The wind was stopped and all the earth smelled of dust, and Filon understood very well that what I had done with him I could not have done so well with another. And the look — the look in the eyes — "

"Ah-ah — !"

I have always said, I will say again, I do not know why at this point the Walking Woman touched me. If it were merely a response to my unconscious throb of sympathy, or the unpremeditated way of her heart to declare that this, after all, was the best of all indispensable experiences; or if in some flash of forward vision, encompassing the unimpassioned years, the stir, the movement of tenderness were for me —but no; as often as I have thought of it, I have thought of a different reason, but no conclusive one, why the Walking Woman should have put out her hand and laid it on my arm.

"To work together, to love together," said the Walking Woman, withdrawing her hand again, "there you have two of the things; the other you know."

"The mouth at the breast," said I.

"The lips and the hands," said the Walking Woman. "The little, pushing hands and the small cry." There ensued a pause of fullest understanding, while the land before us swam in the noon, and a dove in the oaks behind the spring began to call. A little red fox came out of the hills and lapped delicately at the pool.

"I stayed with Filon until the fall," said she. "All that summer in the Sierras, until it was time to turn south on the trail. It was a good time, and longer than he could be expected to have loved one like me. And besides, I was no longer able to keep the trail. My baby was born in October."

Whatever more there was to say to this, the Walking Woman's hand said it, straying with remembering gesture to her breast. There are so many ways of loving and working, but only one way of the first-born. She added after an interval that she did not know if she would have given up her walking to keep at home and tend him, or whether the thought of her son's small feet running beside her in the trails would have driven her to the open again. The baby had not stayed long enough for that. "And whenever the wind blows in the night," said the Walking Woman, "I wake and wonder if he is well covered."

She took up her black bag and her blanket; there was the ranchhouse at Dos Palos to be made before night, and she went as outliers do, without a hope expressed of another meeting and no word of good-bye. She was the Walking Woman. That was it. She had walked off all sense of society-made values, and, knowing the best when the best came to her, was able to take it. Work — as I believed; love — as the Walking Woman had proved it; a child — as you subscribe to it. But look you: it was the naked thing the Walking Woman grasped, not dressed and tricked out, for instance, by prejudices in favor of certain occupations; and love, man love, taken as it came, not picked over and rejected if it carried no obligation of permanency; and a child; any way you get it, a child is good to have, say nature and the Walking Woman; to have it and not to wait upon a proper concurrence of so many decorations that the event may not come at all.

At least one of us is wrong. To work and to love and to bear children. That sounds easy enough. But the way we live establishes so many things of much more importance.

Far down the dim, hot valley, I could see the Walking Woman with her blanket and black bag over her shoulder. She had a queer, sidelong gait, as if in fact she had a twist all through her.

Recollecting suddenly that people called her lame, I ran down to the open place below the spring where she had passed. There in the bare, hot sand the track of her two feet bore evenly and white.

Stewed Beans

MARY AUSTIN

Now I TELLIN' you thiss stewed beans story. Thass Apache story. Iss very fonny. You savvy stewed beans; how they make everybody go in his insides r-r-r-ru, phutt-phutt! Only if you not cook him right; if you pour the water off while they cooking two-three times, they not make. But if water is not poured off, then they make phutt-phutt! Well, I tellin' you.

There iss man in Apache Village in the Chirricahua Mountains and his wife she not likin' him any more. She likin' 'nother man, only she don' tell him that, 'cause he don' live in her village. There iss three villages that make the same talk an' have one council, an' thiss man an' her husband they both bein' members of that council. So when thiss man from Lone Spring Village come over to Chirricahua Council, he visitin' that woman, an' some other times when he come on business. Thiss man is name Two-Comes-Over-the-Hill, an' thiss woman's husband is named Spotted Horse. Spotted Horse he think maybe Two-Comes-Over-the-Hill is comin' to see his wife, only he not sure. He never catch him; an' maybe he no like to catch him; only to make so that man don' think he not knowin'. He don' want to lose hees wife; only to make so that everybody been laughin' at thiss man an' not at Spotted Horse. So then there is a Council, an' Spotted Horse he think maybe so Two-Comes-Over-the-Hill will be visitin' hees wife. He watch an' he seein' hees wife makin' big supper, like when company comin', an' he stay 'roun' the house all afternoon. Hees wife she cookin' stewed beans; an' she want to go out an' pick some greens; so she say, 'I go pickin' greens, you watch those beans, an' make sure you pour the water off two-three times.'

So that man say, 'All right.' Well, he stayin' there while his wife pickin' greens, an' he don' pour that water off those beans, not one time. But when his wife come askin' him, he say, 'Yes, the water is pour off, two times.' So she fixin' the beans good; meat an' everything; an' when supper ready, he say he feel sorta sick an' he not carin' to eat any beans. Then he go to that Council, and when men sayin', 'How come you so early?' he sayin', 'Well, I didden eat much supper tonight 'cause my wife left me to pour the water off the beans an' I forgot, so I not eatin' any beans,' an' everybody laugh an' make jokes with him 'bout those beans.

So it gettin' dark an' the Council wait until those mans from Lone Spring Village come, an' by an' by Two-Comes-Over-the-Hill come along an' sit in the Council. An' he sayin', 'You gotta excuse me 'cause I was eatin' supper with beans with meat an' greens,' so of course they excused him. Iss not polite for mans invited to supper to eat too fast an' not eat a lot. So Spotted Horse say, 'I was goin' to ask you to supper at my house, but my wife left me to pour the water off the beans an' I forgot. You are a lot better off.' So they went on with the Council, an' by an' by the beans began to go r-r-r-ru in Two-Comes-Over-the-Hill's insides, an' pretty soon he begins to go phutt-phutt! An' Spotted Horse he kinda laughin' an' he say, 'Sounds like you been eatin' some of my wife's beans,' an' Two-Comes-Over-the-Hill he sayin', 'Oh, no, no, not at all.' An' the beans go phutt-phutt! An' pretty soon phutt-phutt-phutt — phu — uttt! An' everybody begin sort of laughin', so when the Governor of the Council calls for a vote, the beans goin' r-r-r-ru, phutt! An' somebody say, 'The beans don' got no vote.' Which make everybody laugh. An' Two-Comes-Over-the-Hill say, 'You gotta excuse me; I ain't feelin' so well.' An' Spotted Horse say, 'I gotta see my wife about this'; an' all the Council is laughin'. Every time Two-Comes-Over-the-Hill goes phutt-phutt! they laugh, an' Spotted Horse say, 'If you told me you were comin' to my house to supper, I would have poured the water off.' An' he act sorry like, so they all laugh an' laugh. So the Headman he say, 'You are excuse from this Council,' 'cause he don' like they all laughin' all the time.

So Two-Comes-Over-the-Hill he gathers up hees blanket an' he goes away from there. They watch an' see that he goes in the direction of Spotted Horse's house, an' go 'way from it in a few minutes. An' Spotted Horse when he get home see that his wife has been cryin'. 'Iss not your fault,' he say. 'I forgot to pour the water off. Next time old *Phutt-Phutt* is comin', I think you better tell me.' She say, 'There ain't goin' to be no next time. That Two-Comes-Over-the-Hill, he iss got no highness.' Sure 'nough, he is not comin' there again where he is call *Phutt-Phutt*, an' somebody always ask him if he would like some stewed beans. That's very fonny story.

Papago Wedding

MARY AUSTIN

There was a Papago woman out of Panták who had a marriage paper from a white man after she had borne him five children, and the man himself was in love with another woman. This Shuler was the first to raise cotton for selling in the Gila Valley — but the Pimas and the Papagos had raised it long before that — and the girl went with him willingly. As to the writing of marriage, it was not then understood that the white man is not master of his heart, but is mastered by it, so that if it is not fixed in writing it becomes unstable like water and is puddled in the lowest place. The Sisters at San Xavier del Bac had taught her to clean and cook. Shuler called her Susie, which was nearest to her Papago name, and was fond of the children. He sent them to school as they came along, and had carpets in the house.

In all things Susie was a good wife to him, though she had no writing of marriage and she never wore a hat. This was a mistake which she learned from the Sisters. They, being holy women, had no notion of the *brujería* which is worked in the heart of the white man by a hat. Into the presence of their God also, without that which passes for a hat they do not go. Even after her children were old enough to notice it, Susie went about the country with a handkerchief tied over her hair, which was long and smooth on either side of her face, like the shut wings of a raven.

By the time Susie's children were as tall as their mother, there were many white ranchers in the Gila country, with their white wives, who are like Papago women in this, that, if they see a man upstanding and prosperous, they think only that he might make some woman happy, and if they have a cousin or a friend, that she should be the woman. Also the white ones think it so shameful for a man to take a woman into his house without a writing that they have no scruple to take him away from her. At Rinconada there was a woman with large breasts, surpassing well-looking, and with many hats. She had no husband, and was new to the country, and when Shuler drove her about to look at it, she wore each time a different hat.

This the Papagos observed, and, not having visited Susie when she was happy with her man, they went now in numbers, and by this Susie understood that it was in their hearts that she might have need of them. For it was well known that the white woman had told Shuler that it was a shame for him to have his children going about with a Papago woman who had only a handkerchief to cover her head. She said it was keeping Shuler back from being the principal man among the cotton-growers of Gila Valley, to have in his house a woman who would come there without a writing. And when the other white women heard that she had said that, they said the same thing. Shuler said, "My God, this is the truth, I know it," and the woman said that she would go to Susie and tell her that she ought to go back to her own people and not be a shame to her children and Shuler. There was a man of Panták on the road, who saw them go, and turned in his tracks and went back, in case Susie should need him, for the Papagos, when it is their kin against whom there is *brujería* made, have in-knowing hearts. Susie sat in the best room with the woman and was polite. "If you want Shuler," she said, "you can have him, but I stay with my children." The white woman grew red in the face and went out to Shuler in the field where he was pretending to look after something, and they went away together.

After that Shuler would not go to the ranch except of necessity. He went around talking to his white friends. "My God," he kept saying, "what can I do, with my children in the hands of that Papago?" Then he sent a lawyer to Susie to say that if she would go away and not shame his children with a mother who had no marriage writing and no hat, he would give her money, so much every month. But the children all came in the room and stood by her, and Susie said, "What I want with money when I got my children and this good ranch?" Then Shuler said, "My God!" again, and, "What can I do?"

The lawyer said he could tell the Judge that Susie was not a proper person to have care of his children, and the Judge would take them away from Susie and give them to Shuler. But when the day came for Susie to come into court, it was seen that, though she had a handkerchief on her hair, her dress was good, and the fringe on her shawl was long and fine. All the five children came also, with new clothes, well-looking. "My God!" said Shuler, "I must get those kids away from that Papago and into the hands of a white woman." But the white people who had come to see the children taken away saw that, although the five looked like Shuler, they had their mouths shut like Papagos; so they waited to see how things turned out.

Shuler's lawyer makes a long speech about how Shuler loves his children, and how sorry he is in his heart to see them growing up like Papagos, and water is coming out of Shuler's eyes. Then the Judge asks Susie if she has anything to say why her children shall not be taken away.

"You want to take thees children away and giff them to Shuler?" Susie asks him. "What for you giff them to Shuler?" says Susie, and the white people are listening. She says, "Shuler's not the father of them. Thees children all got different fathers," says Susie. "Shuler — "

Then she makes a sign with her hand. I tell you if a woman makes that sign to a Papago he could laugh himself dead, but he would not laugh off that. Some of the white people who have been in the country a long time know that sign and they begin to laugh.

Shuler's lawyer jumps up. . . . "Your Honor, I object — "

The Judge waves his hand. "I warn you the court cannot go behind the testimony of the mother in such a case . . . "

By this time everybody is laughing, so that they do not hear what the lawyer says. Shuler is trying to get out of the side door, and the Judge is shaking hands with Susie.

"You tell Shuler," she says, "if he wants people to think hee's father of thees children he better giff me a writing. Then maybe I think so myself."

"I will," said the Judge, and maybe two-three days after that he takes Shuler out to the ranch and makes the marriage writing.

Then all the children come around Susie and say, "Now, Mother, you will have to wear a hat."

Susie, she says, "Go, children, and ask your father."

But it is not known to the Papagos what happened after that.

The Coroner Story

WILLIAM A. BAILLIE-GROHMAN

This macabre little tidbit is from one of the many western travel books of its time, Camps in the Rockies, published in 1882 and described in the subtitle as a narrative of life on the frontier and sport in the Rocky Mountains together with an account of the cattle ranches of the West. Baillie-Grohman tucked this piece into a discussion of how rapidly "good stories" — hearty verbal anecdotes — skipped about the country acquiring regional flavors. He included it as an example whose germinal notion sprang from a true case that occurred on Staten Island, New York, and within a few weeks had been "westernized" in California. He claimed it was reported as he gave it "by a 'Frisco paper" — but he cites a New York paper by name and exact date for the Staten Island start and fails to identify the "'Frisco paper" in any way. My guess is that he polished up the story in its 'Frisco form himself. Maybe it is "good" and maybe it isn't. At least it is typical of many "westernized" stories current in the period — and more neatly framed than most. Make up your own mind.

T HE FACT OF IT is," said old Dr. Potts, the Los Angeles Coroner, the other day, as he strolled through the morgue with Judge Van Snyder, "the fact of it is, that these San Francisco coroners don't really understand how to work up their business for all it's worth, and make it boom as it were."

"What do you mean?" said the Judge, somewhat horrified.

"Why, they don't know how to really run a corpse for all the coin that is in it. They don't handle 'em scientifically, so to speak. Now we do that sort of thing better down our way."

"Do, eh?"

"Yes. For instance, there was a Chinaman killed by smoking opium a few months ago, out in the suburbs of our town, and of course I was around there and had sworn in a jury before the cadaver got cold, and what with summoning witnesses, taking testimony, &c., before night I had a bill against the county for $96.50."

"More than the Chinaman was worth, I should think," said the Judge.

"But wait. I opened the grave in the county burial-ground the same night, rushed the corpse down to the laboratory and had it embalmed, and all ready for emergencies. Well, about three nights after that they had a free fight out at the Digger Indian encampment, and so I had the Celestial pigtail cut short, a few feathers twisted in it, and hid him in a bush out that way. Of course it was discovered pretty soon, and reported; and as the jury couldn't agree as to the particular tribe of Indians the deceased belonged to, I impaneled another one — nearly double the fees, don't you see? — and gave the papers a rousing good item. It's a way-up plan to keep in with the reporters, by the way."

"How much did you make?"

"Well, I was about $240 ahead on the speculation then, so I waited until a lot of Dago emigrants passed through the town, and the next day one of 'em was found dropped dead on the road of heart-disease — don't you see? Same old corpse, with a big felt hat and rawhide boots, and his pocket full of macaroni. I think I squeezed about $175 more out of the taxpayers that time. Well, I kinder let up for about a week after that, and then had the remains doubled up in a packing-box and found among the unclaimed freight down at the railroad station. The papers wrote it up as a 'Mysterious Murder Case,' and we had a ten days' examination. Lemme see, I think it was $445.50 the whole thing panned out before we were through that time. What do you think of that?"

"Why, it's the most extraordinary — "

"Why, that's nothing, my dear sir, nothing. I haven't got half through with that Chinaman yet. When I left home I just kinder wedged him in among the top branches of a tree in the woods just out of town, dressed in a suit of complete black with an old telescope in his coat-tail pocket, and a pair of big green spectacles on his nose. Catch the idea, don't you?"

"Can't say I do."

"Why, that's the aeronaut dodge, don't you see? Unknown scientific party fallen out of a balloon. My own design entirely. Splendid, isn't it? The corpse is a little worn by this time, I know; but what are you going to do with such an infernally unhealthy climate as Los Angeles? I expect to send the old lady and the girls to Paris on those remains yet, if I have to wire 'em together to do it. No, my dear sir, depend upon it what those metropolitan coroners lack is push, enterprise, sir, and ingenuity."

And the doctor reluctantly stopped poking a defunct stock speculator with his cane, and permitted the Judge to take him out for a drink.

Ba'tiste's Story of the Medicine Bag

GEORGE CATLIN

This is a brief excerpt from Catlin's long book with the long title, Letters and Notes on the Manners, Customs and Conditions of the North American Indians, originally published by Catlin himself in 1841. That is a wild and wordy and fascinating work, full of moralizing and sentimentality and brilliant descriptions and infor- mation and several of these Ba'tiste tales and some four hundred fine paintings — just such a book as might have been expected from an impulsive, dedicated artist who set out to capture in his pic- tures all the tribes of North America and swung into writing and lecturing in an effort to win sympathy and better treatment for them. His wanderings are unraveled and the puzzle why he, a native of Wilkes-Barre, Pennsylvania and a staunch American, should have published his book in London and spent thirty years abroad is ex- plained in a recent (1948) biography, Pursuit of the Horizon, by Loyd Haberly.

THIS AMUSING STORY is one that my man Ba'tiste used to tell to Bogard and others with great zest; describing his adventure one night, in endeavouring to procure a medicine-bag, which I had employed him to obtain for me on the Upper Missouri; and he used to prelude it thus: —

"Je commence — "

"Dam your commonce (said Bogard), tell it in English — "

"Pardón, Monsieur, en Americaine — "

"Well, American then, if you please; anything but your darned 'parlez vous.' "

"Bien, excusez — now Monsieur Bogard, you must know first place, de 'Medicine-Bags' is mere humbug, he is no *medicine* in him — no pills; he is someting mysterieux. Some witchcraft, súppose. You must know que tous les sauvages have such tings about him, pour for good luck. Ce n'est que (pardón) it is only *hocus pocus*, to keep off witch, súppose. You must know ces articles can nevare be sold, of course you see dey cannot be buy. So my friend here, Monsieur Cataline, who have collect all de curiosités des pays sauvages, avait made strong applique to me pour for to get one of dese *medicine-bags* for his Collection curieux, et I had, pour moimême, le curiosité extreme pour for to see des quelques choses ces étranges looking tings was composí.

"I had learn much of dese strange custom, and I know wen de Ingin die, his *medicine-bags* is buried wis him.

"Oui, Monsieur, so it can never be got by any boday. Bien. I hap to tink one day wen we was live in de mous of Yellow Stone, now is time, and I avait said to Monsieur Cataline, que pensez vous? *Kon-te-wondu* (un des chefs du) (pardón, one of de chiefs, of de Knisteneux) has die tó-day. Il avait une *medicine-bag* magnifique, et extremement curieux; il est composé d'un, it is made (pardón, si vous plait) of de wite wolf skin, ornement et stuff wid tousand tings which we shall see, ha? Good luck! Suppose Monsieur Cataline, I have seen him just now. I av see de *medicine-bag* laid on his breast avec his hands crossed ovare it. Que pensez vous? I can get him to-night, ha? If you will keep him, if you will not tell, ha? 'Tis no harm — 'tis no steal — he is dead, ha? Well, you shall see. But, would you not be afraid, Ba'tiste (said Monsieur Cataline), to take from dis poor fellow his medicines (or mysteries) on which he has rest all his hopes in dis world, and de world to come? Pardón, je n'ai pas peur; non, Monsieur, ne rien de peur. I nevare saw ghost — I have not fear, mais, súppose, it is not right, éxact; but I have grand disposition pour for to obligé my friend, et le curiosité moimeme, pour for to see wat it is made of; suppose tó-night I shall go, ha? 'Well, Ba'tiste, I have no objection (said

Monsieur Cataline) if your heart does not fail you, for I will be
very glads to get him, and will make you a handsome present for
it, but I think it will be a cold and gloomy kind of business.' Nevare
mind, Monsieur Cataline (I said) provide he is well dead, *perfect
dead!* Well, I had see les Knisteneux when dey ave bury de chap —
I ave watch close, and I ave see how de medicine-bags was put. It
was fix pretty tight by some cord around his bellay, and den some
skins was wrap many times áround him — he was put down in de
hole dug for him, and some flat stones and some little dirt was
laid on him, only till next day, wen some grand ceremonays was
to be pérform ovare him, and den de hole was to be fill up; now
was de only time possible for de *medicine-bag*, ha? I ave very pretty
little wife dat times, Assineboin squaw, and we sleep in one of de
stores inside de Fort, de Trade-house, you know, ha?

"So you may súppose I was all de day perplex to know how I
should go, somebody may watch — súppose, he may not be dead!
not quite dead, ha? nevare mind — le jour was bien long, et le nuit
dismal, *dismal!* oh by gar *it was dismal!* plein (pardon) full of
apprehension, mais sans *peur, je n'avais pas peur!* So some time
aftere midnights, wen it was bout right time pour go, I made start,
very light, so my wife must not wake. Oh diable l'imagination! quel
solitude! well, I have go very well yet, I am pass de door, and I am
pass de gate, and I am at lengts arrive at de grave! súppose 'now
Ba'tiste, courage, courage! now is de times come.' Well, súppose I
am not afraid of *dead man*, mais, perhaps, dese *medicine-bag* is give
by de Grande Esprit to de Ingin for someting? possible! I will let
him keep it. I shall go back! No, Monsieur Cataline will laughs
at me. I must have him, ma foi, mon courage! so I climb down
very careful into de grave, mais, as I déscend, my heart rise up into
my mouse! Oh mon Dieu! courage Ba'tiste, courage! ce n'est pas
l'homme dat I fear, mais le *medicine*, le *medicine*. So den I ave lift
out de large stones, I ave put out my head in de dark, and I ave
look all de contré round; ne personne, ne personne — no bodé in
sight! Well, I ave got softly down on my knees ovare him (oh,
courage! courage! oui) and wen I have unwrap de robe, I ave all
de time say, 'pardon, courage! pardon, courage!' until I ad got de
skins all off de bodé; I ave den take hold of de cord to untie, mais!
(dans l'instant) two cold hands seize me by de wrists! and I was just
dead — I was petrifact in one instant. Oh St. Esprit! I could just
see in de dark two eyes glaring like fire sur upon me! and den (oh,
eugh!) it spoke to me, 'Who are you?' (Sacré, vengeance! it will

not do to deceive him, no,) 'I am Ba'tiste, poor Ba'tiste!' 'Then thou art surely mine, (as he clenched both arms tight around my boday) lie still Ba'tiste.' Oh, holy Vierge! St. Esprit! O mon Dieu! I could not breathe! miserable! je sui perdu! oh pourquoi have I been such a fool to get into dese cold, cold arms! 'Ba'tiste? (drawing me some tighter and tighter!) do you not belong to me, Ba'tiste?' Yes, súppose! oh diable! belong? Oui, oui, je suis certainment perdu, lost, lost, for evare! *Oh, can you not possible let me go?* 'No, Ba'tiste, we must never part.' Grand Dieu! c'est finis, finis, finis avec moi! 'Then you do not love me any more, Ba'tiste?' Quel! quoi! what!! est ce vous, *Wee-ne-on-ka?* 'Yes, Ba'tiste, it is the *Bending Willow* who holds you, she that loves you and will not let you go? Are you dreaming Ba'tiste?' Oui, diable — "

The Buck in the Hills

WALTER VAN TILBURG CLARK

*I*t seems to me that the important biographical facts about Walter
Van Tilburg Clark are not that he was first an easterner (born in
Maine, early boyhood in West Nyack, New York) and that later in
life he has again been an easterner (graduate work at the University
of Vermont, ten years of schoolteaching in a New York town). The
important facts are that in between he was a westerner, that his
family moved to Reno, Nevada, when he was seven and for the next
fifteen years, or until he graduated from the University of Nevada,
he was really at home in that territory. As he himself says somewhere, the deserts and mountains of Nevada and the adjoining California area became "my country." Those were the years he absorbed
that sure, sensitive "feel" for western atmosphere that pervades all
his western stories.

But atmosphere is only incidental in Walter Van Tilburg Clark's
stories. He is the man who confounded the critics by proving with
The Ox-Bow Incident in 1940 that a book which had to be labeled
a western could also be a psychological study of mature significance
— and then double-riveted that proof with The Track of the Cat
in 1949. His short stories are few, each separate, individual, completely original in concept and execution. I have never read one that
I would not instantly place on the top level of any list. This one
first appeared in the Rocky Mountain Review and is included in his

collection, The Watchful Gods and Other Stories, 1950. *Length alone dictated the choice. Without that simple measuring stick I would still be puzzling between it and "Hook" and "The Indian Well" and "The Wind and the Snow of Winter."*

I LEFT THE PEAK about two o'clock, drank the very cold, shale-tasting water coming down from last winter's snow in the notch, went on down, and then south through the marshy meadow, already in shadow from the col, the grass yellowing and the sod stiffening from the fall nights, so that I could walk straight across and feel only the first solidity and then a slight give which didn't spring back. It was strange in the meadows, walking in the shadow, but with the sky still bright blue, as in the middle of the afternoon, and the sunlight, when I stopped to look back at the peak, just beginning to look late. It was chilly in the shadow too, but I didn't hurry. The peak was sacred to me, the climb was pilgrimage, and five years is a long time. I had been very happy all day, climbing with the sun on my neck and shoulders, and I was very lonely happy now. I took my time, and looked at everything, and remembered a lot, and would have yodelled sometimes, but the quiet was better.

I climbed over the big rock barrier, which a million winters had cracked into terraces, saw the dry, shrivelled clumps of leaves and single dead stems in the cracks, and remembered times I had come up there in the summer, which is spring at that height, and seen it pouring with green, like cascades, and lighted by flowers. I remembered the dark girl who knew all the flowers, and who, when I bet her she couldn't find more than thirty kinds, found more than fifty. I remembered how we had eaten our pocket lunch dry, in a niche on the east side of the peak, out of the strong wind we could hear among the rocks and more heavily in the notch below. We couldn't see it then, but the image was new in our minds of the big basin to the west, with its rolling of dark green to pale blue, heavily timbered hills, and the wide, dark-blue flat of Tahoe, rough with wind and jointed exactly into all the bays and coves, and the little lakes at different heights around it, also fitted like single pieces into a relief puzzle. In front of us, way down, squared with fields and pencilled by the straight roads, was the chain of ranching valleys, and then the lesser, burned mountains rolling to the east, and in the far northeast just a sky-colored sliver of Pyramid Lake showing through the last pass. I remembered that the clouds that day had gone all around the horizon in a narrow band, flat underneath, all at exactly the same level, with clear sky between them and the mountains, and with their tops standing up in little firm bosses and domes, and not a single cloud in the field of sky above them, so that we sat high up in the center of a great circle of distant cloud. This seemed to mean something, and gave our thoughts, and the big arch of world we looked at, a different quality that made us uneasy and happy too, the way I was now.

I went on through the sparse trees and the rocks over two ridges, and could see from them, and from the little valley between, the rock castle at the end of the high col to the west, where I had eaten at noon another time, when I was alone, and then stayed for two hours to watch a hawk using the wind over the hollow to the west of me, feeling myself lift magnificently when he swooped up toward me on the current up the col, and then balanced and turned above.

I was feeling like that when I got back to the little grassy lake where I'd left my pack. The pack was still there all right, under the bench nailed between two of the three trees on the hump at the farther side. Beyond the three trees, which were stunted and twisted by wind, I could see the wall of the col, very dark now, with a thin gold sky above it. Besides the bench, there was a pine-bough bed and a rock fireplace in the shelter of the trees. I hadn't made them, just found them there, but in the dusk the place gave me the hawk lift again. I had the night here alone, and another day in the mountains. That was a lot. And I had already stacked my firewood; brought it down that morning from the east slope.

I went around to the camp side and stood looking at the lake, thinking about swimming before I made a fire and ate. It was cold, and the water would be cold too. The lake was really just a pool of snow water, with no outlet, and no regular inflow, shallow enough so the dead grasses showed up through at the edges. But I like that kind of clean, cold feeling, and it had been warm climbing in the middle of the day. I peeled off, and stood liking the cold on my body, and the frozen, pebbly earth under my feet, and then, when I went nearer the edge, the wiry grass. It was very still in the valley, and the water reflected, exactly and without break, the mountains and the last of that thin, yellow light. I got that lift again. This time I would take it out. I ran splashing till I was thigh deep, and then rolled under. The water was even colder than I had expected, and hardened my whole body at once. For a minute or two I swam rapidly in circles in the small center that was deep enough. Then I was all right, and could roll easily, and even float looking up. The first stars were showing above the ridge in the east. I let go a couple of bars of high, operatic-sounding something. It came back at me from under the col, sounding much better, sweet and clear and high. God, I was happy. This was the way I liked it, alone, and clean cold, and a lot of time ahead. I rolled over to dive and start one more fast turn, when I heard the yodel that wasn't an echo.

I stood up, feeling the cold rim of the water around my chest, and even in the dusk could see the shape of the man coming over the hump and down towards the lake. When he was part way down, I could tell by the walk, a little pigeon-toed and easy, giving at the knees all the time, that it was Tom Williams. He had his pack on, and his rifle over one shoulder, with a thumb in the sling, the way Tom always carried it. The remainder of ecstasy went out of me. I'd rather have Tom than almost anyone I know for outside company, but I didn't want anybody now. And Tom meant Chet McKenny, and I didn't want Chet now or any other time. Chet was a big-boned, tall Scotchman, probably ten years older than either Tom or I, with gray in his stiff hair. He had a kind of stubborn originality that wouldn't use a joke somebody else had told, but he couldn't make a good one, so he was laughing all the time over bad jokes of his own. But that wasn't what I disliked, though it got tiresome. What I didn't like about McKenny was deeper than stupidity. You saw it when you saw that his eyes were still watching you when he laughed; you were always on guard against McKenny.

The three of us had come up in Tom's car, and they'd left me at the summit meadows. They were going on over to the flat to start a deer hunt. I was supposed to have today and tomorrow and then be back out at the meadows by sunset to wait for them.

Tom came down to where I'd dropped my clothes, and unslung his rifle and pack and put them down.

"Cold?" he asked. He didn't have to speak loudly.

"Plenty," I said.

I kept looking for Chet to come over the rise too.

Tom peeled off and came in, but slowly, and then just lying out and letting himself sink under. He came up slowly too, as if the water weren't cold at all, and just stood there, not even rubbing himself. There was something wrong.

"Where's Chet?" I asked. It would even be pleasant, with a fire after supper, to have Tom to talk to, if he was alone.

"That bastard," Tom said. Then he let himself down into the water again, and came up a few feet farther off, his thin, blond hair streaming down and the springy, blond mat on his big chest holding a few drops.

"He won't be here, anyway," he said, "so you don't have to worry."

He began to swim hard, and I took another turn, to get the blood stirring again. Then we walked up out of the water. Tom didn't say anything more, and I didn't either. I knew it would come. Tom doesn't often talk much, except about engines, but this was different. It was working in him, hard. He went up to his pack, and I could see the muscles in his heavy white shoulders working while he hunted in it. He got out a towel and threw it to me. Then he went back down to the water, and I saw he had a cake of soap in his hand. But he didn't bathe. I stood there wiping off and watching him, and he just bent over in the shallows and washed his hands. He washed them hard, three or four times, rinsing them between. That was queer for Tom. He was an auto mechanic, ran a little shop of his own, and he'd long ago given up hoping to have his hands really clean. Often on trips like this he'd go two or three days without washing them at all.

He still didn't say anything, though, when he came up; just took the towel from me and began to wipe himself slowly.

It felt good to be in the warm flannel shirt and cords again, and shod heavily. Maybe that's even the best feeling, the cold that makes you feel thin and single, with no waste matter, but beginning to get warm. I lit a cigarette with stiff fingers, and saw against the match flame how dark it was getting. The cigarette tasted very good too. I was all set to be happy again, if Tom was right.

Tom didn't talk while he was dressing, or while we went up to the camp, or while he was cooking and watching the coffee and I was putting some new boughs and the sleeping bags on the bed. The bed was a good one, wide enough for three, and in a pit a foot deep. I went down to the lake to get two cans of beer out of the water. They're a lot of weight to carry in a pack, and I'd thought maybe I was pampering myself when I'd put them in, one for each evening. Now I was glad I'd brought them. When I came back up with them, he was just letting the things cook, and standing away from the fire, looking at the stars over the valley and in the little lake.

"This is a swell place," he said in an easier voice. "Gee, I haven't been in here for years, I'd forgot what a swell place it was."

Then I knew it was going to be all right, once he got around to telling me, and I had to sing a little while I put the beers between roots and took the eggs and beans off the fire; not loudly, but just about like the crackling of the fire.

When he came back and sat down on the bench, the light on his face with its fine mouth and big, broken nose and blue eyes, and its hard weather lines, he looked at me because I was singing, and I could see he was still thinking, but not feeling the same way about it.

When we'd started to eat, I asked, "How did the hunting go?"

"Don't you worry," Tom said. "I didn't get anything. I didn't even get a shot. I didn't see a thing."

He looked closed up again, as he had when he came into the water. He finished his beans, staring into the fire. Then he said suddenly, "That McKenny is a first-rate bastard."

"What's he done now?" I asked.

Tom looked right at me for a moment, as if he'd start, but then he said, "Oh, hell, let it go."

He got up and went down to the edge of the lake slowly, and after a moment I saw his match flare, and then, every now and then, the fire point of his cigarette moving.

I'd never seen Tom let anything eat in him like that before. He made up his mind very hard about what was wrong and what was right, especially about people, but he did it carefully, and he was usually gentle about it, even afterwards. It was the first time I'd heard him speak out like that. Whatever had happened, it must have been pretty bad.

Well, I was sure now that McKenny wasn't coming. I stopped thinking about it, put more wood on the fire, and lay on my back where the light wouldn't be in my eyes. Then I could see the silhouette of the col, where it walled out the stars, and the big peak glimmering in the starlight in the north. The size of the place, and the cold quiet, came back on me, and I was happy again.

I'd forgotten about Chet when Tom came back up and sat down on the bench. He stared at the ground for a moment. Then he looked across at me.

"You always thought so, didn't you?"

"Thought what?"

"That Chet McKenny was a first-rate bastard?"

I didn't like to say so.

"All right," Tom said. "I guess he is, at that."

He didn't say anything more, so I sat up.

"Have a beer?"

"No, thanks."

I had to get him started.

"Did Chet get anything?" I asked.

Tom looked at me hard.

"Yeah, he got one, all right, a good big buck, better than two twenty, I'd guess. Ten points." He looked down.

Then he looked up again, and said suddenly, and loudly for that place, "You know what that bastard did? He —" but stopped.

"He what?"

"No," Tom said. "I'll tell you the way it was. Maybe I'm wrong.

"I worked down south, toward the lake meadows. I didn't see a thing all day; not even a doe; not even a fresh track or droppings. I figured it had been worked over and got disgusted and went back to the flat in the afternoon to get some sleep. I was washing up at the brook, and when I stood up and turned around, there was this big buck, a mule, on the edge of the trees across the flat. Even from there I could tell he was a big one, and I cussed, because there was my rifle up against a tree thirty yards from me, and the buck had spotted me. You know, his head was up and right at me, and those big ears up too. He was trying the wind. I figured if I moved he'd be back in those trees before I could take a step. So I held it. After a while he let his head down, way low, and began to go along the edge of the flat toward the pass. Then I saw there was something the matter with him. He wasn't using his left front leg; just bucking along on the other one, in little jumps. He was tired out, too, stopping every few jumps and taking the wind again, and then letting his head drop that way, like he couldn't hold it up. I figured somebody'd made a bad shot. I started for the gun. He saw me then, but he was so far gone he didn't even care, just kept hopping and resting. Then I didn't know whether I wanted him or not. Only I might as well, if his leg was really busted.

"I was standing there on the edge of the flat, wondering, when I heard this yell. It was Mac, coming down through the trees. He yelled at me to head the buck off. Your lousy shot then, I thought.

"When I went right out at the buck, it tried to hurry. I yelled at Mac did he want me to finish it, and he yelled at me, hell no, it was his buck. The buck stood there with his head up when we yelled; he didn't try to do anything.

"I don't know. It made me mad. But it was Mac's buck. I started to work around so as not to hurry it any more than I had to. Mac was working along in the timber to get right above him. When I got around in front, we worked in closer, and then the buck saw us both, and just stopped and stood there. He was shivering all over, and didn't have any fight left in him. I could see now that he'd been hit in the leg, right up against the body. The blood was mostly dried on black, but there was a little fresh blood coming out all the time too. The bad leg was all banged up from being dragged on things too, and he was soaked with sweat on the hind-quarters and under the throat, and making cotton at the muzzle."

Tom stopped.

Then he said, "It's funny the way they look at you like that. I don't know. There wasn't anything, no fight, no panic, no hope, no nothing. He just looked at you. But you couldn't move. They got such big eyes. I don't know."

Tom kicked at a stone with his boot.

"Well, anyway, I couldn't move. But Mac could. He came up close behind. He had his cap on the back of his head and he was grinning. He said wasn't it a nice one. Ten points, he said.

"When he talked, the buck got going again, that same way. It was headed across the meadows toward the camp. I got ready to finish it, but Mac yelled at me to mind my own damn business and let it go or he'd damn well lather hell out of me. You know the way he does, grinning, but mad as the devil. I asked him what he thought he was doing, but he said that was his business, and to mind my own.

"The buck was going so slow you could pass it walking; had to wait on it. And it stopped two or three times. Mac could have killed it a long time before it got to the flat; I was sure of that. I began to think he wanted to take it in alive, or something. But it wasn't that."

Tom stopped talking and sat there.

"No?" I said.

"No," Tom said. "When the buck stopped, near where we'd had the fire, Mac said that was good enough, like he was pleased, and unslung his rifle and took mine too, and stood them up against a tree. Then he told me to hold the buck's head."

After a moment Tom went on again.

"I don't know why I did it. I just did. I never felt that way before. I guess I thought he was going to operate, as near as I thought anything. He just said to hold it, and I did, like I was in a daze. The buck kind of backed a little, and then, when I had hold of his antlers, he stood still; didn't make a move. Holding on to the antlers, I could feel him shivering all over, you know, like putting your hand on a telephone pole. Mac had his skinning knife out.

" 'Hold his head up,' he said.

"He was kind of leaning over and looking at the bullet hole when he said it, and I did.

"Then all of a sudden he leaned down on the buck's neck with one hand, and slit its throat wide open with the knife in the other. Leaning on it that way, he put all his weight on the buck's one leg, and the buck fell over front, and I didn't get out of the way fast enough. It knocked me onto my knees too, and the blood came out all over my hands and arms. It kept coming, in big spurts; there was an awful lot of it. I don't know."

Tom got out a cigarette and lit it. I didn't have anything to say. The story made a difference though, as if it were a lot darker all at once, and we were farther away from other people than before, and there were things alive in the rocks, watching us. I noticed there was a wind coming up too, but didn't think about it, just heard it in the trees as if it had been going all the time.

"It's funny," Tom said. "When the buck got pushed down, it stretched way out; you know. Its muzzle was right in my face, and it blew. It made a little spray of blood, but it had a sweet-smelling breath, you know, like a cow's. And then all that blood came out, hot."

Finally he asked me, "You know what Mac said?"

"No."

"Well, he laughed like hell when the buck pushed me over, and then he said, 'I never take more than one shot,' and then he laughed again.

"I was mad enough, I guess. I told him it was a hell of a shot, and he said two inches to the right would've killed him, and pointed at the hole, and laughed again and said hell, it was per-fect. The bullet had busted the joint all to pieces. There was splinters sticking out where they'd worked through."

I was looking at Tom now.

"You mean he meant to?" I asked.

"That's right," Tom said. "He thought he was real clever. He boasted about it. Said he'd spotted the buck way up in that little meadow under the castle rocks; what's its name? The buck was on the north edge of the meadow, and up wind of him, what wind there was. He said he figured it all out, that it was eight miles back to camp, and the buck was a big one. He couldn't see carrying it all that way, so he just laid down there on the edge of the timber, to make his shot good, and waited till the buck was broadside to him, and then busted that foreleg. Said he'd never made a better shot, that it was a hundred and fifty yards, if it was an inch, and uphill. He was set up about that shot."

"Well," I said, letting out my breath.

"Yes," Tom said.

"He told me all about how he drove it, too," he said angrily. "How it kept trying to run at first, and falling over so he had to laugh, and then how it tried to turn on him, but couldn't stand it when he got close, and what a hell of a time he had driving it out of a couple of manzanita thickets where it tried to hole up. Then he figured if he stayed off it, it would keep going steadier, and it did.

"So, I guess you were right," Tom said, making it a question.

"I didn't think he was that bad," I said. "You have to keep it up a long time to do a thing like that."

"He was still going strong," Tom said. "Only excited and talking a lot.

"Like I am now," he added.

I didn't want to ask. I figured anything he'd done wasn't enough. But I still looked at Tom.

"No," he said. "You don't have to worry. I didn't touch him.

"I don't know," he said doubtfully, "I wanted you to know the way it was, first."

"He had it coming to him," I said. But I was scared, so I nearly laughed when Tom told me.

"I told him if he'd been saving himself so careful, he could damned well carry his buck home, and I left him there."

"I'd like to have seen his face," I said.

"I didn't even look at him," Tom said. "I just put my things into the car and got out.

"He knew better than to say anything, too."

"Well," I said finally, "I wouldn't say you were too hard on him."

"No," Tom said. "But he'll try to bring that buck out."

"Sure," I agreed, "he wouldn't let it go if it was killing him."

Tom heeled his cigarette out carefully and said, "You wouldn't care to go up the mountain again tomorrow, would you?"

"Sure I would," I told him. "Now you quit worrying. He had it coming to him."

Tom said he was going to take another swim, and we undressed by the fire, and went down together, and came back up wet. It felt very cold then, and the wind was stronger. But we piled more wood onto the fire, so it threw shadows of the three trees way up the hump, and when we'd dried off it felt so good we didn't get dressed, but just put on shorts and stayed close to the fire.

"I'll have that beer now," Tom said. He was cheerful.

In the morning the wind was down, but it was snowing. We couldn't even see the mountain. I felt worse about the buck than I had when Tom told me, and kept thinking about it. We packed up and went back down the trail, single file and not talking. Snow makes a hush that's even harder to talk in than the clear silence. There was something listening behind each tree and rock we passed, and something waiting among the taller trees down slope, blue through the falling snow. They wouldn't stop us, but they didn't like us, either. The snow was their ally.

Bank Holiday

EDWIN CORLE

*T*he story is a short sample from the book that started Edwin
Corle's writing career back in 1934: Mojave, A Book of Stories.
Perhaps that volume lacks the more mature mastery of such later
works as People on the Earth, Burro Alley, An American Dream. . . .
But it has its own special flavor. Some of the stories are smart-
alecky, deliberately contrived for effect — but the effect is usually
good. This one has remained clear in my mind while the others,
except in very general terms, have faded. It would be difficult to
explain exactly why, unless because it illustrates with such direct
simplicity an aspect of southwestern Indian character that has
always baffled the conquering whites.

TOM LOBO, whose real name was Gray Wolf, walked up to the
door and looked in. The door, that he had learned was always
open at certain hours, was locked. Tom Lobo's unimaginative mind
found nothing exciting in this unexpected order of events. He
stood still in the bright sunlight and did nothing. He was thinking,
"This place is not open: therefore I cannot go in." He walked to
the curb and stood looking at the building.

He thought it was a nice white building. He thought it had pretty gold letters on the windows. He thought it was a pretty hot morning. He thought he would like a glass of beer.

And so Tom Lobo stood before the First National Bank of the little desert town of Coachella and waited. Several merchants and ranchers went by and some commented about the bank. If Tom Lobo had cared to listen he might have caught phrases — "Until they get things straightened out" — "Checks ain't worth a whoop" — "Roosevelt" — "Congress" — "Scrip money" — "Be open in three days" — "Won't be open in three months" — but he didn't listen. He was thinking that it was a nice white building.

Charley Joe came down the street. He and Tom Lobo said good morning by looking at each other and not by speaking. Then Charley Joe went to the door of the bank. He wasn't very surprised to find it closed. He didn't try to peek in the way the white men did. He walked to where Tom Lobo was standing. Charley Joe wore a pair of blue overalls and a gray shirt with no tie. Tom Lobo wore an old pair of dark blue trousers and a gray shirt with no tie. There was little or no difference between them, except that Tom Lobo wore a dirty white hat of the "Panama" variety, while Charley Joe wore no hat at all. Presently Charley Joe took a pipe from a shirt pocket and began to pack it with tobacco.

"Closed," said Tom Lobo.

"Mmm," agreed Charley Joe.

He struck a match and lit the pipe.

"Good terbacker," said Tom Lobo.

"Mmm," agreed Charley Joe.

They stood in silence for some minutes. They both seemed perfectly at ease and there was no attempt at small talk. After a while it became clear to both of them that the white men, who came to the bank and found it closed, went away more excited than they had come. Many of them raised their voices and asked questions and talked fast.

"Why bank closed?" asked Charley Joe.

"Don't know," replied Tom Lobo.

"Maybe John Whitewater know," said Charley Joe.

"Maybe," agreed Tom Lobo.

That ended the banking situation for the moment. After another minute of smoking Charley Joe said, "Got new horse."

"Where old horse?" inquired Tom Lobo.

"Dead," said Charley Joe.

Then Black Eye, who had been sitting in the shade by the freight station, came down the street. Black Eye was a very old Indian with a wrinkled face and gray hair. He wasn't quite as tall as Tom Lobo and Charley Joe. But he was thought to be very wise. The three men greeted each other without words. Black Eye didn't go to the door of the bank. He simply looked at it and at two passing ranchers who were jokingly and nervously reassuring themselves that "everything was O.K." The ranchers climbed into a Ford truck and drove off. Other white men appeared. They rattled the doors and even peered in the windows.

"Bank no work," said Black Eye.

"Mmm," agreed Tom Lobo and Charley Joe.

"Charley Joe got new horse," said Tom Lobo.

"Old horse dead," added Charley Joe.

"Mmm," said Black Eye.

The three of them stood in silence. They turned and faced the citadel of the white man's economic system. Townspeople were talking in groups and rushing up and rushing away. They seemed frightened. "The First National Bank of Coachella," spelled the gold letters on the windows. The information was hardly necessary. It was the only bank in Coachella, or in the entire Coachella Valley. It was the only bank within a radius of seventy five miles. But the Indians weren't reading the imposing title, nor the names of the executives printed on the door. They were just looking at the bank.

"Why bank close?" asked Charley Joe.

"Why, Black Eye?" asked Tom Lobo.

"Don't know," admitted Black Eye.

"Bank got money. Saw money there yest'day," said Tom Lobo.

"Sure, bank got money," said Charley Joe. "I put money there."

"Maybe John Whitewater know," said Black Eye.

"Maybe," agreed Tom Lobo.

"Wait see," said Black Eye.

And so they waited as the morning went on, and the brilliant desert sun became hotter toward the middle of the day. John Whitewater did not arrive. But Tony Gee did. Tony Gee was working at a date ranch, or date "garden" as they are locally called, not far from Indio. Tony Gee was a prosperous Indian, but he was not the authority that was John Whitewater. John Whitewater had been a friend of old Fig Tree John, and Fig Tree John had been the wisest Indian in the methods of the white men in all the

Colorado Desert. Fig Tree John was reputed to have been one of Frémont's scouts, and to have killed five men. Nobody knew if that were true, and nobody cared any more because old Fig Tree was dead. But his wisdom lived after him in the person of John White-water. Whenever anybody wanted to learn anything he looked up John Whitewater. So naturally John Whitewater would know why the bank was closed and why the ranchers were excited. The thing to do was to wait for John Whitewater. Nevertheless, the arrival of Tony Gee at noon brought a shred of explanation.

Tony Gee drove into town in his rattly old Ford. It sputtered up the street and nosed into the curb. Tony Gee sat very erect in the seat and held the steering wheel with both hands, and with elbows wide apart. He drove his rattletrap car with ridiculous dignity. He abandoned it at the curb and walked to the door of the bank. Tony Gee wore dirty corduroy pants, a gray shirt with no tie, and a straw hat. He looked at his friends and they looked their greeting back to him.

Tony Gee stopped at the door of the bank and gave serious consideration to a sign on the door. None of the others had looked at the sign.

"Bank H-O-L-I-D-A-Y — " he spelled out. "Until next M-O-N-D-A-Y. By order of the G-O-V-E-R-N-O-R."

Tony Gee thought about the message. He turned the significance of it over in his mind. The white man's governor had said to close the bank. His money was in this bank. The governor had said he couldn't have his money. Vaguely he wondered why. He wasn't belligerent, but he was curious. He had worked for a white man and had earned money. He had been told to put this money in a white man's bank. Now the G-O-V-E-R-N-O-R said he couldn't have the money he had earned. Tony Gee couldn't quite puzzle it out. He turned to the three men at the curb. They were looking at him. He knew they couldn't read the sign.

"Bank closed," said Tony Gee.

"Why?" asked Tom Lobo.

Tony Gee waited a long time. He wanted to get it all clear to his own satisfaction.

"Bank closed because man says so."

"What man?" asked Charley Joe.

"Big man say close bank."

"Why close bank?" asked Black Eye.

Tony Gee was not used to questions. He was not at all sure of his ground. He was a little bit afraid of Black Eye.

"Bank closed," he insisted. Then he said no more, but proceeded to roll himself a cigarette. The other three men said nothing. A white man in Tony Gee's place would have felt embarrassed and would have made some excuse and left. But Tony Gee found refuge in stoicism. The bank was closed. His friends knew it was closed. He knew it. He told them the sign said so. That took care of all that could be said about it. He smoked his cigarette in silence. The four of them stood together and waited.

"John Whitewater know," said Tom Lobo after a long wait.

"Maybe," said Tony Gee.

"One time Fig Tree John know, now John Whitewater know," remarked Charley Joe in an unusually complex line of thought.

"Maybe," said Black Eye.

For several days John Whitewater had been camping near La Quinta. He had been cutting mesquite wood and working hard at it. He arrived in Coachella about two o'clock in the afternoon. He saw the group before the bank and he gave the men no immediate thought. He had business in town. He wanted to buy a new shovel, and a small ax to chop away the short stubborn desert mistletoe that was parasitic to the profitable mesquite. But first he had to go to the bank and get some cash. He was very rich with almost a hundred dollars in the bank, and was very proud of it. He liked going to the bank. It was beyond mere vanity. It was pride and self-esteem. The group watched him approach and they saw him stop at the door. Not even John Whitewater could go any further.

He read the sign.

"Bank Holiday until next Monday by order of the Governor."

He went over it several times. Beyond the fact that the bank was closed, it didn't mean very much to him. He wanted a shovel and a small ax. His money was in the bank, and if he could just get inside, he knew what he had to do to get the clerk to give him money. But there was no clerk inside. The bank was empty. His money was locked up. It was something that had never happened before. He really didn't understand it.

Thinking hard, he turned to the men who awaited him. They didn't ask him any questions. They respected his experience and they waited to hear from him. He knew that he was expected to explain the situation. But first he had to explain it to himself. They stood together in a little group and looked at one another and at the bank.

"Bank closed," began John Whitewater as if he were bringing

a new truth to the world. There was a slight pause while they waited. John Whitewater did not seem to be disposed to speak further.

"Why?" asked Black Eye. He enjoyed this, and his question was almost accusatory. He was the only one of them who had no money in the bank. He had no money at all.

"Why?" he repeated.

"Bank closed because gov'ment close him up. Gov'ment say bank close, so he close. Gov'ner of gov'ment close bank up because he can. So he did until Monday."

"Why he close bank?" asked Tom Lobo.

John Whitewater considered. He had vaguely heard of bank failures.

"Maybe bank close because no money. Don't know. Maybe no money in bank."

Tony Gee didn't agree with this.

"Money in bank," he said. "I got money in bank. Tom Lobo got money in bank. Charley Joe got money in bank. Plenty money in bank."

"Sure, money in bank," added Black Eye.

John Whitewater's first theory was blasted. He had no creative imagination so he was unable to think of a second. They all stood and waited for him to go on. John Whitewater did not mind. If he couldn't answer a question, that was the fault of the question. He shrugged his shoulders and simply remarked, "Bank closed."

His friends were disappointed. They expected more information. For over three hours they had known that the bank was closed. And all this business of the governor and the government sounded like a lot of words, and no more. Still, John Whitewater was John Whitewater, and if he couldn't explain any better than that, possibly there was no other explanation. John Whitewater had been the friend of Fig Tree John, and that was authority enough. They stood helplessly and waited for further ideas. They watched ranchers and townspeople become nervous and panicky, and they watched them scurry to and fro using many words.

John Whitewater was turning the course of events over in his mind. He felt that it was reasonable that the bank must have money, for, as his friends had pointed out, they had all put money in it except Black Eye. So money was there. That was one point.

Now John Whitewater went from the general to the particular. He took up his own case. Before he could do any more work he

wanted a shovel and an ax. That was a point. To get these he
wanted his money which was in the bank. That was another point.
To get the money he had to transact certain business within the
bank. So that was the basic point, and everything evolved from
that. Everything depended upon the opening of the bank. ,

The other Indians had similar lines of thought, but their ideas
were not as clean-cut and as orderly as John Whitewater's. They
supposed that some step had to be taken, but just what it was to be
they did not know. But with the advent of John Whitewater
things reached a crisis. His opinion would be their opinion.

"What we do, John?" asked Black Eye, speaking for the majority.

John Whitewater considered. He thought, without any change
of expression coming over his face. He thought of the mesquite,
the shovel and the ax, the money, and the opening of the bank. All
depended upon the opening of this bank. The ways of the white
man were often an enigma. There was no accounting for some of
his devices. Acceptance and patience seemed the method of least
trouble. Sometime the white man must open his bank. Perhaps
in an hour, perhaps next Monday, perhaps next year. Just now the
white man, and many of their women, were coming and going to
and from the closed door of the bank. They were all talking all the
time. There were many words John Whitewater didn't understand.
There seemed to be a great deal of excitement and gesticulating
and a lot of unnecessary perspiring. There was nothing for John
Whitewater to do about it. He wasn't at all sure of what was going
on in the white man's world, and a noncommittal acceptance of
whatever the white man wanted to do seemed to be the only solution. Then he reached the conclusion that was to determine their
policy.

"Maybe sometime bank open," said John Whitewater. "We
wait."

And so all five Indians sat down on the curb in the warm sunshine and waited.

The Bride Comes to Yellow Sky

STEPHEN CRANE

Crane was a random New York newspaperman in 1894 when a syndicate sent him on a jaunt through the west and Mexico. Among the results were three top-rank western stories, The Bride and Horses — One Dash in his 1898 collection, The Open Boat and Other Tales of Adventure, and The Blue Hotel in his 1899 collection, The Monster and Other Stories. Some people might add The Five White Mice, also in the 1898 volume, which is definitely western in flavor though it takes place in Mexico City. The Blue Hotel is in some respects the prize, but it runs to length and lacks the clean-cut craftsmanship of The Bride.

THE GREAT PULLMAN was whirling onward with such dignity of motion that a glance from the window seemed simply to prove that the plains of Texas were pouring eastward. Vast flats of green grass, dull-hued spaces of mesquit and cactus, little groups of frame houses, woods of light and tender trees, all were sweeping into the east, sweeping over the horizon, a precipice.

A newly married pair had boarded this coach at San Antonio. The man's face was reddened from many days in the winds and sun, and a direct result of his new black clothes was that his brick-coloured hands were constantly performing in a most conscious fashion. From time to time he looked down respectfully at his attire. He sat with a hand on each knee, like a man waiting in a barber's shop. The glances he devoted to other passengers were furtive and shy.

The bride was not pretty, nor was she very young. She wore a dress of blue cashmere, with small reservations of velvet here and there, and with steel buttons abounding. She continually twisted her head to regard her puff sleeves, very stiff, straight, and high. They embarrassed her. It was quite apparent that she had cooked, and that she expected to cook, dutifully. The blushes caused by the careless scrutiny of some passengers as she had entered the car were strange to see upon this plain, under-class countenance, which was drawn in placid, almost emotionless lines.

They were evidently very happy. "Ever been in a parlour-car before?" he asked, smiling with delight.

"No," she answered; "I never was. It's fine, ain't it?"

"Great! And then after a while we'll go forward to the diner, and get a big lay-out. Finest meal in the world. Charge a dollar."

"Oh, do they?" cried the bride. "Charge a dollar? Why, that's too much — for us — ain't it, Jack?"

"Not this trip, anyhow," he answered bravely. "We're going to go the whole thing."

Later he explained to her about the trains. "You see, it's a thousand miles from one end of Texas to the other; and this train runs right across it, and never stops but four times." He had the pride of an owner. He pointed out to her the dazzling fittings of the coach; and in truth her eyes opened wider as she contemplated the sea-green figured velvet, the shining brass, silver, and glass, the wood that gleamed as darkly brilliant as the surface of a pool of oil. At one end a bronze figure sturdily held a support for a separated chamber, and at convenient places on the ceiling were frescos in olive and silver.

To the minds of the pair, their surroundings reflected the glory of their marriage that morning in San Antonio; this was the environment of their new estate; and the man's face in particular beamed with an elation that made him appear ridiculous to the negro porter. This individual at times surveyed them from afar with an amused and superior grin. On other occasions he bullied them with skill in ways that did not make it exactly plain to them that they were being bullied. He subtly used all the manners of the most unconquerable kind of snobbery. He oppressed them; but of this oppression they had small knowledge, and they speedily forgot that infrequently a number of travellers covered them with stares of derisive enjoyment. Historically there was supposed to be something infinitely humorous in their situation.

"We are due in Yellow Sky at 3:42," he said, looking tenderly into her eyes.

"Oh, are we?" she said, as if she had not been aware of it. To evince surprise at her husband's statement was part of her wifely amiability. She took from a pocket a little silver watch; and as she held it before her, and stared at it with a frown of attention, the new husband's face shone.

"I bought it in San Anton' from a friend of mine," he told her gleefully.

"It's seventeen minutes past twelve," she said, looking up at him with a kind of shy and clumsy coquetry. A passenger, noting this play, grew excessively sardonic, and winked at himself in one of the numerous mirrors.

At last they went to the dining-car. Two rows of negro waiters, in glowing white suits, surveyed their entrance with the interest, and also the equanimity, of men who had been forewarned. The pair fell to the lot of a waiter who happened to feel pleasure in steering them through their meal. He viewed them with the manner of a fatherly pilot, his countenance radiant with benevolence. The patronage, entwined with the ordinary deference, was not plain to them. And yet, as they returned to their coach, they showed in their faces a sense of escape.

To the left, miles down a long purple slope, was a little ribbon of mist where moved the keening Rio Grande. The train was approaching it at an angle, and the apex was Yellow Sky. Presently it was apparent that, as the distance from Yellow Sky grew shorter, the husband became commensurately restless. His brick-red hands were more insistent in their prominence. Occasionally he was even rather absent-minded and far-away when the bride leaned forward and addressed him.

As a matter of truth, Jack Potter was beginning to find the shadow of a deed weigh upon him like a leaden slab. He, the town marshal of Yellow Sky, a man known, liked, and feared in his corner, a prominent person, had gone to San Antonio to meet a girl he believed he loved, and there, after the usual prayers, had actually induced her to marry him, without consulting Yellow Sky for any part of the transaction. He was now bringing his bride before an innocent and unsuspecting community.

Of course people in Yellow Sky married as it pleased them, in accordance with a general custom; but such was Potter's thought of his duty to his friends, or of their idea of his duty, or of an unspoken form which does not control men in these matters, that he felt he was heinous. He had committed an extraordinary crime. Face to face with this girl in San Antonio, and spurred by his sharp impulse, he had gone headlong over all the social hedges. At San Antonio he was like a man hidden in the dark. A knife to sever any friendly duty, any form, was easy to his hand in that remote city. But the hour of Yellow Sky — the hour of daylight — was approaching.

He knew full well that his marriage was an important thing to his town. It could only be exceeded by the burning of the new hotel. His friends could not forgive him. Frequently he had reflected on the advisability of telling them by telegraph, but a new cowardice had been upon him. He feared to do it. And now the train was hurrying him towards a scene of amazement, glee and reproach. He glanced out of the window at the line of haze swinging slowly in towards the train.

Yellow Sky had a kind of brass band, which played painfully, to the delight of the populace. He laughed without heart as he thought of it. If the citizens could dream of his prospective arrival with his bride, they would parade the band at the station and escort them, amid cheers and laughing congratulations, to his adobe home.

He resolved that he would use all the devices of speed and plainscraft in making the journey from the station to his house. Once within that safe citadel, he could issue some sort of vocal bulletin, and then not go among the citizens until they had time to wear off a little of their enthusiasm.

The bride looked anxiously at him. "What's worrying you, Jack?"

He laughed again. "I'm not worrying, girl; I'm only thinking of Yellow Sky."

She flushed in comprehension.

A sense of mutual guilt invaded their minds and developed a finer tenderness. They looked at each other with eyes softly aglow. But Potter often laughed the same nervous laugh; the flush upon the bride's face seemed quite permanent.

The traitor to the feelings of Yellow Sky narrowly watched the speeding landscape. "We're nearly there," he said.

Presently the porter came and announced the proximity of Potter's home. He held a brush in his hand, and, with all his airy superiority gone, he brushed Potter's new clothes as the latter slowly turned this way and that way. Potter fumbled out a coin and gave it to the porter, as he had seen others do. It was a heavy and musclebound business, as that of a man shoeing his first horse.

The porter took their bag, and as the train began to slow they moved forward to the hooded platform of the car. Presently the two engines and their long string of coaches rushed into the station of Yellow Sky.

"They have to take water here," said Potter, from a constricted throat and in mournful cadence, as one announcing death. Before the train stopped his eye had swept the length of the platform, and he was glad and astonished to see there was none upon it but the station-agent, who, with a slightly hurried and anxious air, was walking toward the water-tanks. When the train had halted, the porter alighted first, and placed in position a little temporary step.

"Come on, girl," said Potter, hoarsely. As he helped her down they each laughed on a false note. He took the bag from the Negro, and bade his wife cling to his arm. As they slunk rapidly away, his hang-dog glance perceived that they were unloading the two trunks, and also that the station-agent, far ahead near the baggage-car, had turned and was running toward him, making gestures. He laughed, and groaned as he laughed, when he noted the first effect of his marital bliss upon Yellow Sky. He gripped his wife's arm firmly to his side, and they fled. Behind them the porter stood, chuckling fatuously.

The California express on the Southern Railway was due at Yellow Sky in twenty-one minutes. There were six men at the bar of the Weary Gentleman saloon. One was a drummer who talked a great deal and rapidly; three were Texans who did not care to talk at that time; and two were Mexican sheep-herders, who did not talk as a general practice in the Weary Gentleman saloon. The barkeeper's dog lay on the board walk that crossed in front of the door. His head was on his paws, and he glanced drowsily here and there with the constant vigilance of a dog that is kicked on occasion. Across the sandy street were some vivid green grass-plots, so wonderful in appearance, amid the sands that burned near them in a blazing sun, that they caused a doubt in the mind. They exactly resembled the grass mats used to represent lawns on the stage. At the cooler end of the railway station, a man without a coat sat in a tilted chair and smoked his pipe. The fresh-cut bank of the Rio Grande circled near the town, and there could be seen beyond it a great plum-coloured plain of mesquit.

Save for the busy drummer and his companions in the saloon, Yellow Sky was dozing. The new-comer leaned gracefully upon the bar, and recited tales with the confidence of a bard who has come upon a new field.

" — and at the moment that the old man fell downstairs with the bureau in his arms, the old woman was coming up with two scuttles of coal, and of course — "

The drummer's tale was interrupted by a young man who suddenly appeared in the open door. He cried: "Scratchy Wilson's drunk, and has turned loose with both hands." The two Mexicans at once set down their glasses and faded out of the rear entrance of the saloon.

The drummer, innocent and jocular, answered: "All right, old man. S'pose he has? Come in and have a drink, anyhow."

But the information had made such an obvious cleft in every skull in the room that the drummer was obliged to see its importance. All had become instantly solemn. "Say," said he, mystified, "what is this." His three companions made the introductory gesture of eloquent speech; but the young man at the door forestalled them.

"It means, my friend," he answered, as he came into the saloon, "that for the next two hours this town won't be a health resort."

The barkeeper went to the door, and locked and barred it; reaching out of the window, he pulled in heavy wooden shutters, and barred them. Immediately a solemn, chapel-like gloom was upon the place. The drummer was looking from one to another.

"But say," he cried, "what is this, anyhow? You don't mean there is going to be a gun-fight?"

"Don't know whether there'll be a fight or not," answered one man, grimly; "but there'll be some shootin' — some good shootin'."

The young man who had warned them waved his hand. "Oh, there'll be a fight fast enough, if any one wants it. Anybody can get a fight out there in the street. There's a fight just waiting."

The drummer seemed to be swayed between the interest of a foreigner and a perception of personal danger.

"What did you say his name was?" he asked.

"Scratchy Wilson," they answered in chorus.

"And will he kill anybody? What are you going to do? Does this happen often? Does he rampage around like this once a week or so? Can he break in that door?"

"No; he can't break down that door," replied the barkeeper. "He's tried it three times. But when he comes you'd better lay down on the floor, stranger. He's dead sure to shoot at it, and a bullet may come through."

Thereafter the drummer kept a strict eye upon the door. The time had not yet been called for him to hug the floor, but, as a minor precaution, he sidled near to the wall. "Will he kill anybody?" he asked again.

The men laughed low and scornfully at the question.

"He's out to shoot, and he's out for trouble. Don't see any good in experimentin' with him."

"But what do you do in a case like this? What do you do?"

A man responded: "Why, he and Jack Potter — "

"But," in chorus the other men interrupted, "Jack Potter's in San Anton'."

"Well, who is he? What's he got to do with it?"

"Oh, he's the town marshal. He goes out and fights Scratchy when he gets on one of these tears."

"Wow!" said the drummer, mopping his brow. "Nice job he's got."

The voices had toned away to mere whisperings. The drummer wished to ask further questions, which were born of an increasing anxiety and bewilderment; but when he attempted them, the men merely looked at him in irritation and motioned him to remain silent. A tense waiting hush was upon them. In the deep shadows of the room their eyes shone as they listened for sounds from the street. One man made three gestures at the barkeeper; and the latter, moving like a ghost, handed him a glass and a bottle. The man poured a full glass of whisky, and set down the bottle noiselessly. He gulped the whisky in a swallow, and turned again toward the door in immovable silence. The drummer saw that the barkeeper, without a sound, had taken a Winchester from beneath the bar. Later he saw this individual beckoning to him, so he tiptoed across the room.

"You better come with me back of the bar."

"No, thanks," said the drummer, perspiring; "I'd rather be where I can make a break for the back door."

Whereupon the man of bottles made a kindly but peremptory

gesture. The drummer obeyed it, and, finding himself seated on a box with his head below the level of the bar, balm was laid upon his soul at sight of various zinc and copper fittings that bore a resemblance to armour-plate. The barkeeper took a seat comfortably upon an adjacent box.

"You see," he whispered, "this here Scratchy Wilson is a wonder with a gun — a perfect wonder; and when he goes on the war-trail, we hunt our holes — naturally. He's about the last of the old gang that used to hang out along the river here. He's a terror when he's drunk. When he's sober he's all right — kind of simple — wouldn't hurt a fly — nicest fellow in town. But when he's drunk — whoo!"

There were periods of stillness. "I wish Jack Potter was back from San Anton'," said the barkeeper. "He shot Wilson up once — in the leg — and he would sail in and pull out the kinks in this thing."

Presently they heard from a distance the sound of a shot, followed by three wild yowls. It instantly removed a bond from the men in the darkened saloon. There was a shuffling of feet. They looked at each other. "Here he comes," they said.

A man in a maroon-coloured flannel shirt, which had been purchased for purposes of decoration, and made principally by some Jewish women on the East Side of New York, rounded a corner and walked into the middle of the main street of Yellow Sky. In either hand the man held a long, heavy, blue-black revolver. Often he yelled, and these cries rang through a semblance of a deserted village, shrilly flying over the roofs in a volume that seemed to have no relation to the ordinary vocal strength of a man. It was as if the surrounding stillness formed the arch of a tomb over him. These cries of ferocious challenge rang against walls of silence. And his boots had red tops with gilded imprints, of the kind beloved in winter by little sledding boys on the hillsides of New England.

The man's face flamed in a rage begot of whisky. His eyes, rolling, and yet keen for ambush, hunted the still doorways and windows. He walked with the creeping movement of the midnight cat. As it occurred to him, he roared menacing information. The long revolvers in his hands were as easy as straws; they were moved with an electric swiftness. The little fingers of each hand played sometimes in a musician's way. Plain from the low collar of the shirt, the cords of his neck straightened and sank, straightened and sank, as passion moved him. The only sounds were his terrible invitations. The calm adobes preserved their demeanour at the passing of this small thing in the middle of the street.

There was no offer of fight — no offer of fight. The man called to the sky. There were no attractions. He bellowed and fumed and swayed his revolvers here and everywhere.

The dog of the barkeeper of the Weary Gentleman saloon had not appreciated the advance of events. He yet lay dozing in front of his master's door. At sight of the dog, the man paused and raised his revolver humorously. At sight of the man, the dog sprang up and walked diagonally away, with a sullen head, and growling. The man yelled, and the dog broke into a gallop. As it was about to enter an alley, there was a loud noise, a whistling, and something spat the ground directly before it. The dog screamed, and, wheeling in terror, galloped headlong in a new direction. Again there was a noise, a whistling, and sand was kicked viciously before it. Fear-stricken, the dog turned and flurried like an animal in a pen. The man stood laughing, his weapons at his hips.

Ultimately the man was attracted by the closed door of the Weary Gentleman saloon. He went to it and, hammering with a revolver, demanded drink.

The door remaining imperturbable, he picked a bit of paper from the walk, and nailed it to the framework with a knife. He then turned his back contemptuously upon this popular resort and, walking to the opposite side of the street and spinning there on his heel quickly and lithely, fired at the bit of paper. He missed it by a half-inch. He swore at himself, and went away. Later he comfortably fusilladed the windows of his most intimate friend. The man was playing with this town; it was a toy for him.

But still there was no offer of fight. The name of Jack Potter, his ancient antagonist, entered his mind, and he concluded that it would be a glad thing if he should go to Potter's house, and by bombardment induce him to come out and fight. He moved in the direction of his desire, chanting Apache scalp-music.

When he arrived at it, Potter's house presented the same still front as had the other adobes. Taking up a strategic position, the man howled a challenge. But this house regarded him as might a great stone god. It gave no sign. After a decent wait, the man howled further challenges, mingling with them wonderful epithets.

Presently there came the spectacle of a man churning himself into deepest rage over the immobility of a house. He fumed at it as the winter wind attacks a prairie cabin in the North. To the distance there should have gone the sound of a tumult like the fighting of two hundred Mexicans. As necessity bade him, he paused for breath or to reload his revolvers.

Potter and his bride walked sheepishly and with speed. Sometimes they laughed together shamefacedly and low.

"Next corner, dear," he said finally.

They put forth the efforts of a pair walking bowed against a strong wind. Potter was about to raise a finger to point the first appearance of the new home when, as they circled the corner, they came face to face with a man in a maroon-coloured shirt, who was feverishly pushing cartridges into a large revolver. Upon the instant the man dropped his revolver to the ground and, like lightning, whipped another from its holster. The second weapon was aimed at the bridegroom's chest.

There was a silence. Potter's mouth seemed to be merely a grave for his tongue. He exhibited an instinct to at once loosen his arm from the woman's grip, and he dropped the bag to the sand. As for the bride, her face had gone as yellow as old cloth. She was a slave to hideous rites, gazing at the apparitional snake.

The two men faced each other at a distance of three paces. He of the revolver smiled with a new and quiet ferocity.

"'Tried to sneak up on me," he said. "Tried to sneak up on me!" His eyes grew more baleful. As Potter made a slight movement, the man thrust his revolver venomously forward. "No; don't you do it, Jack Potter. Don't you move a finger towards a gun just yet. Don't you move an eyelash. The time has come for me to settle with you, and I'm goin' to do it in my own way, and loaf along with no interferin'. So if you don't want a gun bent on you, just mind what I tell you."

Potter looked at his enemy. "I ain't got a gun on me, Scratchy," he said. "Honest, I ain't." He was stiffening and steadying, but yet somewhere at the back of his mind a vision of the Pullman floated: the sea-green figured velvet, the shining brass, silver, and glass, the wood that gleamed as darkly brilliant as the surface of a pool of oil — all the glory of the marriage, the environment of the new estate. "You know I fight when it comes to fighting, Scratchy Wilson; but I ain't got a gun on me. You'll have to do all the shootin' yourself."

His enemy's face went livid. He stepped forward, and lashed his weapon to and fro before Potter's chest. "Don't you tell me you ain't got no gun on you, you whelp. Don't tell me no lie like that. There ain't a man in Texas ever seen you without no gun. Don't take me for no kid." His eyes blazed with light, and his throat worked like a pump.

"I ain't takin' you for no kid," answered Potter. His heels had not moved an inch backward. "I'm takin' you for a damn fool. I tell you I ain't got a gun, and I ain't. If you're goin' to shoot me, you better begin now; you'll never get a chance like this again."

So much enforced reasoning had told on Wilson's rage; he was calmer. "If you ain't got a gun, why ain't you got a gun?" he sneered. "Been to Sunday-school?"

"I ain't got a gun because I've just come from San Anton' with my wife. I'm married," said Potter. "And if I'd thought there was going to be any galoots like you prowling around when I brought my wife home, I'd had a gun, and don't you forget it."

"Married!" said Scratchy, not at all comprehending.

"Yes, married. I'm married," said Potter, distinctly.

"Married?" said Scratchy. Seemingly for the first time, he saw the drooping, drowning woman at the other man's side. "No!" he said. He was like a creature allowed a glimpse of another world. He moved a pace backward, and his arm, with the revolver, dropped to his side. "Is this the lady?" he asked.

"Yes; this is the lady," answered Potter.

There was another period of silence.

"Well," said Wilson at last, slowly, "I s'pose it's all off now."

"It's all off if you say so, Scratchy. You know I didn't make the trouble." Potter lifted his valise.

"Well, I 'low it's off, Jack," said Wilson. He was looking at the ground. "Married!" He was not a student of chivalry; it was merely that in the presence of this foreign condition he was a simple child of the earlier plains. He picked up his starboard revolver, and, placing both weapons in their holsters, he went away. His feet made funnel-shaped tracks in the heavy sand.

The Cloud Puncher

WILLIAM CUNNINGHAM

*H*ere is another of those typical western tales so tall it takes two men to see the top. Western literature supplies them in plenty, but there are not many as neatly original and colloquially exact as this one. All I know about William Cunningham is that he is an Oklahoman who has been variously a teacher and newspaperman and freelance writer and somewhere along the line has published several novels which I certainly intend to read if I ever come across them. I first encountered this tale in the form of tear sheets from the Windsor Quarterly, sent me by a knowing friend some years back. I have met it once or twice since in anthologies. It deserves to pop up here and there for a long time to come.

A WHILE before the cyclone season, a man with uncommon bow legs arrived and said people usually called him Parenthesis, he didn't know why. He said he would work for the outfit if we furnished a horse.

The foreman said that was real kind of him, and what kind of a horse would he like.

Parenthesis said it made no difference, only he preferred a spirited mount.

The foreman said we've got a spirited mount. The only trouble was he bucks a little when you first get on.

Parenthesis said it made no difference, only he liked one with spirits.

The foreman winked at us and said ketch up the piebald and put the gentleman's saddle on it.

We looked at each other with great surprise, because the last man that tried to ride the piebald was throwed so high that he turned three summersets before he hit the ground. We saddled the piebald. There wasn't nothing wrong with him except he had some cockleburs in his mane and tail.

Parenthesis mounted and took off his hat and waved it and we run to get out of the way. The piebald fooled around for a while, jumping about ten feet in the air and coming down stiff-legged, figuring to jar the rider's teeth out of his upper jaw if he didn't have his mouth shut when they landed. But Parenthesis kept his mouth shut, and so the piebald went to work. He arose straight up and switched ends in midair, figuring to twist the rider's head off if he didn't have a strong neck. But Parenthesis kept his head, and after a half-hour of this, the piebald got tired.

Parenthesis dismounted. When we unsaddled the piebald we noticed he had bucked all the cockleburs out of his mane and tail.

Parenthesis said the piebald would do, unless the outfit had a horse with more spirits. The foreman said well we've got a spirited mount. The only trouble was he bucks a little when you first get on, if you don't mind that.

Parenthesis said he didn't mind.

The foreman winked at us and said saddle the pinto.

We looked at each other with dismay because the last man that tried to ride the pinto got a bad sunburn through the seat of his pants before he hit the ground, his pants being a little threadbare and the sun shining through the cloth. We saddled the pinto. There wasn't nothing wrong with him except he had some of these stick-tight fleas in his ears.

Parenthesis mounted and took off his hat and waved it and we run to get out of the way. The pinto fooled around for a while, jumping about fifteen feet in the air and coming down stiff-legged so hard that he buried his feet in the ground up to the ankles. Then he went straight up and twisted himself in midair, so that his front feet was pointing straight down and his hind feet pointing straight up. This was to throw the rider off balance. But Parenthesis kept his balance and after a half-hour of this the pinto got tired.

Parenthesis dismounted. When we unsaddled the pinto we noticed he had bucked all the fleas out of his ears.

Parenthesis said the pinto would do, unless the outfit had a horse with more spirits. The foreman said well we've got a spirited mount. The only trouble was he bucks a little when you first get on, if you don't mind that.

Parenthesis said he didn't mind that.

The foreman winked at us and said saddle the strawberry roan.

We looked at each other with consternation because the last man that tried to ride the strawberry roan, a couple of sparrows built a nest in his navel. We saddled the strawberry roan. There wasn't nothing wrong with him.

Parenthesis mounted and took off his hat and waved it and we run. The piebald fooled around for a while, jumping about twenty feet in the air and coming down stiff-legged so hard that he buried his feet in the ground up to the knees. Then he went straight up and we never did know just what he done. He seemed to kind of explode into a strawberry roan cloud and then he fell out of the cloud stark naked. He made some kind of a twist up there so sudden that he bucked off all his own hair, including the long hairs in his tail and mane. But he couldn't shake off Parenthesis, so after a half-hour he quit.

Parenthesis said the strawberry roan would do, and he went to work for our outfit. Every time he got on that strawberry roan, they went cavorting off across the alkali, and whatever hair the strawberry roan grew overnight he bucked off the next morning.

You would think Parenthesis would get his spine jarred often enough on a horse like that, but he didn't. He always wanted to ride something that bucked. He would pick out the orneriest, longest-legged steer in a herd and ride up beside him and jump off his horse onto the steer's back, and away they'd go, Parenthesis waving his hat. He didn't seem to need no surcingle, like most fellers do on a steer, or turn around and ride backwards, holding to the tail. You know how a steer is. Seems his hind legs is so much longer than his front legs that you just naturally slide down on his horns. But Parenthesis didn't seem to slide.

The cyclones was bad that year. Every once in a while we'd see one off a little distance, like a big funnel in the sky. It would settle to the ground and suck up everything on the ground for a ways and then lift and travel high for a few miles.

Well one day just when Parenthesis got on his naked horse, a cyclone dipped down. We all fell flat on our faces and dug our fingers into the grass roots to keep from being pulled up. Then we looked up, and there went Parenthesis about a thousand feet in the air, waving his hat. And the naked horse was standing there looking up with the most astonished look you ever seen on the face of a horse, and a grief-stricken look too. I think he was sorry to see Parenthesis taken off that way.

We was all sorry, but we agreed if Parenthesis had to go, that was the best way, up in the sky, waving his hat.

Some said the naked strawberry roan had managed to toss Parenthesis into the air at last and the cyclone took him from there. Others said the cyclone pulled him out of the saddle. We didn't know.

Some thought the cyclone would drop him astraddle of a barbed wire fence and split him lengthways. Some said it would slide him through one along the ground, slicing him like a boloney. We looked for him far and wide but didn't find hide nor hair of him, either split or sliced.

Then one Sunday afternoon when we was all lazing around the bunkhouse, a twister let down in the pasture right over there and come hell-bent right toward us, and we flattened out, but just before it got to the corral it lifted and went over us and the buildings and didn't harm anything. And while we were still on our knees, marveling, we noticed Parenthesis standing beside the corral, rolling a cigarette. There was no mistaking him on account of his uncommon bow legs.

We run to him and asked him where he'd been, and he said he took a little run over to the Rockies and then down to the Gulf of Mexico and back. We asked him was he crazy and he said we couldn't imagine how good a cigarette tasted after all this time. He said he had everything else he needed. He even got so he could dip down and lift a cup of coffee off of a counter in a restaurant, out through the window, without spilling a drop, or damaging anything else. But he couldn't roll a cigarette in the middle of a cyclone.

We asked him if he got a bad knock on the head and he said he knew we thought he was crazy, but he broke that thing to ride. We asked him who did he think would believe that and he said he didn't blame us none for disbelieving, and all he come back for was his saddle. He was tired of riding the cyclone bareback.

We said he better come into the bunkhouse and lay down and get some rest. Somebody asked him what happened, did the horse buck him off, or did the cyclone pull him off of the horse. He said

neither one. The cyclone sort of run up beside him and he got to
wondering if he could ride it, so he jumped off the horse onto the
cyclone.

He said it was real rough for an hour or two. The roughest ride
he ever had. Then he kind of got the cyclone under control, and
it learned fast. In a little while he could guide it by leaning this
way or that way. The hardest thing was to keep it from putting its
foot down where it would do damage. Even now he didn't like to
ride it in a well settled country for fear it would set down on a
house or something, so he kept out here in the cattle country
mostly.

He said he hadn't figured any way to use the cyclone yet, except
just to ride around on and see the country. But he had one idea
that he had tried, and maybe could make a little cash. He could
make a rock silo. He said he knew where there was a well about
fifty feet deep, dug through solid rock, but it was dry and no good
to anybody. So he set the funnel of the cyclone down on it and
turned it wrong side out. It made a pretty silo, although it's way
out in the pasture where there's no ensilage for miles around.

He said well he'd better breeze along, because he realized us boys
would just tie him up and take him to the bughouse if he stayed
around much longer. He went to the shed and got his saddle and
walked out a little ways from the buildings and put his fingers in
his mouth and whistled.

A black cloud come whirling toward us, and the funnel came
down over the buildings, just missing them, and picked up Parenthesis. He took off his hat and waved and he was gone.

We didn't see anything of him for a while, then one day he
dropped in on us again. He was all dressed up, and fat and prosperous, and he had a new silver-mounted saddle. He said he was
really making a good thing out of it, herding rain clouds.

He would go down to the gulf coast where there's lots of clouds,
and cut out a herd of them maybe fifteen, twenty miles wide. Then
he'd push them to west Texas and New Mexico, wherever the
ranchers needed rain. It took a lot of patience to herd rain clouds.
It was like herding milk cows, if you run them they lost their rain.
But after you got the knack of it, it was easy enough.

For rain he charged by the inch. A little spatter to settle the
dust didn't cost much, but a half-inch rain come pretty high. A
inch rain was more than twice as much as a half-inch rain, because
it was so much more work, keeping the clouds bunched up and

quiet for long enough to rain that much. Also you had to take time into consideration. A slow drizzle of say an inch was a lot more expensive than a sudden downpour of the same amount.

He said he had a few old clouds off to the northwest that had been just about all rained out and he would bring them over to cool us off a little, free. He asked about the strawberry roan, if his hair was growing back, and we said the roan was looking good. He said we could have the horse if we would promise to treat him right. Which we did.

Then he left, and soon the sky clouded over and it rained a little spatter, which cooled us off.

We was real sad when we found out how Parenthesis ended. It seems he set his cyclone down on a saloon and lifted the whole stock, including a corkscrew. He wasn't exactly a drinking man, but he couldn't resist all that liquor whirling around him, so he opened a bottle. Seems when he had too much to drink he lost his judgment, like lots of other men, and he rode that cyclone over to the Rockies.

Well a cyclone don't like mountains any more than a horse likes rough ground. They stay mostly in flat land because it's easier going. But Parenthesis didn't figure how hard it was on his cyclone, and he rode it over the mountains and up and down from Canada to Mexico. And he broke its wind.

A wind-broke cyclone ain't any good. Besides, there was another thing. This cyclone was with whirlwind. I don't know whether or not he knew about its condition, but he should have. Anyway it gave birth to a litter of whirlwinds and died on him.

And there he was, five thousand feet up, with nothing to support him but some little whirlwinds not hardly big enough to blow a man's hat off. I guess he was dead drunk by this time and never knew what happened. I hope so. He hit awful hard.

The strawberry roan has got a nice glossy coat of hair now and his tail and mane is as long as any horse's. There's nothing wrong with him except he bucks when you first get on him.

Old Man Isbell's Wife

H. L. DAVIS

H. L. Davis has written so many pieces so vigorously explaining
his work and his attitude toward the West and western writing that
it might be presumptuous for anyone else to try to add to them.
I simply note that he writes his own particular brand of western
story, holding rather steadily to his native northwest country, and
has a habit of regarding any other type of western story as not quite
up to the mark. His unswerving distrust of fake and formula is a
healthy influence in the field.

This is one of his earliest stories, written about 1929 for The
American Mercury at the instigation of then editor H. L. Mencken.
It is reprinted with plenty of good company in his 1953 collection,
Team Bells Woke Me and Other Stories. Most of these were
written before the Pulitzer-prize novel Honey in the Horn, 1935,
but most of them can stand right beside it.

THE COW-TOWN started as an overnight station on the old Military
Road through Eastern Oregon into Idaho. The freighters wanted
a place to unhitch and get the taste of sagebrush out of their
mouths. They were willing to pay for it, and one was built for
them by the people who like, better than anything else, money that

has been worked hard for — not to work hard for it themselves, but to take it from men who do.

The cow-town itself was a kind of accident. When they built it, they had no idea beyond fixing up a place where the freighters could buy what they wanted. They fixed it up with houses — houses to eat in, houses to get drunk in, houses to sleep in, or stay awake in, houses to stable horses in; and, as an afterthought, houses for themselves to live in while they took the freighters' and cattlemen's money. And money came — not fast, but so steadily that it got monotonous. There were no surprises, no starvation years, no fabulous winnings or profits; simply, one year after another, enough to live on and something over. They got out of the habit of thinking the place was an overnight station to make money in. They began, instead, to look at it as a place to live in. That, in Eastern Oregon, meant a change of status, a step up. The risk of the place being abandoned was over; there, straddling the long road between Fort Dalles on the Columbia and Fort Boise on the Snake River, was a town.

The new status had no effect upon its appearance. Ugly and little it had begun, and ugly and little it stayed. The buildings were ramshackle and old, with the paint peeled off; and, including the stack of junk behind the blacksmith shop, the whole thing covered an area of ten blocks. Two acres of town, in the middle of a cattle range of ten thousand square miles. Yet in those ten blocks a man could live his entire lifetime, lacking nothing, and perhaps not even missing anything. Food, warmth, liquor, work, and women; love, avarice, fear, envy, anger, and, of a special kind, belonging to no other kind of life, joy.

Over the ten thousand miles of range, whole cycles of humanity — flint Indians, horse Indians, California Spaniards, emigrants, cattlemen — had passed, and each had marked it without altering its shape or color. The cow town itself was one mark, and not the biggest, either; but that was a comparison which none of the townspeople ever made. They were too much used to it, and they had other things to think about. What interested them was their ten blocks of town, and the people who lived in it.

All country people keep track of each other's business — as a usual thing, because they haven't anything else to think about. But the cow-town people did it, not in idleness, but from actual and fundamental passion. They preferred it to anything else in the world. It was not in the least that they were fond of one another — though, of course, some of them were. That had nothing to do with their preference. It was merely that what their town did was life — clear, interesting, recognizable; and nothing else was. They stuck to what was familiar. It must be remembered that these people were not chance-takers. They were more like the peddlers who follow an army, not fighting themselves, but living on the men who do. The freighters and cattlemen, and the men from the range, were a different race; the range itself was a strange element; and they were too small to have much curiosity about either. The women were the smallest. It was they who backed the movement to ship Old Man Isbell out of town.

Old Man Isbell lived in the cow town because there was no other place he could live. He had ridden the range, at one job or another, for more than fifty years, and the town would have been strange and foreign to him, even if it had made him welcome. It did not. For one thing, he was not a townsman, but a member of the race which they preyed on. For another, he was eighty-five years old, slack-witted, vacant-minded, doddering, dirty, and a bore. It took an hour to get the commonest question through his head, and another hour for him to think up an answer to it. He never tied his shoes, and he had to shuffle his feet as he walked, to keep them from falling off. Nor did he ever button his trousers, which fact was cited by the women as indicating complete moral decay. He ought to be sent away, they said, to some institution where such cases were decently taken care of.

The clerk in the general store agreed with them, and perhaps he, at least, had a right to. It was his job, every day, to sell Old Man Isbell a bill of groceries, and the old man could never remember what it was he wanted. Sometimes it took hours, and while he was there ladies couldn't come in the store, on account of his unbuttoned trousers and his pipe.

His pipe was another just ground for complaint. It was as black as tar and as soggy as a toadstool, with a smell like carrion and a rattle like a horse being choked to death. To get it lit took him hours, because his hand shook so he couldn't hold a match against the bowl. It was his palsy, no doubt, that was to blame for his unbuttoned trousers, his dangling shoestrings, and the gobs of food smeared on his clothes and through his whiskers. But that was not conclusive evidence that he was feeble-minded. Even a sane man would have trouble tying a bow-knot or hitting a buttonhole if his hands insisted on jumping two inches off the target at every heartbeat. The ladies added it to their evidence, but it should not have been allowed to count. Old Man Isbell's chief abnormality was of longer standing. He was simply, and before anything else, a natural-born bore.

The dullness of his speech was a gift of God. He had lived his eighty-five years through the most splendidly colored history that one man could ever have lived through in the world — the Civil War, the Indian campaigns in the West, the mining days, the cattle-kings, the long-line freighters, the road agents, the stockmen's wars — the changing, with a swiftness and decision unknown to history before, of a country and its people; yes, and of a nation. Not as a spectator, either. He lived in the middle of every bit of it, and had a hand in every phase. But, for all the interest it gave to his conversation, he could just as well have spent his life at home working buttonholes.

"I remember Lincoln," he would say. "I drove him on an electioneerin' trip, back in Illinoy. Him and Stephen A. Douglas. I drove their carriage."

One would sit up and think, "Well! The old gabe does know something good, after all!" Expecting, of course, that he was about to tell some incident of the Lincoln-Douglas debates — something, maybe, that everybody else had missed. But that was all. So far as he knew, there hadn't been any incidents. They electioneered. He drove their carriage. They rode in it. That was all that had impressed him.

Or he would remember when there had been no Military Road, and no cow-town, nor even any cattle; only, instead, great herds of deer pasturing in grass belly-deep to a horse. A herd of over a hundred big mule-deer trotting close enough for a man to hang a rope on, right where the town was. But when you tried to work him for something beside the bare fact that they had been there you struck bottom. They had been there. Hundreds of them. He had seen them, that close. That ended the story. I asked him, once, if he remembered anything about Boone Helm, an early-day outlaw and all-round mean egg. He considered, sucked his pipe through a critical spell of croup, and finally said, "They used to be a road-agent by that name. He cut a feller's ears off."

It was not a prelude, but a statement of what he remembered. Some old men remember more than what actually happened; some remember things that never happened at all. Old Man Isbell remembered the exact thing, and, that being done, he stopped. He ought to have been writing military dispatches. Or had he? It never came into his head to tone up or temper down the exact and religious truth, and amplifying what he had seen simply wasn't in him.

To events that went on in the town he never appeared to pay the smallest attention. Indeed, he paid none to the people there, either, and, though they laid that to the condition of his wits, it irritated them. Yet it was no more than an old range-man's indifference to things which he considers immaterial. He was sharp enough when anything was going on that interested him — cattle-branding in the corrals below town, or the state of the water on the range. South of town was a long slope, with a big spring almost at the top, ringed with green grass except when the spring went dry. Then the grass turned brown. The old man never failed to notice that. He would stop people in the street and point it out.

They laughed at him for it, behind his back. What did it matter to him whether the cattle had a dry year or not? He had an Indian War pension to live on, and he would get it whether the cattle throve or died to the last hoof. But, of course, he remembered what cattle looked like when they died of thirst, and swelled and popped open in the unmerciful heat, their burnt tongues lolling in the dust. It excited him to think of it, and he made a nuisance of himself about it. Sometimes he would stop strangers to tell it to them, which gave the town a bad name. Besides, his critics added, he smelled bad. Not being able to wait on himself, and never having been particular about washing or laundry, he did smell bad. The place for him, they agreed, was in some nice home where he could be waited on decently. He needed looking after.

In that they were right. He did need looking after. The trouble was that their plan involved sending him away from the sagebrush country, and that would have been the same thing as knocking him in the head with an ax. He was an old sagebrusher. To take him out of sight of his country — the yellow-flowered, silver-green sage, the black-foliaged greasewood, blossoming full of strong honey; the strong-scented, purple-berried junipers, and the wild cherry shrub with its sticky, bitterish-honied flowers and dark sour fruit; the pale red-edged ridges, and the rock-breaks, blazing scarlet and orange and dead-black — to lose them would have killed him. By these things, an old sagebrusher lives. Out of reach of them, silly as it sounds to say so, he will die. I've seen them do it.

Old Man Isbell, incapable and slack-witted, helpless with age, and, so far as anybody could tell, without any suspicion of what the townspeople were thinking about him or that they were making designs against his life, did the one thing that could save him.

He had nobody to take care of him. It was to see him taken care of that they wanted to send him away; and, surely without knowing it, he stumbled on the way to head them off. He got married.

The wedding threw the town into a perfect panic of delighted horror. This was one of the things that made life a fine thing to live. Other people, other communities, had diversions which the cow-town did without; this made up for them. The justice of the peace, having performed the ceremony, put out for home on a gallop to tell his wife the news. Hearing it, she came out with her hair down, and canvassed the houses both sides of the street, knocking at every door, and yelling, without waiting for anybody to open — "Old Man Isbell's got married! You'll never guess who to!"

The bride alone would have made a rich story. She was about twenty-eight years old — Old Man Isbell being, as I've mentioned, eighty-five — and the rest of her was even more incongruous than her youth. She weighed close to three hundred pounds, being almost as broad as she was tall, and she had to shave her face regularly to keep down a coarse black beard, which showed in the wrinkles of fat where a razor could not reach.

As Old Man Isbell was the town nuisance, she was the town joke. Even in that scantily womaned place, where only the dullest girls lived after they were big enough to look out for themselves, she had never had a suitor. The men were not too particular, but nobody dared pay court to her, for fear of getting laughed at. She was so fat that to walk downtown for Old Man Isbell's order of groceries took her almost an hour. It made one tired to watch her. Even the Indian squaws, riding through town, their matronly bellies overhanging the horns of their saddles, drew rein to admire Old Man Isbell's bride for an adiposity which laid theirs completely in the shade. They were fat, all right, but good heavens! They cackled and clucked to each other, pointing.

Housewives ran to peep through the curtains at the twenty-eight-year-old girl who had been hard up enough to marry an old, dirty, feeble-minded man of eighty-five. Store loafers perked up and passed remarks on her and on the match. But in spite of them all, in spite of the tittering, and the cruelty and the embarrassment, and her own exertion, she carried home the groceries every day. She cooked and cleaned house, too; and kept it clean; and one of the first things she bought after her marriage was a clothesline. It was full every day, and the clothes on it were clean. So were Old Man Isbell's. He sat on his front porch, wobbling matches over his black gaggling pipe, without a thing in the world to bother his mind except his pipe and the spring on the slope south of town. His trousers were fully buttoned, his shoes tied, and his beard and clothing washed, brushed and straightened, without a speck upon them to show what he had eaten last, or when.

Town joke or not, the fat woman was taking care of him. She was being a housewife, attending to the duties of her station exactly as the other married women in town attended to theirs, and that was something they had not expected. There wasn't any fun for them in that. They wanted her to remain a joke; and they couldn't joke about her housework without belittling their own. They took it out on her by letting her alone. There was no woman in town for Old Man Isbell's wife to talk to, except my mother, who, being the schoolteacher's wife, didn't quite belong to the townspeople, and would probably have repudiated their conventions if she had. Across the back fence she got all of the fat woman's story — not all of it, either, but all its heroine was willing to volunteer.

The fat woman had come to the country with her father, who took up a homestead on Tub Springs Ridge. But he got himself in jail for vealing somebody else's calf, and she moved into town to live till he served out his time. For a while she lived by selling off the farm machinery he had left. But it didn't take very long to live that up — "not that I eat so much," she hastened to add, "I really don't eat as much as . . . as ordinary folks do . . . " — and when that was gone she was broke. That was what induced her to listen, she said, to Old Man Isbell, when he first began to talk about getting married. She was desperate. It seemed the only resort, and yet it was so unheard of that she hesitated.

Finally, she borrowed a lift from a stage driver, and went to the county jail to ask advice from her father. He knew the old man. It would be all right, he said, to marry him. But not unless she realized what kind of job she was taking on, and was game to live up to it. She mustn't bull into it and then try to back out. The old man would have to be tended exactly like a small infant — the work would be just as hard, and just as necessary — and, in addition, he was uglier, meaner and dirtier. If she wanted to undertake the contract, all right; but she must either stick to it or let it entirely alone. When Old Man Isbell died, she would get what money he had saved up, and his Indian War pension. Enough to keep her, probably, for life. But it was up to her to see that she earned it.

"He made me promise I would," she told my mother, "and the

Lord knows I have. It's just exactly like pa said, too. He's just like a little baby. To see him set and stare at that spring for hours on end, you wouldn't believe how contrary and mean he can be around the house. All the time. He'll take a notion he wants something, and then forget the name of it and get mad because I don't guess it right. I have to pick up things and offer 'em to him, one at a time, till I manage to hit the one he's set his mind on. And him gettin' madder every time I pick up the wrong thing. Just like a baby. And his clothes — they're the same, too." She sighed into her series of stubbly chins. "It keeps me goin' every minute," she said. "It's mighty hard work."

"You do keep him clean, though," my mother said. "He was so dirty and forlorn. Everybody's talking about how clean you keep him now."

"They talk about how I married him to get his pension," the fat woman said. "How I'm just hangin' around waitin' for him to die. I know!"

"That's only some of them," my mother said. "They don't know anything about it. You work right along, and don't pay any attention to them."

"None of the ladies ever come to call on me," said the fat woman.

"I shouldn't think you'd want them to," my mother suggested. "You must be so busy, you wouldn't have time to bother with visitors. They probably think you'd sooner not be disturbed at your work."

"I do want 'em to, anyway," said the fat woman. "And they call on all the other married ladies, whether they're overworked or not. They call on Mis' Melendy, across the way, and she's got teethin' twins."

"Well, I wouldn't care whether they came to see me or not," said my mother.

"I do, though," the fat woman insisted. "I've got a house, and a husband, just the same as they have. I do my housework just the same, too. I'd like to show 'em all the work I do, and what a care it is to keep things clean, and how clean I keep 'em. If they'd come, they'd see."

My mother assented. There was no earthly chance that any of them would come, and she knew it. But the fat woman didn't know it, and it was the one thing in the world that she had her head set on. Everything else that women take pride in and nourish conceit upon she had given up; and for that very renouncement she stuck all the more fiercely to the idea of being visited by the neighbor ladies — of being received as an established housewife, like the rest of them. There might not be any sense in the notion, but she wanted it. No matter how they came, or why, she wanted them. Even if they came prying for things to discredit her with, to trot around and gabble about, she wanted them anyway. When other women got married, the neighbor ladies came to call. Now she was married, and they didn't.

The worst of it was, there was no way of breaking it to her that they weren't going to. My mother made several tries at letting her down easy, but got nowhere. She wanted it too much to give it up. Some days she would come to the fence elated and hopeful, because one of the ladies had nodded to her; sometimes she would be depressed and glum.

"I know what's keepin 'em away," she told my mother. "It's him!"

She yanked a fat arm in the direction of her husband, sitting in the sun with his mouth hanging open.

"Oh, no!" my mother protested. "Why — "

"Yes, it is!" the fat woman insisted. "And I don't blame 'em, either! Who wants to come visitin', when you've got to climb around an object like that to get into the parlor? I don't blame 'em for stayin' away. I would, my own self."

"But you've got to take care of him," my mother reminded her.

"Yes, I've got to. I promised pa I wouldn't back out on that, and I won't. But, as long as I've got him around, I won't have any visitors to entertain. I might as well quit expectin' any."

She sighed, and my mother tried to console her, knowing how deep her idiotic yearning was, and how impossible it was to gratify it. She had tried to persuade the neighbor ladies to call. There was no use wasting any more time on them. Yet, to come out bluntly with the fact that they had all refused would be silly and cruel. My mother was incapable of that. Concealing it, she did her best with promises and predictions, taking care to be vague, while Old Man Isbell dozed, or poked matches at his choking black pipe without any thought of human vanity or hope or disappointment, or anything but the Winter stand of grass on the range. Nobody could believe, from his looks, that he could have asked the fat woman to marry him. It was much more likely that she had hazed the notion into him. Some day, I thought, we might find out, when he could forget the range long enough.

But we never did. He died before the Winter grass got ripe enough for the cattle to sample.

It was on a morning in October that my mother was awakened, about daylight, by yelling and crying from the Isbells' house. She got up and looked across, and saw, through their windows, a lamp still burning, though it was already light enough to see. As she looked, the lamp went out — not from a draft, but because it had run dry. That meant that something was up which was keeping them too busy to tend to it. My mother dressed, and hurried over.

Old Man Isbell was dying. The fat woman had been up watching him all night. She sat beside the bed, while he plunged and pitched his thin hairy arms and yelled. Across her knees lay an old, heavy Sharps plainsman's rifle.

"Watch 'em, watch 'em!" yelled Old Man Isbell. "They cut sagebrush, and push it along in front of 'em to fool you while they sneak up! If you see a bush move, shoot hell out of it! Shoot, damn it!"

The fat woman lugged the immense rifle to her shoulder and snapped the hammer. "Bang!" she yelled.

"That's you!" approved the old man, lying down again. "That's the checker! You nailed him that time, the houndish dastard! You got to watch 'em, I tell ye."

"He thinks he's standin' off Indians," the fat woman explained. "He's young again, and he thinks he's layin' out on the range with the hostiles sneakin' in on him. I've had to — All right, I'm watching close," she told him. "Bang!"

My mother got her something to eat, and built a fire, so that when the neighbor ladies came to help they could have a warm room to sit in. Their resolution to stay away held good only in life. When anybody was dying, social embargoes collapsed. Besides, a death was something they couldn't afford to miss. They came; all the women whom the fat woman had set her heart on being friends with; and nobody thought to remark that, instead of being responsible for their staying away, it was Old Man Isbell who had the credit of bringing them there, after all.

But the fat woman was past bothering about whether they came or stayed away. Even their remarks about the cleanness of her house went over her unnoticed. She had livelier concerns to think about. The old man was driving stage. He was going down the Clarno Grade, and a brake-rod had broken. The stage was running wild, down a twenty percent grade full of hairpin switchbacks. He was flogging his horses to keep them out from under the wheels. He yelled and swore and pitched and floundered in the bedclothes, screaming to his wife that she must climb back and try to drag the hind wheels by poking a bar between the spokes.

"And hurry, damn it!" he yelled. "Drag 'er, before that off pointer goes down!"

The neighbor women gaped and stared. This was something they had never heard of. They didn't even understand what kind of emergency the old man was yelling about. But the fat woman paid no attention to them, and did not hesitate. She climbed along the edge of the bed, reached a broom from the corner, and, poking the handle down as if into a wheel, she set back hard. Her mouth was compressed and firm, and she breathed hard with excitement. She appeared to be taking the game almost as seriously as the old man did, crying back to him that she was holding the wheel, as if it meant the saving of both their lives, though hers was in no danger, and his was burning out like a haystack flaming in a gale.

The women brought food and put it into her mouth as if she was something dangerous. They weren't used to games like this, except in children and dying men. Being neither, the fat woman had no business playing it; and they poked buttered bread into her mouth sharply, frowning as if to show her that they saw through her nonsense, and considered it uncalled for. Neither their buttered bread nor their disapproval made any impression on her. The old man was yelling that she must hold the wheel, and she, with her chins trembling with fatigue and sleeplessness, cried back that she had it where it couldn't get away.

In the afternoon he had another one going. He was in a range-camp at night, and there was a herd of wild mustangs all around his fire, trying to stampede his pack-horses. The fat woman pretended to throw rocks to scare them off.

"There's the stud!" he mumbled. "Where in hell is that gun of mine? Oh, God, if it wasn't for bringin' down them damned Siwashes, wouldn't I salivate that stud? Don't shoot! Don't you know them Injuns'll be all over us if they hear a shot? Hit him with a rock! Watch that bunch over yon! Look how their eyes shine, damn their souls! Throw! Do you want to lose all our horses, and be left out in Injun country afoot?"

All day, and till after dark, the neighbor women watching her, she threw when he ordered; and when, at dark, he switched to

heading a stampede of cattle, she charged with him to turn them,
swinging an imaginary rope with her fat arm, yelling and ki-yi-ing as
he directed, and jouncing the bed till the whole house rocked.

About midnight he had burned his brain down to the last nub,
and there the fat woman was no longer needed. He lifted himself
clear of the bed, and said, "Well, hello, you damned old worthless
tick-bit razor-back, you! How the hell did you get out to this
country?" He sounded pleased and friendly. It had never occurred
to the townspeople that he had ever had any friends. Even as it
was, the fact was lost on some of them, for while he spoke he
looked straight at one of the visiting women, as if he were addressing her. Somebody tittered, and she left indignantly, banging
the door. Everybody jumped, and looked after her. When they
looked back, Old Man Isbell was lying on his pillow, dead.

The fat woman did not want to leave him. She was dull and
almost out of her head with weariness, but, when they took hold of
her, gently, to put her to bed where she could rest, she fought them
off.

"He might come to again," she insisted. "You can't tell, he
might flash up again. And he might think of something he'd need
me for. You leave me be!"

They explained to her that it wasn't possible, and that, even if it
was, she must have some sleep. She mustn't kill herself to humor a
man out of his mind.

"I want to!" she said. "I want to do that! All them things he's
done, and been in, and seen — he never let on a word to me about
'em, and I want to hear 'em! I never knew what an adventured and
high-spirited man he was. I like to do what I've been doin'!"

She fought them until they quit trying, and left her. When they
came back, she had gone to sleep by herself, beside her dead husband; a fat woman, twenty-eight years old, beside the corpse of a
man eighty-five.

She came to call on my mother after the funeral. Her mourning
habit had come from a mail-order house, and, though there were
yards of it, enough, I judged, to make three full-size wagon-sheets,
it needed to be let out in one or two places, and she wanted advice.

"How to fix it so I can wear it, right away," she explained. "I
could send it back, but I don't want to wait that long. I want to
show 'em that my husband was as much loss to me as theirs would
be to them. He was, too. He was a sight better man than any of
theirs."

She rubbed the tears out of her eyes with the back of her wrist. My mother consoled her, and mentioned that now, at least, everybody knew what care she had taken of him.

"I don't care whether they know it or not," said the fat woman. "None of 'em come to see me, and they can all stay away for good, as far as I'm concerned. The way they acted the one time they did come settled 'em with me."

"But they helped out during your bad time," my mother said. "They meant kindly."

"Yes. Helped out. And then they come smirkin' and whisperin' around how I ought to be glad my husband was out of the way. How I must have hated takin' care of him, and what a mercy it was to be rid of him. I told 'em a few things. They'll stay away from me a spell, I can promise you that!"

She sat straight in her chair, and dropped the mourning dress on the floor.

"I was glad to take care of him," she said. "Yes, sir! I was proud of my husband. The things he'd done, and the risks he'd been through, when the men in this town was rollin' drunks and wrappin' up condensed milk. . . . "

She drew a breath, and, forgetting that my mother had been there, began to tell about the time when he had been surrounded by Indians, creeping in on him with sagebrush tied to their heads. He fought them back and outgamed the whole caboodle of them; and her voice rose and trembled, shrilling the scenes she had enacted with Old Man Isbell when his numb old brain was burning down through the pile of his memories, spurting a flame out of each one before they all blackened and went to nothing.

She shrilled the great scenes out defiantly, as if it were her place to defend them, as if they belonged to her, and were better, even at second hand, than anything that any of the townspeople had ever experienced. None of their common realities had ever touched her. Beauty had not; love had not, not even friends. In place of them, she had got an eighty-five-year-old dotard and the ridicule of the townspeople. Watching over the old man when he died was the one time when she had come anywhere within reach of heroism and peril and splendor; and that one time, being worthy of it, she passed them all. And that one time was enough, because she knew it.

"The hostiles a-prowlin' around," she cried, her voice blazing. "The houndish dastards! . . . "

Death in October

ROBERT EASTON

*I*n 1943 Robert Easton published The Happy Man, a memorable book, a modern western in a double sense: a good example of modern writing and about the modern mid-twentieth-century West. He dedicated it, perhaps appropriately, to Frederick Faust, who, as Max Brand, wrote quite a few westerns in his own time, among them the perenially popular Destry Rides Again. But Robert Easton goes well beyond Max Brand in understanding of his material, in appreciation of the meanings in it.

The Happy Man is a series of stories about the men of the El Dorado Investment Company, the modern cattle empire, the dream-made-reality of the great man, Thomas S. Ordway. The El Dorado is no ranch in the old sense of that term; it is a vast streamlined, mechanized cattle-factory. But the stamp of the old West lingers and is transmitted to the young drifter who there finds a place. My choice is the last story, the account of what happened when T. S. Ordway died and the anthrax struck and old Rube dreamed his ancestral dream.

AFTER THE DEATH of T. S. Ordway the El Dorado Investment Company continued as before. The mill ground just as much feed; the cattle in their pens went right on eating, getting fat, being sold

at a good profit; and the boys that made the wheels go round were
on the job at seven every morning when the whistle blew. They
earned their three dollars; but at the end of the month the pay
checks came out signed, not by T. S. Ordway, but by So-and-So,
trustee.

One thing the great man never failed to do through all his wide
realm of ownership was to sign the pay checks personally — hundreds of them. It cost him the last week of every month, but he
did not complain. "I never paid a man in anything but cash," he
said. "If I can't see his face, I want to know his name." You see,
this was later in his career, when the meetings got in his way, the
papers, dividends, debentures.

After he died, the river ran on down. The days began out of the
east, broke over the high Sierra, and passed on down with the
river out to sea, just as they always had done. The great green delta
on an afternoon swayed and muttered and lapped, as the wind
played in the reeds around the islands — the islands with their levees
built by Thomas Ordway, master-architect, who worked in earth, not
wood or stone.

Yet after he went, there was a difference. People said so. Perhaps they looked for one; and where you seek, you find, as the
Good Book says. But in the noises of the wind there was an echo
as it talked across this wide city of boards and cattle; in the grinding of the mill there was an echo, a different sound when you listened. It seemed the feed-trucks moved more slowly, the men
stopped more often to talk. Little things made a bigger difference.
When steers went off a quarter of a cent, it was generally decided
that the market would not have dared to do that in the time of
T. S. Ordway. When school children passed through in caravans,
and on Sundays when pleasure cars lined the county road that runs
along the yards, the people made no sound, but looked with wide-
open eyes, for this might be the last time anyone would see the
El Dorado Investment Company, about which everybody had
heard.

In the bunkhouse, in the cookhouse, we wondered what was going to happen. During the day we gathered often at the barn to
talk — the old gray shelter, eaten by the wind and rain, that was
a derelict when T. S. Ordway found it standing on a mound
above the sloughs. There he had his dream and built his city out
of mud and reeds, the richest land in all the world, where wealth
lay in the decay of centuries, alluvium, waiting for a man who
could see, but waiting not alone, as we found out.

Day after day strange cars glided up and down the alleys, filled with men in city suits smoking good cigars — trustees, appraisers, inspectors, heirs nobody ever had seen — all of them foreigners that didn't belong. It hurt you some way just to see them. Rumors came with every car-load: the yards were being sold for taxes to Swift, to Armour, to the government for an experiment in cattle like those they had made in electricity. But nobody knew.

All that summer was unusually cool. Sea fogs blew in and lay all day. On clear evenings after sunset, off westward towards the blue hills, a cloud formation was observed several times like a great red spear thrust in the sky; and people said this was a sign, and others said it was because of the war raging far over the sea.

Archibald Jacks ran the yards as he had always done, but his shoulders drooped a little and there was no smile in him. Reuben Child, earliest made and latest left of all the helpers of the great man, came to the barn the first few days and lingered like an old dog around the place he had seen his master last; and then he left and was seen no more. At evening his white cottage by the slough had no light; and some said he had gone away into the hills to die, and some said he had gone back home to Texas where he had been born so long ago and where he had first met Thomas Ordway.

Summer blended into fall, the lonely time of year. The days came hot and still, with a hush and everlasting echo, and the sound of wind passing somewhere up above that never touched the earth. From the ventilator on the mill dust rose and spread a fan across the sky. You could hear the heavy, hollow grinding of the gears digesting cattle feed. . . . The things T. S. had set going kept on after him.

Daylight on those mornings found dry ground. There was no dew, no night that mattered. No wind blew, yet in the reeds there was a rattle dry as death. You could hear the endless roaring of a tractor in the fields beside the river where it dragged a great disk plough to break the ground for next year's crop, and here a shroud of yellow dust rose up and hung above the field.

On the sixth day of October the great disks ripped open an Indian burial mound and the skeletons came up like white roots out of the ground. For a day or two there was a good deal of excitement over this, because the sixth came on a Friday, and during the week end people from Bird Town and the nearest villages came down to collect trophies. Later all this was carefully remembered and retold, together with the facts that cats had eaten grass and for three nights straight a ring had lain around the moon. But for the moment the novelty passed and would have been forgotten except for what happened Monday.

Ten minutes after ten the anthrax struck. The first steer went down in Pen 78, close beside the water, and a little blood ran from its nose. Pen 77 was next, the steers dropping as if they had been poled over. Few lived more than half an hour. Not till afternoon did we know what they had. There had been no anthrax in the valley for fifty years. The veterinary stocked no serum; he wired San Francisco.

Old Jacks cruised around the alleys in his pick-up looking the way he did the afternoon news of Ordway's death was brought to him.

The cattle dropped like flies. All Monday night we stood and heard them moving in the dark, kicking in the dust a little when they fell, and soon all would be quiet but for the restless moving of the other cattle up and down the pens. By morning the water troughs were ringed with dead.

Then the serum came and we went to vaccinating. All day long the columns of cattle choked the alleys, moving to the pens around the branding chute, and the yellow dust rose as it does from armies marching. There was no sound. This was the quiet death, taking some even as they moved to safety. Only the grinding of the mill went on; and the plough, breaking the land, its sound falling on the out-turn, coming louder on the way back; and over it the dust rose yellow too.

We put the needle into better than a thousand head a day, but thirteen thousand cattle take a lot of vaccinating. The biggest, fattest ones came first — they cost the most. Around the chute there was a milling red-and-dusty mass, the press and clatter of the cattle on the boards, the sharp bellow of pain as the needle struck them, and the white-and-silver flash of Dynamite's bare forearm with the syringe, for it was he who did the vaccinating.

"Die and prove it!" he would yell, driving home the needle in the soft necks; and the steers would buck and squeal.

Nazi Joe was there, working the drop-gate at the far end of the chute where the cattle went out when Dynamite finished them. Joe was a roly-poly little old German with a battered dun-colored felt hat, stained with sweat, which he always managed to keep jaunty on his head, cocked up a bit behind, so that he looked like a poor Bavarian mountaineer. Actually Joe came out of Prussia, I think. He wore his shirt-sleeves short, cut off at the elbows like a little boy's; his face was red from years of weathering and his eyes were as blue as Dynamite's, only they didn't move — they stuck and stared. A Dutchman stiff and stubborn, with a streak of astrology in him, Joe had a mind that was a whiz on a column of figures, but on other things got just so far on the right track — and then off into either air or water.

Uncle Arky Bill was there, Cherokee and Sims, and Jacks himself, coming and going in the pick-up, his face growing longer with the lines of cattle.

Outside in the alleys the dead-wagons went about their business hauling the bodies, chained behind in tandem, to the fields where they were piled with straw and gasoline, and burnt. Their smoke rose and mingled with the dust the tractor made, until the sun turned red and the stench of roasting meat hung in the air all day.

So it got to be the thirteenth, our lucky day, and we waited by the chute after our noon meal for Jacks to come. He said it was our lucky day; we had eleven hundred head to go, but he didn't come and he didn't come; so we talked it over and went ahead without him, Dynamite in charge. Since Ordway died, Jacks had been like a man walking in a dream, and all the yards for him were like a great house he had known well, furnished in a way he'd seen a thousand times, every chair in place — but nobody home. You'd find him sometimes in the evening sitting in his pick-up alone by the mill or on the docks where the barges tie up and leave their sacks of grain, where the hustle and the bustle is all day, with no time to think and remember. Jacks liked to find these places after work; there was no telling where he was now, so we went ahead.

"Stack 'em up, you guys!" sang Dynamite. "Cattle, *cattle*, ten head to a chute!" And Cherokee and Sims and I shoved them in with terrible shouts, waving our gunny sacks, shaking our sticks.

Dynamite worked from a platform built three feet off the ground along the chute. Uncle Arky Billy helped him, filling the syringes. Nazi Joe worked his drop-gate at the far end. He said slowly after a while, "Jacks, he got zee anthrax." Joe came out of Germany in 1912; his English still had a buzz in it.

"Anthrax?" said Dynamite. "You're crazy. Men, zey don't take anthrax."

"Yes, zey do too," said Joe, yanking down the bar that raised the gate. "Dat's just where you mistaken. Zee anthrax is one of zee most terrible diseases known to man."

"What makes you think he's got it?" said Dynamite to Joe; and to a steer: "Die, you son-of-a-bitch! Die and prove you're hurt!"

Joe kept right on, you couldn't put him off once he got track of an idea, and he never hurried and never let his voice get up or down: "Zee stars say it is his time."

"Stars! . . . Stars my foot; stars don't talk, they shine. Goddammit, Joe, you're gonna break your back out there by the cookhouse some night. I've seen you, bent like a barrel hoop."

"Zee stars never tell a lie," said Joe. "If you study dem, you would be money ahead of zee game. Take Jacks, he don't know, you see . . . October is his month. In zee first part he stand good chance for success; in zee middle part, especially zee thirteenth day or fourteenth, he should be careful, watch his step. Zee stars never say 'You must' only 'You should' . . . there is a good chance of things to happen dis way, happen dat way."

"Horse-water," said Dynamite.

"Man," said Joe, "Man he is a product of zee sun. If he be born when sun is overhead, zee upright position of zee cornstalk, he has more chance of success; he be like a tide coming in. But October is not very good month, sun is changing, he is tired. . . . You find a quarter-shadow around noon . . ."

"I bet you Jacks ain't got the anthrax," said Dynamite. "What makes you think he has?"

Sims piped up, "I seen a black sedan parked by his house at noon."

"Doctor Hartley's car," said Joe. "Jacks went into his room before lunch, lock zee door, don't let nobody in. They telephone zee doctor."

"You've been listening to that Thelma Jenkins' talk," said Dynamite. "I seen her coming to the cookhouse after noon to get her eggs and butter for Old Lady Jacks. You'd better not listen to her; she'll have you b'lieving stars is stripes before she's through."

There was no talking while Sims and I and Cherokee crammed home another chute.

"Anthrax is zee most terrible death," said Joe. "One time on 2 Street, Sacramento, last April ven I vas dere, I talked vid a fellow who has only one eye; half his face vas cut away — you know — big scar. 'Vat's de matter your eye?' I says. 'Oh,' he says, 'I hadda

anthrax.' 'How does dat disease operate?' I says. 'Very simple,'
he says. 'Anthrax of zee human being is de most terrible disease.
Once de germ is in de blood dere is no hope — only chance,' he
says. He says he owns a bunch of cattle, one of dem die; him and
anudder fellow, dey chop it up, zee knife slip, cut him on de hand,
and dat vas de way zee germ obtain entrance to zee body. Dey
rush to a doctor; doctor he say: 'Can do nudding; first we must
follow zee germ.' He put him on de table, under zee X-ray. Ven-
ever zee germ come near surface of zee blood zey try to catch him.
If he come to zee heart — too bad. Zis time dey have good luck;
he come out in zee eye and zey catch him with a knife."

"God Almighty," said Dynamite, "I hope they don't do that to
old Jacks."

"Maybe so, maybe not," said Joe. "Maybe he die. Remember
der is nudding accomplished but vat der is destruction first."

Joe kind of had us there, and we thought a bit about many
things, and Sims said half-aloud: "Jacks cut his hand this morning
. . . on that steer, remember? He was cutting the screw-worm out
of its back."

Jacks *had* nicked his hand; we all remembered.

"Once zee germ has entrance to zee human body," said Joe, "a
man is gone. Dat is why information of zee stars is useful."

"The stars don't know that much," said Dynamite. "There ain't
nobody knows about death only God Almighty."

Joe didn't answer; when he wanted to call you a liar, he could
do it with the back of that blunt head of his, he was that stubborn.

"No sir, Joe, you're full of hop and star dust," Dynamite went on.
"Death ain't in the sky. . . . Death — death's like a lariat-rope and
you're on one end and God, he's on t'other. You're born thataway,
strung up; and that way you run your life. . . . Like I've let many
a steer go along after I had him roped, till I found a place to bust
him out; and then I took my dallies and made my pony squat and
hold. Same with death — you have your run and take your spill.
Ain't it so, Uncle Billy?"

"That's right, Dyney boy," the old Arkansawyer said. "Yessir,
that's about it, I reckon, for the most part. We're on one end, God
Almighty, Lord of Jacob, he's on the other. . . . Reckon he had
time to repent?" said Uncle Billy. "Jacks, I mean. He weren't
much of a church-going man, you know."

"Oh, I think he would," said Dynamite. "Jacks' heart was in the
right place, though he could be ornery, the old son-of-a-gun.

Many's the time I've wanted to warp his head with a neck-yoke. But I reckon if he has took off, he's up there now a-lookin' down on us boys."

"Sure hope so," said Uncle Billy. "Sure do."

Cherokee said, "You boys is sounding mighty high-falutin' in this here argyment, like you'd all been to college. Seems to me this death come right out of the ground."

Cherokee didn't often say much, but he made sense when he opened his mouth. We took a look around our feet, and I remember it was quiet just then, between two fillings of the chute, and you could see the tower of dust built by the plough and hear the tractor going faintly; and then, in a second, we got fear. Nobody said so; we just had it. It ran quicker than any disease; and we were looking at our hands for cuts and shifting on our feet without intending to, as though we stood on something hot.

Up Long Alley by the mill the boys were bringing us more cattle, the last ones, and their dust in the air looked worse than poison gas.

"Well, I dunno," said Dynamite, but his heart wasn't in it. "Cattle," he hollers. "Whatsa matter with you guys? Gimme some cattle." He grabbed a syringe from Uncle Billy and he rolled his right sleeve up a notch as though he was ready for the anthrax then and there, by God.

We began to move slow motion.

Two trucks came up empty from the mill, whining on the turn of the road and passing us right by as they did a hundred times a day, but this was different — it seemed as though they were running from something.

"Here's your wife, Dynamite," said Sims.

The top-heavy Packard sedan rolled down the slope from the barn and made the dust burn with its brakes. Maxine got out. She was in a hurry; there was a handkerchief across her face.

She ran and jumped up on the fence and leaned our way and she was screaming mad. "Don't any of you men come home!" she yelled. "Not one, not any one of you . . . Sims, Annabelle told me to tell you; and Cherokee, your Mary says the same — it's *anthrax!* . . . Jacks has it! . . . He locked the door, wouldn't let them in, but they took the axe — No!" she said, seeing Dynamite start toward her. "No," and it made your spine go cold to hear it, wife to man, "Stay back!"

Dynamite went all the faster.

Maxine was off that fence and into that car quicker than the light of day. She put her head outside and called back once, "You can't come near the babies; don't you *dare!*"

Dynamite stopped at the gate, looking after her and cussing.

Sims started to run.

"Where-ya-going?" Dynamite's voice would have taken off your ear.

"*The dust!*" screamed Sims.

Dynamite knocked him down and he rolled in the dust.

Cherokee said, "Say, Dyney — reckon we outta stop that plough, and them trailing cattle down the alley there? Don't you reckon we outta stop them just a while till we get all this straight?"

"We ain't a-stoppin' nothin'," said Dynamite.

Sims got up and looked like he wanted to run again, but Dynamite said to him, "There'll be no running while I'm here, understand?"

"Listen," said Uncle Arky Billy, "listen, boys!"

We looked into the sky. There was no wind; the sun up there was red and evil as the heart of a boil. We listened, but the sound we tried to hear had gone. "The mill," said Cherokee. "She's quit."

"We ain't a quittin'," said Dynamite.

"It was the plough made the dust," said Sims, half-whimpery.

Now that the noise was gone, it seemed the air had died like a body does when the blood goes out of it. All those alleyways and mangers, all that valley, river, and the hills beyond were empty veins of air, and only the cattle moved or made a sound. Two were dead just beyond us in the holding pen, Bar-Seven steers.

Hank and Jerry, who'd been helping out there, had taken off. I saw them hurry out the back way behind the scales, up toward the barn. Uncle Billy filled a syringe, matter of fact as biscuits and ham-gravy. Nazi Joe tightened up a little in the face, but he stuck to the handle of his drop-gate, ready for that destruction he'd talked about.

"Lookie," said Dynamite, and his voice picked us up.

Gliding low, cruising down the alley from the barn, a pick-up truck was coming in just the easy way Jacks always drove.

The little truck stopped by the outer gate; the door opened and a man got out, but it wasn't Jacks or even his ghost. It was Reuben Child, whose day was gone, whose face was like the side of a mountain where the rains have been. "Howdy, fellers," he said. "Vaccinatin'?"

He hobbled over; he needed a cane to walk. "Understan' ye got the anthrax in your herd," he said, and hardly got his voice above a little girl's.

All his strength was in his face and eye, but he made you want to knock down mountains, that old Rube. "Just thought I'd lend a hand," he said. "Not doin' much these days."

We began to vaccinate.

"Haven't seen you lately, Rube," said Dynamite. "Where you been?"

"Me?" said Rube. "Oh, here-and-there."

He was looking mighty fit for a man who's just been here and there. Those wide gray eyes, always finding some horizon, had got hold of one they liked, and it had lit him up inside in a way we'd never seen. If Rube had been a drinking man, I'd have said he'd taken a few.

He held the syringes; Uncle Arky Billy, who, though he had good legs under him like old Rube, would never see sixty again, got out behind with us into the crowding pen, and then even Sims was ashamed and went to work. We crammed those cattle through. The dust rose up so thick you really couldn't see. Your face turned black; your hollers turned to croaks. We used up all the water in the bottles and didn't dare take the time to send for more.

The anthrax never slackened. It stole the cattle out from underneath our sticks. Here a heifer, there a steer — down like a hog with an axe on its head; then a twitch, a little blood. We let them lie, forgot about the dead-wagon not coming. The boys brought the last pens of cattle up Long Alley and took off without a word, drifting in the dust like shadows, but we never cared.

All of a sudden it got very dark. The wind that for two weeks had wandered up there trying to get down came now, and the dust was made up into sheets and spirals and went everywhere. The wind stopped; the dust cleared off and there was the sky all brown and rotten as though the wind had gone up there with all its dust. The first rain brought thunder. Then the sky broke open.

We wallowed in it, thankful at first, till we saw the mud sticking and thought of germs that live for fifty years, and then I think some of us would have prayed if we could, or had had the time. But things were happening. The cattle couldn't make the chute. The slick board bottom, polished by their hooves, greased with the mud and dung, was no good footing. They went down; they stacked up on one another. A little heifer broke her neck. We spent twenty minutes clearing out the chute, while thunder smashed the hills across the river and the raindrops hit us big as dimes.

Rube called it off. "There's one place we can go," he said, waving a cane toward the barn.

"Not with all these cattle," said Dynamite. "What good will it do? This here's the only chute."

"We'll use our loops," said Rube, "if we ain't forgot quite how. Otherwise these little cattle won't make it till morning. We only got two hundred left."

So we turned the others in the holding pens and took our two hundred little Double Arrow steers and drove them to the barn. We made the horse-corral a holding pen. We cleared the inside of the barn all across one end, moved the bales of hay, dragged an old harvester, kicked out some mangers so there was room to move between the walls from one side to the other, across thirty yards of dirt. This was our crowding pen.

We lit the lanterns and brought the little steers inside, a bunch at a time.

Rube said to Dynamite, "Get me your horse."

"Hell, Rube," said Dynamite, "better let me do the roping."

"I'll do her," the old man said.

We helped him onto Dynamite's renegade nag that might have got a pint of Texas Steeldust in him generations back. He hurt Rube; that broken hip hadn't been in a saddle for ten years, but the old man straightened himself up bit by bit. He wanted to do it. There was something about Rube this night we all remembered — a rising in him and a kind of light, and he moved clean-cut out of the air, smoothly, like he knew just where he was going.

Dynamite whispered, "Rube's sure ridin' high. What's the matter with him? What's he got?" But at that time I didn't know myself.

He took his stand, old Rube, half-way along the mangers from the little steers, where they'd have to run between him and the wall, and began to build his loop; did it from the wrist, with a flick over and a flick back, and gave the signal down the barn for the boys to let the cattle come.

The wind blew the lantern light all cockeyed, splashed it on us, and rocked the barn and made the floor smoke dust.

Rube sat his horse. From Canada to Mexico his name was known; hardly a brand that hadn't felt his loop in olden days,

Hooleyann or straight, and no maverick that ever ran was quicker than his hand and eye.

Dynamite and I stood back; Cherokee cut and pushed a little steer and let him scamper down the wall, under the lanterns, harness, and old blankets.

The hempen loop ran out like light, spun underhanded, and ringed the yearling with a gentle slap. Rube had his dallies fast before the animal took a step. Dynamite put a loop on both hindlegs. I shot the syringe in the soft neck, handed the gun to Arky Billy, loosened Rube's rope, and pulled it off.

"That weren't so good," said Rube. "I meant to lay a figure-eight."

Next time he did, and the animal stepped through with right fore-foot and tied himself. Rube set him down without so much as a finger's help. And so on with the next and the next. Once we took a rest; once Rube missed a loop. Other than that, every throw but half-a-dozen was a perfect figure-eight; and Dynamite, on the ground waiting, had only to shake his head and smile, or lay down his rope to help me.

The two hundred-odd head took us so far into the night that we never knew how long it was.

The storm kept us company; and the tromping of the cattle, the rustle of the running loop, and the squeak and rubbing of Rube's saddle when his pony took a squat and laid the critters down.

The old man never showed his pain. The hours wore away and made him young. He took off the blue denim jumper and tightened his silver-studded belt, a prize from some rodeo long forgotten, and with the work he straightened in the saddle till the patient smile we always knew him by had gone and he wasn't bearing something any more — he was doing it himself.

I wish I could tell just how he looked. Nobody could who hasn't seen a man inside his job or a woman with a child.

We finished and the little steers that had begun at one end of the barn were all crowded at the other.

"Turn 'em out," said Rube. "Let the rain have 'em; the anthrax never will."

We sat along the bench by the door where the boss's saddle hangs, along with some pairs of extra stirrups, a couple of bits, and a strip of hose for ramming down the throats of critters when they choke.

"Death?" said Dynamite to Rube, one eye on Nazi Joe. "You sure beat him out of that one, Rube. Your loop is quicker than the Evil Eye."

Rube was tired; he smiled now the old way.

"Hurt your hip any?" said Cherokee.

"Little," said Rube, "But shucks, just shows what a feller can do when he wants. I should have been on a horse years back."

"How come," said Dynamite, "how come ye took to it tonight?"

"Oh, I dunno," said Rube, lifting his Stetson and wiping his high white forehead where the sun never reached. "I dunno . . . I guess because I had a dream."

"A dream?" said Dynamite.

"Yeah," said Rube. "Funny, my old daddy had one like it years ago, spring of '92, I think it was, or '93. We trailed 'em from the Pecos to Wyoming, two thousand longhorn steers and Dad and me and eight good boys. Crossed the Republican River on the first of May. That night we bedded on a grassy knoll by water where the bluestem went for miles knee-high to horse and man. We bedded just at dark after a long day and laid the wagon tongue for the North Star so we could find the morning's trail.

"I remember how old Tigue, the cook, got out his Dutch oven that night, wiped it with his special cloth made of a flour sack, and baked us bread — bread and beans and jerky stew. We lived like kings.

"Dad dreamed that night. Some way he was in a house alone, a room all bare but warm. It was late afternoon, 'bout four o'clock. From where he sat there was a window and a quarter-angle view up a long rise to some blue hills where night was beginning to gather and creep down. That ground was funny too; it was all bare, low brush and stones.

"He set quite a while, he said, wondering why nobody come and then he realized that house was empty, bare and empty as a house can be, yet full of yellow light . . . the afternoon, you know. And as he set and got his view out quartering from the window in a long slice up, it seemed he just couldn't quite see enough, that just around the edges of that window was the home he knew; the green alfalfa patch, the orchard trees, the good red barn and horses standing, the windmill pumping water — ker-blong ker-chug, ker-chug ker-blong — and the spatter from the leaky leathers as it hit the stones.

"There was all this goodness just on either side of where he looked, but that slice of ground he had to see, it was just a desert, bare as anything, with night creeping down along it 'mongst the little stones.

"Seemed like the sun'd set already, he says, but he couldn't figure it, felt sure it was just four o'clock, half-day half-night.

"So he set. He waited a long time, said he never did know why, wanted to get up and look around the edges of that window and see all the good things he heard and smelt and knew was there, but he just couldn't do it. Said he began to listen for something, something special, and then he heard it coming on the walk outside, crunching in the gravel step by step, heard the door open and latch shut and the jingle of spurs hung on the buckthorn by the wall.

"And then he said he knew and he felt happy. Directly the steps come near and give him leave to look and there stood his old daddy, and his face was all one smile like he was powerful glad to see his son again. He touched my daddy's shoulder and just says, 'Howdy, Son!' . . .

"This was the dream my daddy had that night," said Rube. "At daylight we moved on. In seven days he died, and far in old Wyoming, on the Crazy Woman beyond Ten Sleep, we laid him in the ground."

Rube stopped talking, but outside the wind kept on, lightly now, with a good deal of rain in it. The gusts caught water falling from the gutter that runs along the eaves, and hammered it against the barn one second and let it slosh on down the next. Rube began rolling a cigarette. He never used two hands. We watched him roll and lick and smear the tangled weed-and-paper, then hold a match until it glowed.

"That was the dream you had?" said Dynamite.

"That was the dream I had," said Rube. . . . And after a while: "Well, reckon I'll call on Jacks before I go along. He's poorly; took the chickenpox, you know."

Mister Death and the Redheaded Woman

HELEN EUSTIS

Western writing is well peppered with humorous stories and tall tales. Fantasy is relatively rare. You will have trouble finding a finer example than this galloping yarn of Mr. Death and his granny and the redheaded woman. It is as fresh and timeless as the day it appeared in the Saturday Evening Post for February 11, 1950. I know nothing more of Helen Eustis' work except that she has written two novels, The Horizontal Man and The Fool Killer, and ought to be writing more short stories.

MISTER DEATH come aridin' in from the plains on his pale stallion, ashootin' off his pistols, bangety-bang-bang, till you'd 'a' thought some likkered-up Injun was on a spree. Hoo-ee! We was scared, all us little uns, and the grown folks, too, only to them he seemed more familiar.

But he never touched nary a soul that day but Billy-be-damn Bangtry, the one the girls was all crazy for. An' Mister Death no more'n just laid a finger on him, so he didn't die right off, but lay there cold and sweatin', dyin' of a bullet in his belly which was shot off by a drunken cowpoke in a wild euchre game.

Now, many a girl in our town wet the pillow with her tears

when she heard how young Billy was like to die, for he was a handsome man and drove all women wild; but the one that cried and carried on the worst was pretty little Maude Applegate with the freckles and the red hair.

Old Injun Mary was anursin' Billy with poultices and healin' herbs, and wouldn't let no other woman near his door, so there wasn't nary a thing Maude Applegate could do for him. But you can't expect a redheaded woman to jest sit around and fret, like you would another color girl, an' Maude was no exception to that rule. Though she cried and carried on for a while, she pretty soon decided something had to be done, so she dried her eyes on her pettishirt, saddled up her daddy's pinto pony and took out across the plains after Mister Death.

Maude Applegate, she rode high and she rode low; she rode through the cow country into the sheep country; through the sheep country into the Injun country; through the Injun country to the far mountains, and there at last she caught up with Mister Death, jest about a mile down the trail from the little ole shack where he lived with his granny, up above the timber line.

When Maude Applegate spied his pale stallion, she was mighty tired and mighty weary; her red hair was all tumbled down her back, and her daddy's pinto wasn't no more'n skin and bone.

But she caught her breath and sang out loud, "Oh, wait up, Mister Death! Wait up for me!"

Mister Death, he pulled up his pale stallion and looked around, surprised-like, for there isn't many that call out to halt him.

"Why, what you want, missy?" he asked Maude Applegate as she rode up alongside. "Jumpin' Jehoshaphat, if you don't look like you rode clean through the brier patch!"

"Oh, Mister Death," Maude panted out, "I rode high and I rode low after you! I rode through cow country into sheep country; through sheep country into Injun country; through Injun country to the far mountains, and all to ask you would you spare Billy-be-damn Bangtry, my own true love!"

At that, Mister Death throwed back his head so's his black sombrero slipped off and hung around his neck by the strings, and he laughed loud.

"Now ain't that cute!" said Mister Death. "Honey, I reckon you're jest about the cutest thing I'm likely to see!"

But Maude Applegate, she'd rode high and she'd rode low, she'd stood thirst and she'd stood hunger, she'd like to killed her daddy's pretty little pinto; furthermore, she was a redheaded woman, and

she wasn't goin' to be laughed at so. She took and cussed out
Mister Death good. She tole him that where she come from, no
gentleman laughed at no lady in her true trouble, and she'd thank
him to mind his manners with her, and she'd like to know who
brought him up anyhow? Why, she knew dirty nekkid Injun
bucks acted better'n him. She'd lay his mammy's aspinnin' in
her grave, an' so on.

Well, Mister Death, he sobered down shortly and set up straight
in his saddle and listened real still, with only his eyes ablinkin'.
When Maude give out of breath, he took out his 'baccy bag,
licked a paper an' rolled him a smoke.

"What'll you give me for Billy-be-damn Bangtry?" said he.

But Maude Applegate, she was really wound up. She tossed
her red hair like a pony's mane and made a sassy mouth. "I ain't
agonna talk business until I've washed my face and had me a bite
to eat," said she. "I've rode high and I've rode low — "

"All right, all right!" said Mister Death. "Ride along now, and
I'll take you to my cabin, where my ole granny'll take care of you."

So Maude and Mister Death they rode up the slope, Mister
Death reinin' in his pale stallion to keep down to the pore tired
pinto, until presently they come to a little ole shack with smoke
comin' out of the stovepipe. There was Mister Death's granny
astandin' in the door, as pleased as Punch to see some company.

"Why, you're right welcome, missy!" she sang out, soon's they
were within callin' distance. "The pot's on the stove and the
kettle's abilin'. Come right in and rest yourself a while!"

So they pulled up, and Mister Death swung down off his pale
stallion, come around by Maude and lifted her right down to
the ground, with his two big hands ameetin' around her little
waist.

"Oh, ain't she the purty little thing?" his granny kept asayin'
all the while, and hobblin' around the dooryard on her crutch like
a bird with a broken wing. Then she taken Maude inside and
give her warm water, and a ivory comb, and a pretty white silk
wrapper from out of her ole brass-bound chest, and when Mister
Death come in from seein' to the hosses, there's Maude Applegate
asettin' like a redheaded angel, drinkin' tea.

Maude, she perked up soon's she got some vittles inside her,
and presently she had Mister Death and his granny laughin' fit
to bust with her comical tales of the folks back home.

Soon Mister Death, he set in to yawnin' and gapin'. "I've rode
a far piece today," he said to his granny. "I been twice around

the world and back, and I think I'll lay my head in your lap and catch forty winks." And shortly he was asnorin'.

Then Death's granny begun to talk low to Maude Applegate, questionin' her all about herself, and where she come from, and why she come. So Maude tole her all about how Billy-be-damn Bangtry, her own true love, lay adyin' of a bullet in his belly, so what could she do but take out after Mister Death to beg him to stay his hand? When Death's granny had heard the whole story, she fetched a great sigh.

"Well," she said, "it's a great pity to me you got your heart set, for you're like the girl I once was, and if I had my way, you're the girl I'd choose for my grandson to marry, for I'm ole and tired and would like to see him settled before I go to my rest. You're young, and you're purty, and you don't stand for no sass, and if my ole eyes don't deceive me, you can do a bit of witchin' too. Now ain't that true?"

"Well," Maude answered her modestly, "jest a little of the plain."

"Like what now?" said Death's granny. "White or black?"

"Little o' both," said Maude. "Witched my little brother into passin' his arithmetic, and I also witched the preacher's wife so she tripped on her shoestring and fell in the horse trough."

Once more Death's granny fetched a sigh. "That's a good start for a young'un," said she. "Don't look to me like a girl like you ought to waste herself on no drunken gamblin' cowhand gets hisself shot up in some fool card game. Howsomever, if you got your heart set, I'll help you. Whenever Death catnaps this way, he shortly begins to talk in his sleep, and when he talks, he'll answer three questions truly, and then wake up. What shall I ask him for you?"

"Ask him," said Maude right away, "what is his price to let off Billy-be-damn Bangtry."

"That's one," said Death's granny. "You got three questions. What else?"

At this, Maude had to think, and presently she said, "Ask him why he took my baby sister from her cradle."

"Very well, chile," said Granny. "And one more."

Then Maude Applegate bent her red head near to the red fire and was still, but at last she said, kinda low and slow, "Ask him what he does when he's lonesome."

To this, Death's granny answered nothing at all, and so they set in quiet until shortly Death begun to mumble in his sleep.

Then his granny took aholt of a lock of his coal-black hair and tweaked it, gentle-like.

"Yes?" Death said, but without wakin' up. "Yes?"

"Tell me, son," Death's granny said, bendin' over his ear. "What will you take to let off Billy-be-damn Bangtry?"

At this, Death twitched and turned in his sleep. "Oh, granny," he said, "she's such a pretty girl! If it was some, I'd make it an eye. An' if it was others, I'd make it ten years o' life. But for her, I'll make it that she must ride with me two times around the world and give me a kiss on the lips."

At this, Maude drew a great deep breath and leaned back in her chair.

"Well, son," said granny, "here's another question she asks of you. Why did you take her baby sister from the cradle?"

Then Death twisted and turned in his sleep again. "She was sick," he said. "She was full of pain. I took her so she need never cry no more."

At this, Maude bowed her head and hid her cheek in her hand.

"Well, son," said Death's granny, "an' here's the last. What is it you do when you're lonesome?"

At this, Death give a regular heave and a great groan, and turned his face from the light of the fire. For a long time he whispered and mumbled, and finally he said real low, "I peep through the windows at how the human bein's sleep in each other's arms."

And with this last, he woke up with a jerk, give a mighty yawn, sayin', "My stars, I must of dropped off!"

Now Mister Death and his granny was cheerful folks in spite o' his profession, and that evenin' they gave Maude Applegate such a high ole time that she was almost glad she come. Death's granny, she tole some mighty edifyin' stories about her young days, and furthermore, she got out a jug of her blackberry wine, and Death, he played such merry tunes on his fiddle that Maude Applegate got right out of her chair, picked up her skirts and danced. It was late that night when Death's granny showed Maude to the little trundle bed all made up fresh beside her own four-poster.

In the mornin', Death's granny had Maude's own dress all mended and pressed for her, and a fine breakfast of coffee and ham and grits to stay their stomachs for their long trip, and when Mister Death brought round his pale stallion, all saddled and bridled to go, the tears was standin' in his granny's eyes as she kissed Maude Applegate good-by.

"Good-by," Maude said. "I thank you for your fine hospitality, and if it wasn't for Billy-be-damn Bangtry, my own true love, I'd be right sorry to go."

Mister Death, he lifted Maude up to his big stallion and leaped astride; then away they rode, right up the snowy mountaintop into the sky, and Maude Applegate was surprised to find herself warm and comfortable, ridin' pillion with her arms wrapped around Mister Death's waist.

Then didn't they have a ride! Mister Death, he rode his pale stallion up the mountains of the storm to the pastures of the sky, where the little clouds was grazin' beside their big fat white mammies, and the big black daddy clouds kept watch around the edge. And he rode right up in the fields where the stars grow, and let Maude Applegate pluck a few to wear in her red hair. He rode past the moon, and when Maude Applegate reached out and touched it, it was cold as snow, and slippery too. They couldn't go too near the sun, Mister Death said, lest they might get burned.

But Mister Death, he had his business to tend to, so pretty soon they set out across the wide ocean on their way to twice around the world. Mister Death, he wrapped Maude in his cloak of invisibility, and he took her to all sorts of houses in all sorts of climes — houses where Chinee folks lived, and Rooshian, and Japanee, and African, and folks that never spoke a word of English since the day they was born. He showed her castles and dirty little huts the like of which she never seen in all the state of Texas; he showed her kings and princes and poor folks and all, and maybe she didn't just open her eyes! But in one respect she noticed they was all alike: when Mister Death come, the living couldn't see him, and wept and wailed, but the folks that was dyin' rose up to greet him, and smiled at him on their way, like they knew him for a friend. She was right glad to see that everybody didn't take him for such a bad fellow after all. While they rode, Mister Death, he tole Maude Applegate many a pretty tale about his far travels, and it was plain to see he was a man knew more'n likker and women and ridin' herd.

And when they was on their last lap around and on their way home, Mister Death, he rode out over the ocean and showed Maude Applegate where the whales played — she saw 'em just as plain, aplowin' through the clear green water like a herd of buffalo on a grassy plain. And he rode over the North Pole, for her to see the polar bears, which was all white but for their noses, and he showed her the crocodiles of Egypt driftin' down the Nile, and the tigers of India, too, and every strange creature with his mate. And at last Maude Applegate couldn't help feeling sorry for Mister Death, that he was the only one who had to be alone in all the whole wide world.

But at last they was lopin' back over the plain toward our town; they seen the smoke arisin' from the stovepipes and chimleys into the pale blue sky; they rode right down the main street past Tarbell's Emporium, past the Wells Fargo office, and reined up before the Blue Bird Saloon.

"Why, what you pullin' up here for?" Maude Applegate asked of Mister Death, feelin' surprised, but Mister Death only answered, "Ne'mind; you'll see," and swung down out of the saddle.

Then he reached up and lifted Maude down from off his pale stallion, and he wrapped her once more in his cloak of invisibility, and he said to her, "Now fer the rest of the bargain."

So Maude stood there with her eyes shut, kinda stiff, and steelin' herself for his kiss, but nothin' happened at all, so she opened 'em again, and Mister Death said to her, "No, Maude, the bargain was that you was to kiss me."

So Maude, she was obliged to ask Mister Death to lean down his head, which he did, and she was obliged to reach up and put her mouth on his. Now maybe she thought it would be cold, and maybe she thought it would be fearful to kiss Mister Death — I don't know, I'm sure — but it surely come as a great surprise to her when she found her two arms around his neck without her knowin' how they got there, and her own two lips on his, and the truth of the matter is, it was Mister Death stepped away the first, and tole her, soft and low, "Run along now, Maude. Billy-be-damn Bangtry, your own true love, is settin' right in there in the Blue Bird Saloon."

Then Mister Death unwrapped her from his cloak of invisibility, so's she couldn't see him no more — only hear his spurs jinglin' as he walked away — and Maude Applegate was left standin' by herself before the Blue Bird Saloon, where, inside the window, she could see Billy-be-damn Bangtry, her own true love, settin' at a table drinkin' whisky with a bunch of fly young women of a kind doesn't mind settin' in saloons. Oh, then Maude Applegate's bosom was so full of a thousand feelin's she thought she would bust, and she didn't know whether what she wanted most was to wrench up the hitchin' rail, bust into the Blue Bird Saloon and lambaste her own true love, or whether she'd simply like to melt of shame and sink through the ground. Then she noticed that her daddy's pinto, all groomed and saddled, was tied up by the Blue Bird door. She was jest about decided to mount him and gallop off home before anybody seen her, when Billy-be-damn Bangtry caught a sight of her through the window, and come pushin' out the swingin' doors, swaggerin' and hitchin' his pants like he'd never been half dead in his life.

"Why," he sings out, "if it ain't little Maude Applegate waitin' for me outside the Blue Bird Saloon! Where you been, honey? Heared you was away."

Maude Applegate, she felt the red comin' up in her face. She snapped back at him, "Heared you was mighty sick."

"Mighty sick," Billy said, shakin' his head. "Mighty sick and like to die, but ole Injun Mary, she doctored me good as new with her poultices and herbs!"

Now this was the last straw to Maude Applegate. She'd rode high and she'd rode low; she'd rode through cow country to sheep country; through sheep country to Injun country; through Injun country to the far mountains, all to stay the hand of Mister Death from taking Billy-be-damn Bangtry, her own true love; she'd rode twice around the world and back and give a kiss on the lips to a strange man, and all to save a feller which turned out to be this horse-smellin', whisky-breathin', tobaccer-chewin', loose-livin', gamblin', no-good cow hand standin' here lookin' at her like she was a ripe peach an' all he had to do was shake the tree. Maude Applegate was so mad she could of cried, but she didn't do no such of a thing, since she was a redheaded woman, and besides, somethin' better come to her mind.

Just then she seen ole Pap Tarbell lean outen the upstairs winder of Tarbell's Emporium, and Maude, she took and witched a spell. When Pap let fly with his tobaccer juice, Maude, she witched it straight into Billy-be-damn Bangtry's eye. And while he was still standin' there acursin' and aswearin' in such language as no lady cares to hear, Maude unhitched her daddy's little pinto pony and leaped astride. She dug in her heels and set the dust aflyin' as she galloped down the street out of town. She rode through cow country into sheep country, through sheep country into Injun country, through Injun country to the far mountains, until she caught sight of Mister Death on his pale stallion.

Then she sung out, "Oh, wait up, Mister Death! Wait up for me!"

And when Mister Death heard her he turned and rode back

down the trail — though he is one who turns back for no man —
and he snatched her off her little pinto and onto his pale stallion,
he held her close and he kissed her good and pretty soon he said,
"I guess granny'll be mighty proud to see you."

And Maude Applegate said to him, "Jest don't let me hear no
talk about peepin' through folks' windows never no more."

Now Maude Applegate she lived long and happy with Mister
Death, and from all I hear, she's with him yet. Fact is, she took
to helpin' him with his work, and when we was little uns, and
cross at bedtime, and startin' to cry, our mammies'd tell us, "Hush,
now, honey, close your eyes, and pretty soon Maude Applegate'll
sit by your bed and sing you a lullaby."

And she used to too. Heard her myself.

Spoil the Child

HOWARD FAST

*H*oward Fast has skipped all over American history in his books. He settled briefly on the West in 1941 with The Last Frontier, a novelized version of the heroic northward flight of the Cheyennes under Dull Knife in 1878–1879, but within a year he was back in revolutionary times along the eastern coast. "Spoil the Child" was first printed in the Saturday Evening Post for August 6, 1938. In its terse dramatic restraint it tells more about travel across the plains in the early migration days than many another writer has crowded into a long book. It is the only western short story by Howard Fast I have ever read. There ought to be more, and readily available.

THE FIRST MORNING pa was gone, I tried to ride one of the mules. I didn't think that would hurt, because the mules were unharnessed anyway. But Maude told ma, and ma licked me. Ma was in the wagon, and she wouldn't have seen. I told Maude I'd remember.

Pa left about six in the morning while ma still slept. "Goin' after meat?" I asked him. He had his rifle.

He nodded.

"Kin I go?"

"Stay with ma, sonny," he said. "She ain't well."

"You said I could hunt —"

"You stay with ma, sonny."

Maude got up a few minutes after that. I could see pa like a black dot out on the prairie. I pointed to him.

I said: "That's pa out there huntin'."

Maude was combing her hair, not paying a lot of attention to me. Then I tried to ride the mule. Pa would never let me ride his horse. It was only half-broken, cost four hundred dollars. Ma was always saying we could have lived a year on what that horse cost.

Maude woke ma. My mother was a tall, thin woman, tired looking. She wasn't well. I could see that she wasn't well.

"Dave, get off that mule," she said. "Where's pa?"

"Went out to hunt."

"Come here. Can't ever get it into your head to behave." I went over, and she slapped my face. "Don't bother them mules. When'll he be back? We can't stay here."

"He didn't say."

"Get some chips for a fire," ma told me. "My land, I never seen such a lazy, shiftless boy." But she didn't say it the way she always did, as if she would want to bite my head off. She seemed too tired to really care.

I guess ma licked me every day. She said I was bad — a lot worse than you'd expect from a boy of twelve. You didn't expect them to be bad that young.

"You learn to leave the mules alone," Maude called.

"You shut up," I told her. Maude was fifteen, and pretty. She had light hair, and a thin, delicate face. Ma said that someday Maude would be a lady. She didn't expect much from me. She said I would be like pa.

I walked away from the wagon, looking for chips. By now, pa was out of sight, and where he had gone the prairie was just a roll of yellow and brown, a thread of cloud above it. It frightened me to be alone on the prairie. Pa laughed at it, and called it a big meadow. But it frightened me.

We had been on the prairie for a week now. Pa said in another few weeks we'd reach Fort Lee, due west. He said that if he had cattle stock, he'd settle down right on the prairie. This way, he'd cross the mountains, grow fruit, maybe, in California. Ma never believed much he said.

I went back to the wagon and started a fire. Ma had gone inside, and Maude sat on the driver's seat.

"You might gimme a hand," I told Maude.

"I don't see you overworking," Maude said.

"You'd better learn to shut up."

From inside the wagon, ma yelled: "You hold your tongue, Dave, or I'll wallop you!"

"You're a little beast," Maude said.

"You wait," I told her.

I went to the keg, drew some water, and set it up to boil. I could tell by the sound that there wasn't a lot of water left in the keg. Pa had said we'd reach water soon.

When I came back to the fire, I glanced up at the sky. It was an immense bowl of hot blue, bare except for a single buzzard that turned slowly, like a fish swimming. I guess I forgot. I kept looking up at the buzzard.

Ma climbed down from the wagon slowly. "You're the same as your pa," she said. "Lazy an' bad." Her face was tight-drawn. For the past few weeks she had hardly smiled, and now it seemed that she wouldn't smile again.

"And fresh," Maude said.

I put the water on the fire, not saying anything.

"Spare the rod and spoil the child," ma said.

Then her face twisted in pain, and she leaned against the wagon. "Well, don't stand there," she told me. "Water the mules."

I went to the keg. I knew there wasn't enough water for the mules. I hoped Pa would come back soon; I had a funny, awful fear of what would happen if he didn't come back soon. I kept glancing out at the prairie.

Pa had an itch in his feet. Ma said I would grow up the same way — having an itch in my feet. She was always sorry that she had married a man with an itch in his feet. Sometimes she said that the war had done it, that after the war between the North and the South, men were either broken or had to keep moving, like pa. Always west.

We lived in Columbus. Then we moved to St. Louis; then to Topeka. Pa couldn't stop, and ma got more and more worn out. She said that a wild land was no place to raise children. It was hard on ma, all right. Pa didn't do much, except when we were moving west, and then he would be like a different person. Ma never complained to him. She licked me instead.

I gave the mules enough water to cover the bottoms of their pails.

Ma came over, said: "That's not enough water."

"There ain't a damn sight more."

"Don't swear!" ma exclaimed. She clapped a hand across my head.

"He's always swearing," Maude said. "Thinks he's grown up."

Ma stared at me a moment, dully; then she went over and prepared breakfast. It was gruel and hardtack.

"Fresh meat would be good," ma said. She looked over the prairie, maybe looking for pa. I knew how much she cared for pa. She would talk a lot about itching feet, but that didn't matter.

After breakfast, I gave the mules some oats, and Maude cleaned up the dishes. I kept glancing at Maude, and she knew what I meant. She didn't care, until ma went back into the wagon. It hurt me to look at ma.

"He'll be back soon, I guess," ma said. Then she climbed into the wagon. It was a big sixteen-foot wagon, the kind they called freighters, with a hooped top, covered over with dirty brown canvas.

Maude said: "You leave me alone."

"I'll leave you alone now," I told Maude. "I gotta leave you alone now. Maybe you know what's the matter with ma?"

"That's none of your business," Maude said.

"It's my business, all right."

"You're just a kid."

I went to the back of the wagon and pulled out pa's carbine. It was the one he had used during the war, a short cavalry gun.

Ma saw me; she lay inside, and I could hear her breathing hard. She said: "What're you up to now; pa back?"

"Not yet."

"Well, you tell me soon as he gets back. And don't get into any mischief."

"All right."

In front of the wagon, I sat down on a feed box, and cleaned the gun with an old rag. Maude watched me. Finally, she said: "I'm gonna tell ma you're fooling with pa's gun."

"You keep your mouth shut."

Ma groaned softly then, and we both turned around and looked at the wagon. I felt little shivers crawl up and down my spine. Where was pa? He should have been back already. I put down

the gun and walked around the wagon. In a circle, the prairie rose
and fell, like a sea of whispering yellow grass. There was nothing
there, no living thing.

Maude was crying. "Why don't pa come back?" she said.

I didn't answer her. I guess it occurred to me for the first time
that pa might not come back. I felt like crying. I felt like getting
into a corner and crying. I hadn't felt so small for a long time. It
would be a comfort to have ma lick me now. You get licked,
and you know you're a kid, and you don't have to worry about
anything else.

I said to Maude: "Go inside the wagon and stay with ma."

"Don't you order me around."

"All right," I said. I turned my back on her. I didn't hold much
with girls when they're that age.

Then Maude went inside the wagon. I heard her crying, and
I heard ma say: "You stop that crying right now."

I loaded the carbine. I untethered one of the mules, climbed
onto it, and set out across the prairie in the direction pa had taken.
I didn't know just what I'd do, but I knew it was time pa came
back.

It wasn't easy, riding the mule just with harness straps. Mules
have a funny gait. And we didn't go very fast. I was glad ma and
Maude were in the wagon, otherwise ma would probably lick the
pants off me.

In about a half hour, the wagon was just a tiny black dot. It
might have been anything. I kept glancing at the sun to remember the direction I had taken. Then a swell hid the wagon. I
kept on going. I knew that if I stopped, even for a little while,
I'd cry my head off.

I saw a coyote. He stood like a dog and watched me. An antelope hopped close, and I might have shot at him. But I couldn't
bring myself to fire a rifle there. It would have done something
to me.

I found pa. I guess I had been riding for about an hour when
I saw him, over to one side. A buzzard flapped up, and I felt my
throat tighten until I thought it would choke me. I didn't want
to go over to him. I got down from the mule, and I walked over
slowly. But I didn't want to; something made me.

He was dead, all right. Maybe it was Indians and maybe it
wasn't; I didn't know. He was shot four times, and his gun was
gone.

The buzzard wouldn't go away; I shot the buzzard. I didn't cry. The carbine kicked back and made my shoulder ache. I was thinking about how pa always called me an undersized, freckled little runt. He said I wouldn't grow up. Maybe that's why I didn't cry.

I went away a little distance and sat down. I didn't look at pa. I tried to remember where we were, what pa had told me about going west. When I thought of ma, I had a sense of awful fear. Suppose it happened now.

The mule walked over and nuzzled my shoulder. I was glad the mule was there then. If he wasn't, I don't know what I would have done.

Pa had to be buried. I knew that men had to be buried, but I couldn't do it. The prairie was hard, baked mud. I went back to pa and stood over him; I guess that was the hardest thing I had ever done in my life. I straightened his clothes. I pulled off his boots. Men in the West were always talking about dying with their boots on. I didn't know how it meant anything, one way or another, but I thought pa would be pleased if he didn't have his boots on.

Then I climbed up on the mule and started back for the wagon. I tried not to think that I was twelve years old. If you get to thinking about that, then you're no good at all. When I got back, ma would lick me plenty.

The mule must have found its way back, because I didn't pay much attention to that. I let the reins loose, holding onto the harness straps, and I kept swallowing. Then I saw the wagon.

I thought: "I can't tell ma now — maybe later." Nobody had ever told me about a thing like that, but I knew it wouldn't do to tell ma now. I guess I only felt it instinctively, but I knew that the importance wasn't in pa any more. All that was important was life, and life was just a fleck of dust in the prairie. It was like a nightmare to think of the distance of the prairie, and how we were alone.

I rode up to the wagon, and Maude and ma were both standing next to it. I could tell from ma's face how worried she had been about me.

"There he is!" Maude screamed.

Ma said: "I guess there ain't nothing a body can do with you, Dave. Get off that mule."

I slipped off, tethered the mule. My whole body was twisted up with the strain of keeping what I had seen off my face. I came over to ma.

"Where you been?" she demanded.

"Hunting."

"I reckon there's nothing else for a little loafer like you. Spare the rod and spoil the child. Come here."

I went over and bent down, and she walloped me a bit, not too hard. She wasn't very strong then, I guess. I cried, but I wasn't crying because of the licking. I had had worse lickings than that and never opened my mouth. But it seemed to break the tension inside of me, and I had to cry. I went over and sat down with my back against one of the wagon wheels.

Maude walked past me and said: "I guess that learned you."

I just looked at her, without answering. I took out my jack-knife and began to pare at one of the wagon boards. Then my eyes traveled to the water keg.

I got up and went around to ma. She was still standing there, staring off across the prairie in the direction pa had gone.

Without turning, she said to me: "Seen anything of your pa?"

"No."

The sun was westward now, a splotch of red that blazed the whole prairie into a fire. I could get a little of how ma felt; I could see the loneliness.

"Get a fire going," she said. "He ought to have enough sense to come back early. Stop that whimpering. God help a woman when a man has itching feet."

I gathered chips and started the fire. When I took water from the keg for mush, the keg was just about empty. I didn't mention that to ma. She went about preparing supper slowly, awkwardly, and Maude watched her, frightened.

Ma kept glancing at the west.

"Be dark soon," I said.

"Guess pa'll be here any minute," ma said dully. I could tell that she didn't believe that.

"I guess so," I nodded.

We ate without speaking much. Ma didn't eat a great deal. As soon as we had finished, she went into the wagon.

Maude was saying: "I don't see how I can clean dishes without water. You fetch some water, Dave."

"There ain't no water," I said.

Maude stared at me, her eyes wide and frightened. She had heard stories, just the same as I had, about pilgrims who ran out of water. She opened her mouth to say something.

"What about ma?" I asked her quietly, nodding at the wagon.

"Why don't pa come back?"

"Ain't no sense thinking about pa if he ain't here. What about ma? I guess it won't be long."

She shook her head.

"You don't need to be scared," I muttered. "It won't do no good to be scared. I reckon the worst part of this trip is over."

"Where's pa?" she whispered. "What happened?"

"How do I know what happened? You girls make me sick. I never seen anything to beat you girls."

I got up and went over to the water keg. I shook it, hoping, without having any reason to hope. I knew it was just about empty. We had plenty of food — dried meat and meal and dried beans — enough to last a month, I guess. But ma would need water.

Maude was crying.

"Why don't you go to bed?" I told her.

"Don't order me around."

"Well, you go to bed," I said. "Go in and sleep with ma. I'll stay out here."

"You're not big enough to stay out here alone," Maude said, but I knew she was afraid to stay inside the wagon with ma. I knew how she felt, and I didn't blame her for the way she felt, she was such a kid, with ma petting her all the time. We couldn't talk it over between ourselves, and that would have made it a lot better. But we couldn't.

"I'm plenty big enough," I said.

Inside the wagon ma groaned, and out on the prairie a coyote was barking. There's nothing like a coyote barking to make your insides crawl. I was all shivers, and I could see that Maude wanted to stay close to me. But that wouldn't have made it any better.

"Get in the wagon, damn you!" I cried. I was glad ma couldn't hear me swear. Ma would lick me good and plenty when I swore like that.

Surprised, Maude stared at me. Then, without a word, she went into the wagon.

I stood there, outside, for a while. It had grown quite dark. In the sky there was a faint, reflected light of the sun, but it was quite dark. I walked over to the wagon and picked up one of the mule blankets that hung on the shafts. It was a warm night, summertime; I decided to put the blanket under the wagon and lie down on it.

I heard Maude saying her prayers in the wagon, but no sound from ma. I couldn't say my prayers. Usually, ma saw to it that I did, but tonight I couldn't say a word aloud. I tried, opening my mouth, but no words came out. I thought them, as much as I could. I tried not to think about pa. Spreading the blanket, I lay down on it, holding the carbine close to me. It seemed a part of pa and all that was left; I hugged it.

I couldn't sleep. I tried for a long time, but I couldn't sleep. It was quite dark now, with no moon in the sky. The mules were moving restlessly; probably because they wanted water.

I think I dozed a little. When I opened my eyes again, the moon was just coming up, yellow and bloated. I felt chilled thoroughly. Bit by bit, what had happened during the day came back, and now it was all more real than it had been in the daytime. While I lay there, thinking about it, I heard horses' hoofs; at first not noticing them, and only becoming aware of them when the horses bulked out of the night, two men riding slowly.

They were in the moonlight, and I was hidden in the shadow of the wagon. They didn't see me. They stopped just about a dozen yards from the wagon, sitting on their horses and eyeing the mules. The mules moved restlessly.

When I realized they were Indians I couldn't move, just lay there and watched them. They were naked to the waist, with their hair in two stiff braids to their shoulders. They both carried rifles.

I thought of pa. I thought of screaming to wake Maude and ma. I thought: "If they shot pa — "

They were cutting loose the mules.

I felt for the carbine, twisted around, so I lay on my belly. One of the men had dismounted and was coming toward the wagon. He held his gun in one hand and had drawn a knife with the other. I sighted the center of his breast and fired.

I remember how the sound blasted out the silence of the prairie. In the wagon, someone screamed. The Indian stopped, seemed to stare at me, swayed a bit, and crumpled to the ground. I remember the sharp pain in my shoulder from the blow of the recoil.

The mounted man's horse had wheeled about. He pulled it back, and fired at me. The shot threw sand in my face. I had a few cartridges and caps in my pocket, and I tried frantically to reload. The cartridges slipped through my fingers.

Then the Indian was gone. He had taken the other horse with him, and I heard their hoofs thundering across the prairie. I dropped the carbine. My shoulder ached terribly. Inside the wagon, Maude was whimpering, my mother groaning.

I climbed from under the wagon. The Indian lay on his back, his face hard and twisted. I stood there, looking at him.

Maude climbed down out of the wagon. "What is it?" she cried. Then she saw the Indian and screamed.

"All right — I shot him."

She stood there, holding her hand to her mouth.

"You get back in the wagon. I guess he killed pa, all right. Don't tell that to ma."

She shook her head. Ma was groaning. "I can't go back," Maude said.

"Why?"

And then I knew. I should have known from the way ma was groaning. I went up to Maude and slapped her face. She didn't seem to feel it. I slapped her again.

"Get in there with ma."

"I can't — it's dark."

"Get in there!" I yelled.

We had lanterns on the outside of the wagon. I took one and lit it. I wasn't trembling so much now. I gave the lantern to Maude, who was still standing the way she had been before.

"Go inside," I said.

Maude climbed into the wagon, taking the lantern with her. Then I cried. I crouched under the wagon, clutching the carbine and crying.

Finally, I went over to the Indian. I forced myself to do that. He lay half across the rifle he had carried. I pulled it out, and it was my father's rifle, all right.

I don't know how long I stood there holding the rifle. Then I put it under the seat, along with the carbine. I didn't want to look at the wagon.

I walked over to the mules, led them over to the shafts. It was hard to harness them. I had to balance myself on the shafts to get at their backs. When it was done, I ached all over, and my shoulder was swollen where the carbine had rested.

I climbed to the driver's seat. The curtains were down, and I couldn't see into the wagon, but the light still burned. Taking down pa's whip, I let it go onto the mules' backs. I had seen pa do that, and sometimes he let me try. The whip was fourteen feet long and I couldn't do much with it, but I got the mules moving. They had to keep moving. We had to find water.

At night, under the moon, the prairie was black and silver at the same time. Somehow, it didn't frighten me, the way it had during the day. I sat there thinking, I guess, of nothing at all, only awfully aware of the change inside me.

We drove on like that. I kept the mules at a slow pace, so the freighter wouldn't roll much. I was very tired, and after a while I didn't use the whip at all.

Then Maude came out of the wagon, sat down next to me. She looked at me and I looked at her, but she didn't say anything. She pressed close to me.

I whistled at the mules.

Inside the wagon something was whimpering. It made me tremble to hear that.

"Reckon we'll find water soon," I told Maude.

She nodded mechanically. Her head kept nodding and I dozed, myself. I guess I kept dozing through the night, fell asleep toward morning.

Maude woke me. The wagon had stopped, and the sun was an hour up. The mules had stopped on the bank of a slow, brown stream, lined with cottonwoods as far as I could see.

Maude was pointing at the water.

"Don't you start crying now," I said, rubbing my eyes.

"I won't," Maude nodded.

Ma called me, not very loud: "Dave, come here."

I climbed inside the wagon. Ma was lying on the bed, her arm curled around something. I peered at it.

"Do you know?" she said.

"I reckon I do. I reckon it's a boy. Girls ain't much use."

Ma was crying — not much; her eyes were just wetting themselves slowly.

"Where are we?" ma asked me.

"We been traveling through the night. There's a river out there. I guess we don't need to worry about water."

"All night — pa back?"

I said, slowly: "I killed an Indian last night, ma. He had pa's gun."

Then she just stared at me, and I stood there, shifting from one foot to another, wanting to run away. But I stood there. It must have been about five minutes, and she didn't say anything at all. The baby was whimpering.

Then she said: "You harnessed the mules?"

"Uh-huh. Maude didn't help me — "

Ma said: "You don't tease Maude. You don't tease Maude, or I'll take a stick to you. I never seen a boy like you for teasing."

"Uh-huh," I nodded.

"Just like your pa," ma whispered. "It don't pay to have a man whose heels are always itching — it don't pay."

"No use cryin'," I said.

Ma said: "What are we going to do?"

"Go on west. Ain't hard now to go a few hundred miles more. Reckon it won't be hard. Pa said — "

Ma was staring at me, her mouth trembling. I hadn't ever seen her look just like that before. I wanted to put my head down on her breast, hide it there.

I couldn't do that. I said: "Pa told me. We'll go west."

Then I went outside. I sat down on the wagon seat, looking at the river. I heard the baby making noises.

I said to Maude: "A man feels funny — with a kid."

The Scarecrow

VARDIS FISHER

*V*ardis Fisher is a westerner, an Idahoan, bred and born and raised and resident, and also an able writer of unusual honesty and sincerity. He does not write often about the West or in short story form, but when he does there is another addition to authentic western fiction. I first encountered this story in an anthology, New Stories for Men, published in 1943. I returned to it for this collection and was not disappointed. Quite the contrary. It is a story about a horse — and it is also a story about some of the fundamental impulses of the human spirit.

W<small>E WERE THRESHING</small> on the ranch of Jon Weeg and when we went to the machine one morning we discovered that a stray animal had been to the piled sacks of grain and had ripped several of them wide open. Around the pile were the hoofprints of a horse. We searched the yard and the outlying land, expecting to find the beast foundered; but there was no trace of it. In the evening of this day we built around the stacks of wheat a fence of barbed wire. "That'll hold him," we said.

But on the next morning we found another half-dozen sacks torn open; for the prowler had returned during the night, had leapt our three-wire fence, and had gone. In this evening we added two wires to the fence. It was now chin-high and we didn't think that even an elk could jump it. Our astonishment on the third morning left us speechless. The beast had come again, had vaulted our five-wire fence, and had plundered another half-dozen sacks. On the top wire was a little hair but that was all. And it was at this point that the matter began to be a little unreal for all of us. For Joe Burt, a huge and feeble-witted youth, it was nothing less than a miracle. Because ordinarily, as in turn we declared to one another, an animal does not gorge itself upon grain without foundering; does not come slyly under cover of darkness and vanish before daylight; and does not leap a five-wire fence.

"Mebbe it's a mule," said Curt Obbing. We searched and found tracks but they were not the tracks of a mule.

"I'm going to sleep out here," I said. "I'll find out."

And on the third night I laid my bed in the grain yard and waited for the thief. I fell asleep; and later was awakened by a terrific screeching of wire; and upon looking up, I saw a very tall gaunt horse caught on the fence. In the moonlight it seemed to be nothing but hide and bones and eyes. It had jumped and now stood with its front legs over the wire and with the taunt wire under its belly; and a more forlorn and helpless creature I had never seen. I rose and went over to it, intending to flog the ungainly beast off the place, but something in its eyes made me pause. It was a kind of sad resignation, a hopeless surrender, mixed with shame for having got into such a predicament. And instead of flogging the thief I patted its gaunt and ancient head and looked at its eyes. "You old fool," I said. "Don't you know enough to keep off a wire fence?" I went over and stirred the torn sacks of wheat and watched the beast's eyes, but it gave no sign. It did not even lift an ear or turn its eyes to watch me. Then I put a halter on it and cut the wires to get it off the fence and tied it to a post.

On the next morning the men walked around the drooping skeleton and wondered what should be done. There was no agreement among us. Joe Burt wanted to tie cans to its tail and set the dogs on it; Curt wanted to turpentine it; and Jack Brody wanted to put a girth around it, with sharp nails set to the flesh and turn it loose. And as they spoke, the men smote the beast or cuffed its ears, but it did not flinch. It seemed to be a dead horse, tied to a post. I persuaded the men to let me take it down the road and point its nose valleyward. "It's a good Christian practice," I said, "to give all pests to your neighbors."

And I took the creature a mile down the road and threw clubs at it and as far as I could see that horse, it was going patiently westward and out of sight. But on the next morning, there that beast was, stuffed and contented, before those bags of grain. Even my patience was gone now.

"I suppose," Curt said, "you wanta play with it some more."

"Let me fix him," said Jack Brody. "Put a spiked cinch around him and then give him all the water he'n drink. He'll move plenty fast."

"No, if we're going to do anything we'll kill it."

We talked of the matter and decided it would be best to kill it; and in this night, which was very dark, we got Jon Weeg's double-barreled shotgun and led the horse into a patch of timber. And now all of us, I observed, were very quiet and mysterious, as if we plotted some crime. Joe Burt laughed queerly a time or two but none of us said a word. Curt took the horse and we followed in single file. The old beast led easily, never drawing back or turning aside, as if he had spent all his years on the end of a rope. I think it was his dumb surrender to our wish, the almost eager way in which he went with us, that explains what happened later.

Because after Curt stopped in a dark recess of the woods none of us wanted to be the executioner. This in itself was rather unusual; for we had all slain animals before and none of us thought anything of twisting the head off a rooster or putting pups in a sack with stones and throwing them into water. This execution was different somehow, and I am still at a loss to explain the difference. I don't know why we hesitated as if there would be guilt on our souls. We seemed to share a common friendliness for this old vagabond that had outraged our fence and another's property. Or perhaps it was because Joe began to whimper and put his hands to his ears.

No matter: I am convinced now that none of us would have slain this animal if there had been a protest. If Curt had led him back to the yard, I imagine we would have set food and drink to the thief. But we had brought this horse out to murder and none of us would confess any weakness or any change of mind. We were men and we were doing a man's job. And when Curt said, "Who's got the gun?" we all stepped forward, as though eager to slay the beast; but we did not look at one another.

One of the men stepped forward with the gun and there was another pause. We were waiting for a volunteer.

"Well," said Curt, "who's to blow his head off?"

"It don't make any difference," Jack Brody said.

But Joe Burt, shaking from head to feet, put his hands to his ears and chattered:

"It's — it's a cinch I don't want to!"

This declaration made us hesitate again. Then Curt swore a mighty oath and said we were a fine bunch of men.

"What's the matter you guys? Give me that gun!"

We all stepped back and Curt loaded both barrels. He took the halter off and threw it at our feet and then dug into a pocket for his tobacco and bit off a huge quid. He tongued the tobacco for a moment and looked at us and then raised the gun to his shoulder. We all stepped farther back and Joe, with fingers thrust into his ears, began to babble.

"I can't see the sights!" Curt shouted. "Someone light a match."

"You don't have to see," said Jack. "Just put it against his head."

"Light a match!"

I struck a match and in its feeble light we saw the horse like a gaunt shadow, waiting patiently with his head drooping. The match sputtered and went out. I struck another. We could all see the gleaming barrel of the gun and Curt squinting along the sights. Then there was a thundering roar, the match went out, and we stood in overwhelming darkness. I struck another match and we saw the beast, standing there as if propped, with blood running down its face. I stepped forward quickly with the light and Curt fired the other barrel. The horse squealed and dropped to earth.

On our way back we said nothing. Curt went ahead, with gun smoking on his shoulder; and as before, we followed him in single file. After we had gone fifty yards I stopped and listened but could hear no sound. We took our several ways to bed and I lay sleepless for a long while, thinking of that dead beast out in the woods.

What happened later is very strange and a little incredible and I am not sure that I can make it clear. On the next morning we went to the yard and found that horse again within our fence, standing forlornly before the bags of wheat. Still, this is not exactly the way it happened. As a matter of fact, Joe Burt went out first and made the discovery. He came running to the house, pale and gibbering; and like a frenzied fellow he tried to tell us what he had seen. "He's been dreaming," we said; and we jested with him and did not believe his story at all.

"You're all cracked," Curt said. "You big simple lubber, stop that shakun around!" And Joe babbled at us and his teeth chattered.

And when we did go out, still unconvinced, we saw that creature before the grain. We all stopped and looked at him and looked at one another. He had not torn any sacks or eaten any wheat. Blood from his skull had run down to the bags, suggesting that he had been here most of the night: and the upper part of his head seemed to be a mass of clotted blood. One eye had been shot out and one ear had been blown off.

It is of what happened next that I cannot be certain, because it all seemed strange to me then and it seems strange to me now. None of us ate much breakfast and none of us said anything after our first amazement. I went to the timber to be sure that this was the horse we had shot. I found signs of a terrific struggle, as if it had taken the beast a long while to recover its legs; and I found the bloody trail back to the yard. I also found the halter which in our excitement we had forgotten.

On this day we did not work and for hours we did not talk. We sat in the yard, smoking cigarettes one after another; or looking with fresh astonishment at the horse; or with shame at the world around us. For it seemed to be a new world and we did not understand it. And all the while the animal stood there without moving, and apparently without pain, like a horrible apparition from the dead. More than his return, I think, was the way he stood that filled us with strange emotion. He possessed the yard and the pile of grain in spite of all opposition. He seemed to have a serene, an almost unearthly, unconcern about his victory; and he looked as if he would stand there forever, having by some privilege unknown to us claimed his heritage and his rights.

Harold Dow sat on the doorstep with his chin in his hands. It occurred to me, time and again while walking around, that the whole situation was more comic than tragic; but Dow would not look at me, nor would Curt or Jack, when I passed them. Curt, in fact, pretended to be very busy tinkering with machinery in the yard. Jack lay in the sun with his hands under his head. But it was Joe Burt who acted most queerly and who made us all feel queer. During the whole forenoon he hid behind the bags of wheat and peered at that horse, his big round face like a moon against the sky. The big lubber with his stricken eyes and gibbering tongue made us all feel disembodied and lost. I have wondered since if what took place later would have happened if Joe had not been with us. I don't know. I do know that something persistent and inexplicable was busy in our minds and hearts; a notion which slowly took hold of us; the same thought. And when at last I said, "Fellows, let's get busy," they all knew what I meant. They all rose and followed me as if we had talked of the matter and planned what to do; and we went to the horse and looked at it. For a long moment we did not speak, but I knew that every one of us was thinking the same thing. And it is this part of the experience that baffles me. I've no idea why we wanted to save that creature's life; for it was worthless and homeless and a nuisance to everybody. But here we were, who had suggested one torture and another, who had tried to blow its head off, now resolved to save its life. It may be that our experience — the attempt to kill the beast and then fetch it back to health — became in some strange way symbolic: a struggle between ourselves and all the blind forces of life which we did not understand. Death was our enemy, too, and against it we matched all our cunning and all our skill. And the fight we made here was more than a fight on the Antelope Hills. It was infinitely more than that to every one of us.

For three days and three nights we labored to save that horse's life. Not one of us suggested that we should call a veterinarian: this was our fight, our small epic of cunning and devotion, and we did not want professional skill. If a doctor had come the matter would not have been the same at all. There would not have been those tremendous implications that made silent men of us and chastened our hearts and hands. And so we devoted ourselves to this struggle and everything else in our lives stood aside and waited. With a pile of empty sacks we made a bed and forced the horse to lie; and we put liniments and salves on the wound and bandaged it; and hunted in coves for tender grass. We took turns sitting up with the creature, as if it were a human being, as if our whole life and happiness depended on it. And in everything that we did we moved and felt in common and were driven by the same overwhelming desire. In these three days we achieved the deepest kinship that I have ever known to exist among men.

On my night with the horse I did not sleep at all. I sat by it and looked at the sick eye and wondered what else I could do to relieve the pain and bring healing blood to the wound. Early in the morning Jack called to me from the bunkhouse where the men slept.

"How is he?"

"Better, I think."

"Does he — seem to be in much pain?"

"No, he's resting easily."

And then Curt appeared. "You say he's all right?"

"Yes, I think so."

At break of day they all left the bunkhouse and came to the yard. They looked at the horse and patted his lean hide or studied the sick eye. Jack went away and returned with an armful of grass, though the beast had not in forty-eight hours eaten a mouthful; and Curt warmed a pail of water. The horse drank on this morning and we were sure it was better. We smiled at one another and said the horse would be well soon; and when we sat to breakfast we ate with a little of our former appetites.

But in spite of all our efforts the animal died on the fourth day. Joe Burt wept, and the eyes of the other men, I observed, were as misty as my own. We ate no breakfast on this morning. Upon all of us there fell a depressing sadness; a great loneliness that ached in our throats, as if everything good and beautiful had been taken from life. Out in the woods we searched for a spot to dig a grave; and Curt said, "Here," and upon the ground where we had shot the horse we dug a grave. We did not drag it to the grave, as is the custom, with a log chain around its neck. We rolled it to some planks and hauled it to the grave; and over the unsightly skull we placed a box, so that nothing would strike the wound; and upon the carcass we let the earth fall gently. . . .

And then as one man we returned to the yard and tore the fence down.

Lone Wolf's Old Guard

HAMLIN GARLAND

Garland's West was the Middle West, what he called the "middle border," and he wrote many books about it with a mixture of affection and realism and indignation that it was not willing to become an obedient province of Boston culture. He sometimes pushed on into the "wilder" West and wrote stories that could qualify as westerns. His style suggests that he was a right-handed man who wrote with his left elbow, but he had, in his own way, an earnest, dogged competence. This sample is from The Book of the American Indian, 1923, a handsome volume generously illustrated with reproductions of some of Remington's best pictures.

Now IT HAPPENED that Lone Wolf's camp was on the line between the land of the Cheyennes and the home of his own people, the Kiowas, but he did not know this. He had lived there long, and the white man's maps were as unimportant to him as they had been to the Cheyennes. When he moved there he considered it to be his — a gift direct from the Creator — with no prior rights to be overstepped.

But the Consolidated Cattle Company, having secured the right to enclose a vast pasture, cared nothing for any red man's claim, provided they stood in with the government. A surveying party was sent out to run lines for fences.

Lone Wolf heard of these invaders while they were at work north of him, and learned in some mysterious way that they were to come down the Elk and cut through his camp. To his friend John, the interpreter, he sent these words:

"The white man must not try to build a fence across my land. I will fight if he does. Washington is not behind this thing. He would not build a fence through my lines without talking with me. I have sent to the agent of the Kiowas, he knows nothing about it — it is all a plan of the cattlemen to steal my lands. Tell them that we have smoked over this news — we have decided. This fence will not be built."

When "Johnny Smoker" brought this stern message to the camp of the surveyors some of them promptly threw up their hands. Jim Bellows, scout and interpreter, was among these, and his opinion had weight, for he wore his hair long and posed as an Indian fighter of large experience.

"Boys," he began, impressively, "we got to get out o' here as soon as darkness covers us. We're sixty miles from the fort, and only fifteen all told, and not half-armed. Old Lone Wolf holds over us, and we might as well quit and get help."

This verdict carried the camp, and the party precipitately returned to Darlington to confer with the managers of the company.

Pierce, the chief man, had reasons for not calling on the military authorities. His lease was as yet merely a semi-private arrangement between the Secretary of the Interior and himself, and he feared the consequences of a fight with Lone Wolf — publicity, friction, might cause the withdrawal of his lease; therefore he called in John Seger, and said:

"Jack, can you put that line through?"

"I could, but I don't want to. Lone Wolf is a good friend of mine, and I don't want to be mixed up in a mean job."

"Oh, come now — you mustn't show the white flag. I need you. I want you to pick out five or six men of grit and go along and see that this line is run. I can't be fooling around here all summer. Here's my lease, signed by the Secretary, as you see. It's all straight, and this old fool of an Indian must move."

Jack reluctantly consented, and set to work to hire a half dozen men of whose courage he had personal knowledge. Among these was a man by the name of Tom Speed, a borderman of great hardihood and experience. To him he said:

"Tom, I don't like to go into this thing; but I'm hard up, and Pierce has given me the contract to build the fence if we run the line, and it looks like we got to do it. Now I wish you'd saddle up and help me stave off trouble. How does it strike you?"

"It's nasty business, Jack; but I reckon we might better do it than let some tenderfoot go in and start a killin'. I'm busted flat, and if the pay is good, I jest about feel obliged to take it."

So it happened that two avowed friends of the red man led this second expedition against Lone Wolf's camp. Pierce sent his brother as boss, and with him went the son of one of the principal owners, a Boston man, by the name of Ross. Speed always called him "the Dude," though he dressed quite simply, as dress goes in Roxbury. He wore a light suit of gray wool, "low-quartered shoes," and a "grape box hat." He was armed with a pistol, which wouldn't kill a turtledove at fifteen feet. Henry Pierce, on the contrary, was a reckless and determined man.

Moving swiftly across the Divide, they took up the line on Elk Creek, and started directly towards Lone Wolf's camp. As they were nearing the bend in the river where Lone Wolf was camped, a couple of young warriors came riding leisurely up from the south. They were very cordial in their greeting, and after shaking hands all around pleasantly inquired:

"What are you doing here?"

"Running a line to mark out the land which the cattlemen have leased of the Cheyennes."

"We will go along and see where you are going," they replied.

A couple of hours later, while they were still with the camp, two others came riding quietly in from the east. They said, "We are looking for horses," and after shaking hands and asking Seger what the white men were doing, rode forward to join their companions, who seemed deeply interested in the surveyors and their instruments. Turning to Pierce, Jack said:

"You noticed that these four men were armed, I reckon?"

"Oh, yes, but they are all right. Didn't you see how they shook hands all round? They're just out hunting up ponies."

"Yes, I saw that; but I noticed they had plenty of ammunition and that their guns were bright. Indians don't hunt horses in squads, Mr. Pierce."

Pierce smiled, giving Seger a sidewise glance. "Are you getting nervous? If you are, you can drop to the rear."

Now Seger had lived for the larger part of his life among the red people, and knew their ways. He answered, quietly:

"There are only four of them now; you'll see more of them soon," and he pointed away to the north, where the heads of three mounted men were rising into sight over a ridge. These also proved to be young Kiowas, thoroughly armed, who asked the same question of the manager, and in conclusion pleasantly said:

"We'll just go along and see how you do it."

As they rode forward Seger uttered a more pointed warning.

"Mr. Pierce, I reckon you'd better make some better disposition of your men. They are all strung out here, with their guns on their backs, in no kind of shape to make a defense."

Pierce was a little impressed by the scout's earnestness, and took trouble to point out the discrepancy between "a bunch of seven cowardly Indians" and his own band of twenty brave and experienced men.

"That's all right," replied Seger; "but these seven men are only spies, sent out to see what we are going to do. We'll have to buckle up with Lone Wolf's whole band very soon."

A few minutes later the seven young men rode quietly by and took a stand on a ridge a little in front of the surveyors. As he approached them, Seger perceived a very great change in their demeanor. They no longer smiled; they seemed grim, resolute, and much older. From a careless, laughing group of young men they had become soldiers — determined, disciplined, and dignified. Their leader, riding forth, held up his hand, and said:

"Stop; you must wait here till Lone Wolf comes."

Meanwhile, in the little city of tents, a brave drama was being enacted. Lone Wolf, a powerful man of middle age, was sitting in council with his people. The long-expected had happened — the cattlemen had begun to mark off the red man's land as their own, and the time had come either to submit or to repel the invaders. To submit was hard, to fight hopeless. Their world was still narrow, but they had a benumbing conception of the power and the remorseless greed of the white man.

"We can kill those who come," said Lone Wolf. "They are few, but behind them are the soldiers and men who plough."

At last old White Buffalo rose — he had been a great leader in his day, and was still much respected, though he had laid aside his chieftainship. He was bent and gray and wrinkled, but his voice was still strong, and his eyes keen.

"My friends, listen to me! During seventy years of my life I lived without touching the hand of a white man. I have always opposed warfare, except when it was necessary; but now the time has come to fight. Let me tell you what to do. I see here some thirty old men, who, like me, are nearing the grave. This thing we will do — we old men — we will go out to war against these cattlemen. We will go forth and die in defense of our lands. Big Wolf, come — and you, my brother, Standing Bear."

As he called the roll of the gray old defenders, the old women broke into heart-piercing wailing, intermingled with exultant cries as some brave wife or sister caught the force of the heroic responses, which leaped from the lips of their fathers and husbands. A feeling of awe fell over the young men as they watched the fires flame once more in the dim eyes of their grandsires, and when all had spoken, Lone Wolf rose and stepped forth, and said:

"Very well; then I will lead you."

"Whosoever leads us goes to certain death," said White Buffalo. "It is the custom of the white men to kill the leader. You will fall at the first fire. I will lead."

Lone Wolf's face grew stern. "Am I not your war chief? Whose place is it to lead? If I die, I fall in combat for my land, and you, my children, will preserve my name in song. We do not know how this will end, but it is better to end in battle than to have our lands cut in half beneath our feet."

The bustle and preparation began at once. When all was ready the thirty gray and withered old men, beginning a low humming song, swept through the camp and started on their desperate charge, Lone Wolf leading them. "Some of those who go will return, but if the white men fight, I will not return," he sang, as they began to climb the hill on whose top the white man could be seen awaiting their coming.

Halfway up the hill they met some of the young warriors. "Go bring all the white men to the council," said Lone Wolf.

As the white men watched the band leaving the village and beginning to ascend the hill, Speed turned and said: "Well, Jack, what do you think of it? Here comes a war party — painted and armed."

"I think it's about an even chance whether we ever cross the Washita again or not. Now, you are a married man with children, and I wouldn't blame you if you pulled out right this minute."

"I feel meaner about this than anything I ever did," replied Speed, "but I am going to stay with the expedition."

As Lone Wolf and his heroic old guard drew near, Seger thrilled with the significance of this strange and solemn company of old men in full war-paint, armed with all kinds of old-fashioned guns, and bows and arrows. As he looked into their wrinkled faces, the scout perceived that these grandsires had come resolved to die. He divined what had taken place in camp. Their exalted heroism was written in the somber droop of their lips. "We can die, but we will not retreat!" In such wise our grandsires fought.

Lone Wolf led his Spartan host steadily on till near enough to be heard without effort. He then halted, took off his war-bonnet and hung it on the pommel of his saddle. Lifting both palms to the sky, he spoke, and his voice had a solemn boom in it: "The Great Father is looking down on us. He sees us. He knows I speak the truth. He gave us this land. We are the first to inhabit it. No one else has any claim to it. It is ours, and I will go under the sod before any cattlemen shall divide it and take it away from us. I have said it."

When this was interpreted to him, Pierce with a look of inquiry turned to Speed. "Tell the old fool this line is going to be run, and no old scarecrows like these can stop us."

Seger, lifting his hand, signed: "Lone Wolf, you know me. I am your friend. I do not come to do you harm. I come to tell you you are wrong. All the land on my left hand the Great Father says is Cheyenne land. All on my right hand is Kiowa land. The Cheyennes have sold the right to their land to the white man, and we are here to mark out the line. We take only Cheyenne land."

"I do not believe it," replied the chief. "My agent knows nothing of it. Washington has not written anything to me about it. This is the work of robbers. Cattlemen will do anything for money. They are wolves. They shall not go on."

"What does he say?" asked Pierce.

"He says we must not go on."

"You tell him he can't run any such bluff on me with his old scarecrow warriors. This line goes through."

Lone Wolf, tense and eager, asked, "What says the white chief?"

"He says we must run the line."

Lone Wolf turned to his guard. "You may as well get ready," he said, quietly.

The old men drew closer together with a mutter of low words, and each pair of dim eyes selected their man. The clicking of their guns was ominous, and Pierce turned white.

Speed drew his revolver-holster round to the front. "They're going to fight," he said. "Every man get ready!"

But Seger, eager to avoid the appalling contest, cried out to Pierce:

"Don't do that! It's suicide to go on. These old men have come out to fight till death." To Lone Wolf he signed: "Don't shoot, my friend! — let us consider this matter. Put up your guns."

Into the hot mist of Pierce's wrath came a realization that these old men were in mighty earnest. He hesitated.

Lone Wolf saw his hesitation, and said: "If you are here by right, why do you not get the soldier chief to come and tell me? If the Great Father has ordered this — then I am like a man with his hands tied. The soldiers do not lie. Bring them!"

Seger grasped eagerly at this declaration. "There is your chance, Pierce. The chief says he will submit if the soldiers come to make the survey. Let me tell him that you will bring an officer from the fort to prove that the government is behind you."

Pierce, now fully aware of the desperate bravery of the old men, was looking for a knothole of escape. "All right, fix it up with him," he said.

Seger turned to Lone Wolf. "The chief of the surveyors says: 'Let us be friends. I will not run the line.' "

"Ho, ho!" cried the old warriors, and their faces, grim and wrinkled, broke up into smiles. They laughed, they shook hands, while tears of joy filled their eyes. They were like men delivered from sentence of death. The desperate courage of their approach was now revealed even to Pierce. They were joyous as children over their sudden release from slaughter.

Lone Wolf, approaching Seger, dismounted, and laid his arm over his friend's shoulder. "My friend," he said, with grave tenderness, "I wondered why you were with these men, and my heart was heavy; but now I see that you were here to turn aside the guns of the cattlemen. My heart is big with friendship for you. Once more you have proved my good counselor." And tears dimmed the fierceness of his eyes.

A week later, a slim, smooth-cheeked second lieutenant, by virtue of his cap and the crossed arms which decorated his collar, ran the line, and Lone Wolf made no resistance. "I have no fight with the soldiers of the Great Father," he said: "they do not come to gain my land. I now see that Washington has decreed that this fence shall be built." Nevertheless, his heart was very heavy, and in his camp his heroic old guard sat waiting, waiting!

Tennessee's Partner

BRET HARTE

*B*ret Harte was an easterner, a city man, and he never particularly wanted to be anything else. He went to California at fifteen because his mother took him there. He spent seventeen years there and never liked it much and as soon as he was successful left the West and never returned. He was never really part of it, even in spirit, and remained always a self-conscious, slightly superior outside observer. Yet he was the first to give the western story a firm foundation of popularity, and one of the first to have a definite attitude toward western material in fiction and use it for deliberate artistic purpose — for what he called "a peculiarly characteristic Western American literature." His work can be ridiculed by modern critics as devastatingly as he ridiculed the Victorian novelists in his own Condensed Novels. But the best of it remains, has the vitality to weather all changes in critical fashion.

In 1870, when he was editor of the Overland Monthly and published in it his "The Luck of Roaring Camp," he was suddenly hailed as the new light on the literary horizon. When he published "The Luck" with five other tales in a small book in 1871 he was famous. He wrote steadily for another thirty years, poetry, more tales, endless California romances, more poetry, even a play or two, enough in all to fill nineteen fat volumes of collected works, but he never surpassed those early tales. "The Luck," of course, *and "The Outcasts of Poker Flat" and perhaps "Miggles" are old anthology warhorses. "Tennessee's Partner" happens to be my favorite. Like the others but not quite so much, it is mannered and dated — just as the writing of today will seem mannered and dated in another eighty years. If you let that stand in your way, you are simply cheating yourself.*

I DO NOT THINK that we ever knew his real name. Our ignorance of it certainly never gave us any social inconvenience, for at Sandy Bar in 1854 most men were christened anew. Sometimes these appellatives were derived from some distinctiveness of dress, as in the case of "Dungaree Jack"; or from some peculiarity of habit, as shown in "Saleratus Bill," so called from an undue proportion of that chemical in his daily bread; or from some unlucky slip, as exhibited in "The Iron Pirate," a mild, inoffensive man, who earned that baleful title by his unfortunate mispronunciation of the term "iron pyrites." Perhaps this may have been the beginning of a rude heraldry; but I am constrained to think that it was because a man's real name in that day rested solely upon his own unsupported statement. "Call yourself Clifford, do you?" said Boston, addressing a timid newcomer with infinite scorn; "hell is full of such Cliffords!" He then introduced the unfortunate man, whose name happened to be really Clifford, as "Jaybird Charley," — an unhallowed inspiration of the moment that clung to him ever after.

But to return to Tennessee's Partner, whom we never knew by any other than this relative title. That he had ever existed as a separate and distinct individuality we only learned later. It seems that in 1853 he left Poker Flat to go to San Francisco, ostensibly to procure a wife. He never got any farther than Stockton. At that place he was attracted by a young person who waited upon the table at the hotel where he took his meals. One morning he said something to her which caused her to smile not unkindly, to somewhat coquettishly break a plate of toast over his upturned, serious, simple face, and to retreat to the kitchen. He followed her, and emerged a few moments later, covered with more toast and victory. That day week they were married by a justice of the peace, and returned to Poker Flat. I am aware that something more might be made of this episode, but I prefer to tell it as it was current at Sandy Bar, — in the gulches and bar-rooms, — where all sentiment was modified by a strong sense of humor.

Of their married felicity but little is known, perhaps for the reason that Tennessee, then living with his partner, one day took occasion to say something to the bride on his own account, at which, it is said, she smiled not unkindly and chastely retreated, — this time as far as Marysville, where Tennessee followed her, and where they went to housekeeping without the aid of a justice of the peace. Tennessee's Partner took the loss of his wife simply and seriously, as was his fashion. But to everybody's surprise, when Tennessee one day returned from Marysville, without his partner's wife, — she having smiled and retreated with somebody else, — Tennessee's Partner was the first man to shake his hand and greet him with affection. The boys who had gathered in the cañon to see the shooting were naturally indignant. Their indignation might have found vent in sarcasm but for a certain look in Tennessee's Partner's eyes that indicated a lack of humorous appreciation. In fact, he was a grave man, with a steady application to practical detail which was unpleasant in a difficulty.

Meanwhile a popular feeling against Tennessee had grown up on the Bar. He was known to be a gambler; he was suspected to be a thief. In these suspicions Tennessee's Partner was equally compromised; his continued intimacy with Tennessee after the affair above quoted could only be accounted for on the hypothesis of a copartnership of crime. At last Tennessee's guilt became flagrant. One day he overtook a stranger on his way to Red Dog. The stranger afterward related that Tennessee beguiled the time with interesting anecdote and reminiscence, but illogically concluded the interview in the following words: "And now, young man, I'll trouble you for your knife, your pistols, and your money. You see your weppings might get you into trouble at Red Dog, and your money's a temptation to the evilly disposed. I think you said your address was San Francisco. I shall endeavor to call." It may be stated here that Tennessee had a fine flow of humor, which no business preoccupation could wholly subdue.

This exploit was his last. Red Dog and Sandy Bar made common cause against the highwayman. Tennessee was hunted in very much the same fashion as his prototype, the grizzly. As the toils closed around him, he made a desperate dash through the Bar, emptying his revolver at the crowd before the Arcade Saloon,

and so on up Grizzly Cañon; but at its farther extremity he was
stopped by a small man on a gray horse. The two men looked
at each other a moment in silence. Both were fearless, both self-
possessed and independent, and both types of a civilization that
in the seventeenth century would have been called heroic, but in
the nineteenth simply "reckless."

"What have you got there? — I call," said Tennessee quietly.

"Two bowers and an ace," said the stranger as quietly, showing
two revolvers and a bowie-knife.

"That takes me," returned Tennessee; and, with this gambler's
epigram, he threw away his useless pistol and rode back with his
captor.

It was a warm night. The cool breeze which usually sprang up
with the going down of the sun behind the chaparral-crested mountain was that evening withheld from Sandy Bar. The little cañon
was stifling with heated resinous odors, and the decaying driftwood
on the Bar sent forth faint sickening exhalations. The feverishness
of day and its fierce passions still filled the camp. Lights moved
restlessly along the bank of the river, striking no answering reflection from its tawny current. Against the blackness of the pines
the windows of the old loft above the express-office stood out
staringly bright; and through their curtainless panes the loungers
below could see the forms of those who were even then deciding
the fate of Tennessee. And above all this, etched on the dark
firmament, rose the Sierra, remote and passionless, crowned with
remoter passionless stars.

The trial of Tennessee was conducted as fairly as was consistent
with a judge and jury who felt themselves to some extent obliged
to justify, in their verdict, the previous irregularities of arrest and
indictment. The law of Sandy Bar was implacable, but not
vengeful. The excitement and personal feeling of the chase were
over; with Tennessee safe in their hands, they were ready to listen
patiently to any defense, which they were already satisfied was in-
sufficient. There being no doubt in their own minds, they were
willing to give the prisoner the benefit of any that might exist.
Secure in the hypothesis that he ought to be hanged on general
principles, they indulged him with more latitude of defense than
his reckless hardihood seemed to ask. The Judge appeared to be
more anxious than the prisoner, who, otherwise unconcerned, evidently took a grim pleasure in the responsibility he had created.
"I don't take any hand in this yer game," had been his invariable

but good-humored reply to all questions. The Judge — who was also his captor — for a moment vaguely regretted that he had not shot him "on sight" that morning, but presently dismissed this human weakness as unworthy of the judicial mind. Nevertheless, when there was a tap at the door, and it was said that Tennessee's Partner was there on behalf of the prisoner, he was admitted at once without question. Perhaps the younger members of the jury, to whom the proceedings were becoming irksomely thoughtful, hailed him as a relief.

For he was not, certainly, an imposing figure. Short and stout, with a square face, sunburned into a preternatural redness, clad in a loose duck "jumper" and trousers streaked and splashed with red soil, his aspect under any circumstances would have been quaint, and was now even ridiculous. As he stooped to deposit at his feet a heavy carpetbag he was carrying, it became obvious, from partially developed legends and inscriptions, that the material with which his trousers had been patched had been originally intended for a less ambitious covering. Yet he advanced with great gravity, and after shaking the hand of each person in the room with labored cordiality, he wiped his serious perplexed face on a red bandana handkerchief, a shade lighter than his complexion, laid his powerful hand upon the table to steady himself, and thus addressed the Judge: —

"I was passin' by," he began, by way of apology, "and I thought I'd just step in and see how things was gittin' on with Tennessee thar, — my pardner. It's a hot night. I disremember any sich weather before on the Bar."

He paused a moment, but nobody volunteering any other meteorological recollection, he again had recourse to his pocket-handkerchief, and for some moments mopped his face diligently.

"Have you anything to say on behalf of the prisoner?" said the Judge finally.

"Thet's it," said Tennessee's Partner, in a tone of relief. "I come yar as Tennessee's pardner, — knowing him nigh on four year, off and on, wet and dry, in luck and out o' luck. His ways ain't aller my ways, but thar ain't any p'ints in that young man, thar ain't any liveliness as he's been up to, as I don't know. And you sez to me, sez you, — confidential-like, and between man and man, — sez you, 'Do you know anything in his behalf.' and I sez to you, sez I, — confidential-like, as between man and man, — 'What should a man know of his pardner?' "

"Is this all you have to say?" asked the Judge impatiently, feeling, perhaps, that a dangerous sympathy of humor was beginning to humanize the court.

"Thet's so," continued Tennessee's Partner. "It ain't for me to say anything agin' him. And now, what's the case? Here's Tennessee wants money, wants it bad, and doesn't like to ask it of his old pardner. Well, what does Tennessee do? He lays for a stranger, and he fetches that stranger; and you lays for *him*, and you fetches *him*; and the honors is easy. And I put it to you, bein' a fa'r-minded man, and to you, gentlemen all, as fa'r-minded men, ef this isn't so."

"Prisoner," said the Judge, interrupting, "have you any questions to ask this man?"

"No! no!" continued Tennessee's Partner hastily. "I play this yer hand alone. To come down to the bed-rock, it's just this: Tennessee, thar, has played it pretty rough and expensive-like on a stranger, and on this yer camp. And now, what's the fair thing? Some would say more, some would say less. Here's seventeen hundred dollars in coarse gold and a watch, — it's about all my pile, — and call it square!" And before a hand could be raised to prevent him, he had emptied the contents of the carpetbag upon the table.

For a moment his life was in jeopardy. One or two men sprang to their feet, several hands groped for hidden weapons, and a suggestion to "throw him from the window" was only overridden by a gesture from the Judge. Tennessee laughed. And apparently oblivious to the excitement, Tennessee's Partner improved the opportunity to mop his face again with his handkerchief.

When order was restored, and the man was made to understand, by the use of forcible figures and rhetoric, that Tennessee's offense could not be condoned by money, his face took a more serious and sanguinary hue, and those who were nearest to him noticed that his rough hand trembled slightly on the table. He hesitated a moment as he slowly returned the gold to the carpetbag, as if he had not yet entirely caught the elevated sense of justice which swayed the tribunal, and was perplexed with the belief that he had not offered enough. Then he turned to the Judge, and saying, "This yer is a lone hand, played alone, and without my pardner," he bowed to the jury and was about to withdraw, when the Judge called him back: —

"If you have anything to say to Tennessee, you had better say it now."

For the first time that evening the eyes of the prisoner and his strange advocate met. Tennessee smiled, showed his white teeth, and saying, "Euchred, old man!" held out his hand. Tennessee's Partner took it in his own, and saying, "I just dropped in as I was passin' to see how things was gettin' on," let the hand passively fall, and adding that "it was a warm night," again mopped his face with his handkerchief, and without another word withdrew.

The two men never again met each other alive. For the unparalleled insult of a bribe offered to Judge Lynch — who, whether bigoted, weak, or narrow, was at least incorruptible — firmly fixed in the mind of that mythical personage any wavering determination of Tennessee's fate; and at the break of day he was marched, closely guarded, to meet it at the top of Marley's Hill.

How he met it, how cool he was, how he refused to say anything, how perfect were the arrangements of the committee, were all duly reported, with the addition of a warning moral and example to all future evil-doers, in the "Red Dog Clarion," by its editor, who was present, and to whose vigorous English I cheerfully refer the reader. But the beauty of that midsummer morning, the blessed amity of earth and air and sky, the awakened life of the free woods and hills, the joyous renewal and promise of Nature, and above all, the infinite serenity that thrilled through each, was not reported, as not being a part of the social lesson. And yet, when the weak and foolish deed was done, and a life, with its possibilities and responsibilities, had passed out of the misshapen thing that dangled between earth and sky, the birds sang, the flowers bloomed, the sun shone, as cheerily as before; and possibly the "Red Dog Clarion" was right.

Tennessee's Partner was not in the group that surrounded the ominous tree. But as they turned to disperse, attention was drawn to the singular appearance of a motionless donkey-cart halted at the side of the road. As they approached, they at once recognized the venerable "Jenny" and the two-wheeled cart as the property of Tennessee's Partner, used by him in carrying dirt from his claim; and a few paces distant the owner of the equipage himself, sitting under a buckeye-tree, wiping the perspiration from his glowing face. In answer to an inquiry, he said he had come for the body of the "diseased," "if it was all the same to the committee." He didn't wish to "hurry anything"; he could "wait." He was not working that day; and when the gentlemen were done with the "diseased," he would take him. "Ef thar is any present," he added, in his simple, serious way, "as would care to jine in the fun'l,

they kin come." Perhaps it was from a sense of humor, which I
have already intimated was a feature of Sandy Bar, — perhaps it
was from something even better than that, but two thirds of the
loungers accepted the invitation at once.

It was noon when the body of Tennessee was delivered into the
hands of his partner. As the cart drew up to the fatal tree, we
noticed that it contained a rough oblong box, — apparently made
from a section of sluicing, — and half filled with bark and the
tassels of pine. The cart was further decorated with slips of
willow and made fragrant with buckeye-blossoms. When the body
was deposited in the box, Tennessee's Partner drew over it a piece
of tarred canvas, and gravely mounting the narrow seat in front,
with his feet upon the shafts, urged the little donkey forward.
The equipage moved slowly on, at that decorous pace which was
habitual with Jenny even under less solemn circumstances. The
men — half curiously, half jestingly, but all good-humoredly —
strolled along beside the cart, some in advance, some a little in
the rear of the homely catafalque. But whether from the narrow-
ing of the road or some present sense of decorum, as the cart
passed on, the company fell to the rear in couples, keeping step,
and otherwise assuming the external show of a formal procession.
Jack Folinsbee, who had at the outset played a funeral march in
dumb show upon an imaginary trombone, desisted from a lack of
sympathy and appreciation, — not having, perhaps, your true hu-
morist's capacity to be content with the enjoyment of his own fun.

The way led through Grizzly Cañon, by this time clothed in
funereal drapery and shadows. The redwoods, burying their mocca-
sined feet in the red soil, stood in Indian file along the track,
trailing an uncouth benediction from their bending boughs upon
the passing bier. A hare, surprised into helpless inactivity, sat
upright and pulsating in the ferns by the roadside as the cortège
went by. Squirrels hastened to gain a secure outlook from higher
boughs; and the blue-jays, spreading their wings, fluttered before
them like outriders, until the outskirts of Sandy Bar were reached,
and the solitary cabin of Tennessee's Partner.

Viewed under more favorable circumstances, it would not have
been a cheerful place. The unpicturesque site, the rude and un-
lovely outlines, the unsavory details, which distinguish the nest-
building of the California miner, were all here with the dreariness
of decay superadded. A few paces from the cabin there was a
rough inclosure, which, in the brief days of Tennessee's Partner's

matrimonial felicity, had been used as a garden, but was now overgrown with fern. As we approached it, we were surprised to find that what we had taken for a recent attempt at cultivation was the broken soil about an open grave.

The cart was halted before the inclosure, and rejecting the offers of assistance with the same air of simple self-reliance he had displayed throughout, Tennessee's Partner lifted the rough coffin on his back, and deposited it unaided within the shallow grave. He then nailed down the board which served as a lid, and mounting the little mound of earth beside it, took off his hat and slowly mopped his face with his handkerchief. This the crowd felt was a preliminary to speech, and they disposed themselves variously on stumps and boulders, and sat expectant.

"When a man," began Tennessee's Partner slowly, "has been running free all day, what's the natural thing for him to do? Why, to come home. And if he ain't in a condition to go home, what can his best friend do? Why, bring him home. And here's Tennessee has been running free, and we brings him home from his wandering." He paused and picked up a fragment of quartz, rubbed it thoughtfully on his sleeve, and went on: "It ain't the first time that I've packed him on my back, as you see'd me now. It ain't the first time that I brought him to this yer cabin when he couldn't help himself; it ain't the first time that I and Jinny have waited for him on yon hill, and picked him up and fetched him home, when he couldn't speak and didn't know me. And now that it's the last time, why" — he paused and rubbed the quartz gently on his sleeve — "you see it's sort of rough on his pardner. And now, gentlemen," he added abruptly, picking up his long-handled shovel, "the fun'l's over; and my thanks, and Tennessee's thanks, to you for your trouble."

Resisting any proffers of assistance, he began to fill in the grave, turning his back upon the crowd, that after a few moments' hesitation, gradually withdrew. As they crossed the little ridge that hid Sandy Bar from view, some, looking back, thought they could see Tennessee's Partner, his work done, sitting upon the grave, his shovel between his knees, and his face buried in his red bandana handkerchief. But it was argued by others that you couldn't tell his face from his handkerchief at that distance, and this point remained undecided.

In the reaction that followed the feverish excitement of that day, Tennessee's Partner was not forgotten. A secret investigation had cleared him of any complicity in Tennessee's guilt, and left only a suspicion of his general sanity. Sandy Bar made a point of calling on him, and proffering various uncouth but well-meant kindnesses. But from that day his rude health and great strength seemed visibly to decline; and when the rainy season fairly set in, and the tiny grass-blades were beginning to peep from the rocky mound above Tennessee's grave, he took to his bed.

One night, when the pines beside the cabin were swaying in the storm and trailing their slender fingers over the roof, and the roar and rush of the swollen river were heard below, Tennessee's Partner lifted his head from the pillow, saying, "It is time to go for Tennessee; I must put Jinny in the cart"; and would have risen from his bed but for the restraint of his attendant. Struggling, he still pursued his singular fancy: "There, now, steady, Jinny, — steady, old girl. How dark it is! Look out for the ruts, — and look out for him, too, old gal. Sometimes, you know, when he's blind drunk, he drops down right in the trail. Keep on straight up to the pine on the top of the hill. Thar! I told you so! — thar he is, — coming this way, too, — all by himself, sober, and his face a-shining. Tennessee! Pardner!"

And so they met.

A Question of Blood

ERNEST HAYCOX

E rnest Haycox wrote twenty and more good, standard western novels, well above the average in style and pervasive atmosphere but not necessarily in material. Many of them seem formularized magazine serials rather than independent novels and simply play rather well disguised variations on the familiar sun-god-hero theme. Then, just before his death in 1950, he finished The Earthbreakers, a big novel of pioneering in Oregon, which is a permanent addition to western literature. But his best work, I think, emerges in his short stories, scattered over the years in the writing. I would not hesitate to pick for this collection any one of the nine in Pioneer Loves, 1948, or of the matching nine in By Rope and Lead, 1951. My choice here is the shortest of them all because rarely have I read, in any field, a story which says so much in so little and with the same right, inevitable, perfect touch.

THAT FALL OF 1869 when Frank Isabel settled in the Yellow Hills the nearest town was a four-day ride to the north and his closest white neighbor lived at the newly established Hat ranch, seventy miles over in Two Dance Valley. The Indians were on reservation but it was still risky for a man to be alone in the country.

It made no difference to Isabel. He was young and self-willed and raised in that impoverished and faction-torn part of Missouri where manhood came to a male child almost as soon as he could lift a gun. He had a backwoodsman's lank loose height, his eyes were almost black and though he kept a smooth-shaven face there was always a clay-blue cast to the long sides of his jaw. The land was free, well grassed and watered and ideal for a poor man who had ambition. This was why he had come.

Yet self-sufficient as he was he had made no calculation for the imperious hungers that soon or late come to a lonely man. And presently, seeing no hope of a white woman in the land for many years, he went down to the reservation and took unto himself a Crow girl, the bargain being sealed by payment to her father of one horse and a quart of whisky.

She was quick and small and neat, with enormous eyes looking out of a round smooth face. The price paid was small and that hurt her pride for a little while, yet it was a white man who wanted her and the hurt died and she moved quietly into Frank Isabel's log house and settled down to the long, lonesome days without murmur.

She was more than he had expected in an Indian woman: quick to perceive the way his mind ran, showing him sudden streaks of mischief-making gaiety, and sometimes a flash of affection. Before the boy baby was born he drove her three hundred miles to Cheyenne and married her in the white way.

It was a sense of justice that impelled him to do this rather than any need in her eyes. For he was learning that the horse and bottle of whisky were as binding as any ceremony on earth; and he was also learning that though an Indian woman was a dutiful woman, immemorial customs guided her in a way he could not hope to touch or change. A man's work was a man's; a woman's work was hers and the line was hard and clear. In the beginning he had shocked her by cutting the firewood and by dressing down the game he brought in. It had shamed her for a while that he should descend to those things; and only by angry command had he established the habit of eating at table instead of crosslegged on a floor blanket. She was faithful to the discharge of the duty she owed him, but behind that girlish face was an adamant will. The ways of a thousand generations were ingrained in her.

Often at night, smoking before the fire and watching his boy crawl so awkwardly across the floor, he felt a strangeness at seeing her darkly crouched in a corner, lost in thoughts he could never reach. Sometimes the color and the sound of his early days in Missouri came strongly to him and he wished that she might know what was in his head. But he talked her tongue poorly and she would speak no English; and so silence lay between them.

Meanwhile Two Dance town was born on the empty prairie sixty miles away and the valley below him began to fill up with cattlemen long before he had thought they would come. Looking down from the ramparts of the Yellows he could see houses far off under the sun and dust spiral up along the Two Dance road, signals of a vanishing wilderness. His own people had finally caught up with him. And then he knew he had become a squaw man.

One by one the few trappers who had pioneered the Yellows began to send their squaws and their half-breed children back to the reservation as a shamefaced gesture of a mistake that had to be righted. He said nothing of this to the Crow woman, yet when fear showed its luminous shadow in her eyes he knew she had heard. He said then: "Those men are fools. I am not ashamed of you." And was happy to see the fear die.

This was why he took her to Two Dance. It pleased him to have her be seen in that lively little cattle town for she was a pretty woman with her black hair braided and her clothes neat and colorful under the sun. But he had forgotten her customs and when they walked up the street she followed behind him as a squaw always did, obediently and with her head faintly lowered. He knew how Two Dance would see that and anger colored his talk to her on the way home. "A white man's wife walks beside him, not behind."

He saw that dark fear in her eyes again, and had no way of softening it. Never afterwards did she come to town.

He knew then how it was to be. At hay time when he went down to help out on Hat he could feel that faint line drawn between him and the others; at the roundup fire he sat apart, with the strangeness there — a white man who was yet not quite white. One fall night at town he stepped in to watch the weekly dance and felt all the loose bitterness of his position rise and grow to be a hard lump in his chest. Once he would have had a part in this, but the odor of the blanket was upon him now and those fair, pleasant girls went wheeling by and he saw their eyes touch him and pass on. Over the whisky bottle in Faro Charley's saloon later he understood how fatal his mistake had been; and how everlastingly long its penalty would be.

He went home late that night quite drunk. In the morning the Crow girl was gone with her boy.

He didn't follow, for he knew that either she would return or she wouldn't, and that nothing he did could change her mind. Late in the third day she came back without a word. When he went in to supper that night he sat down to a single plate on the table. Her own plate and the boy's were on a floor blanket in a corner of the room.

It was, he saw, her decision. He had told her nothing of the misery in his mind, but she knew it without need of speech and so had answered him. He was white and might eat at his table. But she was Indian and so was the boy, and the table was not for them.

There was a kindness in Frank Isabel that governed the strongest of his emotions and this was what held him still as the days went on. He was remembering back to the horse and bottle of whisky and to the time when her lips had been warm with humor. In those days the Yellows had been wild and his world had not caught up with him, but he could see the depth and the length of his mistake now. He had committed it and could stand it. Yet it had passed beyond him and touched the Crow girl and the boy who was neither Crow nor white. For himself, Frank Isabel thought, there was no help. For the girl, none. It was the boy he kept weighing in his mind, so slowly and so painfully.

One winter night at meal time Jim Benbow of Hat dropped in for a cup of coffee. There was a little talk of cattle snowed into the timber and afterwards Benbow put on his hat and went to the door. As he left his glance crossed to the Crow woman and to the boy crouched in the corner and he said briefly: "Your youngster's growin' up, Frank," and left.

There was the rush of wind along the cabin eaves and deep silence inside. Isabel sat with his arms idle on the table remembering Benbow's words, which had contained a note of judgment. Presently he rose and brought another chair to the table and went over to where the Crow girl crouched mutely in the corner. He lifted the boy and put him in the chair at the table and stood there a moment, a long man throwing a thin shadow across the room. He said: "Hereafter he eats at the table."

She drew farther and farther back into the corner, like a shadow vanishing. And then, with his face turned suddenly away, he heard her stifled and terrible crying tremble the room's silence.

Scars of Honor

DOROTHY JOHNSON

*H*ere is the old and the new, the old West and the new West,
the old traditions striking forward into this era of world wars, in
about as fine a western story as any other in this book. And yet
it is only its timeliness, its placing in contemporary calendared
time, that has ruled the choice. For Dorothy Johnson has written
others ranging back through the western frontier years that can
match it by any standards. You will find them in her 1953 collection, Indian Country. Quietly, simply, with a rare depth of
feeling, she is adding to the authentic literature of the West.

I have chosen "Scars of Honor" from among the others simply
because it seems to me such a fine example of a modern western
story dealing with modern material that retains the imprint of
the past to give it meaning. I know no better example of such
work than this haunting tale of Joe Walking Wolf, the twentieth-
century Cheyenne, who went to his country's war in the one way
that he could, who gave his only pony to old Charley Lockjaw and
swung to the pole in sacrifice as his ancestors had done when the
buffalo peopled the plains.

C<small>HARLEY</small> L<small>OCKJAW</small> died last summer on the reservation. He
was very old — a hundred years, he had claimed. He still wore

his hair in braids, as only the older men do in his tribe, and the braids were thin and white. His fierce old face was like a withered apple. He was bent and frail and trembling, and his voice was like a wailing of the wind across the prairie grass.

Old Charley died in his sleep in the canvas-covered tepee where he lived in warm weather. In the winter he was crowded with the younger ones among his descendants in a two-room log cabin, but in summer they pitched the tepee. Sometimes they left him alone there, and sometimes his great-grandchildren scrambled in with him like a bunch of puppies.

His death was no surprise to anyone. What startled the Indian agent and some of Charley's own people, and the white ranchers when they heard about it, was the fact that some of the young men of the tribe sacrificed a horse on his grave. Charley wasn't buried on holy ground; he never went near the mission. He was buried in a grove of cottonwoods down by the creek that is named for a dead chief. His lame great-grandson, Joe Walking Wolf, and three other young Indians took this horse out there and shot it. It was a fine sorrel gelding, only seven years old, broke fairly gentle and nothing wrong with it. Young Joe had been offered eighty dollars for that horse.

The mission priest was disturbed about the killing of the horse, justifiably suspecting some dark pagan significance, and he tried to find out the reason the young men killed it. He urged Joe's mother, Mary, to find out, but she never did — or if she did, she never told. Joe only said, with a shrug, "It was my horse."

The white ranchers chuckled indulgently, a little shocked about the horse but never too much upset about anything Indians did. The rancher who told the story oftenest and with most interest was the one who had made the eighty-dollar offer to Joe Walking Wolf. Joe had said to him, "Ain't my horse." But Joe was the one who shot it on old Charley's grave, and it didn't belong to anyone else.

But the Indian agent guessed what had been going on. He knew more about Indians than the Federal Government required him to know. The horse was not government property nor the tribe's common property; everybody knew it belonged to Joe. The agent did not investigate, figuring it was none of his business.

That was last summer, when old Charley died and the young men took the horse out to where he was buried.

The story about the killing of the horse begins, though, in 1941, before that horse was even born. The young men were being drafted then, and the agent explained it all, over and over again, through an interpreter, so nobody would have an excuse for not understanding. In the agent's experience, even an Indian who had been clear through high school could fail completely to understand English if he didn't happen to want to.

Some of the white ranchers explained it, too. Some of them were expecting to go, or to have their sons or hired cowboys go, and the draft was a thing they mentioned casually to the Indians who worked for them at two or three dollars a day, digging irrigation ditches or hoeing in the kitchen garden or working in the hay fields. So the Indians understood the draft all right, with everybody talking about it.

The agent kept telling them, "In the World War you were not citizens, so you did not have to go in the Army." (He meant the First World War, of course. The United States hadn't got into the second one yet; there was only the draft.) "Many of your fathers enlisted in the Army anyway and they were good fighters. They did not have to go, but they wanted to. Now you are citizens, you can vote, and some of you will have to go in the Army. When the letters come for you, we will talk about it again."

Well, some of the young men didn't want to wait until the letters came. Fighting was part of their tradition. It was in the old men's stories, and the names of their long-dead warriors were in history books, as well as in the stories the old men told around the cabin stoves when snow was deep outside and the cabins were crowded with many people and the air foul with much breathing and not much bathing. (Long ago, before any of these young men were born, their forefathers had bathed every morning in rivers or creeks, even if they had to break the ice, but that custom had passed with their glory.)

The middle-aged men of the tribe remembered the white man's war they had fought in, and some of them still had parts of their old uniforms put away. But the stories they told were of places too distant for understanding, foreign places with no meaning except for the men who had been there. The stories the grandfathers told were better. They were about the stealthy approach through the grass after the men had prayed and painted, the quick, sharp action on riverbanks that were familiar still or in tepee camps where white men now live in brick houses.

The grandfathers' stories were of warriors who never marched or drilled but walked softly in moccasins or rode naked on fleet war ponies. They had no uniforms; they wore mystic painted symbols on face and body. In those battles there was the proud waving of eagle-feathered war bonnets and the strong courage of warriors who dared to carry a sacred buffalo shield, although a man who carried one was pledged not to retreat. They were battles without artillery, but with muzzle-loading rifles and iron-tipped lances and the long feathered arrows hissing out from a horn bow. Killing was not paramount in those old battles; more important was proof of a man's courage in the face of death, and the bravest were those few who dared to carry no weapon at all, but only a whip, for counting coup on a living, unhurt enemy. Nobody was drafted for those battles, and death was often the price of glory.

Only two or three of the old men remembered so far back. One of them was Charley Lockjaw. He was suddenly important. If he had not lived two generations too late, he would have been important simply because he was old. His people would have taken it for granted that he was wise, because his medicine had protected him for so long against death. They would have listened respectfully when he spoke. There was a time when it was a good thing to be an Indian, and old. But Charley was cheated — almost — of his honors, because he lived at the wrong time.

Suddenly he was needed. He was sitting in front of his summer tepee, nodding in the sun, with the good warmth seeping into his joints, when four young men came to him. They were modern Indians, with white men's haircuts. They wore torn blue jeans and faded shirts and white men's boots, because they were all cowboys, even the lame one, his great-grandson, Joe.

Charley looked up, ready to be angry, expecting some disrespectful, hurried greeting, like "Hey, grampa, look here."

They did not say anything for a while. Embarrassed, they shuffled their boots in the dust. Joe Walking Wolf took off his broad-brimmed hat, and the other three took their hats off, too, and laid them on the ground.

Joe cleared his throat and said in Cheyenne, "Greetings, my grandfather." It was the way a young man talked to a wise old one in the buffalo years that were gone.

Old Charley blinked and saw that Joe was carrying, with awkward care, an ancient ceremonial pipe of red stone.

Joe asked gravely, "Will you smoke with us, my grandfather?"

Charley was at first indignant, thinking they meant to tease him, because they were atheists who did not believe in the old religion or any of the new ones. He railed at them and said, "Goddam!"

in English. But they did not go away; they stood there respectfully with their heads bent, accepting what he said and, in the
old, courteous way, not interrupting.

He looked at their sober faces and their steady eyes, and he was
ashamed for his own lack of courtesy. When he understood that
they were sincere, he would have done anything for them, anything they asked. There was not much he could do any more, and
nobody had asked him to do anything for a long time.

If he took the pipe and smoked, that said, "I will do whatever
you ask." He did not know what they were going to ask, but he
would have let them cut him into pieces if that was what they
wanted, because his heart was full at being approached in the remembered, ceremonial way, clumsy as these modern Indians were
about it. He answered in his reedy voice, "I will smoke with you."

They were going to do it all wrong. One of the young men
brought out a sack of tobacco, and that was all right if there was
none that had been raised with the right prayers said over it. But
Joe pulled out a pocket lighter a white man had given him and
another young man brought out some kitchen matches and old
Charley could not endure such innovations.

He made them build a fire in the center of his summer tepee,
under the fire hole in the peak, and he sat down with a groan of
stiffness at the back, in the honor seat, the place of the lodge
owner. The young men were patient. They sat where he told
them to, on the old ragged carpet his granddaughter had put on
the earth floor.

He filled the pipe with pinches of tobacco without touching the
bowl and lighted it with a coal from the fire. With slow, remembered ceremony he offered the pipestem to Heammawihic, the
Wise One Above, to Ahktunowihic, the power of the earth below,
and to the spirits of the four directions — where the sun comes up,
where the cold wind goes to, where the sun comes over and where
the cold wind comes from.

He spoke reverently to each of these. Then he himself took
four puffs and passed the pipe, slowly, carefully, holding the stem
upright, to young Yellowbird, who was on his left.

Yellowbird smoked, though awkwardly, in the sacred manner
and passed the pipe to Joe Walking Wolf. When Joe had finished,
he stood up to take the pipe to the two young men on the other
side of Charley, but the old man corrected him patiently. The
pipe must not cross the doorway of the lodge; it must be passed

back from hand to hand, first to Robert Stands in Water and then on to Tom Little Hand.

The young men were humble when he corrected them. They thanked him when he told them how to do things right.

When he signified that the time had come for them to talk, young Joe, the lame one, said formally in Cheyenne, "My grandfather has told of the old times long ago, and we have listened. He has told how the warriors used to go on a hilltop with a wise old man and stay there and dream before they went on the warpath."

Old Charley said, "I told you those things and they were true. I dreamed on a hilltop when I was young."

Joe Walking Wolf said, "We want to dream that way, my grandfather, because we are going to war."

The old man did not have to promise to help them. He had promised when he took the pipe. He sat for a while with his eyes closed, his head bowed, trying to remember what his instructors had said to him the three times he had gone through the wu-wun, the starving. How would anyone know the right way if the old men had forgotten? But he was able to remember, because he remembered his youth better than yesterday.

He remembered the chanted prayers and the hunger and thirst and the long waiting for mystery to be revealed. He remembered the grave warnings, the sympathetic teaching of the wise old men seventy years before.

"It is a hard thing to do," he told the young men. "Some men cannot do it. Alone on a high place for four days and four nights, without food or water. Some men dream good medicine, and some dream bad medicine, and some have no dream. It is good to finish this hard thing, but it is no disgrace not to finish.

"A man lies on a bed of white sage," he told them, "and he is alone after his teacher, his grandfather, has taught him what to do. After four days, his grandfather goes up the hill and gets him — if he has not come back before that time."

Charley Lockjaw remembered something else that was important and added firmly, "The young men bring the grandfather a gift."

And so they went through the wu-wun, each of them alone on a high hill, hungering and thirsting for four days and nights. First they brought Charley gifts: four silver dollars from one, new moccasins from another, and two bottles of whiskey. (After the ordeals were over, he spent the four silver dollars for whiskey, too, getting it with difficulty through a man who was going off the reservation and who did not look like an Indian, so he could buy it, though it was against the law. An Indian could vote and be drafted, but he could not buy whiskey.)

The whole thing was secret, so that no one would complain to anybody who might want to interfere. Charley Lockjaw had been interfered with so much that he was suspicious. All his long life, white men had been interfering with him and, he thought, his own granddaughter might go to the priest if she knew what was going on, or the other young men's families might make trouble. No good would come of telling what went on.

Because of the secrecy, the old man had to ride horseback several times. Usually he had to be helped into a saddle because his joints were stiff and his legs hurt, so that if he did not stop himself and remember that now he could be proud again, he might groan.

He took each young man out separately to a hill chosen because of its height, its loneliness and its location. It had to be south or west of a river; that had always been the rule. He had never known the reason, and neither did anyone else. It was one of the things that was right, that was all, and he was very anxious to do everything right.

At the foot of the hill, he and the young man left the horses hobbled. The young man helped Charley up the hill, respectfully and with great patience. He made a bed of white sage, and Charley sang his prayers to the Spirit above.

He added a humble plea that had not been in the ritual when he was young. "If I make a mistake," he cried to the blue sky, "it is because I am old. Do not blame the young man. He wants to do right. If he does wrong, it is my fault. Give him good medicine."

Then he stumbled down the hill and got on the borrowed horse by himself and rode home. If the young man should give up before his time had passed, he could catch up the horse that was left.

None of them gave up, and none of them cheated. Each of them lay alone on the sage bed on the hill, singing the songs Charley Lockjaw had taught him, sometimes watching the sky (and seeing airplanes more often than wheeling eagles) and three times a day smoking the sacred pipe.

The first was Joe Walking Wolf. Charley was proud of him when he toiled up the hill with a canteen of water and a chunk of dry bread. He was proud when the boy first splashed water on his face and then drank, unhurriedly, from the canteen.

When Joe's tongue was moistened enough so he could talk, he said briefly, "I dreamed a horse was kicking me."

"I do not know what that means," Charley told him. "Maybe you will know after you think about it."

He was afraid, though, that the dream was bad. The reason Joe limped was that a horse had kicked him when he was three years old.

The second man was Yellowbird. He was impatient. He was standing up, watching, when Charley Lockjaw came in sight on his old bag-of-bones, borrowed horse, and he came down the hill to gulp the water the old man had brought. But he had endured the whole four days.

He said in English, "I dreamed I was dead and gone to hell." Then he said it in Cheyenne, except "hell," and Charley knew what that word was. There was no hell for Cheyennes after they were dead, according to the old religion.

Charley said, "That may be good medicine. I do not know."

The third man was Robert Stands in Water. He was sick and he vomited the first water he drank, but he got better in a little while and they went home. He didn't say what his dream was.

The fourth and last was Tom Little Hand, a laughing young man except when there were white people around. He was a proud rider and a dandy; he wore green sunglasses when he went outdoors, and tight shirts like the white cowboys. When Charley brought the water, he was no dandy any more. Naked to the waist, he lay flat on the sage bed, and the old man had to help him sit up so he could drink and eat.

"There was a bright light," he said when he felt like talking. "It floated in the air and I tried to catch it."

Charley didn't know what kind of medicine that was, but he said Tom Little Hand would probably be able to understand it after a while.

Anyway, they had all done the best they could, the right thing, and they were ready to be warriors. They had endured in the old fashion.

When they got back to the cabin settlement beside the creek that is named for a dead chief, old Charley dug up his whiskey and went into his lodge and drank, and slept, and drank some more. A teacher is worthy of his hire, and Charley Lockjaw was tired out from all that riding and climbing of high hills. For all that time, four days for four men, sixteen days altogether, he had not slept very much. He had been singing in his lodge or in front of it, in his reedy voice like the wailing of the wind across the prairie. The little boys had not bothered him by crowding in to tumble around like puppies. They were afraid of him.

While Charley was having his drunk, the four young men went down to town to enlist in the Army. He did not know that. When he was sober again, two of them had come back — his grandson Joe and Tom Little Hand, the dandy.

Tom said, "They don't want me. I don't see so good."

Joe Walking Wolf didn't say anything. He went around with his bad limp and got a job for a few days on a white man's ranch, sawing branches off some trees in the yard. The cook gave him his meals separate from the white hired hands, but he heard them talking about the draft and joking with each other about being 4F. Some were 4F because cowboys get stove up by bad horses. Joe felt better, knowing he was not the only one.

In the winter the war clouds broke with lightning and thunder, and the Army decided Tom Little Hand could see plenty well enough to go to war. The Army began to take some married men, too, and almost all the single ones except lame Joe Walking Wolf, and a couple who had an eye disease, and six who had tuberculosis and one who was stone-deaf.

Then for a couple of years old Charley Lockjaw wasn't important any more. The people who were important were those who could read the letters that came to the cabin settlement, and those who could write the answers.

Some of the young men came back on furlough, hitchhiking eighty miles from the railroad. In wartime people would pick up a soldier, even if he was an Indian. They strolled around the settlement and rode over to the agency in their uniforms and went to the white men's store, and some of the white ranchers went out of their way to shake hands with them and say, "Well, boy, how goes it?" They were important, the fledgling warriors.

Old Charley, sitting in front of his peaked lodge in the summer, saw them strut, saw the shawl-wrapped, laughing girls hang around them. He saw them walk down the road after dark, and he felt bad about some of the girls. When he was a young man, the Cheyennes took pride in the virtue of their women. His first wife had worn the rope of chastity until he removed it himself, the fourth night after her father had accepted his gift of captured horses.

He was ashamed of the Cheyenne girls, but not of the young

warriors. He pitied them a little, remembering the proud nodding eagle-feathered war bonnets and the tall, straight men who wore them. He remembered his own courting; for five years it had gone on. There were many other gallants who had stood in front of the girl's lodge, blanket-wrapped, waiting for her to come out.

One of the letters that came to the reservation had bad news in it. It was in a yellow envelope, and the agent brought it over himself and explained it to the mother of Tom Little Hand.

Tom had been wounded, it said, and was in a hospital.

The next morning Joe Walking Wolf, the lame one, made a ceremonial visit to old Charley, carrying the old stone pipe. He was not embarrassed this time, because he knew how to smoke in the sacred way.

Charley drew in a breath sharply and was ashamed because he trembled.

"The gift for that, to the grandfather," he cautioned, "must be a big gift, because it is a hard ceremony."

"The gift is outside with the pole," Joe said humbly.

And outside was picketed Joe's good sorrel colt.

There was a time when the Cheyennes, the Cut Arm people, could be lordly in their generosity with gifts of captured horses, sometimes bought with their blood. They could be splendid in their charity, giving buffalo meat to the needy and fine robes to the poor. But that time was when Charley Lockjaw was young. He had not owned a horse of his own for thirty years. And this was the only horse his great-grandson had, for the old mare this colt belonged to had died.

Charley blinked at the horse, a beautiful colt without a blemish. He walked over to stroke its neck, and the colt threw its head back and tried to get away. Charley spoke to it sharply, with approval. The colt was no stable pet, but used to running across the prairie with its mane flying in the wind and the snow. It would throw a rider before it was broke, Charley thought.

He nodded and said, "The gift is enough."

When he was a young man, he had paid many fine horses to the old one who taught him the ceremony for swinging at the pole and whose hard, gentle hands had supported him when he fainted. But he had had many horses to give, and plenty of them left. This was a finer present than he had given, because it was all Joe had.

"We will have to wait," Charley said. "We cannot do this

thing today. We will wait four days."

He chose four because it was the sacred number and because he needed time to remember. He had been a pupil for this sacrifice, but never a teacher.

"Come back in four days," he said.

In the time while he was remembering and praying for a return, in some part, of his old strength and steadiness, he fasted for one whole day. His granddaughter fretted and murmured, coming out to the lodge to bring soup because he said he was sick and could not eat.

"I will send one of the children to tell the nurse at the agency," she decided, but he waved her away, promising, "I will be well tomorrow."

He was afraid, not only because he might forget something important or his hand might slip, but because someone might find out and try to stop him. Somebody was always interfering. For years the old religion had been outlawed by the government in Washington. For years no one dared even to make the Medicine Lodge when the grass was tall in summer, so those years passed without the old, careful ceremony of prayer and paint and reverence that brought new life to the tribe and honor to the Lodge Maker.

This was no longer true by the time of the Second World War, though. Every year now the Medicine Lodge was made by some man who could afford it and wanted to give thanks for something. Perhaps his child had been sick and was well again. A man who made the Lodge, who learned the ritual, could teach another man. So that was not lost, though some of it had changed and some was forgotten, and it was very hard to find a buffalo skull to use in the ceremony.

The white ranchers and their guests came to the reservation in July to watch the making of the Lodge and see the prayer cloths waving from the Thunderbird's nest, and Charley took part in those ceremonies. The white people vaguely approved of the Indians keeping their quaint old customs.

But the Medicine Lodge, the Sun Dance, was a public ceremony. Swinging at the pole, as Joe Walking Wolf wanted to do it, was private suffering.

It was a long time since a young man had wished to swing at the pole. There was no one left in the tribe, except Charley Lockjaw, who could instruct a pupil in the ceremony. No one could teach it except a man who had himself endured it. And only Charley had on his withered breast the knotted scars of that ordeal.

Now that Joe was going to do it, Charley could not keep this great thing to himself. A man who suffered at the pole gained honor — but how could he be credited if no one knew what he had done?

At sunrise on the fourth day, Joe and Charley rode far out to a safe place among the sandstone cliffs.

Then Charley was shaken by terror. He denied his gods. He said, "Do not be too sure about this thing. Maybe the spirits will not hear my voice or yours. Maybe they are all dead and will never hear anything any more. Maybe they starved to death."

Joe Walking Wolf said, "I will do it anyway. Tom Little Hand has a bad wound, and he is my friend. I will make this sacrifice because maybe it will help him get well. Anyway, I will know what it is to be wounded. I did not go to war."

Charley dug a hole to set the pole in. He told Joe how to set up the pole and fasten a lariat to it, and all the time he was thinking about long ago. He could not remember the pain any more. He remembered his strong voice crying out prayers as he jerked against the thong. He had not flinched when the knife cut or when the thong jerked the skewers in the bloody flesh.

He said, "I did this to pay a pledge. My wife, Laughing Woman — my first wife — she was very sick, and I pledged this sacrifice. The baby died, because it was winter and the white soldiers chased our people through the snow in the bitter cold. Lots of people died. But Laughing Woman lived, and in the spring I paid what I had promised."

He had Joe make a bed of white sage. When everything was ready, Joe said, "Fasten it to my back. I don't want to see it."

Charley said, "Kneel on the sage bed."

He made his gnarled hands as steady as he could and pinched up the skin on Joe's right shoulder. He tunneled through the pinched part with a sharp knife, and the bright blood sprang to the dark skin. Through the tunnel he thrust a wooden skewer three inches long. Joe did not move or murmur. Kneeling on the sage bed, with his head bowed, he was silent as a stone.

Charley put another skewer under the skin on the left shoulder, and over each skewer he put a loop of rawhide, which he tied to the lariat that hung from the pole. The skewers would never be pulled out as they had been put in.

He lifted Joe to his feet and made him lean forward to see that the rope was tight and the pull even. Joe walked a quarter of a circle to the right four times, and back, sagging forward hard on the lariat's pull, trying to tear the skewers through. Then he walked four times to the left, with his blood running down his back.

Charley left the red stone pipe where he could reach it and said, "Three times before the sun goes down, stop and smoke for a little while."

His heart was full of Joe's pain. He ached with tenderness and pride.

"Break away if you can," he urged, "but if you cannot, there is no wrong thing done. If you cannot break away, I will cut you free when the sun goes down. Nobody can take away the honor."

Joe said, "I am not doing it to get honor. I am doing it to make Tom Little Hand get well again."

He kept walking with his bad limp and pulling mightily, but he could not break through the tough flesh that stretched like rubber.

"I will come back when the sun goes down," Charley Lockjaw said.

Back in the settlement he went around and told a few safe, religious men what was happening in the sandstone cliffs. They said their hearts were with Joe, and Charley knew that Joe would have his honor among his people.

When he went back to the pole at sunset, Joe was still walking, still pulling.

Charley asked, "Did you have a dream?"

Joe said, "I saw Tom Little Hand riding a horse."

"What a man dreams when he swings at the pole," Charley told him, "is sure to come true. I saw myself with thin, white braids, and I have lived to be old instead of being killed in battle." He got out his knife and said, "Kneel down."

He cut out a small piece of skin from the right shoulder and the left, freeing the skewers, and laid the bits of bloody skin on the ground as an offering.

He touched Joe's arm and said gently, "It is ended."

Joe stood up, not even giving a deep breath to show he was glad the suffering was over.

Charley did something new then. He bandaged the wounds as well as he could, with clean gauze and tape from the white man's store. These were new things, not part of the ceremony, but he saw that some new things were good as long as there were young men strong enough to keep to the old ones.

"Tonight," he said, "you sleep in my lodge and nobody will bother you." In the sagging bed in the cabin where Joe slept, there were also two or three children who might hurt those wounds.

"Now," Charley said, "I am going to give you something."

He brought from a hiding place, behind a rock, a pint whiskey bottle, still half full, and said, "I am sorry there is not more here."

He told Joe, "Now you can teach the ritual of swinging at the pole. Two men can teach it, you and I, if anyone wants to learn. It will not be forgotten when my shadow walks the Hanging Road across the stars."

The spirits may be dead, he thought, but the strong hearts of the Cheyenne people still beat with courage like the steady sound of drums.

Charley never rode his sorrel horse, but when it was three years old, Joe broke it. The horse threw him two or three times, and the old man cackled, admiring its spirit, while Joe picked himself up from the dust, swearing. Joe used the horse, but he never put a saddle on that sorrel without first asking Charley's permission.

Some of the short-haired young men never did come back from the Army, but Joe's three friends came back, wearing their uniforms and their medals. Tom Little Hand walked on crutches the first time he came home, with a cane the second time, but when he came home to stay he needed only a brace on the leg that had been wounded, and a special shoe on that foot.

The three soldiers went to the agency to show off a little, and to the white man's store off the reservation, to buy tobacco and stand around. The white ranchers, coming in for the mail, shook hands with them and called each one by name and said, "Glad to see you back, boy! Sure glad to see you back!"

The Indian soldiers smiled a little and said, "Yeah."

The ranchers never thought of shaking hands with Joe Walking Wolf. He had been around all the time, and the marks of his honor were not in any medals but in the angry scars under his faded shirt.

After all the girls had had a chance to admire the uniforms, the young men took off their medals, to be put away with the broken-feathered war bonnets and the ancient, unstrung bows. They wore parts of their uniforms to work in, as the white veterans did, and they went back to raising cattle or doing whatever work they could get.

Tom Little Hand, that proud rider, never wore his old cowboy boots again because of the brace on his leg. He could not even wear moccasins, but always the special shoe. But he walked and he rode, and pretty soon he married Joe's sister, Jennie, whose Cheyenne name was Laughing Woman, the same as her great-grandmother's.

That's all there is to the story, except that last summer Charley Lockjaw died. He had thought he was a hundred years old, but his granddaughter told the Indian agent that he had always said he was born the year a certain treaty was made with the white chiefs. The agent knew what year that treaty was, and he figured out that Charley must have been ninety when he died.

The agent was interested in history, and so he asked, "Was Charley in the fight with Yellow Hair at the Little Big Horn?" Charley's granddaughter said she didn't know.

Her son, Joe Walking Wolf, knew but did not say so. Charley Lockjaw had been there, a warrior seventeen years old, and had counted coup five times on blue-coated soldiers of the Seventh Cavalry that June day when General Custer and his men died in the great victory of the Cheyennes and the Sioux. But Joe did not tell everything Charley Lockjaw had told him.

When Charley died, he left his horse to Joe. So Joe wasn't lying when, after he shot the beautiful eighty-dollar sorrel on Charley's grave, he simply said, "It was my horse."

The three other young men were there when Joe killed it. That was the right thing to do, they agreed soberly, because in the old days when a warrior died, his best horse was sacrificed for him. Then he would have it to ride as he went along the Hanging Road to the place where the shadows of the Cheyenne people go. The place is neither heaven nor hell, but just like earth, with plenty of fighting and buffalo and horses, and tall peaked lodges to live in, and everybody there who has gone before. It is just like earth, as Charley Lockjaw remembered earth from his young days.

When Joe had shot the horse, the young men took the sharp knives they had brought along and peeled the hide off. They butchered the carcass and took the great hunks of horse meat home to their families.

Because the buffalo are gone from earth now, and in the dirt-roofed cabins of the Cheyennes, the conquered people, there is not often enough food to get ready a feast.

All The Young Men

OLIVER LA FARGE

*T*o think of Oliver La Farge is to think of Indians, North American and Central American Indians, not only because the bulk of his writing has been about them but also because he has for most of his adult career been associated with Indian Affairs institutions and research expeditions. Laughing Boy, his prize-winning novel, is of course a classic in the field. He is always the conscious and conscientious artist — and almost always his artistry succeeds. There have been later short stories, but the best are still to be found in All the Young Men, 1935. This is the title piece.

OLD SINGER was one of those Indians the trader would point out to strangers whenever he came into the store. "See that old buck there? That's the real thing, a medicine man, too. You'd never think he was eighty, would you?" The trader would nod, and then add the fact which is a special badge of distinction among the Navajos: "He was one of Haskinini's men; you know, the band that never was caught when Kit Carson rounded up the tribe and took them into exile."

He dressed well, in the later Navajo style of velveteen, calico, and silver; he carried himself with easy pride, his strong, dark face was stamped with the kindness and control of a religious man. His word carried weight in council.

As a young man, in the long past warlike days, he had been called "Hasty Arrow." Whatever the hastiness was, it disappeared after he became a medicine man, governed by the precepts of the Navajo religion. He was known as "Mountain Singer," and latterly "Old Singer."

When his wife died he began to go to pieces. From being a tall, straight old man he became bent and aged and frail. Not even the trader had realized how completely his wife had managed their business, Old Singer being wrapped up in the mysteries of his chants and dances. Now he made little or no effort to collect his fees, pawned his jewelry thoughtlessly, seemed to have become oblivious of material things.

He talked a great deal about old times, when the Navajos were true to themselves; and occasionally to men he knew well, like the trader, he would tell about the terror of that day when artillery opened on them, when they thought they had the Americans trapped and beaten, and they broke and fled under the shrapnel at Segi Chinlin.

His wife's clan divided her sheep. He let them all go, saying, "Take them. She herded them. I don't want them." With the flocks gone, and his carelessness, and a habit he developed of buying real turquoise and mother-of-pearl for his ceremonial offerings, he became poor quickly. It meant nothing to him that his clothes were ragged, that he had no jewelry, that he lived in a leaky hogahn, sometimes cooking for himself, more often eating with the Indians roundabout.

The trader urged him to change his ways. Old Singer made a cigarette and smoked nearly half of it before he answered.

"As a man full of needs and wants, I am finished," he said. "I know so many songs and prayers, and the stories that stand behind them, that it would take me from the first frost to the first thunderstorm just to think them all over to myself.

"Behind all those stories, in turn, is a greater truth than they have on their faces. I am thinking about that. It is all that really matters. I am thinking about the faces that are behind the masks of the gods. I am reaching behind Nayeinezgani's mask to the one great thing."

The trader sighed. Since he was a young man Old Singer had been especially concerned with Nayeinezgani. The name means "Slayer of Enemy Gods." He is the great war god.

The trader said: "I have better than five hundred dollars' worth of your jewelry in pawn. I won't sell it, but it stands for so much goods which I bought, and I have to pay for them."

The next time Old Singer held a mountain chant he collected his full fee, and paid the trader fifty sheep on account, which released almost all his pawn. He didn't want to embarrass his friend, so when he borrowed on his goods again, he did it at other trading posts, with men he did not know so well.

He looked so poor and unworldly that the Indians stopped listening to his counsel, but as a singer — a medicine man — his reputation remained great. When he was not holding ceremonies, he meditated, or discussed with other old man like himself, who had worked on the philosophy of their religion so long, and penetrated so deep into its mysteries, that no ordinary Indian would have understood what they were saying.

His granddaughter heard how poor and ragged he was, and finally she sent for him to live with her and her husband, Homer Wesley. They were a smart pair of educated Indians who dressed well and spoke good English, and affected to despise Navajo ways. Sometimes they professed Christianity, but really they had no religion save, in the secret part of their hearts, a little longing for and a real fear of the old gods.

Wesley might have made a warrior once — he had strength and brains — but, like so many school Indians, he wanted chiefly to be slicker than white men in their manner, and he was pretty slick. It was trying to be up to the minute, and wanting a new car, that got him started running liquor into the reservation. That was dangerous work, but he did it well, drank little himself, and made big money.

They lived south of the reservation, in one of those sections where Indian allotments and white homesteads and public domain were all mixed together, the breeding grounds of continual trouble. Old Singer did not care. It was right that his granddaughter should house him. He wouldn't have to go visiting for his meals any more; he would have more time for his religion. That was enough.

But he was seriously disturbed when he found out what Wesley was doing. He'd tried liquor when he was young, knew it was fun, and a bad thing when it got going the way it had among the Navajos in recent years. He had seen the spread of drinking, and was worried about it. He hated to see bootlegging right in his family, and tried to persuade them to stop.

Even down in that section there was reputation to be gained from a famous medicine man, and Wesley was careful to collect the fees, so they bore with his talk. When Old Singer would hammer at them about being Navajos, and being true to themselves, and how completeness inside a man or a woman was all that mattered, the young man would grow sullen.

He minded being lectured by an old back number, and minded doubly because fragments of belief, and his voiceless blood, responded to what was said. In anger he conceived the idea of getting Old Singer to drink, and he finally managed it. He had known a Kiowa once, who belonged to the peyote cult, and, borrowing the idea from that man's talk, claimed that his liquor would bring beautiful, mystic experiences and religious communions, and thus persuaded the medicine man to try it.

Old Singer did have an extraordinary experience. For an hour or two he recaptured the full flavour of the old days, and later thought he was talking almost directly to Nayeinezgani. Wesley kept at it, building up the habit, aided by a nasty, raw, wet autumn. By midwinter Old Singer was drinking regularly.

His granddaughter objected at first, but Wesley convinced her. He said he was afraid of the old man's telling on them, but his taking to drink would keep his mouth shut. Besides, they could chalk off the value of the liquor against his fees if he ever tried to claim what they had collected. So she let things slide until it was too late, and her grandfather was a drunkard.

Early the next winter he got drunk in the course of conducting a hail chant, and messed things up so that another singer had to be called in to do it all over again. After that no one sent for him. Leading the prayers and chants was the breath of his nostrils. He felt more and more empty and lonely as the months went by without a call. He attended many ceremonies, watching how the younger medicine men were careless and cut things short.

He was utterly apart from his granddaughter and Wesley, who began to let him see that he was a nuisance to them. The liquor did not bring him such happy experiences now. He would catch the glorious feeling, but it was confused, and then he would fall to thinking of the old days, and the decay of his nation, and at last would have a kind of horrors, talking disconnectedly about the boom of the field-pieces at Segi Chinlin and the white man's lightning, which destroyed the lightning of Slayer of Enemy Gods.

They built him a small hogahn at some distance from the house,

and fed him what was convenient when he came round. Wesley
let him have liquor, hoping he would drink himself to death. As
he grew decrepit, he lived further and further into the past until
he was surrounded by the shades of his youth, against which the
miserable present was thrown in sharp relief.

That winter and summer went by. The first frosts of autumn
came, bringing again the longing for the ceremonies, his mind full
of the sacred names which could not be spoken in the thunder
months. He fingered his medicine bundle sadly. It contained the
strongest kinds of medicine, and was wrapped in a perfect buckskin, which is the hide of the animal killed without wounding,
absolutely unblemished.

Wesley, feeling cheerful over a big profit he had made, brought
the old man two bottles of whiskey. He hadn't had a drink for
nearly a week, and he needed it badly. Now he took a big pull,
and sat back, looking at his bundle. It was the time for ceremonies.
He took another drink and began softly singing a song for Nayeinezgani.

> Now, Slayer of Enemy Gods, I come
> Striding the mountain tops . . .

This was a bad country. These people here might be Navajos,
but they were lost. Living with them, he, too, had lost his way. In
Zhil Tlishini, on the slopes of Chiz Lan-Hozhoni, were still Navajos who were men, he knew. There he could find himself; he
could give them the message, to keep the gods, the power of the
gods, the strength of Nayeinezgani. He started reciting the names
in a half chant:

> Slayer of Enemy Gods, Child of the Waters, White Shell
> Woman, House God, Dawn Boy, Thunders All Around — their
> names fall down; the great power of their names falls down. Here
> the people turn them back, here the air turns them back, here
> the earth turns them back, here the water turns them back, their
> great names, the great power of their names.

He took a long drink. Quite steady and not apparently drunk,
he went to the house. Standing to his full height, so that he filled
the door, he said to Wesley:

"I am going away for good. Give me a horse."

Wesley stared at him. He said, "Take the pinto mare in the
corral."

By the time he had his rickety saddle on the mare he was
stooped again; his hands were uncertain. On the saddle he tied

his blanket, with the untouched bottle in it, and his medicine bundle. That was all he owned. He took another drink and mounted.

He was dressed in cast-off overall trousers and a grotesquely ragged coat. Of his ancient style remained only the long hair, knotted behind and wrapped in a dirty, red turban, and his moccasins. The toes of one foot came through, and, having long ago sold his silver buttons, the footgear was tied on with bits of rag around the ankle.

The mare followed a cart track leading from Wesley's house to the road, then turned south. Old Singer took no heed of her direction. Whenever the liquor began to die in him he took a drink, so that by mid-afternoon he had emptied the first bottle. Everything he saw made him feel worse — badly dressed Indians, automobiles, men on horseback in the clothes of white labourers, usually pretty ragged.

Always he saw short hair and the stupid-smart expression of the young men. They wore clothes over clothes. No one stood up clean and straight in breechclout and moccasins; no one let the sun strike on strong chest and shoulders; no one wore the dignity of the old, strong blankets.

These shapes moved in and out through his dream of the past, so that he rode in a nightmare. The Navajos were dead; these were the children of dead people. He and a few others had been condemned to go on moving around after the big guns on wheels had killed them all. The lucky ones were the ones who stopped right there.

With that he remembered Hurries-to-War, who had been his friend. He remembered with longing how they had hunted and gone on the warpath together, and the warrior's figure as he stood ready for battle. He remembered this, and looked at a boy going by in an old flivver. He groaned, and started on the second bottle.

About sunset he reached a town. At first the houses had no reality to him, then he realized he was entering a white settlement, and drew rein by the roadside. The houses were strange to him. Raising his eyes, he saw cliffs to the eastward, very bold in the level sunlight with their banding of dull, greenish-white and orange strata. He recognized the cliffs. This was Tseinachigi. They passed this way when they raided Zuñi, two hundred men, when he and Hurries-to-War were just beginning to be warriors.

This was country over which the Navajos swept at will, their raiding ground and their plaything. Now here was a big town, and the railroad. He began to be dismayed, realizing how far he had ridden in the wrong direction, regaining at this sight his urgent intention to head north for country that was still Navajo.

He dismounted and sat down wearily, cradling his medicine bundle. He needed to think. He took a little more whiskey, having reached the stage of weary intoxication where each drink braced and confused him, then quickly died away. He decided he must not sleep yet, drunk as he was, and knowing in what condition he would wake.

White men spoke just behind him; he turned to see two coming toward him. They had badges on their shirts, and one carried a gun. They spoke to him in English, then in Spanish, out of which he understood something about liquor and being drunk. He told them in Spanish that he was a good Indian, the Americans' friend.

They laughed, and took away his bottle. He let it go. Then they reached for his bundle, but he clutched it to him. They laughed again. Each took one of his elbows and hustled him along to a house, into which they took him. There was a desk, at which sat a big Mexican, also wearing a badge. He and the Americans talked together, and he wrote something in a book. Old Singer stood all hunched up, hugging his bundle. Now they went seriously about taking it away from him.

After they got it, one of them had to hold him. He went on struggling and protesting in mixed Navajo and Spanish. When they opened the bundle and saw its contents, they seemed to find it funny. They poked around with their fingers among the sacred objects and made jokes. Old Singer was frantic. One of them said something. The Mexican nodded, wrapped the bundle carelessly, and gave it back. Old Singer held it tight and mumbled over it. They took him along a corridor, opened a door, shoved him into a room, slammed and locked the door.

He sat down with his bundle in his lap. For several minutes his mind was blank. Then he looked around. The room was narrow and quite bare. The door was of metal. There was one small, high, barred window. This was jail, then; they were going to keep him in jail. With the Navajos' horror of being enclosed, he went into a panic. At last, wearily, he set his bundle on the dirt floor.

This was his end; he might at least pray. This was his great need. He might at least meet his end talking with the gods, if they would hear him, if he had not cut himself off from them forever. He had everything here — prayer sticks, breath plumes, sacred jewels.

As his hands performed the familiar acts of arrangement, he gained a little courage. Life pollen, sacred cigarettes, Nayeinezgani's cigarette, clear stones, blue feathers, yellow feathers and a perfect buckskin.

That was the keystone of his power, to pray sitting before the unwounded skin. Having taken everything out of it, he began smoothing it out, his hands moving slowly. Then his hands stopped; his heart jumped downward, and his eyes ceased seeing. It was torn, ripped wide across near the head.

After sunset the cell grew dark and chilly in a short time. In the complete blackness, with the fumes of liquor and great fatigue, his fear reached fantastic depths and grew into a kind of exaltation. His right hand began to move forward with a slight downstroke, and back, as though he were shaking a rattle. His lips formed a prayer to Slayer of Enemy Gods. By the second verse his voice had risen to a soft whisper. His eyes were closed and his ears were stopped.

The cold slid in along his skin; he might as well have had no clothes on. As though in opposition to the reality, he began the prayer, "Dawn Boy, little chief." It was very chilly.

He would have done well to have brought a blanket, but then one would not want to seem soft. It had been long and slow, lying out on the mesa, watching just that one line of pass against the night sky for a movement, a quiver of the horizon, that would mean the Americans were coming. Now when he rose and stretched he was stiff. He reached his arms out to the white line in the east, intoning his prayer softly.

Day seeped into the sky overhead, but had not yet touched the cañon below him. The east was brilliant. He looked to the south again, and his blood leaped. A column of smoke rose from Tletsosenili — broke, rose, broke, rose. He read the code, twanged his bowstring, and ran down the gully to where his pony was tethered.

In the cañon he met Hurries-to-War on his blue roan.

"Come along," his friend said; "it is time."

They rode together. Hasty Arrow was surprised to see how handsome the man was. Everything was familiar, but he seemed to have new eyes, a new perception. He felt a sharp pleasure at the sight of a warrior stripped for battle, at the long hair on his brown shoulders, his muscles, his lance. The rich, strong colours of his blanket almost sang.

He saw Segi Cañon, too, as though it had just been made, the wide valley and high, red cliffs with spruce trees on the upper ledges; the brilliant, gold sunlight touching the highest places. They loped, feeling the morning air tingle against their chests.

More and more men joined them until they had an army. Hasty Arrow looked back at the tossing, feathered spears, the bright headbands, the brown torsos and strong blankets and lively horses. He felt the vigour of his people. We cannot be beaten, he thought.

Hurries-to-War said, "Over here."

They turned into a narrow side cañon and mounted a precipitous trail where their horses climbed like goats, now at a fast walk, now at a scrambling trot. They came out on a high, small mesa where a clump of spruce trees stood by a clear spring. Halting, the two friends looked about them.

From here one could see all around to the blue, distant boundary mountains at the extreme ends of the four directions. Mesa and cañon and plain, the immensity of the Navajo country was under their hands. From Tletsosenili the smoke of the signal fire still rose.

"Make a prayer for us," said Hurries-to-War. "You have everything."

Hasty Arrow put his hand behind his saddle and felt the bundle. Dismounting, he spread the objects around his buckskin, just as though he were an initiated singer. The young men gathered behind and on each side of him, save Hurries-to-War, who sat his horse just in front. Hasty Arrow looked around, half smiling, at the familiar, grave faces, thinking about their true names, concentrating himself.

He offered the cigarettes and threw the life pollen, then he began to sing. He did not follow a prescribed ceremony. Songs came to his lips in an order which seemed to be dictated by them.

> Now Slayer of Enemy Gods, alone I see him coming;
> Down from the skies, alone I see him coming.
> His voice sounds all about,
> His voice sounds divine!

He went on through the four verses, calling the warrior gods. Looking up at his friend, he was disturbed by his beauty. It was almost intolerable.

> Now with a god I walk,
> Striding over mountains . . .

It was not just his friend, not just a man. The blue pony stood on the ground, but it was high above them. Hasty Arrow swung into another song.

> Now, Nayeinezgani, on my turquoise horse I ride . . .

He sat above them on his horse, standing on the end of a bent rainbow; not the masked impersonation of the dances, but the great, young war god himself in majesty. The turquoise horse struck lightning with his hoofs. His mane and tail were rain; lightning rustled as it played around the arrows in the god's quiver; sunbeams were gathered above his head. He looked down, smiling.

Hasty Arrow was rent with joy and exalted fear. His heart was high above him.

> Lightnings flash out from me; they zigzag
> Four times.
> Striking and returning, they zigzag
> Four times.

He began the final song.

> I am thinking about the enemy gods . . .

An alien voice sounded somewhere, and heavy footsteps. A cold fear without meaning rose in him. Behind what he saw was something trying to be seen. He sang louder. The heavy voice spoke again, and there was pounding. The big guns began to boom, the white men's lightning flashed in the air, and Nayeinezgani's arrows stayed in his quiver.

He was two things at once; he was fighting down a knowledge in his mind. All the young men were dead long ago; they faded before his eyes, and the war god was high upon his rainbow. He clung desperately to his song, singing with all his voice and all his being. The young men, the beauty of the Navajos, were riding off into the sky. He was alone, making a prayer with a torn buckskin.

> The enemy gods, the enemy gods, I wander among their weapons.

He sang, trying to keep that vision, to keep away the cell walls. He was an old man praying in agony. White men were opening the door to do something to him. Over Nayeinezgani came a mask of a ragged, drunken Indian with a bottle in his hand. Old Singer's voice rose frantically:

Now on the old-age trail, now on the path of beauty walking,
The enemy gods, the enemy gods . . .

Slayer of Enemy Gods leaned down, smiling, and picked him up as one might pick up a child. He placed Old Singer behind the saddle on his turquoise horse, wheeled on the rainbow, and galloped up after the warriors, beyond the reach of the white men.

Oh, Once in My Saddle

DAVID LAMSON

This story, in a sense, is slipped in here under special visa. David Lamson's western stories take place in the Canadian West. But their usual locale is not far from the United States border and, their usual chief character, the father of the boy narrator, was once an American cowboy and is a true product of the American West. This is the first of the stories and I first read it when it appeared in the Saturday Evening Post for September 30, 1938. Others have followed, all with the same flavor, and a group of them have been published in a book titled from this first one.

I REMEMBER the day was Sunday, because my mother and sisters had taken the light team and driven uptown to church, and were going on to have dinner with the Finleys if the river was not too high to ford. And it was the end of July, because my father made me stay home to help sharpen the mowing-machine blades. We were going to start cutting timothy next day.

It took an endless time of turning the heavy grindstone before my father was satisfied with the edge on all the little triangles along the cutter bar. There was an uneven place in the grindstone over which the steel skipped quickly, so that the sound of steel

on stone was cadenced and not an even blur. Some of the time
my father made it easier for me by singing in time to this beat.
One favorite song of his fitted the rhythm especially well:

> Oh, once in my saddle I used to go dashing,
>   Oh, once in my saddle I used to be gay;
> I first took to drinking and then to card playing,
>   Got shot through the body, and now here I lay.

My father had been a cowboy before he married my mother and
took up a homestead in Northern Alberta and became a farmer.
He knew quite a lot of cowboy songs, but I liked that one best.

He ground the blade that was in the mowing machine first;
and when we finished it, I went over to the well and pulled up
a bucket of water and stood leaning against the poplar tree by
the curb, sipping the icy water and looking at the blister on my
palm and wondering if my father would want to start on the spare
blade right away.

But the spare blade had two broken teeth. My father went
over to the blacksmith shed and started cutting them out, and I
began to walk toward the house, as if I weren't going anywhere
in particular. But he called me back.

"You might go hunt up Sam and Bess," he said. "I want to
have a look at their shoes. We'll put them in and give 'em a feed
of oats."

So I got a halter and a pan of oats for bait, and went down
through the woods looking for Sam and Bess, our work team. I
did not hurry, because I kept thinking about that grindstone.

I followed the cowbell first; Sam and Bess often grazed near
the cows. But they were not there. Then I went past the head
of our clearing, over to the thick growth of spruce and jack pine
in the northeast corner, where they might have taken shelter from
the mosquitoes and bulldog flies. But they weren't in there either.

I went back through the woods, looking along the fence for
a break, or for sign that they had jumped the fence, although
neither of them was breachy and it was a good fence. It was made
of poplar rails nailed to tamarack posts, the rails put on green and
the bark slit along the top, so the rain would peel the bark off
and let the rails season.

I told my father the horses were gone. He looked as though
he didn't believe me, but he came with me and we looked along
the west side. There was one place where the pasture came right

out to the road, but to get to that place the horses had to cross a little neck of muskeg swamp, which they did not like to do. But there were tracks beside the fence here.

My father walked slower and slower then, looking at the fence, and pretty soon he stopped beside a panel and pointed to some marks on the rails next the post.

He said the top rails had been knocked off and the horses taken out and the rails put back. I was not sure of this, but my father was sure. I mean I found it hard to believe, because that meant our horses had been stolen, and people in our country did not steal. But there were nicks in the rail, and in the nicks were little streaks and flecks of red paint. The man who knocked down the rails had used a new ax with paint on the head.

And my father showed me places outside the fence where the kinnikinnick bushes were scuffed and broken; and in the bare ground beside an anthill there was the mark of shoes, one calked, the other smooth. Sam and Bess were shod rough in front and smooth in back.

We could not tell anything by tracks in the road, because a lot of teams had driven along it during the day, but it looked as though our horses had been taken northward toward Willow Creek, because whoever stole them would not be likely to take them south past our place and toward town.

My father squatted on his heels beside the tracks for a few minutes, thinking, and he didn't say anything, and I didn't say anything either, because of the way he stuck out his jaw and made his eyes narrow. By and by he stood up and started back to the house, walking very fast, so I had to trot to keep up.

I said, not very loud, "You want me to get Corporal Macey?"

Corporal Macey was the Northwest Mounted policeman in our district. He wore a red coat and blue breeches with a yellow stripe down each leg, and he looked fine. He was in charge of all the country between the Saskatchewan River and the Rocky Mountains, a strip eighty miles wide and I don't know how long, but with not many people in it except around our town and over at Willow Creek. Everyone in our country thought Corporal Macey was quite a man, which he was.

But when I asked my father if I should go for Corporal Macey, he grunted. "Huh!" he said. "I guess not! I guess I can still make out to handle my own affairs." And in a minute he began to hum that song: "Oh, once in my saddle I used to go dashing — "

Back at the house he took down his .30-30 carbine from the rack behind the kitchen door. I said, "What you going to do?"

He said, "Do? I'm going to go after that team, of course! Go saddle a horse!"

I said, "What horse? Ma's got the other team at church."

He knew that as well as I did, but he had forgotten. He had gone back in his mind to the days when he was a cowboy and there were horses all over the place.

"That's right," he said. "I plumb forgot. I can't go afoot after a horse thief! Go see if Bellows will lend me a horse. Hustle!"

So I hustled. I knew how my father hated to borrow from anybody, especially from Fred Bellows, because Bellows was shiftless, and if we borrowed from him then, he'd feel free to borrow from us. But there wasn't anybody else within two miles, except Old Man Thrush, and he was a remittance man and didn't have any horses or anything else except a lot of big plans in his head.

The Bellows house was only a quarter of a mile south, a rackety old cabin made of little fire-killed spruce logs. Mr. Bellows wasn't home, but his wife was, and I asked her for the loan of a couple of horses. I told her ours had strayed.

There was no use telling her everything; she talked too much, and, besides, all the little runny-nose Bellows kids were standing there listening, with their fingers in their mouths.

She said I could take the two horses in the corral. I knew, without looking, which ones she would give me.

They had several pretty good horses, and these two old crowbaits. One was a big, rangy bag of bones named Bill, a gray; he had been a cavalry horse in the Boer War. The other was Nancy, a fat old mare, so sway-backed she could hardly get over a barn doorsill without touching.

I thanked Mrs. Bellows and put a bridle on Bill and climbed on him; and when I was out of sight of the house I managed to kick him into a trot, although sitting that sharp backbone of his was like riding a ridgepole in an earthquake.

Father was waiting down by the barn. The carbine was leaning against the wall, and father was wearing his old six-gun and cartridge belt, and he had on his high-heeled cowboy boots. Never but once had I seen him wear those boots. That was at a Dominion Day celebration uptown three years before. Father had got all dressed up for it, chaps and all, and had gone up riding Stub, my buckskin pony. In the middle of the parade Stub had stumbled and thrown father into the dirt street. Father had gone over to the wagon, his face very red under the dust, and pulled off his chaps and boots, and driven home in his stocking feet. He sold Stub and had not been on a horse since.

Father looked at old Bill and Nancy, and snorted. "I was afraid of that," he said. "Well, beggars can't be choosers." Then he looked at me sharply. "I thought I told you to get a horse."

I said, "I thought you meant a horse apiece."

His eyes crinkled up and he grinned on one side of his face. "All right then," he said. "After all, you're fourteen."

I ran back to the house and got my little .22 rifle and a box of shells.

I saw a note that he had left on the kitchen table for my mother: "Gone looking for horses. Back when we find them." So he had meant for me to go, all along.

When I came out I saw my father had got his rope out of the granary and was tying it to his saddle. He had put the rope away when he did his boots, and wouldn't let me touch it. It was a good rope. He grinned again when he saw my rifle, but he didn't say anything about it — just shoved his carbine into the boot.

With one foot in the stirrup, he remembered something. He said, "Hey, Bub, where's my spurs?"

I said, "I don't know, father," which was true.

He said, "Sure you ain't seen 'em?"

I said, "Not for a long time." Which was also true, and I'd been trying for a month to remember where I left them. But I couldn't see any good reason to say that.

He climbed up on old Bill rather slowly, because old Bill was very high and my father was getting rather portly.

About a mile up the road we overtook Mr. McKenzie, driving his ox team with a load of dry poles from the strip where the fire went through two years before.

Mr. McKenzie was a hairy little Scotchman who talked with his lungs instead of his mouth and lips. He worked all the time, Sundays and all. So did the other Scotchmen in our country, which may be why they went on living there while other people got starved out.

When my father saw Mr. McKenzie ahead of us, he hitched his gun around in back of him a little and let his arm down over it, as if he were embarrassed to be seen wearing it. The oxen stopped when we got near the wagon, and Mr. McKenzie looked around. His bushy eyebrows twitched when he saw our guns and the horses we were riding, but he was too polite to ask questions. My father and Mr. McKenzie had known each other for eight years, but they still called each other "Mister." Now they talked for a while about the weather, and haying, and the new hay shed for which Mr. McKenzie was hauling poles.

Then my father said, "Well, I can't start cutting if I don't find that team of mine. They got out last night or this morning. You haven't seen anything of 'em, have you?"

"That 'ud be a white mare and a bay gelding, no?" said Mr. McKenzie. "Nay, I ha'na seen 'em. Perhaps Jim or Alan might, though they said naught to me; but ye might ask of them as ye pass by."

He looked at the cartridge belt and at the butt of the carbine sticking out of the boot. He said, slowly and unwillingly, "Now, I had it in mind that ye bought that team from over Calder way."

My father said, "That's right." He and Mr. McKenzie looked at each other. Mr. McKenzie knew that when horses stray, they go back to their home range. He knew that Calder was fifteen miles south. But we were riding north. So Mr. McKenzie understood why my father carried a pistol and a rifle to look for his horses.

He wanted to say something. He moved uncomfortably and smoothed his mustache and rubbed his nose. "Maybe," he said, "ye'll be gettin' a shot at a deer, eh?"

"Might happen," said my father. "Or some kind of varmint. There's still some around here."

"Aye," said Mr. McKenzie. He looked attentively at the brown rumps of his oxen. "A'weel, Corpor-r-ral Macey is a fine man. Be sure he does'na catch ye shootin' out o' season."

That was as close as politeness would let him come to remonstrating with my father.

For a time my father had a sober, thoughtful look, but presently his eye lighted up again and he prodded old Bill along and began to whistle softly.

We met other teams, and we stopped to inquire at houses beside the road, but no one had seen our horses. And none of those to whom we spoke were as wise as Mr. McKenzie, nor as well acquainted with my father, so they made nothing of the fact that he went armed. In those days people commonly carried rifles or shotguns, for there was still plenty of game in our country. And even six-shooters were not really uncommon.

Homesteaders' cabins became more and more infrequent. Beyond Ed Johnson's place, seven miles north of our ranch, we came to a clear, sandy stretch over a jack-pine ridge. My father swung out of the saddle and knelt in the road, looking at the tracks there.

"They been through here, all right," he told me. "I'd know those shoes in a thousand."

A mile farther on we came to Ed Davis' cabin, the last one south of the muskeg country that separated our district and the Willow Creek settlement. Davis was an American who had filed on this homestead only the year before. No one knew very much about him.

Davis had made a start at a clearing, but he had not got very far with it. The timber in that section was heavy — poplar and spruce, with some jack pine.

When we came up to the cabin my father called, "Hello there! Anybody home?"

Davis came out.

"Howdy?" he said. "Somethin' I c'n do for you?"

It was not polite in our country to ask a question like that. A polite man would have waited for my father to say what he wanted.

My father said, "I'm lookin' for some strays. Haven't seen anything of 'em, have you?"

Davis looked up and down the road as if he expected to see them there. "Why, no," he said. "No, I haven't seen any horses up this way at all. Tell you the truth, though, I ain't been out around much today. Fact is I ain't been out at all — got a touch of grippe or somethin'. What's your team look like?"

"Pair of brown geldings," my father said. Davis glanced up quickly, with a surprised look, but my father wheeled old Bill around toward the road. "I got to be gettin' on home to do the milkin'. They wouldn't hardly have come this far anyway, I reckon."

"Well," said Davis, "I hope you find 'em. If I see anything of 'em, I'll let you know."

My father nodded, and we turned south the way we had come. Davis stood in the door, watching us go.

By trying hard, I kept from saying a word. When we were out of sight of the cabin, my father looked over at me and grinned.

"Well?" he said. "Anything on your mind?"

"Yes," I said. "How come we're going home?"

"What makes you think we're going home?" he asked me. "You see anything funny about that coot?"

I had, but I wasn't sure just what it was. And my father had lied in describing our lost horses.

"How'd he know I was lookin' for a team of horses? I said strays; not what kind or how many. Another thing, he had too much 'the fact is' and 'tell you the truth.' Man ain't lyin', he don't need to say he ain't. . . . You go back up the road like you'd dropped a jackknife, see if you can see what our friend Davis is up to."

He took Nancy's rein. I slipped out of the saddle and ran back up the road, head bent. But I was looking all around and feeling very important, like an Indian scout. I came up behind a big fir tree, stealthy as Kit Carson, and peeked out at the cabin. In a minute Davis came out, carrying a shotgun. He went across his clearing and into the woods in back of it, following a path through the mountain currants and young poplars.

I told my father what I had seen. He looked as cheerful as the day before Christmas. "Ah!" he said. "Now we're getting down to it!" He pulled Bill around. "Come on, jug head!" he said. "Let's see you travel!"

He laid into Bill with the rein ends until the dust flew, and I pounded on Nancy with my willow switch, and I was really surprised at the way they rattled along.

I expected him to turn in past the cabin and follow Davis, but he stayed in the road.

I asked him, "Don't we follow Davis, father?"

He gave me a disgusted look. "We're goin' where Sam and Bess went," he said. He pointed to the road. "There's their tracks. If you can't be smart, be as smart as you can." After a minute he must have felt sorry, for he went on: "Don't never come up behind a man that might be lookin' for you to come up behind him. Thing to do is surround him," he said.

By and by we came to a section marker — a heap of dirt with an iron stake driven in it. The marker was almost at the edge of the big muskeg. Beside the marker there was a footpath into the woods on the east side of the road. My father sat looking at that path. I looked, too, but I couldn't see anything, although it was only about six o'clock and the sun was still well up. In our country in summer you can see to read until nine o'clock or after, and it doesn't really get dark all night because it is so far north the sun can hardly get out of sight.

Father showed me where a strawberry plant was torn up, and looking closer I could see the outline of a hoof-print. Then we started down the foot-path, letting the horses walk. And while we rode, he talked to me in a very low voice.

"This quarter," he said, "is all swamp. But the one next to it, cornering on Davis' place, there's high land, a hundred acres or so, sticks out into the muskeg, kind of a finger of poplar ridge. I heard there was a couple of young fellows settled on it a while back. We'll go look in on 'em."

Pretty soon he left the path and rode down toward the swamp. All the sloughs and muskegs in our country have little fir trees growing around the edges, a belt about twenty feet wide with the trees so close together nothing bigger than a rabbit can get through them. But every so often there will be a break where deer and moose went through when the trees were younger. When we came to one of these breaks my father rode through it to the other side of the fir belt, and we went along the edge of the muskeg toward the poplar ridge he had mentioned.

The horses made no noise at all on the thick brown-and-green moss inside the fir belt. There was no noise at all, anywhere in that whole country, not so much as a bird song. All I could hear was the creak of the saddles, and the hum of the mosquitoes.

It was so quiet I began to get scared. I felt very angry with the horse thief for getting me into this mess. I envied old Nancy, slogging along over the soft moss and groaning every once in a while — envied her because she didn't have any imagination, and so did not know what she might be getting into. If she had known all I knew, she would have turned around and run away with me. And that would have been all right with me too.

I had a severe case of the gollywobbles. Most of all I was afraid of having my father know I was scared. So I rode Nancy over as close to Bill as I could get her, and clamped on to my little rifle until my whole arm ached, and kept my hat pulled down so my father couldn't see my face.

We came to where the poplar ridge curved out into the muskeg, and we followed along the edge of this finger until we came to the point, where it curved back. My father rode cautiously here, expecting to find a break in the fir belt at the point. Sure enough, it was there. He stopped just inside it and looked, and then he pulled old Bill back beside me.

"They're in there," he whispered. "Sam and Bess. Over a ways, staked out, I think. What'll we do now, Bub?"

"Whatever you say."

"Their shack'll be back at the other end of the ridge," he said, as if to himself. "I really ought to go warm their jackets for 'em — and Davis — he was in on it. . . . Still, there's no use lookin' for trouble, and the cows need milkin'. . . . Imagine puttin' horses on a long line, in woods like that. . . . Maybe we better just take 'em and get along home. Take the picket ropes with us and whoever owns 'em can come ask for 'em, huh?"

I was strongly in favor of that program, but before I could say so my father put his hand up to be quiet. Somebody was coming along the ridge in back of us — somebody in a hurry.

"Too late now," my father said, looking pleased. "They come to move 'em — just one, it sounds like. Davis was in it sure enough. . . . You stay here 'til I call you. I'm goin' to put the fear of God into those dudes."

He waited until we could hear someone walking along the ridge opposite the opening in the fir belt. Then he gathered up the ends of the reins and belted old Bill as hard as he could. Bill jumped clear out of his tracks, out into the open, and my father had his gun out and was hollering:

"Get your hands up, horse thief! Reach for it, blast you!"

Of course I was right along behind him, in spite of what he said. I saw this young fellow, this Charlie Semple, standing too startled and frightened even to put up his hands. My father had his pistol pointed at him, and he was booting old Bill up to him and calling him a lot of names. Charlie Semple's eyes were popped away out, and his jaw was trembling and his mouth making queer twisting motions, and he really looked green. He had yellow hair and a long nose and not very much chin. He wore an old black pullover sweater with a big hole in the side.

Sam and Bess were over a little farther, below the curve of the ridge. Sam whinnied a couple of times when he saw the other horses, but neither Bill nor Nancy answered him. I looked down the ridge the way Charlie had come, in case Davis or Willie Bemis, Charlie's pardner, might be following him. But I didn't see anything, so I watched Charlie Semple.

I had never seen a man really frightened, so frightened that he had lost track of everything and didn't care any more, and couldn't think enough to care. When a man is only a little scared, he is ashamed of being scared at all, and he will try to cover it up. He may act bold and blustery, or he may try to laugh it off. But Charlie Semple was scared sick and witless. At first he couldn't say anything at all, but my father kept prodding him, cursing him out and asking him what he meant by stealing our horses, and waving that big pistol in front of him. And pretty soon Charlie began saying "Don't!" in a weak, moaning voice. That was all he could say: "Don't! Don't! Don't!"

It made me feel a little sick to see Charlie Semple like that, because he was a human being and not acting like one. I guess my father felt the same way. He stopped yelling at Charlie Semple and just sat and looked him over for a minute, and then he leaned over and spat on the ground in disgust.

"Go on," he said to Semple. "Let's go see that pardner of yours. Where is he — back at the cabin?"

Semple nodded his head helplessly. My father said, "Well, get goin', then." When Charlie Semple didn't move, my father rode old Bill right into him, and then Charlie dodged away and started back up the ridge, hurrying and stumbling.

I thought Davis might have heard Sam whinny and come along with his shotgun, to see if there was anything wrong; but my father did not think so.

"That yahoo ain't smart enough to figure like that, nor brave enough to do anything about it if he did," my father said. "Might as well bring the nags along with us, though; save coming back. You go get 'em."

So I went back for Sam and Bess, and overtook my father and Charlie just before they came to what was meant for a clearing. It was only about an acre, and the trees had been whittled down and let fall every which way. They hadn't even been trimmed up. It was a very pitiful sight, even for a tenderfoot's homestead. There was no way to get through the tangle, so we rode around the edge of it, toward the cabin.

The cabin was not much more than a brush heap with a chimney stuck in it and a pile of marsh hay for a roof. The walls were all whopper-jawed, and it looked about ready to fall to pieces, although you could tell it had not been up long. There was one little window in it, with a flour sack nailed over it instead of glass.

When we came in range of the cabin my father rode up close to Charlie Semple, in case Davis was tempted to let off his shotgun, then yelled, "Come out of it, you horse-stealin' coyotes! Come out right now, with your hands away up!"

My father was having a good time. I could see he was a rootin', tootin', pistol-shootin' cow-waddie again, in his own mind. Like in another song he used to sing: "I'm a lone wolf from Bitter

Creek, and it's my night to howl!" This was his time to howl. And man, I though it was wonderful. It was living in a wild-West story. I'd forgotten about being scared, I was so proud of my father.

"Come out!" he whooped, and he added some words he'd licked me for saying. Then Willie Bemis came slowly through the door, looking almost as surprised as Charlie had, but more sullen. Willie Bemis was an Englishman, not much more than twenty. He had black, curly hair and he had more chin than Charlie; but he was a weak sister, though not so weak as Charlie.

"Where's Davis?" my father said to Willie Bemis. "Trot him out here!"

"He's gone," said Willie Bemis. He was a Cockney, so the words sounded like " 'E's gorn."

"Gone where?"

"Back 'ome, I suppose, where 'e said 'e was going." Bemis started to put his hands down, but my father would not let him, so he clasped them on top of his head and stared at father defiantly.

My father said, "What do you mean by stealin' my horses out of my pasture and bringing them off up here?"

"We never stole your bloody blasted horses," Willie Bemis said.

"They come in here and tied themselves up back there, I suppose," my father said, sneering.

"We found 'em straying a mile down the road and tied 'em up until we could find out who they belonged to. As you might have found out, you blasted Yankee, if you'd ask questions instead of sneakin' around people's places wavin' a gun and a-usin' bad language! Who do you think you are — Bill Hart? Why, gorblimy, I ought to give you in charge for this!"

He was shaking his fist at my father — although still remembering to keep his hands up — and my father was too surprised to say anything for a minute. Then he got very red, and made a strangling noise in his throat. He looked down at Charlie Semple, who was still standing beside old Bill. "Get over there you!" my father said. "Get over beside that other polecat!"

He took his left foot out of the stirrup and prodded Charlie Semple with it. Then he looked surprised, and grabbed for the horn. Because old Bill suddenly lay down under him. He didn't fall down or collapse; he just lay down, as if that was what he wanted to do, so he did it. I never saw a horse do that before or since. If my father had had his spurs, he would have lifted him up all right; but as it was, all he could do was step clear.

His face got redder and redder, and he looked at old Bill, and then quickly at Willie and Charlie to see if they were laughing at him.

I was careful not to make a sound, because I knew my father was perfectly furious. Old Bill made him look ridiculous, and he hated that above all else.

My father said to Willie Bemis in a level, deadly voice: "Young feller, you lie like hell. Where I come from there's just one thing happens to horse thieves. And this is it."

He shifted his gun to his left hand and reached over to his saddle and took down his rope. He slipped the coil to his left hand holding the gun, and shook out a loop in back of him, stepping away from old Bill as he did so.

I knew — or I was pretty sure — that my father was bluffing. But Bemis and Semple weren't sure at all. What little they knew about the West they had learned from the movies. And my father was mad enough to sound convincing. Willie Bemis' jaw dropped when he saw the rope, and he got deathly pale.

"It's too bad," said my father, "that I only got one rope. One apiece would be easier on you; you'd die quicker. But I got no time to fool around. So — "

His arm gave a twitch, and the loop flew forward. But my father had not stepped far enough away from old Bill. The loop stung his ear, and he lurched up on his feet, spoiling the cast. And as he came up he caught his foot in a root or something, and almost went down again; and in trying to save himself he came lunging right at my father and knocked him down. He sat down, hard, and had to scramble fast to get out from under Bill's feet.

I pretended afterward that I did it to keep Bemis and Semple from taking advantage of my father's accident, but really I was just excited. Anyway, when my father fell down I shot off my little .22. It seemed to me to make a feeble little pop, but it must have sounded more impressive to Willie and Charlie out in front of it. Their hands went back up as high as they could reach, and instead of looking at my father, they watched me.

My father got up on his feet and he was whispering to himself. He jammed his six-gun into the holster and unbuckled the belt and laid it over a log. Then he walked over to Bemis and Semple. He stopped right in front of them, and he began to slap them as hard as he could, first Bemis and then Semple, left hand, right hand. It sounded like a whole colony of beavers smacking the water with their flat tails. When they tried to dodge away from him, he grabbed them and cracked their heads together, and then he smacked them some more.

After a while they were both on the ground in front of him, Charlie spread out face down and crying real tears, and Willie all hunkered up with his arms wrapped around his head.

"Now tell me why you stole my horses," said my father.

So then they told him.

It was quite a story, and all mixed up the way they told it; but it came down to this:

Willie and Charlie had been sailors. A year before, their ship had been in Montreal, and someone had told them about the great opportunities for young men in Northern Alberta. They did not like the sea, so they had pooled their savings and started out together to homestead. They knew nothing at all about farming, much less about the peculiar combination of woodcraft and agricultural skill essential to the homesteader in our country. They didn't even know enough to ask questions — or perhaps they were too proud to ask, out of that contempt which sailors have for landlubbers. Then, too, they were very young.

They had had a bad time. But Willie Bemis had a mother and father in London, and to them he had written brave fairy stories, picturing the homestead, not as it was, but as he wished it to be.

And then his father — a "draper's clark" — had died, and his mother wrote that she was coming out to live with him. His father's insurance had been enough to pay for the funeral and for his mother's passage.

In two more weeks his mother would arrive. Willie was desperate. They had confided in Davis, their neighbor, the only one in the whole country who had shown the slightest interest in them. They had gone uptown with Davis the day before, and Davis had provided them with consolation out of a whisky bottle. They had stayed in town all day and until late at night, and on the way home our horses had been stolen.

It was hard to determine just what part Davis had played in the actual theft. Either they were protecting him or they really could not remember because of the whisky. Willie insisted he did not know whether Davis had suggested the stealing, or who had suggested it. He was sure that Davis was not with them when they got the horses. But he had loaned them the ax and the new well rope which he had bought that day in the town.

When they came past his cabin with the horses, they had told him what they had done and he had advised them where to hide the team until the next night, when he would take them out through Willow Creek and around by Mulvalen and sell them in some distant place where they could not be traced. With the money thus gained they thought they might "fix things up" before Willie's mother arrived.

They took us around to the other side of the cabin, and showed us how they had tried to build a new cabin for her. There are many wrong ways to build a log house, and the two ex-sailors had hit most of them. They took us into their own cabin — a dank, dark, waterlogged hole, smelling like an abandoned root cellar, and everything in it mildewed — even the blankets in which they slept.

My father looked and listened. When he came out of the cabin he sat down on a stump and poked with a twig at some chips. My father had forgotten he was a lone wolf from Bitter Creek. His jaw no longer stuck out, and his eyes were not narrow and keen, but thoughtful. He looked like a middle-aged farmer, a bit on the portly side. He did not look like a cowboy at all.

We three youngsters stood and watched my father prod the chips, waiting for him to speak. We were no longer enemies, nor strangers; but we were not yet friends, we three. We were in the uncertain middle ground of emotion that comes with an abrupt shift in a human relationship. We might become friends, enemies, or nothing. Now everything hung suspended between us, and it was for my father to say which way the balance would fall.

My father said slowly, "God alone knows why the fool-killer didn't get you two long ago. You are ignorant young lunkheads, and you stole my horses. I don't know why that puts it up to me to take care of you; by rights I ought to turn you over to Macey. Anyhow, here's what: There's a cabin on my place, two rooms. I been using it for a storehouse. It can be cleared out. You can come down there and live. Burn this — this hovel down, if you can make it catch. Then you can tell your mother you was burned out, if you want.

"I start haying tomorrow. You can help me with it. When we get the crop in, the four of us'll come up here and put up a decent place to live. One of you can cut wood for me this winter, for grub and some cash and the rent of a team to get this place cleared off and ready to plow next spring.

"There it is, now. Take it or leave it," said my father.

They took it.

When we passed the Davis cabin my father handed me Sam's

bridle rein and told me to ride on ahead, slowly. He went up toward the cabin alone. His pistol was wrapped in his slicker and tied to the back of his saddle. I was afraid again, seeing him go in there and knowing Davis had a shotgun. But my fear was unnecessary. Looking back through the twilight, I saw the cabin door open to his knock. My father stood for a moment, talking, and then lunged forward suddenly. For a little while there was a great tumult within the cabin — the sound of blows, of pounding feet, the crash of breaking furniture. Then Davis ran out the door and across the clearing and into the woods, and that was the last I ever saw of Davis. Next time we passed that way his cabin stood open and deserted.

My father stood in the doorway, watching him go. Then he picked up his hat and came down the road toward me, stuffing his shirttail into his trousers. I rode back to meet him. He sat down beside the road and pulled off his cowboy boots deliberately. He sat there wiggling his toes and weighing the boots in his hand, considering them.

At last he said, "You want these damn things, Bub? I won't be wantin' them no longer. They don't seem to fit good, somehow."

I took them gladly. In his stocking feet my father mounted our brown plow horse, and we rode home to do the milking.

Jake Hoover's Pig

FRANK B. LINDERMAN

*L*inderman *is best known for his work with the Indians, inter-
preting their tales and legends and translating them into interesting books:* Indian Why Stories, *1915;* Indian Old-Man Stories,
1920; Kootenai Why Stories, *1926;* Old Man Coyote, *1931. The
two sketches here show another aspect of his writing. They are
from a little book called* On a Passing Frontier, *1920, dedicated
to "the camps in the Little Rockics where the old west is making
its last stand." They are brief, neat, authentic.*

I*t's* FUNNY lots of men deny sentiment," said Charley Russel, "but
I've found more of it in those that denied it than in others who
advertised themselves as suffering with an overburden of that virtue.

"A man don't look for a lot of sentiment in a trapper. I mean
when it applies to the life and welfare of wild animals. Sometimes
it's there, just the same.

"When I was a kid I threw in with old Jake Hoover. Jake was a
trapper — a skin-hunter, and killed deer, elk, and antelope for the
market. His cabin was in Pig Eye Basin over in the Judith country,
and you could see deer from the door of the shack 'most any day.

"The old man would never kill a deer that stuck about the place, and I've seen the time when there wasn't enough grub in the camp to bait a mousetrap, too, yet Jake would no more think of killing one of the deer that hung around there than he would of taking a shot at me. Squirrels and birds were friends of his at all times, and he often fed them.

"One spring a ranchman traded Jake a small pig for some elk meat, and Jake took the pig to camp. He was little and cute, and a nuisance about the place till Jake finally made a pen for him. Grain was scarce, of course, in those days, and we had to rustle to feed that confounded rooter. But whenever either of us could land on a sack of wheat we got it.

"Eat! well I guess so. And grow! Say! that pig just seemed to swell up over night. He was a great pet. When Jake would go to the pen with food, he'd rub Jake's legs with his head while the old fellow would scratch his back and pet him. Let him out, and he'd trail after Jake all day like a dog. Sometimes we had to ride forty or fifty miles to get grain. And money, well, we didn't have any, but managed to trade meat for wheat when we found it.

"Jake would look at the pig and say: 'Kid, won't he make fine eatin' this fall? He's fat as a fool an' big enough to kill right now, but we'll wait till the cold weather comes, and then, Zowie! we'll bat him with the axe. We'll have grease enough to last us till spring. I'm glad I got him.'

"One day he got out of the pen. We had gone hunting. Of course the cabin door was open, and the pig went inside. We were gone two days. I wish you could have seen that shack when we got back.

"She never was very tidy, but the pig had found the flour and the syrup and the dried apples. Jake's best blanket was on the floor, and it had been walloped around in the mess for hours. A million flies had moved in, too, an' every sticky spot on the blanket was black with them. We were within ten feet of the door when *crash!* went the dishpan.

"That was when Jake cocked his rifle and whispered: 'Bear! Look out, Kid.'

"He slipped up to the door, and I was behind him as he poked the barrel of his Winchester inside. Then he began to swear.

"From the middle of the damnedest wreck you ever saw that fool pig raised his head in welcome. He was a black pig, and flour and syrup had gummed his face until it was white. His eyes were ringed all around an' you'd have sworn he had on a pair of goggles. You know the way the dried apples used to come, in a box? — Well, a round slice with a hole in its centre had stuck fast to his forehead.

"The pig was real glad to see us, an' showed it, but Jake was mad.

" 'That settles it. You die. You won't see the leaves turn yeller, either. You'll be bacon, ye — Look at my blanket, Kid.'

"I was dying to laugh, but I was afraid to. Jake might go to war if I did.

"We cleaned out the shack, and that night we got ready for the killing. Jake got up before daylight and built a fire.

" 'I'm afraid it's too warm to kill that pig yet, Kid,' he said as I pulled on my boots. 'It's too early in the season, an' we can't afford to lose the meat after all the hell we've had with him. Guess we'll wait a spell. Besides, we've got a little wheat left an' there wouldn't be nothin' to feed it to. You bet I won't never have another.'

"So the pig's time was extended. I felt rather glad, for I sort of liked him, even if he was a nuisance.

"But the wheat disappeared at last, and we had to make another rustle. 'It's the last time,' said Jake. 'I'm plumb sick of the contract, an' as soon's this sack is gone — Zowie! we'll bat him. It's comin' to him, ain't it?'

" 'Sure it is,' I told him.

"The weather was growing sharp when the last of the wheat was dished out. 'I'll feed him to-night an' bust his head in the mornin'.' He sharpened his knives and talked of the feast all the evening, but I didn't like to think of the pig at all.

"Jake turned out early. As soon as he got his boots on he took his knives, an axe, and the camp kettle he had always used to feed the pig, and said: 'Come on, Kid, an' we'll git rid of that dirty skunk before we eat. I jest can't put it off no longer. Wheat's all gone, an' I ain't goin' ridin' like a madman to find feed for a dirty hawg no more.'

"We started for the pig-pen. A pine squirrel ran down a fir tree and came to meet us. Jake kicked at him. 'This place is plumb overrun with damned nuisances,' he said, an' stepped over into the pen.

"The pig was tickled to see him and began rubbing his nose on his legs. 'Get out, damn ye,' he cried. 'Get away from me! This ain't no friendly errand. Here, Kid, smash him while I git some water heatin'.'

" 'Not by a damn sight,' I said. 'He ain't my pig.'

" 'Oh, come on, Kid. He's knowed me ever since he was a little feller. We need the meat, an' the wheat's all gone.'

" 'Can't help it,' I said. 'I didn't bring him here, and I won't kill him.'

"Jake leaned the axe against the pen. 'Why, he's nothin' but a hawg, an' a low-down one at that. Look at my blanket.'

" 'Can't help it, Jake. I can't kill him, and I won't.'

"He turned back to the cabin. I saw him come out with his Winchester. He climbed up the hill, and I walked away from the pen. A half hour went by before the pig, wondering why he had not been fed, turned around.

"Bang!

"The pet was no more. A bullet had entered his brain. Jake came down the hill, leaned his rifle against a tree, and cut the pig's throat. " 'I don't reckon he saw me er knowed who done it, do you, Kid?' he said in a low voice that shook a trifle."

The Post-Office at Wolftail

FRANK B. LINDERMAN

THE STAGE STOPPED at a cow ranch far from other human habitation. The driver, after spending some time in pawing over the contents of the front boot, threw an apparently empty mail-sack to the ground before the cabin. Then, gathering up the reins, he expectorated violently, for he was chewing tobacco.

"Wolftail! pardner. Here's where you git off," he called, leaning slightly from his high perch on the Concord coach.

A young man got out. He carried a suitcase, and his tan buttoned shoes and derby hat fairly screamed "tenderfoot" to the silence about him — for the coach had gone its way in a cloud of dust.

The sun was high and hot. The desert-like plains had been baked until they had cracked. The range was drying up. The water-holes were empty now, and as far as the stranger could see there was not a single living thing in sight.

He knocked on the door. There was no answer. Then he tried the knob, and the door opened, for it was unlocked. The coolness of the cabin invited him, and he entered with an air of proprietorship. "Whew!" he said, and setting down his suitcase, he mopped his face with a linen handkerchief.

It was cool in the cabin, for the thick dirt roof was a warrant against the sun. A lone bald-faced hornet, worn out and battered, was crawling laboriously up a grimy window-pane, only to fall back and begin the ascent again.

Besides the stranger, a cat had availed herself of the cabin's shelter, and being awakened, stretched herself listlessly, and then, noting something disappointing about the visitor, crawled away under the bunk in the corner, where from the darkness she gazed at the disturber, her eyes glistening green displeasure.

"Kitty, kitty, kitty," called our friend, invitingly. But the cat would have none of him. So he looked about.

"Guns, guns, guns," he murmured as he surveyed the rack upon which hung an assortment of rifles. There was a colored likeness of Abraham Lincoln and another of Washington at Monmouth. Besides, there was a calendar, and a soap-box that had been nailed to the cabin wall. These furnished the decorations — all of them. The owner's brand had been liberally burned on the door; but this had been done on the outside, so the marks could hardly be included in the decorations within.

The stranger finally sat down and lit a cigarette. "I'll have something to say to Mr. Man when he returns," he mused. "Nice, isn't it? Oh, very nice, indeed, but he will find that I — "

His musing was suddenly interrupted. A cayuse had stopped at the open door, and the roll of the bit in the horse's mouth was an unfamiliar sound to our friend. He watched a man dismount and stoop to pick up the mail-sack, drawing it toward him, while the cayuse backed away with a frightened snort. "Strange," he thought, when the horse, trailing his loose bridle-reins, stopped as he felt their trifling weight.

The rider began to whistle absently as he entered the cabin with the mail-sack. He crossed the floor to the table near the window, secured a key, and unlocked the sack. Then he emptied its contents carelessly upon the table. There were five letters and two wrapped papers. One of the papers, bounding about among the dishes there, upset the sugar-bowl before it landed on the floor. The man swore under his breath. Then he scooped the sugar into a pile with his hand and, holding the sugar-bowl near the edge of the table, scraped the spilled sweetness back into its rightful place. This done, he stooped to recover the refractory paper, and saw the visitor.

"Howdy, stranger," he greeted.

"How are you, sir? Are you the postmaster?"

"Hell, no. I live down on the river. Circle-dot's my iron. I was

just lookin' to see if there was anything fer me, but there ain't."
He gathered up the letters and papers, and crossing the room to
the soap-box, he laid them in it. Then he took up a dozen or
more letters that had been in the box and ran them through,
slowly making sure of every name upon the much-handled enve-
lopes.

Selecting three or four letters and a paper, he tucked them into
his pocket. "I see there's mail for some of the SY outfit, an' I'm
ridin' that way so I'll take it along. Say, what's in yer cigarette
that makes it stink that-a-way?"

"It's a Turkish cigarette, sir."

"Bet it is, all right. Smells like a moccasin afire. Antiose."

He rode away. The young man got out a notebook and in it
made some entries. "Oh, this will be spicy," he murmured, "and
coming in upon him unexpectedly, I'll learn much." Then he
selected another cigarette from a golden case and lighted it.

The sun had settled well toward the horizon when another rider
came to the cabin. He breezed in good-humouredly, sensing company, no doubt.

"Howdy," he said. "And who might you be, stranger? Hungry?"

"Are you the postmaster?" asked the young man severely, ignor-
ing the polite question.

"Yep."

"Well, sir, I am a United States Inspector of post offices,
and — "

"The hell you be!"

"Yes, sir, and I shall have to report the grossest carelessness on
your part to the department. Their — "

"You will!"

The man stuffed the mail-sack into the soap-box and wrenched
the box from the wall.

"I'll jest make it worth yer while to add to yer report, son. They
ain't never heard from me. Tell 'em I said to go to hell. There's
yer damn post-office. Go git it!"

And he threw the box out of the door.

All Gold Canyon

JACK LONDON

During his brief lifetime and for a while afterwards Jack London was a force. Nowadays, except for the stories kept in print for each new generation of boys, he seems to be an acquired taste that not everyone can acquire. Certainly his work, uneven and extreme and prolific (fifty volumes in only sixteen years of writing), is strong and heady stuff, too much so for the fastidious. He was only incidentally a writer of western stories. Most of his, and the best, take place in Alaska or at sea or in the South Sea islands. Even this one may not technically be a western in that he might have had an Alaskan setting in mind. But it could apply to many a gold area of the West of the opening days and it is definitely western in tone and spirit.

It was the green heart of the canyon, where the walls swerved back from the rigid plan and relieved their harshness of line by making a little sheltered nook and filling it to the brim with sweetness and roundness and softness. Here all things rested. Even the narrow stream ceased its turbulent down-rush long enough to form a quiet pool. Knee-deep in the water, with drooping head and half-shut eyes, drowsed a red-coated, many-antlered buck.

On one side, beginning at the very lip of the pool, was a tiny meadow, a cool, resilient surface of green that extended to the base of the frowning wall. Beyond the pool a gentle slope of earth ran up and up to meet the opposing wall. Fine grass covered the slope — grass that was spangled with flowers, with here and there patches of color, orange and purple and golden. Below, the canyon was shut in. There was no view. The walls leaned together abruptly and the canyon ended in a chaos of rocks, moss-covered and hidden by a green screen of vines and creepers and boughs of trees. Up the canyon rose far hills and peaks, the big foothills, pine-covered and remote. And far beyond, like clouds upon the border of the sky, towered minarets of white, where the Sierra's eternal snows flashed austerely the blazes of the sun.

There was no dust in the canyon. The leaves and flowers were clean and virginal. The grass was young velvet. Over the pool three cottonwoods sent their snowy fluffs fluttering down the quiet air. On the slope the blossoms of the wine-wooded manzanita filled the air with springtime odors, while the leaves, wise with experience, were already beginning their vertical twist against the coming aridity of summer. In the open spaces on the slope, beyond the farthest shadow-reach of the manzanita, poised the mariposa lilies, like so many flights of jewelled moths suddenly arrested and on the verge of trembling into flight again. Here and there that woods harlequin, the madrone, permitting itself to be caught in the act of changing its pea-green trunk to madder-red, breathed its fragrance into the air from great clusters of waxen bells. Creamy white were these bells, shaped like lilies-of-the-valley, with the sweetness of perfume that is of the springtime.

There was not a sigh of wind. The air was drowsy with its weight of perfume. It was a sweetness that would have been cloying had the air been heavy and humid. But the air was sharp and thin. It was as starlight transmuted into atmosphere, shot through and warmed by sunshine, and flower-drenched with sweetness.

An occasional butterfly drifted in and out through the patches of light and shade. And from all about rose the low and sleepy hum of mountain bees — feasting Sybarites that jostled one another good-naturedly at the board, nor found time for rough discourtesy. So quietly did the little stream drip and ripple its way through the canyon that it spoke only in faint and occasional gurgles. The voice of the stream was as a drowsy whisper, ever interrupted by dozings and silences, ever lifted again in the awakenings.

The motion of all things was a drifting in the heart of the canyon. Sunshine and butterflies drifted in and out among the trees. The hum of the bees and the whisper of the stream were a drifting of sound. And the drifting sound and drifting color seemed to weave together in the making of a delicate and intangible fabric which was the spirit of the place. It was a spirit of peace that was not of death, but of smooth-pulsing life, of quietude that was not silence, of movement that was not action, of repose that was quick with existence without being violent with struggle and travail. The spirit of the place was the spirit of the peace of the living, somnolent with the easement and content of prosperity, and undisturbed by rumors of far wars.

The red-coated, many-antlered buck acknowledged the lordship of the spirit of the place and dozed knee-deep in the cool, shaded pool. There seemed no flies to vex him and he was languid with rest. Sometimes his ears moved when the stream awoke and whispered; but they moved lazily, with foreknowledge that it was merely the stream grown garrulous at discovery that it had slept.

But there came a time when the buck's ears lifted and tensed with swift eagerness for sound. His head was turned down the canyon. His sensitive, quivering nostrils scented the air. His eyes could not pierce the green screen through which the stream rippled away, but to his ears came the voice of a man. It was a steady, monotonous, singsong voice. Once the buck heard the harsh clash of metal upon rock. At the sound he snorted with a sudden start that jerked him through the air from water to meadow, and his feet sank into the young velvet, while he pricked his ears and again scented the air. Then he stole across the tiny meadow, pausing once and again to listen, and faded away out of the canyon like a wraith, soft-footed and without sound.

The clash of steel-shod soles against the rocks began to be heard, and the man's voice grew louder. It was raised in a sort of chant and became distinct with nearness, so that the words could be heard:

> "Tu'n around an' tu'n yo' face
> Untoe them sweet hills of grace
>   (D' pow'rs of sin yo' am scornin'!).
> Look about an' look aroun'
> Fling yo' sin-pack on d' groun'
>   (Yo' will meet wid d' Lord in d' mornin'!)."

A sound of scrambling accompanied the song, and the spirit of the place fled away on the heels of the red-coated buck. The green screen was burst asunder, and a man peered out at the meadow and the pool and the sloping side-hill. He was a deliberate sort of man. He took in the scene with one embracing glance, then ran his eyes over the details to verify the general impression. Then, and not until then, did he open his mouth in vivid and solemn approval:

"Smoke of life an' snakes of purgatory! Will you just look at that! Wood an' water an' grass an' a side-hill! A pocket-hunter's delight an' a cayuse's paradise! Cool green for tired eyes! Pink pills for pale people ain't in it. A secret pasture for prospectors and a resting-place for tired burros. It's just booful!"

He was a sandy-complexioned man in whose face geniality and humor seemed the salient characteristics. It was a mobile face, quick-changing to inward mood and thought. Thinking was in him a visible process. Ideas chased across his face like wind-flaws across the surface of a lake. His hair, sparse and unkempt of growth, was as indeterminate and colorless as his complexion. It would seem that all the color of his frame had gone into his eyes, for they were startlingly blue. Also, they were laughing and merry eyes, within them much of the naiveté and wonder of the child; and yet, in an unassertive way, they contained much of calm self-reliance and strength of purpose founded upon self-experience and experience of the world.

From out the screen of vines and creepers he flung ahead of him a miner's pick and shovel and gold-pan. Then he crawled out himself into the open. He was clad in faded overalls and black cotton shirt, with hobnailed brogans on his feet, and on his head a hat whose shapelessness and stains advertised the rough usage of wind and rain and sun and camp-smoke. He stood erect, seeing wide-eyed the secrecy of the scene and sensuously inhaling the warm, sweet breath of the canyon-garden through nostrils that dilated and quivered with delight. His eyes narrowed to laughing slits of blue, his face wreathed itself in joy, and his mouth curled in a smile as he cried aloud:

"Jumping dandelions and happy hollyhocks, but that smells good to me! Talk about your attar o' roses an' cologne factories! They ain't in it!"

He had the habit of soliloquy. His quick-changing facial expressions might tell every thought and mood, but the tongue, perforce, ran hard after, repeating, like a second Boswell.

The man lay down on the lip of the pool and drank long and deep of its water. "Tastes good to me," he murmured, lifting his

head and gazing across the pool at the side-hill, while he wiped
his mouth with the back of his hand. The side-hill attracted his
attention. Still lying on his stomach, he studied the hill formation
long and carefully. It was a practised eye that traveled up the
slope to the crumbling canyon-wall and back and down again to
the edge of the pool. He scrambled to his feet and favored the
side-hill with a second survey.

"Looks good to me," he concluded, picking up his pick and
shovel and gold-pan.

He crossed the stream below the pool, stepping agilely from
stone to stone. Where the side-hill touched the water he dug up
a shovelful of dirt and put it into the gold-pan. He squatted down,
holding the pan in his two hands, and partly immersing it in the
stream. Then he imparted to the pan a deft circular motion that
sent the water sluicing in and out through the dirt and gravel. The
larger and the lighter particles worked to the surface, and these, by
a skilful dipping movement of the pan, he spilled out and over the
edge. Occasionally, to expedite matters, he rested the pan and with
his fingers raked out the large pebbles and pieces of rock.

The contents of the pan diminished rapidly until only fine dirt
and the smallest bits of gravel remained. At this stage he began
to work very deliberately and carefully. It was fine washing, and
he washed fine and finer, with a keen scrutiny and delicate and
fastidious touch. At last the pan seemed empty of everything but
water; but with a quick semi-circular flirt that sent the water flying
over the shallow rim into the stream, he disclosed a layer of black
sand on the bottom of the pan. So thin was this layer that it was
like a streak of paint. He examined it closely. In the midst of it
was a tiny golden speck. He dribbled a little water in over the depressed edge of the pan. With a quick flirt he sent the water
sluicing across the bottom, turning the grains of black sand over
and over. A second tiny golden speck rewarded his effort.

The washing had now become very fine — fine beyond all need
of ordinary placer mining. He worked the black sand, a small
portion at a time, up the shallow rim of the pan. Each small portion he examined sharply, so that his eyes saw every grain of it
before he allowed it to slide over the edge and away. Jealously, bit
by bit, he let the black sand slip away. A golden speck, no larger
than a pin-point, appeared on the rim, and by his manipulation of
the water it returned to the bottom of the pan. And in such
fashion another speck was disclosed, and another. Great was his
care of them. Like a shepherd he herded his flock of golden specks

so that not one should be lost. At last, of the pan of dirt nothing remained but his golden herd. He counted it, and then, after all his labor, sent it flying out of the pan with one final swirl of water.

But his blue eyes were shining with desire as he rose to his feet. "Seven," he muttered aloud, asserting the sum of the specks for which he had toiled so hard and which he had so wantonly thrown away. "Seven," he repeated, with the emphasis of one trying to impress a number on his memory.

He stood still a long while, surveying the hillside. In his eyes was a curiosity, new-aroused and burning. There was an exultance about his bearing and a keenness like that of a hunting animal catching the fresh scent of game.

He moved down the stream a few steps and took a second panful of dirt.

Again came the careful washing, the jealous herding of the golden specks, and the wantonness with which he sent them flying into the stream. His golden herd diminished. "Four, five," he muttered, and repeated, "five."

He could not forbear another survey of the hill before filling the pan farther down the stream. His golden herds diminished. "Four, three, two, two, one," were his memory tabulations as he moved down the stream. When but one speck of gold rewarded his washing, he stopped and built a fire of dry twigs. Into this he thrust the gold-pan and burned it till it was blue-black. He held up the pan and examined it critically. Then he nodded approbation. Against such a color-background he could defy the tiniest yellow speck to elude him.

Still moving down the stream, he panned again. A single speck was his reward. A third pan contained no gold at all. Not satisfied with this, he panned three times again, taking his shovels of dirt within a foot of one another. Each pan proved empty of gold, and the fact, instead of discouraging him, seemed to give him satisfaction. His elation increased with each barren washing, until he arose, exclaiming jubilantly:

"If it ain't the real thing, may God knock off my head with sour apples!"

Returning to where he had started operations, he began to pan up the stream. At first his golden herds increased — increased prodigiously. "Fourteen, eighteen, twenty-one, twenty-six," ran his memory tabulations. Just above the pool he struck his richest pan — thirty-five colors.

"Almost enough to save," he remarked regretfully as he allowed the water to sweep them away.

The sun climbed to the top of the sky. The man worked on. Pan by pan, he went up the stream, the tally of results steadily decreasing.

"It's just booful, the way it peters out," he exulted when a shovelful of dirt contained no more than a single speck of gold.

And when no specks at all were found in several pans, he straightened up and favored the hillside with a confident glance.

"Ah, ha! Mr. Pocket!" he cried out, as though to an auditor hidden somewhere above him beneath the surface of the slope. "Ah, ha! Mr. Pocket! I'm a-comin', I'm a-comin', an' I'm shorely gwine to get yer! You heah me, Mr. Pocket? I'm gwine to get yer as shore as punkins ain't cauliflowers!"

He turned and flung a measuring glance at the sun poised above him in the azure of the cloudless sky. Then he went down the canyon, following the line of shovel-holes he had made in filling the pans. He crossed the stream below the pool and disappeared through the green screen. There was little opportunity for the spirit of the place to return with its quietude and repose, for the man's voice, raised in ragtime song, still dominated the canyon with possession.

After a time, with a greater clashing of steel-shod feet on rock, he returned. The green screen was tremendously agitated. It surged back and forth in the throes of a struggle. There was a loud grating and clanging of metal. The man's voice leaped to a higher pitch and was sharp with imperativeness. A large body plunged and panted. There was a snapping and ripping and rending, and amid a shower of falling leaves a horse burst through the the screen. On its back was a pack, and from this trailed broken vines and torn creepers. The animal gazed with astonished eyes at the scene into which it had been precipitated, then dropped its head to the grass and began contentedly to graze. A second horse scrambled into view, slipping once on the mossy rocks and regaining equilibrium when its hoofs sank into the yielding surface of the meadow. It was riderless, though on its back was a high-horned Mexican saddle, scarred and discolored by long usage.

The man brought up the rear. He threw off pack and saddle, with an eye to camp location, and gave the animals their freedom to graze. He unpacked his food and got out frying-pan and coffeepot. He gathered an armful of dry wood, and with a few stones made a place for his fire.

"My!" he said, "but I've got an appetite. I could scoff iron-filings an' horseshoe nails an' thank you kindly, ma'am, for a second helpin'."

He straightened up, and, while he reached for matches in the pocket of his overalls, his eyes traveled across the pool to the side-hill. His fingers had clutched the match-box, but they relaxed their hold and the hand came out empty. The man wavered perceptibly. He looked at his preparations for cooking and he looked at the hill.

"Guess I'll take another whack at her," he concluded, starting to cross the stream.

"They ain't no sense in it, I know," he mumbled apologetically. "But keepin' grub back an hour ain't goin' to hurt none, I reckon."

A few feet back from his first of test-pans he started a second line. The sun dropped down the western sky, the shadows lengthened, but the man worked on. He began a third line of test-pans. He was cross-cutting the hillside, line by line, as he ascended. The center of each line produced the richest pans, while the ends came where no colors showed in the pan. And as he ascended the hillside the lines grew perceptibly shorter. The regularity with which their length diminished served to indicate that somewhere up the slope the last line would be so short as to have scarcely length at all, and that beyond could come only a point. The design was growing into an inverted "V." The converging sides of this "V" marked the boundaries of the gold-bearing dirt.

The apex of the "V" was evidently the man's goal. Often he ran his eye along the converging sides and on up the hill, trying to divine the apex, the point where the gold-bearing dirt must cease. Here resided "Mr. Pocket" — for so the man familiarly addressed the imaginary point above him on the slope, crying out:

"Come down out o' that, Mr. Pocket! Be right smart an' agreeable, an' come down!"

"All right," he would add later, in a voice resigned to determination. "All right, Mr. Pocket. It's plain to me I got to come right up an' snatch you out bald-headed. An' I'll do it! I'll do it!" he would threaten still later.

Each pan he carried down to the water to wash, and as he went higher up the hill the pans grew richer, until he began to save the gold in an empty baking powder can which he carried carelessly in his hip-pocket. So engrossed was he in his toil that he did not notice the long twilight of oncoming night. It was not until he tried vainly to see the gold colors in the bottom of the pan that he realized the passage of time. He straightened up abruptly. An expression of whimsical wonderment and awe overspread his face as he drawled:

"Gosh darn my buttons! if I didn't plumb forget dinner!"

He stumbled across the stream in the darkness and lighted his long-delayed fire. Flapjacks and bacon and warmed-over beans constituted his supper. Then he smoked a pipe by the smouldering coals, listening to the night noises and watching the moonlight stream through the canyon. After that he unrolled his bed, took off his heavy shoes, and pulled the blankets up to his chin. His face showed white in the moonlight, like the face of a corpse. But it was a corpse that knew its resurrection, for the man rose suddenly on one elbow and gazed across at his hillside.

"Good night, Mr. Pocket," he called sleepily. "Good night."

He slept through the early gray of morning until the direct rays of the sun smote his closed eyelids, when he awoke with a start and looked about him until he had established the continuity of his existence and identified his present self with the days previously lived.

To dress, he had merely to buckle on his shoes. He glanced at his fireplace and at his hillside, wavered, but fought down the temptation and started the fire.

"Keep yer shirt on, Bill; keep yer shirt on," he admonished himself. "What's the good of rushin'? No use in gettin' all het up an' sweaty. Mr. Pocket 'll wait for you. He ain't a-runnin' away before you can get your breakfast. Now, what you want, Bill, is something fresh in yer bill o' fare. So it's up to you to go an' get it."

He cut a short pole at the water's edge and drew from one of his pockets a bit of line and a draggled fly that had once been a royal coachman.

"Mebbe they'll bite in the early morning," he muttered, as he made his first cast into the pool. And a moment later he was gleefully crying: "What 'd I tell you, eh? What 'd I tell you?"

He had no reel, nor any inclination to waste time, and by main strength, and swiftly, he drew out of the water a flashing ten-inch trout. Three more, caught in rapid succession, furnished his breakfast. When he came to the stepping-stones on his way to his hillside, he was struck by a sudden thought, and paused.

"I'd just better take a hike down-stream a ways," he said. "There's no tellin' who may be snoopin' around."

But he crossed over on the stones, and with a "I really oughter take that hike," the need of the precaution passed out of his mind and he fell to work.

At nightfall he straightened up. The small of his back was stiff from stooping toil, and as he put his hand behind him to soothe the protesting muscles, he said:

"Now what d'ye think of that? I clean forgot my dinner again! If I don't watch out, I'll sure be degeneratin' into a two-meal-a-day crank."

"Pockets is the hangedest things I ever see for makin' a man absent-minded," he communed that night, as he crawled into his blankets. Nor did he forget to call up the hillside, "Good night, Mr. Pocket! Good night!"

Rising with the sun, and snatching a hasty breakfast, he was early at work. A fever seemed to be growing in him, nor did the increasing richness of the test-pans allay this fever. There was a flush in his cheek other than that made by the heat of the sun, and he was oblivious to fatigue and the passage of time. When he filled a pan with dirt, he ran down the hill to wash it; nor could he forbear running up the hill again, panting and stumbling profanely, to refill the pan.

He was now a hundred yards from the water, and the inverted "V" was assuming definite proportions. The width of the pay-dirt steadily decreased, and the man extended in his mind's eye the sides of the "V" to their meeting place far up the hill. This was his goal, the apex of the "V," and he panned many times to locate it.

"Just about two yards above that manzanita bush an' a yard to the right," he finally concluded.

Then the temptation seized him. "As plain as the nose on your face," he said, as he abandoned his laborious cross-cutting and climbed to the indicated apex. He filled a pan and carried it down the hill to wash. It contained no trace of gold. He dug deep, and he dug shallow, filling and washing a dozen pans, and was unrewarded even by the tiniest golden speck. He was enraged at having yielded to the temptation, and berated himself blasphemously and pridelessly. Then he went down the hill and took up the cross-cutting.

"Slow an' certain, Bill; slow an' certain," he crooned. "Short-cuts to fortune ain't in your line, an' it's about time you know it. Get wise, Bill; get wise. Slow an' certain's the only hand you can play; so get to it, an' keep to it, too."

As the cross-cuts decreased, showing that the sides of the "V" were converging, the depth of the "V" increased. The gold-trace was dipping into the hill. It was only at thirty inches beneath the surface that he could get colors in his pan. The dirt he found at twenty-five inches from the surface, and at thirty-five inches yielded barren pans. At the base of the "V," by the water's edge, he had found the gold colors at the grass roots. The higher he went up the hill, the deeper the gold dipped. To dig a hole three feet deep in order to get one test-pan was a task of no mean magnitude; while between the man and the apex intervened an untold number of such holes to be dug. "An' there's no tellin' how much deeper it'll pitch," he sighed, in a moment's pause, while his fingers soothed his aching back.

Feverish with desire, with aching back and stiffening muscles, with pick and shovel gouging and mauling the soft brown earth, the man toiled up the hill. Before him was the smooth slope, spangled with flowers and made sweet with their breath. Behind him was devastation. It looked like some terrible eruption breaking out on the smooth skin of the hill. His slow progress was like that of a slug, befouling beauty with a monstrous trail.

Though the dipping gold-trace increased the man's work, he found consolation in the increasing richness of the pans. Twenty cents, thirty cents, fifty cents, sixty cents, were the values of the gold found in the pans, and at nightfall he washed his banner pan, which gave him a dollar's worth of gold-dust from a shovelful of dirt.

"I'll just bet it's my luck to have some inquisitive one come buttin' in here on my pasture," he mumbled sleepily that night as he pulled the blankets up to his chin.

Suddenly he sat upright. "Bill!" he called sharply. "Now, listen to me, Bill; d'ye hear! It's up to you, to-morrow mornin', to mosey round an' see what you can see. Understand? To-morrow morning, an' don't you forget it!"

He yawned and glanced across at his side-hill. "Good night, Mr. Pocket," he called.

In the morning he stole a march on the sun, for he had finished breakfast when its first rays caught him, and he was climbing the wall of the canyon where it crumbled away and gave footing. From the outlook at the top he found himself in the midst of loneliness. As far as he could see, chain after chain of mountains heaved themselves into his vision. To the east his eyes, leaping the miles between range and range and between many ranges, brought up at last against the white-peaked Sierras — the main crest, where the backbone of the Western world reared itself against the sky. To the north and south he could see more distinctly the cross-systems that broke through the main trend of the sea of mountains. To the west the ranges fell away, one behind the other, diminishing and fading into the gentle foothills that, in turn, descended into the great valley which he could not see.

And in all that mighty sweep of earth he saw no sign of man nor of the handiwork of man — save only the torn bosom of the hillside at his feet. The man looked long and carefully. Once, far down his own canyon, he thought he saw in the air a faint hint of smoke. He looked again and decided that it was the purple haze of the hills made dark by a convolution of the canyon wall at its back.

"Hey, you, Mr. Pocket!" he called down into the canyon. "Stand out from under! I'm a-comin', Mr. Pocket! I'm a-comin'!"

The heavy brogans on the man's feet made him appear clumsy-footed, but he swung down from the giddy height as lightly and airily as a mountain goat. A rock, turning under his foot on the edge of the precipice, did not disconcert him. He seemed to know the precise time required for the turn to culminate in disaster, and in the meantime he utilized the false footing itself for the momentary earth-contact necessary to carry him on into safety. Where the earth sloped so steeply that it was impossible to stand for a second upright, the man did not hesitate. His foot pressed the impossible surface for but a fraction of the fatal second and gave him the bound that carried him onward. Again, where even the fraction of a second's footing was out of the question, he would swing his body past by a moment's hand-grip on a jutting knob of rock, a crevice, or a precariously rooted shrub. At last, with a wild leap and yell, he exchanged the face of the wall for an earthslide and finished the descent in the midst of several tons of sliding earth and gravel.

His first pan of the morning washed out over two dollars in coarse gold. It was from the centre of the "V." To either side the diminution in the values of the pans was swift. His lines of cross-cutting holes were growing very short. The converging sides of the inverted "V" were only a few yards apart. Their meeting-point was only a few yards above him. But the pay-streak was dipping deeper and deeper into the earth. By early afternoon he was sinking the test-holes five feet before the pans could show the gold-trace.

For that matter, the gold-trace had become something more

than a trace; it was a placer mine in itself, and the man resolved
to come back after he had found the pocket and work over the
ground. But the increasing richness of the pans began to worry
him. By late afternoon the worth of the pans had grown to three
and four dollars. The man scratched his head perplexedly and
looked a few feet up the hill at the manzanita bush that marked
approximately the apex of the "V." He nodded his head and said
oracularly:

"It's one o' two things, Bill: one o' two things. Either Mr.
Pocket's spilled himself all out an' down the hill, or else Mr.
Pocket's so rich you maybe won't be able to carry him all away
with you. And that 'd be an awful shame, wouldn't it, now?" He
chuckled at contemplation of so pleasant a dilemma.

Nightfall found him by the edge of the stream, his eyes wres-
tling with the gathering darkness over the washing of a five-dollar
pan.

"Wisht I had an electric light to go on working," he said.

He found sleep difficult that night. Many times he composed
himself and closed his eyes for slumber to overtake him; but his
blood pounded with too strong desire, and as many times his eyes
opened and he murmured wearily, "Wisht it was sun-up."

Sleep came to him in the end, but his eyes were open with the
first paling of the stars, and the gray of dawn caught him with
breakfast finished and climbing the hillside in the direction of the
secret abiding-place of Mr. Pocket.

The first cross-cut the man made, there was space for only three
holes, so narrow had become the pay-streak and so close was he
to the fountainhead of the golden stream he had been following
for four days.

"Be ca'm, Bill; be ca'm," he admonished himself, as he broke
ground for the final hole where the sides of the "V" had at last
come together in a point.

"I've got the almighty cinch on you, Mr. Pocket, an' you can't
lose me," he said many times as he sank the hole deeper and
deeper.

Four feet, five feet, six feet, he dug his way down into the earth.
The digging grew harder. His pick grated on broken rock. He examined the rock. "Rotten quartz," was his conclusion as, with the
shovel, he cleared the bottom of the hole of loose dirt. He at-
tacked the crumbling quartz with the pick, bursting the disinte-
grating rock asunder with every stroke.

He thrust his shovel into the loose mass. His eye caught a gleam of yellow. He dropped the shovel and squatted suddenly on his heels. As a farmer rubs the clinging earth from fresh-dug potatoes, so the man, a piece of rotten quartz held in both hands, rubbed the dirt away.

"Sufferin' Sardanopolis!" he cried. "Lumps an' chunks of it! Lumps an' chunks of it!"

It was only half rock he held in his hand. The other half was virgin gold. He dropped it into his pan and examined another piece. Little yellow was to be seen, but with his strong fingers he crumbled the rotten quartz away till both hands were filled with glowing yellow. He rubbed the dirt away from fragment after fragment, tossing them into the gold-pan. It was a treasure-hole. So much had the quartz rotted away that there was less of it than there was of gold. Now and again he found a piece to which no rock clung — a piece that was all gold. A chunk, where the pick had laid open the heart of the gold, glittered like a handful of yellow jewels, and he cocked his head at it and slowly turned it around and over to observe the rich play of the light upon it.

"Talk about yer Too Much Gold diggin's!" the man snorted contemptuously. "Why, this diggin' 'd make it look like thirty cents. This diggin' is All Gold. An' right here an' now I name this yere canyon 'All Gold Canyon,' b' gosh!"

Still squatting on his heels, he continued examining the fragments and tossing them into the pan. Suddenly there came to him a premonition of danger. It seemed a shadow had fallen upon him. But there was no shadow. His heart had given a great jump up into his throat and was choking him. Then his blood slowly chilled and he felt the sweat of his shirt cold against his flesh.

He did not spring up nor look around. He did not move. He was considering the nature of the premonition he had received, trying to locate the source of the mysterious force that had warned him, striving to sense the imperative presence of the unseen thing that threatened him. There is an aura of things hostile, made manifest by messengers too refined for the senses to know; and this aura he felt, but knew not how he felt it. His was the feeling as when a cloud passes over the sun. It seemed that between him and life had passed something dark and smothering and menacing; a gloom, as it were, that swallowed up life and made for death — his death.

Every force of his being impelled him to spring up and confront the unseen danger, but his soul dominated the panic, and he remained squatting on his heels, in his hands a chunk of gold. He did not dare to look around, but he knew by now that there was something behind him and above him. He made believe to be interested in the gold in his hand. He examined it critically, turned it over and over, and rubbed the dirt from it. And all the time he knew that something behind him was looking at the gold over his shoulder.

Still feigning interest in the chunk of gold in his hand, he listened intently and he heard the breathing of the thing behind him. His eyes searched the ground in front of him for a weapon, but they saw only the uprooted gold, worthless to him now in his extremity. There was his pick, a handy weapon on occasion; but this was not such an occasion. The man realized his predicament. He was in a narrow hole that was seven feet deep. His head did not come to the surface of the ground. He was in a trap.

He remained squatting on his heels. He was quite cool and collected; but his mind, considering every factor, showed him only his helplessness. He continued rubbing the dirt from the quartz fragments and throwing the gold into the pan. There was nothing else for him to do. Yet he knew that he would have to rise up, sooner or later, and face the danger that breathed at his back. The minutes passed, and with the passage of each minute he knew that by so much he was nearer the time when he must stand up, or else — and his wet shirt went cold against his flesh again at the thought — or else he might receive death as he stooped there over his treasure.

Still he squatted on his heels, rubbing dirt from gold and debating in just what manner he should rise up. He might rise up with a rush and claw his way out of the hole to meet whatever threatened on the even footing above ground. Or he might rise up slowly and carelessly, and feign casually to discover the thing that breathed at his back. His instinct and every fighting fibre of his body favored the mad, clawing rush to the surface. His intellect, and the craft thereof, favored the slow and cautious meeting with the thing that menaced and which he could not see. And while he debated, a loud, crashing noise burst on his ear. At the same instant he received a stunning blow on the left side of his back, and from the point of impact felt a rush of flame through his flesh. He sprang up in the air, but halfway to his feet collapsed. His body crumpled in like a leaf withered in sudden heat, and he came down, his chest across his pan of gold, his face in the dirt and rock, his legs tangled and twisted because of the restricted space at the bottom of the hole. His legs twitched convulsively several times. His body was shaken with a mighty ague. There was a slow expansion of the lungs, accompanied by a deep sigh. Then the air was slowly, very slowly, exhaled, and his body as slowly flattened itself down into inertness.

Above, revolver in hand, a man was peering down over the edge of the hole. He peered for a long time at the prone and motionless body beneath him. After a while the stranger sat down on the edge of the hole so that he could see into it, and rested the revolver on his knee. Reaching his hand into a pocket, he drew out a wisp of brown paper. Into this he dropped a few crumbs of tobacco. The combination became a cigarette, brown and squat, with the ends turned in. Not once did he take his eyes from the body at the bottom of the hole. He lighted the cigarette and drew its smoke into his lungs with a caressing intake of the breath. He smoked slowly. Once the cigarette went out and he relighted it. And all the while he studied the body beneath him.

In the end he tossed the cigarette stub away and rose to his feet. He moved to the edge of the hole. Spanning it, a hand resting on each edge, and with the revolver still in the right hand, he muscled his body down into the hole. While his feet were yet a yard from the bottom he released his hands and dropped down.

At the instant his feet struck bottom he saw the pocket-miner's arm leap out, and his own legs knew a swift, jerking grip that overthrew him. In the nature of the jump his revolver-hand was above his head. Swiftly as the grip had flashed about his legs, just as swiftly he brought the revolver down. He was still in the air, his fall in process of completion, when he pulled the trigger. The explosion was deafening in the confined space. The smoke filled the hole so that he could see nothing. He struck the bottom on his back, and like a cat's the pocket-miner's body was on top of him. Even as the miner's body passed on top, the stranger crooked in his right arm to fire; and even in that instant the miner, with a quick thrust of elbow, struck his wrist. The muzzle was thrown up and the bullet thudded into the dirt of the side of the hole.

The next instant the stranger felt the miner's hand grip his wrist. The struggle was now for the revolver. Each man strove to turn it against the other's body. The smoke in the hole was clearing. The stranger, lying on his back, was beginning to see dimly. But suddenly he was blinded by a handful of dirt deliberately flung into his eyes by his antagonist. In that moment of shock his grip on the revolver was broken. In the next moment he felt a smashing darkness descend upon his brain, and in the midst of the darkness even the darkness ceased.

But the pocket-miner fired again and again, until the revolver was empty. Then he tossed it from him and, breathing heavily, sat down on the dead man's legs.

The miner was sobbing and struggling for breath. "Measly skunk!" he panted; "a-campin' on my trail an' lettin' me do the work, an' then shootin' me in the back!"

He was half crying from anger and exhaustion. He peered at the face of the dead man. It was sprinkled with loose dirt and gravel, and it was difficult to distinguish the features.

"Never laid eyes on him before," the miner concluded his scrutiny. "Just a common an' ordinary thief, hang him! An' he shot me in the back! He shot me in the back!"

He opened his shirt and felt himself, front and back, on his left side.

"Went clean through, and no harm done!" he cried jubilantly. "I'll bet he aimed all right all right; but he drew the gun over when he pulled the trigger — the cur! But I fixed 'm! Oh, I fixed 'm!"

His fingers were investigating the bullet-hole in his side, and a shade of regret passed over his face. "It's goin' to be stiffer'n hell," he said. "An' it's up to me to get mended an' get out o' here."

He crawled out of the hole and went down the hill to his camp. Half an hour later he returned, leading his pack-horse. His open shirt disclosed the rude bandages with which he had dressed his wound. He was slow and awkward with his left-hand movements, but that did not prevent his using the arm.

The bight of the pack-rope under the dead man's shoulders enabled him to heave the body out of the hole. Then he set to work gathering up his gold. He worked steadily for several hours, pausing often to rest his stiffening shoulder and to exclaim:

"He shot me in the back, the measly skunk! He shot me in the back!"

When his treasure was quite cleaned up and wrapped securely into a number of blanket-covered parcels, he made an estimate of its value.

"Four hundred pounds, or I'm a Hottentot," he concluded. "Say two hundred in quartz an' dirt — that leaves two hundred pounds of gold. Bill! Wake up! Two hundred pounds of gold! Forty thousand dollars! An' it's yourn — all yourn!"

He scratched his head delightedly and his fingers blundered into an unfamiliar groove. They quested along it for several inches. It was a crease through his scalp where the second bullet had ploughed.

He walked angrily over to the dead man.

"You would, would you?" he bullied. "You would, eh? Well, I fixed you good an' plenty, an' I'll give you a decent burial, too. That's more'n you'd have done for me."

He dragged the body to the edge of the hole and toppled it in. It struck the bottom with a dull crash, on its side, the face twisted up to the light. The miner peered down at it.

"An' you shot me in the back!" he said accusingly.

With pick and shovel he filled the hole. Then he loaded the gold on his horse. It was too great a load for the animal, and when he had gained his camp he transferred part of it to his saddle-horse. Even so, he was compelled to abandon a portion of his outfit — pick and shovel and gold-pan, extra food and cooking utensils, and divers odds and ends.

The sun was at the zenith when the man forced the horses at the screen of vines and creepers. To climb the huge boulders the animals were compelled to uprear and struggle blindly through the tangled mass of vegetation. Once the saddle-horse fell heavily and the man removed the pack to get the animal on its feet. After it started on its way again the man thrust his head out from among the leaves and peered up at the hillside.

"The measly skunk!" he said, and disappeared.

There was a ripping and tearing of vines and boughs. The trees surged back and forth, marking the passage of the animals through the midst of them. There was a clashing of steel-shod hoofs on stone, and now and again a sharp cry of command. Then the voice of the man was raised in song: —

> "Tu'n around an' tu'n yo' face
> Untoe them sweet hills of grace
>   (D' pow'rs of sin yo' am scornin'!).
> Look about an' look aroun'
> Fling yo' sin-pack on d' groun'
>   (Yo' will meet wid d' Lord in d' mornin'!)."

The song grew faint and fainter, and through the silence crept back the spirit of the place. The stream once more drowsed and whispered; the hum of the mountain bees rose sleepily. Down through the perfume-weighted air fluttered the snowy fluffs of the cottonwoods. The butterflies drifted in and out among the trees, and over all blazed the quiet sunshine. Only remained the hoof-marks in the meadow and the torn hillside to mark the boisterous trail of the life that had broken the peace of the place and passed on.

The Last Thunder Song

JOHN G. NEIHARDT

*N*eihardt is well known to western readers for his long narrative poems: The Splendid Wayfaring, 1920; and The Song of Hugh Glass, 1919, Song of Three Friends, 1921, Song of the Indian Wars, 1925. His prose work, both before and after that poetic period, ought to be better known. This piece is from an early collection of Indian and trapper tales, The Lonesome Road, published in 1907. It is a tragic story of an old Indian — and a parable for all men whatever the color of their skins.

I<small>T IS AN ANCIENT CUSTOM</small> to paint tragedy in blood tints. This is because men were once merely animals, and have not as yet been able to live down their ancestry. Yet the stroke of a dagger is a caress beside the throb of hopeless days.

Life can ache; the living will tell you this. But the dead make no complaint.

There is no greater tragedy than the fall of a dream! Napoleon dreamed; so did a savage. It is the same. I know of the scene of a great tragedy. Very few have recognized it as such; there was so little noise along with it. It happened at the Omaha Agency, which is situated on the Missouri River some seventy miles above Omaha.

The summer of 1900 debilitated all thermal adjectives. It was
not hot; it was *Saharical!* It would hardly have been hyperbole
to have said that the Old Century lay dying of a fever. The un-
tilled hills of the reservation thrust themselves up in the August
sunshine like the emaciated joints of one bedridden. The land
lay as yellow as the skin of a fever patient, except in those rare
spots where the melancholy corn struggled heartlessly up a hillside, making a blotch like a bedsore!

The blood of the prairie was impoverished, and the sky would
give no drink with which to fill the dwindling veins. When one
wished to search the horizon for the cloud that was not there,
he did it from beneath an arched hand. The small whirlwinds
that awoke like sudden fits of madness in the sultry air, rearing
yellow columns of dust into the sky — these alone relieved the
monotony of dazzle.

Every evening the clouds rolled flashing about the horizon and
thundered back into the night. They were merely taunts, like the
holding of a cool cup just out of reach of a fevered mouth; and
the clear nights passed, bringing dewless dawns, until the ground
cracked like a parched lip!

The annual Indian powwow was to be ended prematurely that
year, for the sun beat uninvitingly upon the flat bottom where
the dances were held, and the Indians found much comfort in
the shade of their summer tepees. But when it was noised about
that, upon the next day, the old medicine-man Mahowari (Passing
Cloud) would dance potent dances and sing a thunder song with
which to awaken the lazy thunder spirits to their neglected duty
of rain-making, then the argument of the heat became feeble.

So the next morning, the bronze head of every Indian tepeehold
took his pony, his dogs, his squaw, and his papooses of indefinite
number to the powwow ground. In addition to these, the old men
carried with them long memories and an implicit faith. The
young men, who had been away to Indian school, and had succeeded to some extent in stuffing their brown skins with white
souls, carried with them curiosity and doubt, which, if properly
united, beget derision.

The old men went to a shrine; the young men went to a show.
When a shrine becomes a show, the World advances a step. And
that is the benevolence of Natural Law!

About the open space in which the dances were held, an oval
covering had been built with willow boughs, beneath which the

Indians lounged in sweating groups. Slowly about the various small circles went the cumbersome stone pipes.

To one listening, drowsed with the intense sunlight, the buzzle and mutter and snarl of the gossiping Omahas seemed the grotesque echoes from a vanished age. Between the dazzle of the sun and the sharply contrasting blue shade, there was but a line of division; yet a thousand years lay between one gazing into the sun and those dozing in the shadow. It was as if God had flung down a bit of the Young World's twilight into the midst of the Old World's noon. Here lounged the masterpiece of the toiling centuries — a Yankee. There sat the remnant of a race as primitive as Israel. Yet the white man looked on with the contempt of superiority.

Before ten o'clock everybody had arrived and his family with him. A little group, composed of the Indian Agent, the Agency Physician, the Mission Preacher, and a newspaper man, down from the city for reportorial purposes, waited and chatted, sitting upon a ragged patch of available shadow.

"These Omahas are an exceptional race," the preacher was saying in his ministerial tone of voice; "an exceptional race!"

The newspaperman mopped his face, lit a cigarette and nodded assent with a hidden meaning twinkling in his eye.

"Quite exceptional!" he said, tossing his head in the direction of an unusually corpulent bunch of steaming, sweating, bronze men and women. "God, like some lesser master-musicians, has not confined himself to grand opera, it seems!"

He took a long pull at his cigarette, and his next words came out in a cloud of smoke.

"This particular creation savours somewhat of opera bouffe!"

With severe unconcern the preacher mended the broken thread of his discourse. "Quite an exceptional race in many ways. The Omaha is quite as honest as the white man."

"That is a truism!" The pencil-pusher drove this observation between the minister's words like a wedge.

"In his natural state he was much more so," uninterruptedly continued the preacher; he was used to continuous discourse. "I have been told by many of the old men that in the olden times an Indian could leave his tepee for months at a time, and on his return would find his most valuable possessions untouched. I tell you, gentlemen, the Indian is like a prairie flower that has been transplanted from the blue sky and the summer sun and the pure winds into the steaming, artificial atmosphere of the hothouse! A glass roof is not the blue sky! Man's talent is not God's genius! That is why you are looking at a perverted growth.

"Look into an Indian's face and observe the ruins of what was once manly dignity, indomitable energy, masterful prowess! When I look upon one of these faces, I have the same thought as, when travelling in Europe, I looked upon the ruins of Rome.

"Everywhere broken arches, fallen columns, tumbled walls! Yet through these as through a mist one can discern the magnificence of the living city. So in looking upon one of these faces, which are merely ruins in another sense. They were once as noble, as beautiful as — "

In his momentary search for an eloquent simile, the minister paused.

"As pumpkin pies!" added the newspaper man with a chuckle; and he whipped out his notebook and pencil to jot down this brilliant thought, for he had conceived a very witty "story" which he would pound out for the Sunday edition.

"Well," said the Agency Physician, finally sucked into the whirlpool of discussion, "it seems to me that there is no room for crowding on either side. Indians are pretty much like white men; liver and kidneys and lungs, and that sort of thing; slight difference in the pigment under the skin. I've looked into the machinery of both species and find just as much room in one as the other for a soul!"

"And both will go upward," added the minister.

"Like different grades of tobacco," observed the Indian Agent, "the smoke of each goes up in the same way."

"Just so," said the reporter; "but let us cut out the metaphysics. I wonder when this magical *cuggie* is going to begin his humid evolutions. Lamentable, isn't it, that such institutions as rain prayers should exist on the very threshold of the Twentieth Century?"

"I think," returned the minister, "that the Twentieth Century has no intention of eliminating God! This medicine-man's prayer, in my belief, is as sacred as the prayer of any churchman. The difference between Wakunda and God is merely orthographical."

"But," insisted the cynical young man from the city, "I had not been taught to think of God as of one who forgets! Do you know what I would do if I had no confidence in the executive ability of my God?"

Taking the subsequent silence as a question, the young man answered: "Why, I would take a day off and whittle one out of wood!"

"A youth's way is the wind's way," quoted the preacher, with a paternal air.

"And the thoughts of youth are long, long thoughts; but what is all this noise about?" returned the reporter.

A buzz of expectant voices had grown at one end of the oval, and had spread contagiously throughout the elliptical strip of shade. For with slow, majestic steps the medicine-man, Mahowari, entered the enclosure and walked towards the centre. The fierce sun emphasized the brilliancy of the old man's garments and glittered upon the profusion of trinkets, the magic heirlooms of the medicine-man. It was not the robe nor the dazzling trinkets that caught the eye of one acquainted with Mahowari. It was the erectness of his figure, for he had been bowed with years, and many vertical suns had shone upon the old man's back since his face had been turned toward the ground. But now with firm step and form rigidly erect he walked.

Any sympathetic eye could easily read the thoughts that passed through the old man's being like an elixir infusing youth. Now in his feeble years would come his greatest triumph! Today he would sing with greater power than ever he had sung. Wakunda would hear the cry. The rains would come! Then the white men would be stricken with belief!

Already his heart sang before his lips. In spite of the hideous painting of his face, the light of triumph shone there like the reflection of a great fire.

Slowly he approached the circle of drummers who sat in the glaring centre of the ellipse of sunlight. It was all as though the First Century had awakened like a ghost and stood in the very doorway of the Twentieth!

When Mahowari had approached within a yard of the drums, he stopped, and raising his arms and his eyes to the cloudless sky, uttered a low cry like a wail of supplication. Then the drums began to throb with that barbaric music as old as the world; a sound like the pounding of a fever temple, with a recurring snarl like the warning of a rattlesnake.

Every sound of the rejoicing and suffering prairie echoes in the Indian's drum.

With a slow, majestic bending of the knees and an alternate

lifting of his feet, the medicine-man danced in a circle about the snarling drums. Then like a faint wail of winds toiling up a wooded bluff, his thunder song began.

The drone and whine of the mysterious, untranslatable words pierced the drowse of the day, lived for a moment with the echoes of the drums among the surrounding hills, and languished from a whisper into silence. At intervals the old man raised his face, radiant with fanatic ecstasy, to the meridian glare of the sun, and the song swelled to a supplicating shout.

Faster and faster the old man moved about the circle; louder and wilder grew the song. Those who watched from the shade were absorbed in an intense silence, which, with the drowse of the sultry day, made every sound a paradox! The old men forgot their pipes and sat motionless.

Suddenly, at one end of the covering, came the sound of laughter! At first an indefinite sound like the spirit of merriment entering a capricious dream of sacred things; then it grew and spread until it was no longer merriment, but a loud jeer of derision! It startled the old men from the intenseness of their watching. They looked up and were stricken with awe. The young men were jeering this, the holiest rite of their fathers!

Slower and slower the medicine-man danced; fainter and fainter grew the song and ceased abruptly. With one quick glance, Mahowari saw the shattering of his hopes. He glanced at the sky; but saw no swarm of black spirits to avenge such sacrilege. Only the blaze of the sun, the glitter of the arid zenith!

In that one moment, the temporary youth of the old man died out. His shoulders drooped to their wonted position. His limbs tottered. He was old again.

It was the Night stricken heart-sick with the laughter of the Dawn. It was the audacious Present jeering at the Past, tottering with years. At that moment, the impudent, cruel, brilliant youth called Civilisation snatched the halo from the grey hairs of patriarchal Ignorance. Light flouted the rags of Night. A clarion challenge shrilled across the years.

Never before in all the myriad moons had such a thing occurred. It was too great a cause to produce an effect of grief or anger. It stupefied. The old men and women sat motionless. They could not understand.

With uneven step and with eyes that saw nothing, Mahowari passed from among his kinsmen and tottered up the valley toward his lonesome shack and tepee upon the hillside. It was far past

noon when the last of the older Omahas left the scene of the
dance.

The greatest number of the white men who had witnessed the
last thunder dance of the Omahas went homeward much pleased.
The show had turned out quite funny indeed. "Ha, ha, ha! Did
you see how surprised the old *cuggie* looked? He, he, he!" Life,
being necessarily selfish, argues from its own standpoint.

But as the minister rode slowly toward his home there was no
laughter in his heart. He was saying to himself: "If the whole
fabric of my belief should suddenly be wrenched from me, what
then?" Even this question was born of selfishness, but it brought
pity.

In the cool of the evening the minister mounted his horse and
rode to the home of Mahowari, which was a shack in the winter
and a tepee in the summer. Dismounting, he threw the bridle
reins upon the ground and raised the door flap of the tepee.
Mahowari sat cross-legged upon the ground, staring steadily before
him with unseeing eyes.

"How!" said the minister.

The old Indian did not answer. There was no expression of
grief or anger or despair upon his face. He sat like a statue. Yet,
the irregularity of his breathing showed where the pain lay. An
Indian suffers in his breast. His face is a mask.

The minister sat down in front of the silent old man and, after
the immemorial manner of ministers, talked of a better world,
of a pitying Christ, and of God, the Great Father. For the first
time the Indian raised his face and spoke briefly in English:

"God? He dead, guess!"

Then he was silent again for some time.

Suddenly his eyes lit up with a light that was not the light of
age. The heart of his youth had awakened. The old memories
came back and he spoke fluently in his own tongue, which the
minister understood.

"These times are not like the old times. The young men have
caught some of the wisdom of the white man. Nothing is sure.
It is not good. I cannot understand. Everything is young and
new. All old things are dead. Many moons ago, the wisdom of
Mahowari was great. I can remember how my father said to me
one day when I was yet young and all things lay new before me:
'Let my son go to a high hill and dream a great dream'; and I went
up in the evening and cried out to Wakunda and I slept and
dreamed.

"I saw a great cloud sweeping up from under the horizon, and it was terrible with lightning and loud thunder. Then it passed over me and rumbled down the sky and disappeared. And when I awoke and told my people of my dream, they rejoiced and said: 'Great things are in store for this youth. We shall call him the Passing Cloud, and he shall be a thunder man, keen and quick of thought, with the keenness and quickness of the lightning; and his name shall be as thunder in the ears of men.' And I grew and believed in these sayings and I was strong. But now I can see the meaning of the dream — a great light and a great noise and a passing."

The old man sighed, and the light passed out of his eyes. Then he looked searchingly into the face of the minister and said, speaking in English:

"You white medicine-man. You pray?"

The minister nodded.

Mahowari turned his gaze to the ground and said wearily:

"White God dead too, guess."

A Sketch by MacNeil

FREDERIC REMINGTON

*R*emington the artist is even more famous now than he was in
his lifetime, which was considerable. Remington the writer has
in consequence been overshadowed. But it was Theodore Roosevelt, a fair contemporary judge, who once wrote him: "Aside
from what you do with your pencil, you come closer to the real
thing with the pen than any other man in the western business."
He published, among other things, two novels (one reached
Broadway as a play) and at least three volumes of tales that can
stand close to his paintings and sculpture: Pony Tracks, 1895, which
contains perhaps the only extant story about the First Cycle In-
fantry and which appeared recently (1951) in a handsome new
edition; Crooked Trails, 1898; and Men with the Bark On, 1900.
This short sample was originally published in Harper's Magazine
for May, 1899, and can be found in the last of those three collections. It sketches in prose an episode in the life of one of the
barked men who, according to the dedication, "die like the wild
animals, unnaturally — unmourned, and even unthought of
mostly."

*W*E HAD TO LAUGH. I chuckled all day, it was all so quaint.
But I don't see how I can tell you, because you don't know
MacNeil, which is necessary.

In a labored way, MacNeil is an old frontier scout with a well-frosted poll. He is what we all call a "good fellow," with plenty of story, laugh, and shrewd comment; but his sense of humor is so ridiculously healthy, so full-bloodedly crude, that many ceremonious minds would find themselves "off side" when Mac turns on his sense of jollity. He started years ago as a scout for Sheridan down Potomac way, and since then he has been in the Northwest doing similar duty against Indians, so a life spent in the camps and foot-hills has made no "scented darling" out of old man MacNeil. He is a thousand-time hero, but he does not in the least understand this. If he could think any one thought he was such a thing he would opine that such a one was a fool. He has acted all his life in great and stirring events as unconscious of his own force as the heat, the wind, or the turn of the tide. He is a pure old warrior, and nothing has come down the years to soften MacNeil. He is red-healthy in his sixties, and has never seen anything to make him afraid. The influence of even fear is good on men. It makes them reflective, and takes them out of the present. But even this refinement never came to Mac, and he needed it in the worst way.

So that is a bad sketch of MacNeil.

A little bunch of us sat around the hotel one day, and we were drawing Mac's covers of knowledge concerning Indians. As the conversation went on, Mac slapped his leg, and laughing, said, "The most comical thing I ever saw in my life!"

"What was that, Mac?" came a half-dozen voices, and Mac was convulsed with merriment.

"The last time the Piegans raided the Crows I was out with the First Cavalry. We were camped on the Yellowstone, and had gone to bed. I heard an Injun outside askin' about me, and pretty soon Plenty Coups comes in, sayin' the Piegans had got away with a good bunch of their ponies, but that they had found the trail crossing a little way down the river, and Big Horse and a war-band of Crows was layin' on it, and they wanted me to go 'long with them and help run it. I didn't have anything but a big government horse, and they ain't good company for Injun ponies when they are runnin' horse-thieves; besides, I didn't feel called to bust my horse helpin' Injuns out of trouble. There had got to be lots of white folks in the country, and they wa'n't at all stuck on havin' war-bands of Injuns pirootin' over the range. The Injuns wanted me to protect them from the cowboys, 'cause, you see, all Injuns look alike to a cowboy when they are runnin' over his cows. So Plenty Coups says he will give a pony, and I says, 'Mr. Injun, I will go you one.'

"I fixed up sort of warm, 'cause it was late in the fall, and threw my saddle on the pony, and joined the war-band. It was bright moon, and we ran the trail slowly until morning; and when it come day we moved along Injun fashion, which ain't slow, if you ask me about it. We kept a pushin' until late afternoon, when we saw the Piegans, about seven miles ahead, just streakin' it over the hills. My Injuns got off their ponies, and, Injun fashion, they stripped off every rag they had on except the G-string and moccasins. This is where them Injuns is light-minded, for no man has got any call to go flirtin' with Montana weather at that time of the year in his naked hide. Old man Mac stands pat with a full set of jeans. And then we got on them ponies and we ran them Piegans as hard as we could lather till plumb dark, when we had to quit because we couldn't see. We were in an open sage-brush country. Well, it got darker and darker, and then it began to rain. I sat on my saddle and put my saddle-blanket over my head, and I was pretty comfortable. Then it began to rain for fair. Them Injuns stamped and sung and near froze to death, and I under the blanket laughing at them. 'Long 'bout midnight it began to snow, and them Injuns turned on the steam. The way they sung and stomped round in a ring tickled me near to death. The snow settled round my blanket and kept out the cold in great shape. I only had my nose out, and when it began to get gray morning I had to just yell to see the Injuns out there in five inches of snow, without a rag on, hoppin' for all they was worth. You talk about shootin' up a fellow's toes to make him dance; it wa'n't a circumstance. Them Injuns had to dance or 'cash in.' I have seen plenty of Injun dances, but that dance had a swing to it that they don't get every time.

"We got on the ponies and started back through the falling snow, tryin' to locate them annuity goods of theirn. 'Course we lost the Piegans. We lost ourselves, and we didn't find them clothes till afternoon, 'most eighteen miles back, and then we had to dig them up, and they was as stiff as par-flèche. Them was a funny bunch of warriors, I tell you.

"We found an old big-jaw steer which some punchers had killed, and them Injuns eat that all right; but I wasn't hungry enough yet to eat big-jaw steer, so I pulled along down to the railroad. I got a piece of bread from a sheep-man, and when I got to Gray Cliffs, on the N.P., I was 'most frozen. My feet and knees were all swollen up.

"Whenever I gets to thinkin' 'bout them bucks jumpin' around out there in the snow all that night, and me a-settin' there under the blanket, I has to laugh. She was sure a funny old revel, boys."

And we listeners joined him, but we were laughing at MacNeil, not with him.

Beyond the Desert

EUGENE MANLOVE RHODES

*C*anvass the really ardent readers of westerns and about every one in three will turn out to be a passionate Rhodesian. The man's writing stimulates fanaticism, cultism. To the faithful, he could do no wrong. They cherish every word he wrote. They are ready to jump out fighting at the suggestion his short novel, Pasó Por Acquí, is not the finest western story ever written. Certainly he mastered his material as few others in the field, in any field, have done. The substance of his stories is authentic, as it should be since he lived much of it himself, and over this he cast a glow of creative imagination. The Rhodes country is lower Arizona and New Mexico. But it is not the real Arizona and New Mexico. It is the Rhodes country, a never-never land that begins with reality and is transformed and highlighted and made completely his own somewhat as Faulkner has done with that unpronounceable county in Mississippi. His individual books are hard to find — the cultists have grabbed all readily available — except some that have been reprinted in paperback editions, but a good starting collection appeared in 1949 with the title: The Best Novels and Stories of Eugene Manlove Rhodes. Probably no two Rhodesians would agree that those included are precisely "the best" — except, of course, for Pasó Por Acquí. But all his stories are superb reading. This one gives you MacGregor, Sandy MacGregor of Black Mountain, the sun-god hero with a difference, a man you will not easily forget.

CHAPTER I

Beyond the Desert

MacGregor was in haste. He pressed forward in a close, fine rain. A huge and graceless bulk of a man, he rode craftily, a brisk jog, a brisk walk; where the trail was steep, he slipped from the saddle and led the way to the next smooth bit.

Hard by the head of the pass, where the peaks of San Quentin — monstrous, exaggerated, fantastic — frowned through fog and mist, he paused on a jutting shoulder in a brief lull between showers. The night drew near. The fog lifted for a space as a gust of wind whipped between the hills: far behind and below there was a glimpse of toiling horsemen, a black wavering line where the trail clung to the hillside.

MacGregor lifted the heavy brows that pent his piggy little red eyes. His face was a large red face, heavy, square, coarse-featured, stubbly. It now expressed no emotion. Unhurriedly, he took up a long thirty-forty from the sling below the stirrup leather, raised the sights high, and dropped two bullets in the trail before the advancing party. They shrank back to a huddling clump. The mist shut down.

Under shelter of his long slicker, he wiped the rifle carefully and returned it to the scabbard. "Persons of no experience," he grumbled. "They ride with small caution for a country of boulders and such-like cover. If the half o' them had stayed behind at yonder well and the best few followed, each with a led horse, they might well ha' caught me oop ere I could win across yonder weary plain. No judgment at all!"

The critic clicked his teeth disparagingly as he remounted.

"'Tis plain I have naught to fear from these gentry for all the heavy weight this red horse of mine must carry. For they will think twice and again at each bend and rockfall. Aweell — I hae seen worse days. Thanks to this good rain, I needna fear the desert either for mysel' or the beastie. Hunger and great weariness, pain and jostling death, these I can make shift to bear — but against naked thirst no man can strive for long — But beyont the desert? Ay, there's the kittle bit. There's a telephone line awa' to the north, and if the good folk of Datil be at all of enterprising mind, 'tis like I shall hear tidings."

Dawn found him beyond the desert, breasting the long slow ridges beneath the wooded mountain of the Datils. The storm was passed away. Behind, the far peaks of San Quentin fluttered on the horizon, dream-pale; and then, in one swift moment, flamed at a touch of sudden sun, radiant and rejoicing, sharp against a clean-washed sky. The desert brimmed with a golden flood of light, a flood which rolled eastward across the level, to check and break and foam against the dense, cool shadow of the Datil Range. So dense and so black was the shadow that the rambling building of the C L A ranch scarce bulked blacker; hardly to be seen, save for a thin wisp of wood smoke that feathered in the windless air.

"Ay," said the horseman. "Now the pot boils. And indeed I am wondering if my name is in that pot. For here comes one at a hard gallop — wrangling horses, belike. And now he sees me and swerves this way. Truly, I am very desirous that this man may be Mundy himself. I would ever like best to deal with principals — and Mundy is reputed a man of parts. Be it Clay Mundy or another, yon bit wire has gien him word and warning to mark who comes this way. I must e'en call science to my own employ. Hullo, Central! . . . Hullo! Give me Spunk, please . . . Hullo, Spunk. MacGregor speaking. Spunk, I am now come to a verra strait place, and I would be extremely blithe to hae your company. For to deal plainly wi' you, my neck is set on the venture, no less . . . I am obligit to you. Ye hae aye been dependable. See if you canna bring Common-sense wi' you. Hullo, Central! Gimme Brains . . . What's that? No answer? Try again, Central! Central, gin ye please. The affair is verra urgent."

The oncoming rider slowed down: MacGregor turned to meet him, his two hands resting on the saddle horn.

" 'Tis Mundy's self, thanks be," he muttered. "Now, do you twa walk cannily, Spunk and Common-sense. Here is the narrow bit. Aha, Brains! Are ye there at the last of it? That's weel! I shall need you!"

He rode on at a walk. The riders drew abreast.

"Hands up, you!" Mundy's gun was drawn and leveled with incredible swiftness.

MacGregor's hands did not move from the saddle horn: he leaned on them easily. "And that is no just what ye might call a ceevil greeting, Mr. Mundy. Ye give me but a queer idea of your hospitality. Man, ye think puirly! Do ye see this rifle under my knee? Thirty-forty, smokeless — and had I meant ye ill, it was but stepping behind a bit bush to tumble you from the saddle or e'er ye clapped eyes on me."

"You have my name, I see," said Mundy. "And there is certainly some truth in your last saying. You might have taken a pot shot at me from ambush, easy enough. Guess you didn't know we were expecting you. Unless all signs fail, you are fresh from the loot of Luna. Now I've had about enough nonsense from you. Stick up those hands or I'll blow you into eternity."

"And that is a foolish obsairve," said MacGregor, composedly. " 'Into eternity!' says he! Man, I wonder at ye! We're in eternity just noo — every minute of it — as much as we e'er shall be. For the ambush, you do me great wrong. I was well knowing to yon mischief-making telephone — but I took my chance of finding you a man of sense. For my hands, they are very well where they are. You have me covered — what more would you wish? I have conscientious scruples aboot this hands-up business. It is undeegnified in the highest degree. Man, theenk ye I have nae self-luve at all! Hands up might be all verra weel for a slim young spark like you, wi' looks and grace to bear it off with. But me, wi' my years and the hulking carcass of me, in such a bairnly play — man, I should look just reedeeculous! The thing cannae be done."

"Very well. I am coming to get your gun. Keep your hands on the saddle horn. I have you covered, and if you crook a finger, I'll crook mine."

" 'Tis early yet in the day, Mr. Mundy." MacGregor held the same attitude and the same unmoved composure. "Dinna be hasty in closing in upon me. I was thinking to propose a compromise."

"A compromise? And me with finger on trigger — me that could hit you blindfolded?"

"Nae doot of it at all. I am well acquaint wi' you by repute. Ye have the name of a man of speerit and of one skilly wi' his gun and unco' swift to the back o' that. Myself, I am slow on the draw. 'Tis lamentable, but I must needs admit it. I am no what ye might ca' preceesly neemble of body or of mind — but, man! if I'm slow, I'm extraordinary eefeecient! If you crook that finger you are speaking of, I am thinking that the two of us may miss the breakfast cooking yonder. For myself, I am free to say I had liefer crook elbows wi' you over a thick beefsteak."

"Fool! I can shoot you three times before you get to your gun."

"Nae doot, nae doot," said MacGregor pacifically. "It has been done — yet here am I, little the waur o't. Mr. Mundy, I must deal plainly wi' you. Long ago, that place where your ranch is was pointit oot to me by yon square-capped peak behind for landmark — and I came here the noo rather than to any ither spot round about this wide circle of the plains of San Quentin, preceesly because ye are bespoken a man of parts and experience — and thereby the better able to judge weel and deal wisely with another man as good as yoursel'."

"Sure of that?"

"Positeeve. Now, understand me weel. I am laying no traps to tempt your eye to rove — so dinna look, but e'en take my word for it. But gin ye were free to look ye wad see, as I did just ere you came, some ten-twelve black specks coming this way ahindt me on the plain, a long hour back, or near two — and ye may draw your ain conclusions thereby. To speak the plain truth, I doot they mean me nae guid at a'."

"I should conclude that this was your unlucky day, Mr. Whatever-your-name-is. Quite aside from these gentlemen behind, or from myself — and you may possibly be underrating me — the whole country east of here is warned by telephone. Heavy, heavy hangs over your head!"

"I am a little struck wi' that circumstance myself," said MacGregor simply. "Ye see the seetuation wi' great clearness, Mr. Mundy. But I have seen worse days and have good hopes to come fairly off from this one yet. For if you can eenstruct me in what way I should be any worse off to be shot by you just now, than to be hanged in a tow from a pleasant juniper a little later, after tedious delays and parley-wows, I shall be the more obleegit. For then I can plainly see my way to give myself up to you. If you cannae do this, then I shall expect ye, as a reasoning man yourself, to note that ye can have naught to gain by changing shots wi' one who has naught to lose, and to conseeder the proposeetion I mak to you — as I should surely do and the cases were changed."

"You put it very attractively and I see your point," said Mundy. A slow smile lit up his face. He put his gun back in the scabbard. "Well, let's have it."

"And a verra guid choice, too. If it be not askin' too much, let us e'en be riding toward your ranch gate while ye hear my offer, for when the sun reaches here we should be seen — and yonder weary bodies gain on us while we stand here daffing."

They made a strange contrast: Mundy, smooth, slender and graceful, black of hair and eye, poised, lithe and tense, a man to turn and look after: MacGregor, stiff, unwieldy, awkward, gross, unkempt, battered, year-bitten.

"For the first of it, ye should know that not one of these gentry behind have seen my face, the which I kep' streectly covered durin' my brief stay in Luna. Second, though no great matter, ye may care to know that the bit stroke I pulled off in Luna was even less than justice. For within a year and a day a good friend of mine was there begowked and cozened by that same partnership — yes and that wi' treachery and broken trust to the back of it — of mair then I regained for him by plain and open force at noon-day. So much for that — though I do not hold you squeamish. Third, for your own self, it is far known that you and the Wyandotte Company and Steel-foot Morgan are not agreeing verra weel — "

"You never heard that I've taken any the worst of it, did you?"

"No, but that they keep you well occupied. Also, that hired warriors from the Tonto are to join wi' Webb of the Wyandotte. So hear me now. I need nae ask of ye if ye have ony but discreet persons aboot ye?"

Mundy laughed. "Boys are floating in the Malibu hills with a pack outfit. No one at the ranch today but Hurley, the water-mason. He's all right."

"Verra weel. Do you send him away betimes on that beastie atween your knees, and I will be water-mason to you — the mair that I can run your steam-pump as well as the best, though there will be small need of pumps till these rains be over. The story will be that the outlaw-body passed by night, unseen, liftin' your night-horse as he flitted, and leavin' this sorrel of mine. Your man Hurley can join your outfit and lose himself. That will be my gain, for I shall be blameless Maxwell, your water-mason — and who so eager to run down the rungate robber as he? And when they see how it is, that their man has got clean away, these men from Luna will know that the jig is definitely up and they will be all for the eating and sleeping."

"Very pretty, and it can be done — since they do not know you," agreed Mundy. "They will not be expecting their outlaw to call them in to breakfast, certainly. But I do not see where I am to gain anything."

"You are to hear, then," said the outlaw. "I will praise the

bridge that carries me over, but I will do more too: I will mend
that bridge. I will fight your battles with you against all comers.
Not murder, mind you, but plain warfare against men fit for war."

"A fighting man, and slow on the draw?"

"I am that same, both the one and the other. Slow, I cannot
deny it — slow, in compare with the best. But man, I'm experienced. I'm judgmatical, and I'm fine on the latter end. I'm a
good person to have at your right hand or your left. Some way,
I dinna prosper verra weel as chief man — but as the next best,
there is none better rides leather."

"You come well recommended."

"By myself, you are meaning? And just that you may know
the worth of that recommend, I am telling ye that my name is
no exactly Maxwell. You have had word of me, your ownself,
in El Paso, where indeed I saw your face, though you saw not
mine. And I would have ye to observe, Mr. Mundy, that I keepit
my name streectly to myself for such time as ye might have taken
the sound of it as a threat, and give it to you now only when
it comes mair as a promise. So now I offer to you the naked
choice, peace or war — and the last word is with you. A hundred
miles and twenty, at the least of it, I have now made in sax-and-
thirty hours — and blow high, blow low, I ride no step beyond
yonder gate."

"I am decidedly inclined toward peace," said Clay Mundy,
smiling again, "if only to hear you talk. For you talk convincingly.
My own risk in the matter — which you have been kind enough
not to mention — also moves me that way. And, after all, your
late exploit at Luna is nothing to me. But as to your value in
my little range war — you forgot to mention the name, you know."

"The name is MacGregor."

"Not Sandy MacGregor? Of Black Mountain?"

"That same. Plain shooting done neatly."

"You're on," said Clay Mundy.

So MacGregor became Maxwell, and Mundy's. The search
party came, and swore, and slept; for they were weary. None
mistrusted Maxwell, that kindly and capable cook, who sympa-
thized so feelingly with them concerning the upness of the jig.
In the seven-up tournament organized after that big sleep, Maxwell won the admiration of all and the money of most: and they
went home mingling praises of their new friend with execrations
of the escaped outlaw.

CHAPTER II

Pictured Rock

"AND THE HERDSMEN of Gerar did strive with Isaac's herdsmen, saying, The water is ours."

That was at the well Esek. The patriarchs were always quarreling with their neighbors or with each other over wells, pasturage and other things — mavericks, maybe. Abraham, Laban, Lot, Isaac, Jacob — they led a stirring life, following the best grass. You ought to read about them, sometime.

It is entirely probable that Terah went forth from Ur of the Chaldees either because the grass was short or because he had no friends on the grand jury.

Cattlemen have not changed much since then. They still swing a big loop: it is as risky as ever to let the stock out on shares: and we still have cattle wars wherever there is free range, because of the spirit so justly expressed by Farmer Jones: "He said he wasn't no land-hog — all he wants is just what joins his'n."

Human nature is the same on the plains of Mamre or of San Quentin: so there is no new thing to tell about the Mundy-Morgan war. Wrong and folly and stubbornness; small matter now whose first the blame; this might have been a page of history.

Strong warriors, able leaders, Ben "Steel-foot" Morgan, Webb of the Wyandotte outfit, and Clay Mundy; sharp and bitter hate was in their hearts, and the feud was more savage than the usual run of cattle wars: carried on (of course) upon a higher plane than any "civilized" warfare. For there were restrictions, there were limits. To rise up from a man's table and war upon that man while the taste of his bread was still sweet in your mouth — such dealing would have been unspeakable infamy in the San Quentin country.

Again, you might be unfriendly with a man and yet meet on neutral ground or when each was on his lawful occasions, without trouble. It was not the custom to war without fresh offense, openly given. You must not smile and shoot. You must not shoot an unarmed man, and you must not shoot an unwarned man. Here is a nice distinction, but a clear one: you might not ambush your enemy; but when you fled and your enemy followed, you might then waylay and surprise without question to your honor, for they were presumed to be on their guard and sufficiently warned. The rattlesnake's code, to warn before he strikes, no better: a queer, lop-sided, topsy-turvy, jumbled and senseless code — but a code for all that. And it is worthy of note that no better standard has ever been kept with such faith as this barbarous code of the fighting man.

Roundup season passed with no fresh outbreak of hostilities. After the steer-shipping, Mr. Maxwell had been given a mount, a rope and a branding iron, and so turned loose to learn the range. This was equivalent to letters of Marque and Reprisal.

Mr. Maxwell was camped at Whitewater, alone. So far, he had passed a pleasant day. He had killed a fat buck at daybreak, when he wrangled horses. Later, he had ridden leisurely in nooks and corners, branding two of his employer's calves, overlooked by the roundup, two of the Y calves, and one long-eared yearling — a pleasant total of five for the C L A tally-book. So far his services had been confined to such peaceful activities as these: the war had languished since the rains set in. It was late October now, and the rains were still falling. The desert was glorified with the magic of belated spring.

All day it had been cloudy. While Mr. Maxwell was branding his maverick it began to sprinkle; when he turned it loose the sprinkle had become rain, the clouds were banked dark and sullen against the mountains. He wriggled into his slicker and started for camp, but the rain turned to a blinding storm and he was glad to turn his back to its fury and ride his straightest for the next shelter.

Pictured Rock is an overhanging cliff of limestone, sheltered from three winds. Gray walls and creamy roof are close covered with the weird picture writing of Apache and Navajo, a record of the wars and journeys of generations.

As he turned the bend in the canon, Maxwell saw a great light glowing under Pictured Rock, now veiled by the driving sheets of rain, now beating out in gusts across the murky dark, reflected and magnified by the cliff behind. Another, storm driven like himself, was before him. He paused at the hill-foot and shouted:

"Hullo, the house! Will your dog bite?"

"Hi!" It was a startled voice: a slender figure in a yellow slicker appeared beside the fire. "Dog's dead, poor fellow — starved to death! Come on up!"

The C L A man rode up the short zigzag of the trail to the firelit level. He took but one glance and swept off his hat, for the face he saw beneath the turned-up sombrero was the bright and sparkling face of a girl.

"You will be Miss Bennie May Morgan? I saw you in Magdalena at the steer-shipping."

"Quite right. And you are Mr. Sandy Maxwell, the new warrior for Clay Mundy."

"Faces like ours are not easily forgot," said Maxwell.

Miss Bennie laughed. Her eyes crinkled when she laughed. "I will give you a safe-conduct. Get down — unless you are afraid of hurting your reputation, that is." She sat upon her saddle blankets where they were spread before the fire, and leaned back against the saddle.

The C L A man climbed heavily down and strode to the fire, where he stood dripping and silent. The grinding of boulders in the flooded canon rose louder and louder, swelled to a steady ominous roar by the multitudinous echoes of the hills.

"Well! How about that lunch?" demanded Miss Bennie sharply. "It's past noon."

"Sorry, Miss Morgan, but I have not so much as a crumb. And that is a bad thing, for you are far from home, and who knows when this weary storm will be by? But doubtless they will be abroad to seek for you."

Miss Bennie laid aside her hat and shook her curly head decidedly. "Not for me. Dad thinks I'm visiting Effie at the X L and Effie thinks I'm home by this time. But this storm won't last. The sun will be out by three. You'll see! And now, if you please, since you can't feed me, hadn't you better entertain me? Sit down, do!"

"It is like that I should prove entertaining for a young maid, too!" said Maxwell, carrying a flat stone to the fire to serve for a seat.

"Oh, you never can tell! Suppose, for a starter, you tell me what you are thinking so busily."

"I am thinking," said Maxwell, slowly, "that you are a bonnie lass and a merry one. And I was thinking one more thing, too. The X L is awa' to the southeast and the Morgan home ranch as far to the southwest. Now what may Miss Bennie Morgan need of so much northing, ten long miles aside from the straight way, and her friend Effie thinking she was safe home and all? And then I thought to myself, the folk at San Quentin are very quiet now. It is to be thought that the season of great plenty has put them

in better spunk with the world. And it is an ill thing that a
way cannae be found to make an end of this brawling for good
and all. And, thinks I, the bonny Earl of Murray himself was
not more goodly to the eye than Clay Mundy — and it is a great
peety for all concerned that Clay Mundy is not storm-bound
this day at Picture Rock, rather than I!"

"Well!" Miss Bennie gasped and laughed frankly, blushed red,
neck and cheek. "Oh, you men! And while you were making
this up — "

"It is what I thought," said Maxwell stoutly. "Only I was nae
thinking words, d'ye see? I was just thinking thoughts. And it
is no verra easy to put thoughts into words."

"Well, then — while you were thinking all those preposterous
thoughts, I was seeing a wonderful picture, very much like this
storm, and this cave, and this fire, and us. If I were a painter,
this is what I would try to paint: a hill-side like this — so you
might feel what you could not see, the black night and the wild
storm. The black night, and a red fire glowing in a cave-mouth,
and a wind-bent tree close beside: and by the fire a man straining
into the night at some unseen danger; a cave-man, clad in skins,
with long matted hair, broad-shouldered, long-armed, ferocious,
brutal — but unafraid. He is half-crouching, his knees bent to
spring: he is peering under his hand: the other hand clutches a
knotted club: a dog strains beside his foot, snarling against the
night, teeth bared, glaring, stiff legs braced back, neck bristling:
behind them, half-hidden, shrinking in the shadow — a woman
and a child. And the name of that picture would be 'Home!' "

Maxwell's heavy face lit up, his dull and little eyes gleamed
with an answering spark, his sluggish blood thrilled at the spirit
and beauty of her: his voice rang with a heat of frank admiration.
"And that is a brave thought you have conjured up, too, and I
will be warrant you would be unco' fine woman to a cave-man —
though I'm judgin' you would be having a bit club of your own."
He paused, fixed her with a meditative eye, and spoke again in a
lighter tone. "I recognize myself, and the dog is dead, puir fellow
— starved to death, you said. But I would have you observe that
the thoughts of the two of us differed but verra little when all
is said — forbye it ran in my mind that a much younger person
was to be cave-man to you. And you gave me safe-conduct, too!
Are you to be man-sworn, then, and me trusting to you?"

"Now you are trying to torment me," said Miss Bennie briskly.

"I can't have that, you know. Better give it up. Roll a smoke. I know you want to. The storm is slackening already — we will be going soon."

"A pipe, since you are so kind," said Maxwell, fumbling for it.

"Do you admire your friend Clay Mundy so much?" said Miss Bennie next, elbows on knees, chin in hands.

Maxwell rolled a slow eye on her, and blew out a cloud of smoke. "My employer. I did not say friend, though if I like him no worse it may come to that yet. He has the devil's own beauty — which thing calls the louder to me, misshapen as you see me. He is a gallant horseman, fame cries him brave and proven. But I am not calling him friend yet till I know the heart of him. Fifty-and-five I am, and I can count on the fingers of my twa hands, the names of those I have been willing to call wholly friends — forbye one of those few was my enemy to my overthrow. So you will not be taking Clay Mundy to your cave upon my say-so till I am better acquaint wi' him. But dootless you know him verra well yourself."

Miss Bennie evaded this issue. She became suddenly gloomy. "It is plain that you are a stranger here, since you talk so glibly of any lasting peace in the San Quentin. A wicked, stiff-necked unreasoning pack, they are — dad and all! There has never been anything but wrong and hate here, outrage and revenge, and there never will be. It is enough to make one believe in the truth of original sin and total depravity!"

"No truth at all!" cried Maxwell warmly. "Oreeginal sin is just merely a fact — no truth at a'! Folks are aye graspin' at some puir halflin fact and settin' it up to be the truth. It takes at least three trees to make a row, and it needs at least three facts to make a truth. Mankind is blind, foolish and desperately wicked — yes, take it from me that am an old ruffian. But mankind is also eencurably good — wise and strong and splendid and kindly and brave — in your time of sorrow and danger you will find it so — and there's another glaring fact for you! Wi' endless rain earth would drown, wi' endless sun it would be a cinder: look about you now, see what sun and rain and evil and good have wrought together, grass and flower and bud and fruit, the bonny world and the bonny race o' men! World and man, the machine Works! And there's the third fact for you, lassie, and the weightiest fact. We are a Going Concern: we pay a profit to our Owner! And for the truth behind these three facts, may not this be it: That if we are at once evil and good, it is the good God who made us that way, not in sloth, but because He wanted us to be that way? It is so I think. But it is a strange thing to me that I am most roundly abused for disrespect to the Maker whene'er I dare venture the mild guess that perhaps He knew what He was about!"

"A very fine sermon, reverend sir, though I did not get the text," said Miss Bennie, twinking. "And now if you will give me your benediction, I will be on my way soon. The storm is breaking. It will clear as suddenly as it came on."

Maxwell shook out the saddle blankets and saddled her horse. "For the text it is this: 'And God saw everything that He had made and behold it was very good.' — And I am an old fool as well as an old ruffian," he grumbled, "for I have wearied you."

"Oh, no, you haven't. Your theology took my breath away, rather — that's all. It was so very unexpected."

"Of course, I will be seeing that you get safe home — "

"You mustn't. It would only make you a hard ride for nothing. No need of it at all. There is time for me to get home while the sun is still an hour high."

"It doesn't seem right," protested Maxwell.

"Really, I'd rather you wouldn't," said Miss Bennie earnestly. "I don't want to be rude, but I am still — " She gave him her eyes and blushed to her hair — "am still . . . north of where I should be, as you so shrewdly observed. And your camp lies farther yet to the north."

"Good-bye, then, Miss Morgan."

"Good-bye, Mr. MacGregor."

He stared after her as she rode clattering down the steep. "MacGregor!" he repeated. "MacGregor, says she! And never a soul of the San Quentin kens aught of the late MacGregor save Clay Mundy's own self! Here is news! Is she so unco' chief wi' him as that, then? And who told her whaur my camp was; she was glib to say that she had time enow to go home or sundown — but she was careful she didna say she was gaun there! Little lady, it is in my mind that you are owre far north!"

She waved her hand gaily; her fresh young voice floated back to him, lingering, soft and slow:

> He was a braw gallant,
> And he rid at the ring;
> And the bonny Earl of Murray
> Oh! He might have been a king.

He was a braw gallant,
  And he played at the glove;
And the bonny Earl of Murray
  Oh! He was the Queen's love!

Oh! Lang may his lady
  Luke owre the castle down,
Ere she see the Earl of Murray
  Come sounding thro' the town.

The girl passed from sight down the narrow canon. MacGregor-Maxwell gave his head a shaking then, to clear his thoughts, and put foot to stirrup. When he came to the beaten trail again, where the horse's feet pattered rhythmically on the firm ground, MacGregor half sang, half crooned, a plaintive and wandering air:

Then I pray you do not trust the hawk again,
  The cruel hawk that mocks thy love, like me.
Oh, alone, betrayed and sad although I leave thee,
  Yet the wandering traitor weeps, poor love, for thee —
            Ay! Paloma azul!

"The de'il and his horns! Now why do I sing such an ill-omened and unchancy song as that?" He shook his great shoulders, as if to shake off a weight: he held his cupped hand to his mouth. "Hullo, Central! Can you get Brains for me? . . . Try again, please . . . Now, Brains, you are partly acquaint wi' this day's doings. But did you mark the bonny blush of her at the name of Clay Mundy — and her so far from the plain way, wi' no cause given? . . . Ye didna? . . . Brains, you're but a cauld, feckless, dusty-dry thing, when all's said. Well then, I am telling you of it. And what am I to do in such case as that? . . . A little louder, please! . . . Oh! I am to see where Clay Mundy rides this day, if it is any affair of mine — is that it? . . . Surely it is my business. Any man is natural protector to any woman against any man except himself . . . And if he means her naething but good? . . . It is what I will know. And then I will be best man — and to be best man at this employ should be no empty form. For indeed I think the Morgans are like to be little pleased.

"Aweel, Brains, I will e'en do your bidding, and I will seek proof where Clay Mundy fares this day — though I tell you plainly that I know very well now. And I scorn for a slow-speerit-less, doddering sluggard — you and your proofs! You can but look through a hole in a stone wall, at the most of it. What are walls

for but to leap over — can you tell me that? Show me once a braw
lass and a high hard wall and a lad beyond, and I will show you
a place where there shall be a fine climbing done — the more
when the young folk are so bold and bonny as the twa of them
yonder towards the sunset . . . What's that? How do I know? . . .
Brains, I wonder at ye, I fairly peety you — and that's the truth
of it. Where else should he be?"

Chapter III

Good-Bye

I thought it was you," said Miss Bennie May Morgan. "So I
waited for you. Aren't you rather out of your own range, Mr.
Maxwell? The Morgans'll get you if you don't watch out!"

With elaborate surprise, MacGregor took his bearings from the
distant circling hills. "Why so I am! I was on my way to Datil,"
he explained. "I see now" — he jerked a thumb back over his
shoulder — "that I should have ridden east-like this morning instead of west."

"It is shorter that way — and dryer," she agreed. "This road
to Datil is very damp after you pass California."

"Shall I ride with you a bit on your way?" said MacGregor. "I
can still get back to my camp before sundown. Mind you, I am
not saying at all that I shall go to my camp by that hour, but
only that there is time enough."

Then Miss Bennie Morgan knew where she stood. She flicked
at her stirrup with a meditative quirt. "Why, I said something
about like that to you last week at Pictured Rock, didn't I?"

"Very much like that."

"When you got lost today," said Miss Bennie thoughtfully, "I
suppose you were composing a sermon?"

"Why, no, I wasnae. It was like this. Clay Mundy set off for
Datil early this morning, you see, whilst I staid in camp, shoeing
horses. He was riding his Jugador horse — fine I ken the crooked
foot of him. And when later in the day I came upon the track of
that twisted hoof, I found suddenly a great desire to go after
him to Datil, where I have never yet been. And I said to myself,
'Plainly if you follow this track you will come to that place.' And
so you see me here."

"And now that you're here, Mr. — ?"

"Maxwell — not MacGregor," said MacGregor.

"Thank you; Maxwell. Not MacGregor. I must remember that." She turned clear, unflinching eyes upon him. "Well, let's have it!"

"Er — why — eh!" said MacGregor, and swallowed hard. "I don't quite understand you."

"Oh, yes you do!" said Miss Bennie cheerfully. "Don't squirm. What's on your mind?"

"It is now on my mind that it would be none such a bad scheme for me to turn tail bravely and run awa' from this place," said MacGregor, truthfully; quite taken aback at this brisk and matter-of-fact directness.

In her innermost heart Miss Bennie knew certainly — without reason, as women know these things — that this grim old man-at-arms liked her very well, and came as a friend.

"Blackmail? Oh no — that is not your line. And I do not take you for a tell-tale, either." She looked him over slowly and attentively; a cruel, contemplative glance. It brought a dull glow to MacGregor's leathern face, even before she spoke. "I see!" She dropped the reins and clapped her hands together. "You were planning to take Clay Mundy's place with me — is that it?"

MacGregor plucked up spirit at the taunt. "And that was an unkind speech of you, Miss Morgan."

Her eyes danced at him. "There is but one thing left, then. You have come to plead with me for your friend — your employer — to ask me to spare his youth and innocence — to demand of me, as the phrase goes, if my intentions are honorable. Is that it?"

"It is something verra like that, then, if I must brave your displeasure so far as to say it. And it is my poor opinion that so much was verra needful — though it was in my mind to give you but the bare hint that your secret was stumbled upon. For what one has chanced upon this day another may chance tomorrow. And there was something else besides, which I find ill to put to words to."

The girl dropped all pretense. "I think you meant kindly to me, Mr. MacGregor, and I thank you for it. And you must consider that our case is hard indeed. For where can we meet, if not secretly? Fifty miles each way, every ranch is lined up on one side or the other of this feud. One word to my father's ear will mean bloodshed and death — and then, whoever wins, Bennie Morgan must lose."

"Yet you must meet?" said MacGregor.

She met his eyes bravely. "Yet we must meet!" She said it proudly.

"You two should wed out of hand then, and put the round world between you and this place," said MacGregor.

Miss Bennie sighed. "That is what I tell Clay. It is the only way. Soon or late, if we live here, those two would clash, my father and my husband. If we go away, father may get over it in time. Clay does not want to go. He cannot bear to have it said that he had to run away from San Quentin. But I will never marry him till he is ready to go."

"He is a fool for his pains, and I will be the one who will tell him that same!" declared MacGregor, stoutly. "Him and his pride! He should be proud to run further and faster than ever man rode before on such an argument."

"No — you mustn't say one word to him about me — please! He would be furious — and he is a dangerous man!"

"I thank ye kindly for this unexpected care of my safety," said MacGregor humbly.

"Oh these men! Must you hear that you are so dangerous, too? There would be trouble, and you know it. Clay's as cross as a bear with a sore head, now — so I think he is coming to my way of thinking, and doesn't like to own up. Don't you say anything to him. I'll tell him — not that you have seen me, but that we might easily be seen — and that our meetings must be few and far between. That will help to make up his mind, too, if he feels — " She checked herself, with a startled shyness in her sudden drooping lids: she was only a young girl, for all her frank and boyish courage. "I will warn him, then. And yet I think there is no man who would not think twice before he whispered evil of Ben Morgan's daughter and" — she held her head proud, she lifted her brave eyes — "and Clay Mundy's sweetheart!"

MacGregor checked his horse, his poor, dull face for once lit up and uplifted: whatever had been best of him in all his wasted and misspent life stirred at the call of her gallant girlhood.

"I think there will be no man so vile as to think an evil thing of you," he said. "Miss Morgan, I was a puir meddlin' fool to come here on such an errand — and yet I am glad that I came, too. And now I shall go back and trouble you nae mair. Yet there is one thing, too, before I turn back — and I think you will not laugh."

She faced him where he stood: so that he carried with him a memory of her dazzling youth against a dazzle of sun. "I shall not laugh."

"It is better than fifty years, they tell me, since last the San Quentin knew any such rains as these," said MacGregor slowly. "This place has the ill name of a desert. Yet all this day the air has been heavy with sweetness; all day long I have ridden stirrup-deep in strange bright flowers — and no man knows the name of them! Fifty years they have slept in the blistered brown earth, the seeds of these nameless flowers, waiting for this year of many rains. Lassie, there are only too many men, like me, of deserved and earned ill name, as of waste places where no good thing can flourish. And when you think of us, I would have you remember how this bright, belated spring-tide came to San Quentin. I would have you think there may be hidden seeds of good in us yet — if only the rains might come! And if ever you have any need of me — as is most unlike — I shall be leal friend to you, I shall stick at nothing in your service. It is so that I would have you think of old MacGregor. Good-bye!"

"I shall not forget," said Bennie. "But you said there was something else — something hard to put into words?"

MacGregor took off his hat. "I think there will be no need to say that — to you," he said.

Once more her eyes searched him and this time he did not flinch — so high he held her now in his thought. She read his answering look. "Yes — since this is the day for plain-speaking, let me say it for you. You mean . . . that it is not only whispering tongues I have to fear, or my father's anger — no, nor black death itself — but that I must fear myself most of all? But, Mr. Mac-Gregor — there was need to say that indeed! And now you are my friend, for I have trusted you very greatly."

"Good-bye, then!" said MacGregor again. He bent over her hand.

"Good-bye!"

CHAPTER IV

Skullspring

MacGregor worked out the Whitewater country and moved his camp to Bear Springs, on the southern frontier of the Mundy range. From here he rode the cedar brakes on the high flanks of the mountain, branding late calves. This work was most effectively done at early daybreak and at sundown, when the wild cattle ventured from the thickets into the open glades and valleys.

For a week, Milt Craig had ridden with him. But Milt had made his pack yesterday and moved on to the Cienaga, where Mac-Gregor was to join him later, once he had picked up the few calves that still went unbranded in the Bear Spring country. So today MacGregor rode alone.

Ever drifting from one bunch of cattle to another and then on to another clump of red and white on the next hill-side, as the day wore on he found himself well across in the Wyandotte-Morgan country; prowling in the tangle of hills, south of the Magdalena road, which was the accepted dividing line.

As the sun rode on to afternoon, the prowler turned back, and made his way to Skullspring, with a thought of the trickle of water that dripped from the high cliffs there; and as he came down a ridge of backbone from the upper bench, he saw a little curl of smoke rising above the Skullspring bluff.

MacGregor remarked upon this fact to Neighbor his horse. "We are in a hostile country, Neighbor," said he. "For all we are so quiet and peaceful these days, it will be the part of prudence to have a look into this matter, least we go blundering in where we arenae much wanted." He tied Neighbor in a little hollow of the hill, and went down with infinite precaution to the edge of the cliff above Skullspring.

Three men were by the fire below — all strangers to MacGregor. That gentleman lay flat on the rock, peering through a bush, and looked them over. Clearly, they had only stopped at Skullspring for nooning. Two were cowboys: their saddled horses stood by. The younger of these two stowed a little grub-sack under the seat of a light buggy that stood by the fire. The third person, a tall man of about thirty, had the look of a town-man. He wore a black suit and a "hard-boiled" hat.

"I tell you," said the older cowboy, a sullen-faced young man. "I'll be good and glad a-plenty when this thing is over with. It's a shaky business."

"Don't get cold feet, Joe," advised the tall man. "You're getting big money, mighty big money, for a small risk."

"I notice there's none of these San Quentin *hombres* caring for any of it," grumbled Joe, sulkily.

"Aw, now, be reasonable," said the tall man. "He wouldn't risk letting any of the home people know. Too shaky. You get the chance just because you're a stranger. And because you're a stranger, you can get away without being noticed."

Plainly, here was mischief afoot. It seemed likely to MacGregor that Clay Mundy was to be the object of it.

The younger man of the party spoke up. "I'm not only goin' to get away, but I'm goin' to keep on gettin' away. I'm after that dough all right, all right — but lemme tell you, Mr. Hamerick, this country'll be too hot for me when it's over."

MacGregor barely breathed. It appeared that the tall man was Hamerick, for he answered. "I'm going away myself. But this is too good a chance for easy money, and we don't want to make a hash of it. Keep your nerve. Your part is easy. You take the first right-hand trail and drift south across that saddle-back pass yonder, so you'll get there before I do. You'll find the Bent ranch right under the pass. Nobody there. The Bents have all gone to Magdalena for supplies. Mrs. Bent is going to Socorro and Bent'll wait for her. You're to make yourselves at home, so there won't be anything suspicious — new men working there; sorry the Bents are gone, and all that." He kicked out the dying fire.

"And if anyone comes, then what?" Joe glowered at him with the question.

"Then you're strangers, passing by. It isn't at all likely that anyone'll come. The nearest ranch is twenty-five miles. But if anyone should come, it's all off, for today. We want to have the longest start we can get. And for Mundy, he has his own reasons. You'll ride out to good grass and make camp. If we see your fire, Mundy and me'll turn back. We'll pull it off tomorrow."

Mundy! MacGregor's heart leaped. Were the men to entice Mundy to the Bent ranch and murder him there, while he was off his guard, thinking himself among friends? MacGregor drew his gun, minded to fall upon the plotters without more ado: the vantage of ground more than made up for the odds of numbers. But he put back his gun. They were to separate. He would follow the man Hamerick and deal with him alone.

"I am to meet Mundy at that little sugar-loaf hill yonder, four or five miles out on the plain," said Hamerick. "I'll be late, too — jawing with you fellows this way. Then I'll go on down the wagon road to Bent's with him. The play is that I'm supposed to think the Bent folks are at home. You boys'll have plenty of time to get settled down."

"If we don't run into a wasp's nest," said Joe sulkily.

Hamerick scowled. "I'm the one that's taking the biggest risk, with this damned buggy — but I've got to have it, to play the part. I'll leave it, once I get safe back to my saddle."

"We three want to ride in three different directions," said Joe. "I wish it was over."

Hamerick gave him a sinister look. "You get no money till I get a-straddle of a horse again — I'll tell you that right now, my laddie-buck! This buggy's too easy to track up, if anything goes wrong. You'd like it first-rate to ride off scot-free and leave me to hold the sack."

"I won't, eh!" Joe took a step forward, his ugly face blotched with crimson. "Damn you, I've took just about enough from you!"

Here the younger man interposed. "Oh, you both make me sick!" His voice was cutting and cold, venomous in its unforced evenness. "I guess I'll do a little telling now, myself. If you fellows get to fighting, I'll do my best to kill both of you. Got that?"

MacGregor almost hugged himself with delight. Oh, if they once get to shooting — if they only would! he thought. It would be a strange thing if between the four of us we should not do a good day's work of it!

"Now, now, Tait — "

"Don't Tait me!" said Tait, in the same deadly level. "This is a wise bunch for a ticklish job, ain't it? I know that no one but a dirty skunk would be found in such dirty work — but is that any reason why we should be fools, too? Hamerick's right, Joe. We'll string along with him till he gets to a saddle — and then may the devil take the hindmost! Maybe we'll find a saddle at the Bent ranch. If we do, all the better. The sooner I see the last of you two, the better pleased I'll be. For you, Hamerick — you're engineerin' this thing, but when it comes down to brass tacks, I'm the best man, and don't you forget it. So if you've been plannin' any nice little plans to hold out part of the price on me and Joe, you can throw 'em over for excess baggage, right here. For I'm to put it up to the paymaster, right to your face — you won't have no chance to fool us. Now don't up any more head to me! You'll stick to me against Joe till you're horseback again, with a fair chance for a getaway; Joe'll stick to me till we get a fair divvy on the money — and if either of you don't like it, you can double up on me whenever you feel lucky. I'm ready for you both any turn in the road."

The challenge went unmet. It was plain that Tait was to be master. MacGregor waited for no more. He rolled back from the bare rim with scarce more noise than a shadow would have made. He crawled to the nearest huddle of rocks and hid away. For a little, the muffled murmur of angry voices floated to him; then came the sound of wheels and a ringing of shod feet on rock; Tait and Joe toiled up the trail beyond the cliff-end, paced slowly by, black against the sky line, and dipped down into a dark hollow that twisted away towards Bent's Pass.

The tingling echoes died; and then MacGregor climbed back to Neighbor. The game was in his hands. Keeping to the ridge, he would gain a long mile on the wagon road, deep in the winding pass. He was in high feather as he followed the plunging slope; he laughed as he rode; his eyes drank in the brightness of the day. This would be a rare jest to tell at campfires!

"Now I wonder who can be at the bottom of this bonny scheme?" he chuckled. "It doesnae sound much like the San Quentin folk, who, if reports be true, are accustomed to do their own murders. And, if the man Hamerick tells the whole story, what then? That will be for Mundy to say. Any rate, 'tis a fine thing for Clay Mundy that my dry throttle drove me to Skullspring just at that time."

When he came into the wagon road the buggy was just before him, close to the mouth of the pass. MacGregor struck into a gallop.

The stranger had been going at a brisk gait, but at sight of the horseman he slowed to a prim and mincing little trot.

"A fine day, sir," said MacGregor civilly, as he rode alongside.

"It certainly is," said the stranger. He was plainly ill at ease at this ill-timed meeting, but tried to carry it off. "How far is it to Old Fort Tularosa, can you tell me?"

MacGregor squinted across the plain. "A matter of forty miles, I should say. Goin' across?"

The stranger shook his head. "Not today. I think I will camp here for the night and have a look in the hills for a deer. You're not going to the Fort yourself, are you?"

MacGregor grinned cheerfully. Knowing what he did, he knew that this was Hamerick's device to try to shake off his unwelcome company. "Well, no; not today. The fact is, sir" — he bent over close and sunk his voice to a confidential whisper — "the fact is, if you're for camping here the night, I must even camp here, too."

"What!"

"Just that. And first of all, do you remark this little gun which

I hold here in my hand? Then I will ask you to stop and to get out upon this side, holding to your lines verra carefully lest the beastie should run away, while I search you for any bit weapons of your ain. For you spoke very glibly of hunting a deer — and yet I do not see any rifle."

Hamerick groaned as he climbed out; he had not thought of that. "I haven't any rifle. My revolver is under the cushion — but of course you can search me, if you think I've got another. What the devil do you want anyway? If it's money you're after, you'll get most mighty little."

"All in good time, all in good time," said MacGregor cheerfully. He went through Hamerick for arms; finding none, he went through the buggy, finding the gun under the cushion. He inspected this carefully, tried it, and stuck it in his waistband.

"Will you kindly go aside some few steps, sir?" said MacGregor politely. "I am dry, and I would have a good swig of water from your canteen, but I didnac wish to set myself in that defenseless posture of holding a canteen to my throat whilst ye were still armed."

"You see I have no money, you have my gun, you have your drink — what more do you want of me?" spluttered Hamerick. "Let me go! I have an appointment — I'll be late now."

"With that deer, ye are meaning?" MacGregor sat cross-legged on the ground and whittled off a pipeful of tobacco with loving care. He puffed a while in great satisfaction, watching his fuming captive with twinkling eyes. "Do you know, sir," he said at last, between whiffs, "that in my puir opeenion, if you knew how you are like to keep that appointment of yours, you would be little made up with it?"

Hamcrick stammered. He had no idea of what his captor was driving at, but he had his own reasons for great uneasiness. He pulled himself together with an effort. "I — I don't know what you mean. I see now that you are not a robber, as I first thought. You are mistaking me for some other man. You can't be doing yourself any possible good by keeping me here. I tell you I am waited for."

"Take my word for it, sir — if you knew my way of it, you would be less impatient for that tryst of yours."

"What — what the devil do you mean?"

"I will tell you then, Mr. Hamerick." At this unexpected sound of his own name, Hamerick started visibly. "If Clay Mundy is at all of my mind, this is what we shall do: We will set you on Clay Mundy's horse and put Clay Mundy's hat upon your head; and we two will get in your bit wagon and drive you before our guns — just at dusk, d'ye mind? — to the Bent ranch; and there, if I do not miss my guess, you will be shot to death by hands of your own hiring!"

Here MacGregor, gloating on that pleasant inward vision, was extremely disconcerted by the behavior of his prospective victim. So far from being appalled, Hamerick was black with rage; he stamped, he shook his fist, he struggled for speech in a choking fury.

"You fool! You poor spy! Idiot! Bungler! Why couldn't you tell me you were Mundy's man?"

"Steady, there! Are you meaning to face it out that you did not plan to murder Clay Mundy! Because we are going on now to see him."

Hamerick gathered up the reins eagerly. "Come on, then, damn you — before it's too late!" There was relief and triumph in his voice — and at the sound of it MacGregor sickened with a guess at the whole dreadful business; the bright day faded. "Me, kill Clay Mundy? Why, you poor, pitiful bungler, Clay Mundy brought me here to play preacher for him!"

MacGregor drew back. His face flamed; his eyes were terrible. He jerked out Hamerick's gun and threw it at Hamerick's feet. There was a dreadful break in his voice. "Protect yourself!" he said.

But Hamerick shrank back, white-lipped, cringing. "I won't! I won't touch it!"

"Cur!"

"Oh, don't kill me, don't murder me!" Hamerick was wringing his hands; he was almost screaming.

MacGregor turned shamed eyes away. He took up Hamerick's gun. "Strip the harness from that horse then, take the bridle and ride! And be quick, lest I think better of it. Go back the way you came, and keep on going! For I shall tell your name and errand, and there is no man of Morgan's men but will kill you at kirk or gallows-foot."

He watched in silence as Hamerick fled. Then he rode down the pass, sick-hearted, brooding, grieving. He came to the mouth of the pass: at the plain's edge he saw a horseman, near by, coming swiftly. It was Clay Mundy.

CHAPTER V

No Dwelling More on Sea or Shore

MACGREGOR slowed up. The flush of burning wrath had died away; his face was set to a heavy, impassive mask. He thrust Hamerick's gun between his left knee and the stirrup-leather and gripped it there. He rode on to meet Clay Mundy — and the nameless flowers of San Quentin were stirrup-high about him as he rode.

He drew rein so Mundy should come to his right side; and again, as at their first meeting, he laid both hands on the saddle horn as he halted.

Clay Mundy's face was dark with suspicion.

"Have you seen a fool in a buggy?" he demanded.

"I see a fool on a horse!" responded MacGregor calmly. "For the person you seek, I have put such a word in his ear that he will never stop this side of tidewater. What devil's work is this, Clay Mundy?"

"You damned meddler! Are you coward as well as meddler, that you dare not move your hands?"

"Put up your foolish gun, man — you cannae fricht me with it. The thing is done and shooting will never undo it. There will be no mock-marriage this day, nor any day — and now shoot, if you will, and damned to you! Man! Have ye gone clean daft? Or did ye wish to proclaim it that ye were no match for the Morgans in war? And did ye think to live the week out? That had been a chance had you married her indeed, with bell and book — as whaur could ye find better mate? But after such black treachery as ye meant — Man, ye are not in your right mind, the devil is at your ear!"

"It is hard to kill a man who will not defend himself," said Mundy thickly. "I spared your life once because you amused me —"

"And because it was a verra judeecious thing, too — and you are well knowing to that same. Think ye I value my life owre high, or that I fear ye at all, that I come seeking you? Take shame to yourself, man! Have a better thought of it yet! Say you will marry the lass before my eyes, and I will go with you on that errand; or turn you back and I will go with her back to the house of the Morgans — and for her sake, I will keep your shame to mysel'. Or, if it likes you better, you may even fall to the shooting."

"Fool!" said Mundy. "I can kill you before you can touch your gun."

"It is what I doubt," said MacGregor. "Please yourself. For me there is but the clean stab of death — but you must leave behind the name of a false traitor to be a hissing and a byword in the mouths of men."

"I will say this much, that I was wrong to call you coward," said Mundy, in a changed voice. "You are a bold and stubborn man, and I think there is a chance that you might get your gun — yes, and shoot straight, too. I will not marry the girl — but neither will I harm her. But I will not be driven further. I am not willing to skulk away while you tell her your way of the story. That would be too sorry a part. I will go on alone, and tell her, and send her home."

"You will say your man fled before the Morgans, or was taken by them, or some such lies, and lure her on to her ruin," said MacGregor. "I will not turn back."

"I will give you the minute to turn back," said Mundy.

"It is what I will never do!"

"Then you will die here," said Mundy.

"Think of me as one dead an hour gone," said MacGregor steadily. "My life is long since forfeit to every law of God or man. I am beyond the question. Think rather of yourself. You have the plain choice before you — a bonny wife to cherish, and bairns to your knee — life and love, peace and just dealing and quiet days — or at the other hand but dusty death and black shame to the back of that!"

As a snake strikes, Mundy's hand shot out: he jerked MacGregor's gun from the scabbard and threw it behind him. His face lit up with ferocious joy.

"You prating old windbag! How about it now? I'll be driven by no man on earth, much less by a wordy old bluffer like you."

"You used other speech but now. Ye are false in war as in love. But I carenae for hard words, so you deal justly with the lassie. Wed her with me to witness, or let her go free."

"Talk to the wind!" said Mundy.

"For the last time, Mundy, give it up! In the name of God!"

"Get off that horse and drag it! I give you your life — you're not worth my killing. Never be seen on the San Quentin again!"

"Mundy—"

"Get off, I say!" Mundy spurred close, his cocked gun swung shoulder high.

"Aweel," said MacGregor. He began to slide off slowly, his right hand on the saddle horn; his left hand went to the gun at his left knee; he thrust it up under Neighbor's neck and fired once, twice — again! Crash of flames, roaring of gun shots: he was on his back, Neighbor's feet were in his ribs; he fired once more, blindly, from under the trampling feet.

Breathless, crushed, he struggled to his knees, the blood pumping from two bullet-holes in his great body. A yard away, Clay Mundy lay on his face, crumpled and still, clutching a smoking gun.

"I didnae touch his face," said MacGregor. He threw both guns behind him; he turned Mundy over and opened his shirt. One wound was in his breast, close beside his heart; another was through the heart. MacGregor looked down upon him.

"The puir, mad, misguided lad!" he said between pain-wrung lips. "Surely he was gone horn-mad with hate and wrong and revenge."

He covered the dead man's face, and straightened the stiffening arms, and sat beside him: he looked at the low sun, the splendor of the western range; he held his hand to his own breast to stay the pulsing blood.

"And the puir lassie — she will hear this shameful tale of him! Had I looked forward and killed yonder knave Hamerick, she had blamed none but me. 'Twas ill done . . . Ay, but she's young still. She will have a cave and a fire of her own yet."

There was a silence and a little space, and his hand slipped. Then he opened his dulling eyes:

"Hullo, Central! . . . Give me Body, please . . . Hullo, Body! Hullo! That you, Body? . . . MacGregor's Soul, speaking. I am going away. Good luck to you — good-bye! . . . I don't know where."

Early Marriage

CONRAD RICHTER

This story shows Conrad Richter at the start of a career during which he has gone on to write firm, memorable novels of various American frontiers. It is from Early Americana and Other Stories, 1937, all of which show his ability to present simple, straightforward happenings in a simple, almost plain style, unvarnished and unglamorized, with a cumulative power that brings conviction that this is the way things were, these are the things that happened, in the West of the western story.

FOR TWO DAYS the leathery face of Asa Putman had been a document in cipher to anyone who could read the code. Since Saturday but one traveler had passed his solitary post, a speck of adobe and picket corrals lost on the vast, sandy stretch of the Santa Ana plain. Far as the eye could see from his doorway, the rutted El Paso trail, unfenced, gutterless, innocent of grading, gravels, culverts, or telephone poles, imprinted only by iron tires, the hoofs of horses and oxen, sheep and cattle, and the paw of the loping lobo wolf, lay with dust unraised.

Ordinarily, there were freighters with cracking whips and

trailers rumbling on behind. Army trains to and from the forts set up their tents for the night beyond the springs. The private coaches of Santa Fe and Colorado merchants, of cattle kings and Government officials, stopped long enough for the Putman children to admire the ladies, the magnificent woodwork, and the luxurious cushions inside. Trail herds of gaunt red steers bawled for the water in the earthen tank, and pairs and companies of horsemen rode up and down.

But since Saturday not even a solitary buckboard from the far settlements in the Cedar country had called for supplies or letters. Only a girl from the Blue Mesa had ridden in for her and her neighbors' mail. She had eaten dinner with the Putmans, refused to stay overnight and started her long ride home.

A stranger from the East would have spoken about the stillness, the deadly waiting, and asked uneasily why Uncle Gideon hadn't come as promised. But in the Putman household it was not mentioned.

Asa deliberately busied himself about the post, filling the bin beneath the counter with navy beans and green coffee, leafing through the packet of letters in the drawer, and making a long rite out of feeding the occupants of the picket corrals — four horses of which were fresh for the next stage.

Rife, just turned fifteen, carried water and gathered cow chips in an old hide dragged by a rope to his saddle horn. Ignacita, the Mexican housekeeper, spat sharply on her heavy irons in the torrid kitchen and kept glancing over her shoulder and out of the open door and windows.

And Nancy Belle, going on seventeen, packed and repacked the high, iron-bound trunk that her father had bought for her at Santa Fe and sang softly to herself in the way that women sang fifty and sixty years ago.

Saturday she was being married at Gunstock, two hundred miles away — five days' journey in a wagon, four in a saddle or buckboard.

For six months she had thought of little else. The almanac fell apart at June as naturally as her mother's Bible did at the Twenty-third Psalm. So often had she run her finger down the page that anyone might tell from the worn line of type the very day she and Stephen Dewee would be man and wife. The Dewees lived four hundred miles west across the territory in the Beaverhead country. She and Stephen were taking a mountain ranch near his people, and for the wedding they had compromised on Gunstock, nearly equidistant from both families and convenient to friends scattered up and down the Rio Grande.

She had lighted a candle in the dusk, when a figure appeared reluctantly in her doorway. Asa Putman had never been at ease in his daughter's bedroom. A tall, rawhide man in an unbuttoned, sagging vest, he was visibly embarrassed by any furnishings that suggested refinement. Invariably he kept his hat on in the house. He had it on now, a flat top and a flat brim, not so much like the Western hats you see now. Nancy Belle knew that her mother's people had never forgiven him for bringing his young wife and their two small children to this lonely post, at the mercy of outlaws and the worse Apaches.

Tonight she could see that something bothered him. He gave her a sidewise glance, so sharp and characteristic.

"I don't expect, Nancy Belle, you could put off your weddin'?"

The girl stood quietly gazing at him with a face like the tintype of her mother. But under her sedate gray dress, with tight waist and full skirts to the instep, she had frozen. She looked much older than her years. Her air of gentlefolk and her wide-apart gray eyes came from her mother. But the chin, tipped up with resolute fearlessness, was her father's.

"No, papa!" Her two clear words held all the steady insistence of the desert.

"I figured how you'd feel," he nodded, avoiding her eyes. "I just wanted to put it up to you. I'd 'a' covered the *jornada* on foot to be on time at my own weddin', but I didn't have to count on Gideon to hold me up."

"Are you telling me, papa, that you can't go to Gunstock tomorrow?" Her voice remained quiet, but a coldness had seized her. Of all the people she had visualized at her wedding, the one next to Stephen she could least spare was the tall, grave figure of her father.

"I reckon I kind of ain't, Nancy Belle," he said soberly. "Rife could tend to the stage all right and do the feedin'. But they's men come to this post no boy can handle." He shifted his position. "I figured once on closin' up the post till I got back. But the stage is comin' and the mail. And the freighters count on me for feed and grub. Then I got to protect my own property and the mail and freight for the Cedar country that's in the storage room."

"I know," Nancy Belle said steadily. "I can get to Gunstock all right."

Far back in her father's assaying eyes, she fancied she saw a glint of pride.

"You're pretty nigh a woman now, Nancy Belle. And Rife's a good slice of a man. It's a straight trail to the Rio Grande, once you turn at the old post. Both you and Rife's been over it before. Of course, I'd like to be at the weddin', but the boy can tell me about it." He went to the window. "Rife!" he called.

Nancy Belle's brother came in presently. A slight boy, with his father's blue eyes, he seldom made a fuss over anything, even when he shot a stray duck on the tank or when they braked down the last cedar hill into Santa Fe with all the open doors of the plaza shops in sight. And when his father told him now, he showed neither enthusiasm nor regret — merely straightened.

"Sure. I can take you, Nancy Belle," he said.

Something pulled under his sister's tight basque. She remembered the long miles they would have in the wagon, the camps at lonely places, the ugly shadow ever hovering over the outposts of this frontier country, and the blight that, since Saturday, seemed to have fallen on the trail. Her eyes swam. Now, at the last minute, she yielded.

"If you'll let me ride, papa, I'll wait another day for Uncle Gideon," she promised.

Her father's eyes moved to the ruffled red calico curtains at the shadeless windows.

"I don't hardly count on Gideon comin' any more, Nancy Belle. Besides, it's too long in the saddle to Gunstock — especially for a girl to get married. You'd be plumb wore out, and you wouldn't have your trunk. You couldn't get dressed for your weddin'."

He turned thoughtfully and went out, Rife close behind. Nancy Belle could hear her father's tones, slow and grave, coming from near one of the picket corrals.

It was too far to catch the words; but when they came in, she saw that her brother's features looked a little pale under the tan.

"You better get some sleep, Nancy Belle," her father said. "You and Rife are startin' before daylight. If Gideon comes, I'll ride after."

They had scarcely gone from the room when Ignacita came in from the kitchen, her black eyes glittering over a pile of freshly starched white in her arms.

"Nancy Belle, *chinita!*" she whispered, plucking at the girl's sleeve. "You don't say to your *papacito* I talk to you! I have promise I don't scare you. But I can't see you go far in the wild-

ness alone, *pobrecita!* Sometimes people go safe from one place
to the other, oh, sí! But sometimes, *chinita*, they don't come back.
You have not the oldness like Ignacita. Ay, I tell you these old
eyes have seen men and women quartered from a tree like sheep
or maybe tied over a stove like I don't have the words to say to
you."

Nancy Belle did not answer except to lay, one by one, the ironed
pieces in her trunk — a bride's muslin underwear trimmed with
red and blue feather stitching; long petticoats stiffly flounced with
ruffles, and nightgowns long in the sleeve and high in the neck,
with ruffles at wrist and throat. The Mexican woman went on
hoarsely. The girl folded away her winter's cashmere dress, buttoned up the front and with a white fichu. She unwrapped and
wrapped again in crumpled white tissue the red slippers the
old gentleman on the stage had sent her as a wedding present from
Philadelphia.

When Ignacita had left, she opened her keepsake box covered
with colored shells. The mirror on the inside lid turned back a
face as calm as the little golden clouds that hung of an evening
over the east to catch the desert sunset. But after she had undressed and put on her nightdress, for a long time she was aware
of the soft pound of her heart faintly swaying the bed on its rawhide springs.

At the first sound of Ignacita's hand on the kitchen stove, Nancy
Belle sprang out of bed. She dressed on the brown pool of burro
skin, the only carpet on her adobe floor. Through the west window she could see the morning star burning like a brilliant candle.
It hung, she told herself, over Gunstock and the Beaverhead, where
Stephen, at this moment, in their new log ranch house, lay thinking about her.

They ate in the kitchen by lamplight. She had never been so
conscious of every detail — the great white cups and saucers, the
familiar steel knives, the homey smell of the scorched paper lamp-
shade, the unreadable eyes of her father, Rife, and Ignacita.

Asa Putman himself carried out the trunk. There was already
hay in the wagon, a gunny sack of oats, food in a canned-tomato
box and utensils in another, a water-keg, bed roll tied in a wagon
sheet, an ax, a bridle, and her own side-saddle, made to order over
a man's tree. Her eyes caught the gleam of a rifle leaning up against
the seat in the lantern-light. Tethered to the rear of the wagon
stood her saddle mare, Fancy, with pricked-up ears. She was going

along to their new ranch home. Nancy Belle felt that she was still among intimate things, but outside the little circle of light lay darkness and the unknown.

When she said good-by to her father, he kissed her — something he had not done for years.

"You haven't changed your mind, Nancy Belle?" he asked.

She climbed quickly up over the wheel to the spring seat of the wagon before he might see that she was crying. Rife swung up like a monkey on the other side and pushed the rifle into the crevice behind the seat cushion. The lines tautened and the wagon lurched.

"Dios go with you safe to your husband, Nancy Belle!" she heard Ignacita cry after her.

The morning star had set. They moved into a world of silent blackness. Nancy Belle could not see how the horses remained on the trail. When she looked back, the only light in all these square miles of black, unfriendly earth was the yellow window of her father's post.

It was almost a vision, golden and far away, like all beautiful things. She didn't trust herself to look again.

Two hours later the wagon was a lonely speck of boat rocking in an illimitable sage-green sea beneath the sun. The canvas wagon sheet fastened over the bows was a kind of sail, and eastward the sandy water did not stop rolling till it washed up at the foot of the faintly blue ramparts of the distant Espiritu Range.

Just before they turned west on the cross trail to the Rio Grande, a heavy wagon with a yoke of oxen in front and a cow behind toiled round the crumbling adobe walls of the old, abandoned post house. A bearded man and a thin woman with a white face sat on the seat. She held a baby in her arms, and three black-eyed children peered from under the wagon sheet.

The bearded man saluted and stopped his willing team. Rife did likewise. The woman spoke first. Her tongue was swift and slightly acid.

"You better turn around and follow us if you want to save your hair!" she called. "Yesterday a sheep-herder told us he saw — "

A sharp word from the bearded man caused her to relapse into sullen silence. He asked Rife where he might be going, then climbed down to the trail and said he wanted to talk to him a little. The boy followed reluctantly behind his wagon. Nancy Belle could hear the bearded man's tones coming slow and grave like her father's, while the woman made silent and horribly expressive lip language.

Rife came back, walking stiffly. The bearded man climbed up beside the woman.

"They got to go on," he told her in a low voice, then saluted with his whip. "Good luck, boy! And you, miss!"

Rife raised his whip in stiff acknowledgment. The wagons creaked apart. Nancy Belle saw in front of her the trail to the Rio Grande, little more than a pair of wheel tracks, that lost itself on the lonely plain. Rife seemed relieved that she did not ask what the bearded man had said. But it was enough for her not to be able to forget the woman's fearful signs and mouthings and the horror in the curious eyes of the staring children.

Sister and brother talked very little. Nancy Belle saw her brother's eyes keep sweeping the country, scanning the horizons. Bunches of bear grass that might have been feathers pinioned his blue gaze, and clumps of can cactus that seemed to hold pointing gun barrels. At arroyos thick with chamiso and Apache plume she could see his feet tighten on the footboard. Once he pulled out the rifle, but it was only a herd of antelopes moving across the desert page.

They camped for the night when the sun was still high. Nancy Belle asked no questions as the boy drove far off the trail into a grassy cañada. She sang softly to herself as she fried the salt side bacon and put the black coffee-pot to boil.

Rife hobbled Anton Chico and the Bar X horse and staked out Fancy close to the wagon.

She pretended not to notice when, before dark, he poured earth on the fire till not a spark or wisp of smoke remained. Out of one eye she watched him climb the side of the cañada and stand long minutes sweeping the country from the ridge, a slight, tense figure against the sullen glow of the sunset.

"It's all right," he said when he came down. "You can go to bed."

"What's all right?" she asked him.

"The horses," he said, turning away, and Nancy Belle felt a stab of pain that so soon this boy must bear a man's responsibilities and tell a man's lies.

She prayed silently on her blankets spread on the hay in the wagon box, and lay down with her head on the side-saddle, her unread Testament in her hand. She heard Rife unroll his camp bed on the ground beneath the wagon. It was all very strange and hushed without her father. Just to feel the Testament in her hand helped to calm her and to remember the day at the post when she had first met Stephen.

Her father had never let her come in contact with the men of the trail. Always, at the first sign of dust cloud on the horizon, he would tell both children to heap up the chip-box, fill the water-buckets and carry saddles and bridles into the house. But this day Asa Putman and Rife had gone to Fort Sumner. And to Nancy Belle, Uncle Gideon could seldom say no.

It had been a very hot day. She had been sitting in the shade of the earthen bank of the tank, moving her bare feet in the cool water, watching the ripples in the hot south wind. The leaves of the cottonwoods clashed overhead, and she heard nothing until she looked up, and there was a young man on a blue-gray horse with dust clinging to his hat brim and mustache. His eyes were direct as an eagle's. Firm lines modeled his lean face. But what she noticed most at the time was the little bow tie on his dark shirt.

Instantly she had tucked her bare, wet legs under her red dress. Her face burned with shame, but the young stranger talked to her about her father coolly, as if she, a girl of fifteen, had not been caught barefooted. Then he did what in her mind was a noble thing. When Uncle Gideon came out, he magnificently turned his back for her to run into the house and pull on shoes and stockings.

She thought of Stephen constantly next day and the next. She had grown a little used to the journey without her father now — the still, uncertain nights under the wagon sheet, sitting, lying, listening, waiting; the less uncertain days with the sun on the endless spaces; her never-quiet perch on the high spring seat under the slanted bow; the bumps, creaks, and lumberings of the wagon; the sand sifting softly over the red, turning wheels; all afternoon the sun in their faces; ahead the far haze and heat waves in which were still lost Gunstock and the Rio Grande. Almost she had forgotten the bearded man with the oxen and the curious, detached horror in the eyes of his children.

Since morning of the third day their progress had been slower. The trail seemed level, except for the heavy breathing of the horses. But when Nancy Belle glanced back she could see the steady grade they had been climbing. Abruptly, in mid-afternoon, she found that the long, blue Espiritu Range had disappeared, vanished behind a high pine-clad hill which was its southernmost beginning. It was like the lizard that swallowed itself, a very real lizard. At this moment they were climbing over the lizard's tail.

"Cedars!" Rife said briefly, pointing with the whip to dark sprawling growths ahead.

"You breathe deep up here!" Nancy Belle drank in the light air.

Rife took a sniff, but his blue eyes never ceased to scan the high, black-thatched hill under whose frowning cliff they must pass.

"Soon we can see the Gunstock Mountains," Nancy Belle said.

"And Martin Cross's cabin," Rife nodded. "It's the last water to the Rio Grande."

"He's a nice old man," Nancy Belle ventured casually. "It would be nice to camp by his cabin tonight and talk."

The boy inclined his head. After a few moments he started to whistle softly. At the first cedar Nancy Belle leaped off the moving wagon and climbed back with an evergreen branch. The twig, crushed in her hand, smelled like some store in Santa Fe.

They gained the summit. A breeze was sweeping here from the southwest, and the horses freshened. But Rife had suddenly stopped whistling and Nancy Belle's sprig of cedar lay on her lap. The frowning cliff of the pine-clad hill was still there. But Martin Cross's cabin had turned to a desolate mound of ashes. As they stared, a gust of wind sent wisps of smoke scurrying from the mound, and a red eye opened to watch them from the embers. Nancy Belle felt an uncontrollable twitching in the hair roots at the base of her scalp.

Where Martin Cross's eastbound wheel tracks met the trail, Rife reluctantly halted the horses and wet his air-dried lips.

"The water keg's dry, and the horses. If papa was here, he'd drive over."

"I'm the oldest." Nancy Belle found her voice steady. "I'll ride over. There might be something we can do."

The boy rose quickly. His eyes seemed to remember something his father had said.

"You can drive the wagon over if I wave."

He had thrown her the lines and slipped back through the canvas-covered tunnel of wagon box, picking up Fancy's bridle and the rifle. Barebacked he rode toward the smoldering ashes at the foot of that frowning hill. The chestnut mare's tail and mane streamed like something gold in the wind.

When she looked back to the trail, her eyes were pinioned by a light object in the wheel track ahead of the Bar X horse. It was a long gray feather. Instantly she told herself that it had come from some wild turkey Martin Cross had shot, and yet never had air anywhere become so suddenly horrible and choking as in this canyon.

Rife did not signal her to drive over. She saw him come riding back at full speed. The mare was snorting. As he stopped her at the wagon, her chestnut head kept turning back toward what had once been a cabin. Rife slipped the lead rope about her neck and climbed into the seat with the rifle in his hands.

"The water — you wouldn't want it!" he said thickly. His cheeks, she noticed, were the color of yeso.

"Rife" — Nancy Belle touched his arm when she had driven down the canyon — "what did you see at the cabin?"

The boy sat deaf and rigid beside her, eyes staring straight ahead. She saw that his young hands were still tortured around the barrel of his rifle.

Far down on the pitch-dark mesa she stopped the horses in the trail and listened. There were no stars, not a sound but the flapping of the wagon sheet in the wind and the clank of coffee-pot and water-bucket under the wagon. Half standing on the footboard, she guided the team off the trail in the intense blackness. Her swift hands helped the trembling boy stake out the mare and hobble the team. They did not light a lantern. Rife declined to eat. Nancy Belle chewed a few dry mouthfuls.

The wind came drawing out of the blackness with a great draft. It hissed through the grass, sucked and tore at the wagon sheet, and whistled through the spokes and brake rigging. Rife did not take his bed roll under the wagon tonight. He drew the ends of the wagon sheet together and lay down in the wagon box near his sister. For a long time they were silent. When she heard his heavy breathing, she lifted the rifle from his chest.

The storm grew. Sand began pelting against the canvas and sifted into the wagon box. An invisible cloud of choking dust found its way into eyes, mouth, ears, and lungs. Nancy Belle laid down the rifle a moment to pull a blanket over the face of the boy. He tossed and muttered pitifully, but he slept on.

Magically the rain, when it came, stopped the sand and dust.

The girl drank in the clean-washed air. At daylight she slipped out to the ground. The mesa, stretching away in the early light, touched here and there with feathers of mist, would have been beautiful except for a sharp new loneliness. The horses were gone!

At her exclamation, Rife appeared from the wagon box. His shame at having slept through the night was quickly overshadowed by their misfortune.

Together they found where Fancy's stake had been pulled out and dragged. Yards farther on they could tell by Anton Chico's tracks that his hobbles had parted.

Nancy Belle made her brother come back to the wagon and stuff his pockets with cold biscuits and antelope jerky. She said she would have a hot breakfast ready when he returned. The horses, perhaps, were just down in some draw where they had drifted with the wind.

When he had gone with the rifle, she filled the coffee-pot from a clearing water-hole in the nearest arroyo. She fried potatoes and onions in the long-handled skillet. And when he did not come, she set fresh biscuits in the Dutch oven. Each biscuit held a square of salt bacon in its top, and as it baked, the fat oozed down and incased it in a kind of glazed tastiness.

At noon she thought she heard a shot. Nowhere could she see him on the endless sweep of mesa. By late afternoon she was still alone. She read her Testament and wondered how many women over the world had read it in hours like this. Sitting in the shadow of the wagon, facing the direction in which he had gone, she looked up every few minutes. But all her eyes could find were cloud shadows racing across the lonely face of the mesa. All she could hear were the desolate cries from the unseen lark sparrows.

Darkness, stillness settled down on the empty land. She climbed back into the wagon and sat on the chuck-box, hands rigid on her knees. Again and again she convinced herself that the horses could not have been driven off or she would have seen the drivers' tracks. When wild, sharp barks shattered the stillness and set wires jerking in her limbs, she talked to herself steadily, but a little meaninglessly, of the post — on and on as the darkness was filled with the ringing and counter-ringing of shrill, cracked yappings — not long tones like a dog's, but incredibly short syllables rising, rising, in a mad eternal scale and discord.

"I wish papa had given me two of the chairs," she repeated. "Mamma said they were post oak from Texas. She said they had got white from scrubbing. I liked the laced rawhide seats with the hair left on. It made them soft to sit on. The seats in the parlor were black. And the ones in the kitchen were red. But I liked the brockle one in my room best."

The insane din around the wagon had become terrific. There were only two or three of the animals, Nancy Belle guessed, but they threw their voices and echoes together to make a score.

"When I was little I liked to go in the storage room," her voice went on, scarcely intelligible to her own ears. "It was dark and cool, and smelled of burlap and kerosene and whisky, and sweetish with brown sugar. I can see the fat sacks of green coffee. And the round tins of kerosene had boards on the side. The flour-sacks were printed: 'Rough and Ready' in red letters. Mamma once used to make our underwear out of the sacking. I can smell the salt side bacon in the gunny sacks."

She could tell from the sounds that one of the animals was running insanely back and forth near the wagon tongue. She had never noticed before that they yelped both when breathing in and out. Suddenly came silence. It warned her. Instinctively she felt for the ax.

"Nancy Belle!" a boy's far, anxious voice called from the darkness.

She hallooed and leaned out over the tailboard. Three shadowy forms were coming across the mesa in the starlight. Never had horses looked so good.

"Were you scared?" Rife greeted. "Anything bother you?"

"Nothing," Nancy Belle said. "Just coyotes."

"I had to give Fancy her head after it got dark." He slid wearily to the ground. "She brought us straight back to the wagon."

Nancy Belle had wanted to put her arms around her brother. Now she hugged the mare instead. Rife ate fresh biscuits and a tin plate of cold potatoes. He drank several tin cups of coffee. Nancy Belle had slipped the oats-laden gunny-sack morrals over the horses' heads.

"I had to walk halfway to the mountain," Rife said.

"Just help hitch up; then you can sleep all night," she promised.

It rained again heavily toward midnight. Flashes of lightning lit the drenched plain. For minutes at a time, quivering fingers of blue phosphorescence stood on the ears of the toiling horses. At dawn Nancy Belle still held the reins as the mud-splashed wagon crawled through a world bathed in early purple splendor.

Four days they had been crossing a hundred and seventy miles of desolate plain. Now the end waited in sight. To the west lay a land broken and tumbled by a mighty hand. Hill shouldered hill and range peered over range, all indescribably violet except where peaks tipped by the unseen sun were faroff flaming towers of copper.

It was a new land, her promised land, Stephen's land, Nancy Belle told herself, where nobody burned cow chips, but snapping cedar and pine, where cold water ran in the wooded canyons, and the eye, weary of one flat circle the horizon round, had endless geometric designs to refresh the retina.

She sang softly as the wagon lumbered to the edge of a long, shallow valley, brown and uninhabited, running north and south, and desolate except for a winding ribbon that was white with sky and narrowly bordered with green.

"Rife!" Nancy Belle cried. "The Rio Grande!"

An hour afterwards they pulled out of the sun into the shade of the long cottonwood bosque. Nancy Belle wasn't singing now. Where she remembered wide sandbars glistening with sky and tracked by waterfowl, a chocolate-red flood rolled. Where had been the island, tops of tule and scrub willow swung to and fro with the current.

Anton Chico and the Bar X horse stopped of their own accord in the trail, ears pricked forward at the swirling brown wash. While Rife turned the three horses loose to graze, Nancy Belle silently fried bacon and made coffee. When she had washed skillet and tin dishes in the river, the boy had wired the wagon box to the brake rigging. Now he was tying securely one end of his rope to the center of the coupling pole under the wagon. The other end she knew he would fasten to the inadequate upper horn of the side-saddle.

"I wouldn't mind the river if I just had my own saddle," he mourned.

They hitched up the team silently. Rife cinched the side-saddle on Fancy and straddled it, the single stirrup useless to a man. Nancy Belle climbed into the wagon and picked up the lines. The other bank looked as far away as the Espiritu Range from the post. She wanted to say something to her brother — some last word, in case they didn't make it. But all she did was cluck her tongue to the horses.

Gingerly, one slow foot at a time, the team moved down the trail into the water.

"Give 'em their heads!" Rife called from the right rear.

Nancy Belle held a rein in each hand. The red channel water came to the wagon tongue, covered it, reached the horses' bellies. The team wanted to stop. Nancy Belle swung her whip, a stick tipped with a long rawhide lash. The wagon went on. The collars of both horses kept dipping, but never entirely out of sight. Still barely wading, the slow team reached the firmer footing of the island.

Two-thirds of the river still rolled in front of the wagon. The west bank did not seem to have grown much closer, but the east bank behind them had moved far away. The team had to be whipped into the violent current. The water churned white through the wagon wheels. Suddenly both horses appeared to stumble and drop out of sight. Their heads came up wildly, spray blowing from their nostrils. The muddy water hid their legs, but by their bobbing motions Nancy Belle knew that they were swimming.

"Keep 'em pointed up the river!" Rife shouted.

Already she felt the wagon floating. It swung downstream with the current; then Rife's rope from Fancy's saddle snubbed it. The team was snorting with every breath. The Bar X horse swam high in the water, his withers and part of his back out of the chocolate current. But all she could see of Anton Chico were his nose and ears.

Down between her ankles she saw water in the wagon box. She thought of the hemstitched sheets at the bottom of her trunk, the towels and pillow-cases crocheted with shell lace. Her blue velvet corduroy dress was probably wet already, and all the cunning print aprons with dust caps to match. River water couldn't hurt the little yellow creamer, sugar bowl, and covered butter dish that had been her mother's. And the gingham dresses could be washed. What worried her were her wedding dress and the keepsake box, especially the tintypes, one of which was Rife in a child's suit edged with black braid, his brand-new hat on his knee.

An older Rife was shouting something behind her now. She couldn't catch the words. Then she found what it was. The neck and withers of Anton Chico raised suddenly out of the water and both horses were scrambling up the steep bank below the ford. Only quick work with the lines saved the wagon from turning over. Safe and blowing on the high bank, the dripping horses shook themselves like puppies.

Nancy Belle couldn't go on until she had opened the trunk and appraised the damage. Rife unsaddled Fancy and drove on with the refreshed team. Behind his slight back in the wagon box, the girl changed to her blue velvet corduroy, which was hardly wet at all. Then she combed her hair and rolled into a cranny of her trunk the old felt hat that had been too large for her father.

A half-dozen riders met the wagon some miles down the Gunstock Canyon. All of them, Nancy Belle noticed, carried guns. Stephen wore a new white shirt and a gray hat with curled brim she had not seen before. He stood in his stirrups and swung her down in front of him on the saddle, where he kissed her. She had never felt his lips press into such a straight line.

"Papa couldn't come," she said. "So Rife brought me."

She felt Stephen's rigid arm around her.

"We just got in from the Beaverhead ourselves."

"He means they never get any news out in the Beaverhead or he'd 'a' come further east to meet you!" Uncle Billy Williams put in. He had a lovable, squeaky voice. "The Apaches been breakin' loose again. Funny you didn't hear anything over in your country."

Nancy Belle gave him an inscrutable look with her gray eyes. Uncle Billy pulled out his bandanna and blew his nose.

"They got my old friend Judge Hower and his wife and kid in a buggy on the Upper Espiritu. The man that found what they did to 'em, they say, cried like a baby."

"That's all right, Uncle Billy," Stephen said in a gentle voice.

Nancy Belle glanced at Rife. Her brother's face looked gray, the eyes staring as when he had ridden in the late afternoon sunlight from the smoking ashes of Martin Cross's cabin.

Nearly fifty people, gathered in the big parlor upstairs at the hotel, greeted Nancy Belle. An old man whose young black eyes twinkled out of a bearded face said he was glad to see she had her "hair on straight." Rife stopped with the trunk before driving to the livery, and Stephen's mother showed Nancy Belle to a room to dress.

The guests stopped talking when she came into the parlor in her white wedding dress. Her basque came to a point in the front and back. It fitted like a glove. The silk underskirt came to her instep, and the ruffled overskirt to her knees. She had parted her hair from side to side and brushed the bangs down on her forehead. She felt very light-headed. The wagon still seemed to be jerking under her.

She glimpsed Rife gazing at her, a rapt expression in his reticent blue eyes. She was glad to see that he had brushed his hair. The brass swinging lamp had been lighted and the dark woodwork of the parlor festooned with evergreen branches. White streamers from the wall met in a papier-mâché bell in one corner. She noticed two children peering eagerly from the dark hall.

Stephen came to her, very straight in a long coat and stand-up collar with a black tie. He led her up beneath the papier-mâché bell. In a sibilant, churchlike whisper, the Gunstock preacher made sure of her full name. Then he coughed and began the ceremony. He had a deep voice, but Nancy Belle didn't hear all of the service. Her mind kept going back to a tall, grave man in a lonely adobe post on the wide Santa Ana plain. And after she had said: "I do," her lips moved, but she was not praying for Stephen, her husband.

Dog Eater

CHARLES M. RUSSELL

Yes, this is the Charley Russell who told the tale of Jake Hoover's pig to Frank Linderman. He was a cowboy-artist-writer — an authentic cowboy in his time, an illustrator of the West following close after Remington, and a salty teller of tales in the cow-camp and campfire manner. Rawhide Rawlins, 1921, and More Rawhides, 1926, are two choice collections. The following, with Rawhide himself the spokesman, is from his last book, Trails Plowed Under, 1928.

A MAN THAT AIN'T never been hungry can't tell nobody what's good to eat," says Rawhide Rawlins. "I eat raw sow bosom and frozen biscuit when it tasted like a Christmas dinner.

"Bill Gurd tells me he's caught one time. He's been ridin' since daybreak and ain't had a bite. It's plumb dark when he hits a breed's camp. This old breed shakes hands and tells Bill he's welcome, so after strippin' his saddle and hobblin' his hoss, he steps into the shack. Being wolf hungry, he notices the old woman's cooking bannocks at the mud fire. Tired and hungry like Bill is, the warmth and the smell of grub makes this cottonwood shack, that ain't much more than a windbreak, look like a palace.

" 'Tain't long till the old woman hands him a tin plate loaded with stew and bannocks, with hot tea for a chaser. He don't know what kind of meat it is, but he's too much of a gentleman to ask. So he don't look a gift hoss in the mouth. After he fills up, while he's smokin', the old man spreads down some blankets and Bill beds down.

"Next mornin' he gets the same for breakfast. Not being so hungry, he's more curious, but don't ask no questions. On the way out to catch his hoss he gets an answer. A little ways from the cabin, he passes a fresh dog hide pegged down on the ground. It's like seeing the hole-card — it's no gamble what that stew was made of, but it was good and Bill held it.

"I knowed another fellow one time that was called Dog Eatin' Jack. I never knowed how he got his name that's hung to him, till I camp with him. This old boy is a prospector and goes gophcrin' 'round the hills, hopin' he'll find something.

"I'm huntin' hosses one spring and ain't found nothing but tracks. I'm up on the Lodgepole in the foothills; it's sundown and my hoss has went lame. We're limping along slow when I sight a couple of hobbled cayuses in a beaver meadow. One of these hosses is wearing a Diamond G iron, the other's a Quarter Circle-Block hoss. They're both old cow ponies. I soon locate their owner's camp — it's a lean-to in the edge of the timber.

"While I'm lookin' over the layout, here comes the owner. It's the Dog Eater. After we shake hands I unsaddle and stake out my tired hoss. When we're filled up on the best he's got — which is beans, bacon, and frying pan bread, which is good filling for hungry men — we're sittin' smokin', and it's then I ask him if he ever lived with Injuns.

" 'You're thinkin',' says he, 'about my name. It does sound like Injun, but they don't hang it on me. It happens about ten winters ago. I'm way back in the Diamond range; I've throwed my hosses about ten mile out in the foothills where there's good feed and less snow. I build a lean-to, a good one, and me and my dog settles down. There's some beaver here and I got out a line of traps and figger on winterin' here. Ain't got much grub, but there's lots of game in the hills and my old needle gun will get what the traps won't.

" 'Snow comes early and lots of it. About three days after the storm I step on a loose boulder and sprain my ankle. This puts me plumb out; I can't more than keep my fire alive. All the time I'm running short of grub. I eat a couple of skinned beaver I'd throwed away one day. My old dog brings in a snowshoe rabbit to camp and maybe you don't think he's welcome. I cut in two with him but manlike, I give him the front end. That's the last we got.

" 'Old Friendship — that's the dog's name — goes out every day, but he don't get nothing and I know he ain't cheating — he's too holler in the flanks. After about four days of living on thoughts, Friendship starts watchin' like he's afraid. He thinks maybe I'll put him in the pot, but he sizes me up wrong. If I'd do that, I hope I choke to death.

" 'The sixth day I'm sizin' him up. He's layin' near the fire. He's a hound with a long meaty tail. Says I to myself, 'Oxtail soup! What's the matter with dog tail?' He don't use it for nothing but sign talk, but it's like cutting the hands off a dummy. But the eighth day, with hunger and pain in my ankle, I plumb locoed and I can't get that dog's tail out of my mind. So, a little before noon I slip up on him, while he's sleeping, with the ax. In a second it's all over. Friendship goes yelpin' into the woods and I am sobbin' like a kid, with his tail in my hand.

" 'The water is already boilin' in the pot, an' as soon as I singe the hair off it's in the pot. I turned a couple of flour sacks inside out and dropped them in and there's enough flour to thicken the soup. It's about dark. I fill up, and if it weren't for thinkin' it would have been good. I could have eat it all but I held out over half for Friendship, in case he come back.

" 'It must be midnight when he pushes into the blankets with me. I take him in my arms. He's as cold as a dead snake, and while I'm holdin' him tight I'm crying like a baby. After he warms up a little, I get up and throw some wood on the fire and call Friendship to the pot. He eats every bit of it. He don't seem to recognize it. If he does, being a dog, he forgives.

" 'We got back to the blankets. It's just breaking day when he slides out, whinin' and sniffin' the air with his ears cocked and his bloody stub wobblin'. I look the way he's pointin', and not twenty-five yards from the lean-to stands a big elk. There's a fine snow fallin'; the wind's right for us. I ain't a second gettin' my old needle gun, but I'm playin' safe — I'm coming Injun on him. I use my ram-rod for a rest. When old needle speaks, the bull turns — his neck's broken. 'Tain't long till we both get to that bull and we're both eatin' raw, warm liver. I've seen Injuns do this but I never thought I was that much wolf, but it sure was good that morning.

" 'He's a big seven-point bull — old and pretty tough, but me and Friendship was looking for quantity, not quality, and we got it. That meat lasted till we got out.'

" 'What became of Friendship?' says I.

" 'He died two years ago,' says Jack. 'But he died fat.' "

The Girl in the Humbert

MARI SANDOZ

*M*ari Sandoz plays the whole field, fiction and non-fiction —
short stories, novels, articles, biographies, histories — and her work
rates high, not in number of volumes but in quality. She has written perhaps a dozen short stories during the last twenty-odd years.
They are available right now only in the back issues of various
magazines, but someday some publisher will have sense enough
to offer them in book form. "The Girl in the Humbert," is
from the Saturday Evening Post for March 4, 1939. It handles
one of the old worn western themes, rancher vs. homesteader, in
retrospect, in the aftermath of later years, and does so with none of
the slickness usually associated with the slick magazines, instead
with a quiet fresh conviction of reality.

I*T WAS THE CITY NEPHEWS* who first saw smoke in the Humbert.
They came galloping home through the oppressive spring heat,
bouncing together on the barebacked old pinto, Down's short
arms tight around the middle of his nine-year-old brother before
him. Together they kicked the old mare at every jump, the reins
flapping loose.

When they saw their tall, browned uncle at the ranch-yard
gate, the boys let the pinto drop into a walk. Sliding off on the

far side, they started reluctantly toward him. But almost at once
their eager young legs betrayed them, their legs and the need to
tell the news before they were scolded for running the old mare.

"Somebody's — somebody's in the old house!" Down shouted,
to beat his brother in the telling.

"There's smoke coming from the chimney in the Humbert,"
Dickup said, deliberately explicit.

But Jack Pulmer only snapped Down's transparent ear and
picked beggar lice from the older boy's tousled hair. So his two
young cowpunchers had been seeing a whirlwind and the dust
it can raise?

"But there's a car — there is," they cried together.

The uncle nodded a little, and thumbed imperatively toward
the lathered old mare, standing head down, sides heaving. So the
boys fetched clean corn-cobs from a manger and started to rub
her down, one on a side, while they watched their fine big uncle
swing his empty car away through the sandpass.

Jack Pulmer hoped that it was only dust and a whirlwind the
boys had seen. The Humbert, apparently never Spurwheel ranch
property except by claim of occupation, was his best meadow,
its hay essential if he was to hold off foreclosure on the ranch
another year. Otherwise it would be the last ending of a long
descent since Colonel Pulmer, Jack's grandfather, was killed by
Frenchy Humbert, over thirty years ago. Families and times both
change and the sons of the ruthless old cowman couldn't keep
together much of the empire the old colonel cut from the public
domain and held against all settlement until Frenchy appeared.

But the free range pinched out, the days of cheap beef and
wild cow towns passed. Five years ago, what was left of the Spurwheel and its mortgages fell to young Jack, who had studied voice
instead of ranching. In those five years the colonel's grandson
learned about cattle markets and stock diseases and that a frozen
bit will burn the mouth of a horse. He learned, too, that he
couldn't risk a late April prairie fire from any tin-can tourist,
particularly not through the Humbert.

By the time the rancher emerged from the pass no smoke darkened the early green of the meadow, the winter-bleached rushes of
the swamp, or the high ridge of hills beyond, tawny in the hot
sun. But the windmill at the head of the valley was in gear, the
wheel turning slowly, lopsided and awkward as a tumbleweed on
the prairie, the water gathering in the reservoir Frenchy threw
up years ago. There was a car, too, as the boys had said, and new

shingle patches shone yellow on the roof of the old sod house.

At the door Jack Pulmer was faced by a cool-eyed young woman in overalls and striped jersey, a worn rifle in her hand. Without greeting, she listened to what he had to say over the gray cowman's hat in his hand.

"No," she told him, when he was done. "I do not think I would be more comfortable at the Spurwheel ranch house."

When he attempted a little firmness, she let her palm slide down to the trigger guard of the rifle and pointed out that she was not trespassing here. She was Arille Hombiert, *h* and *t* silent, please, and she happened to own this place he called the Humbert.

So there was nothing for the young rancher to do but to go, heading away toward the county seat to check up on the claims of this girl with the name something like Frenchy's. She couldn't be much over twenty, slim as September bluestem, with hair bright and free as its ripening seed. And on the sill of the window beside her was a small statuette, a mule-deer doe carved from some light-colored wood, the head delicate and shy, the wide ears alert. Alone, poised for flight, the little animal stood silvery pale against the full-drawn curtain of solid black.

At the courthouse Jack Pulmer discovered that Frenchy's name was really Hombiert and that the girl's title to the deserted meadow was as solid as the earth from which the old sod house grew. So went the Spurwheel's last bit of free grass and left the young rancher owing several thousand dollars in back rent to a cool-eyed girl named Arille, granddaughter of a murderer.

But because he had to know what his chances of leasing this year's hay were, he came back through the low-clouded dusk by way of the Humbert. The soddy was a dark blur beside the road, with no ray of light anywhere. Yet somebody seemed to be working at the old outside chimney, somebody who stood against the blackness of the earthen wall until the car was past.

Around midnight the drizzle turned to a light, rattling sleet. Jack Pulmer drew on his sheepskin and went out to throw the gates of the winter pasture, where a few of the older cows, smelling snow, were already breaking through and bawling for their calves to follow them to the corrals. When he came in, the ground was covered, soft-cushioned and silent under his boots.

By morning the wind was up, the air thick and white and sharp with driving snow that shut in the ranch house all around. The two boys ran for the door, incredulous and excited. But the great-aunt who cared for them was a sister of the old colonel's, and they got no farther than the windows.

Three days later the sun was out, the long drifts mushing under the feet of bawling cattle, just right for snow forts. The old aunt sent the boys out, even though she had brought them West to recover from scarlet fever while their mother, not a Pulmer, got a summer's rest.

On his way back from the north range, his sorrel horse dark with snow water to the flanks, Jack Pulmer cut through the Humbert. But the storm hadn't discouraged the pale-skinned Eastern girl. She was out in sunglasses and boots, shooting at a soup can on a gatepost, the bullets well bunched in the center.

"This snow'll be flooding your hay land," the rancher called from the road.

"I suspect it's been flooded before," the girl replied, her teeth white and derisive in her tanning face.

But the man had to have the hay secure, and so he swung a leg over the horn and dickered. The girl from the Humbert was fair enough: Standing hay at the going price, to be measured and paid for after stacking. And before the rancher could unlimber his leg from the horn, the girl was gone through the door of the soddy, leaving only her tracks to show that anyone lived there — firm tracks, some large and deep, as though she had worn big overshoes and carried a heavy load.

As soon as the dark velvet of the earth pushed up wet between the shrinking drifts, Dickup and Down got the old pinto out. They had to see what the storm did to their swamp and the open water in its center, where their uncle had a duck boat they might hope to reach along in July. Jack Pulmer knew the boys shouldn't be playing in the Humbert, no matter how much they liked the chattering ducks along the rising water edge, the flooding muskrat houses, the acres of dead rushes still under snow. But the old aunt was down with a bilious attack and so the man slapped the bony hip of the pinto and let them go.

"Tie your horse solid to a hackberry tree on the slope or you'll be a couple cowpunchers hoofing it in. And don't go near the soddy."

Promising everything, the boys got away. They kicked the old mare and yelled, "Yip-pi!" but hung on tight, Dickup holding the reins close, with both hands buried in the mane, Down's arms gripping his brother's middle. They remembered from the day they got their nicknames, the first time they tried the pinto. Dick had pushed Don up and climbed on behind, the reins hanging loose. The old mare dropped her head, kicked up her heels high and both boys slid off over her ears.

"It's Dickup behind and his brother Down in front!" old Pete roared. When the smaller boy began to cry, the chore man stopped. "Why, sa-ay, all a them old-timers had nicknames — like Lame Johnny an' Fly Speck Billy," he complained.

After that it was all right, with Dickup sitting in front, to pull on the reins, Down hanging on behind, the old pinto plodding along with half-closed eyes.

In the Humbert, summer came hard upon the storm, the greening swamp of evening alive with the soft quack of ducks, the late song of blackbirds and the croak of the awakening frogs. As the noise swelled into night, a thin, white old man often slipped out to sit beside the girl. It was old Frenchy, free after ten years of solitary darkness for successive attempts at prison break and twenty years of darkness by choice when his urge to freedom was stilled at last. In those years he went back to the old, old craft of his people, wood carving. With a knife improvised from a broken hinge, and pieces of his plank bunk for material, he formed little wooden statuettes, mostly small, wild, free things — a saucy prairie dog poised at the mouth of his hole, a young gray wolf trying his voice against the sky, the wide-eared doe on the window sill in the Humbert. All this grew up in darkness, by touch, with the simplicity of line that pleased the fingertips, mass that satisfied the palm.

Free now, and back on his homestead, he returned to his earlier craft, the soil, and when powdery dusk filled the valley and the swamp song began he sat upon the doorstep with his rifle beside him. Sometimes he talked a little to his granddaughter, of plants and weather and earth, with slow, spare words, for speech, too, was almost lost to him in those long years of silence.

In the darkness he chopped up the sod of his old garden plot that the girl hired rebroken. With hoe and rake he worked the soil into a fine seed bed, smooth as any done by light of day, and level for irrigation from the old reservoir. Later he crept along the sprouting rows of green, thinning, transplanting, weeding. He did all these things in darkness, in paths his feet remembered, within the bonds of long, long habit.

And in the meantime he taught his granddaughter to shoot the old rifle, for, to his light-blinded eyes, the Spurwheel ranch over the hill was unchanged, and a settler's risk as great as ever.

One cloudy afternoon the boys came riding home just ahead of a rain. They had a little mud turtle, moss-backed, not as big as a saucer, in Dickup's handkerchief, held safely by the corners. They had news too. There had been hammering all day in the Humbert, somebody on the roof, and the house looking different.

Jack Pulmer poked the wet, soiled handkerchief with a finger. "Hadn't you better keep to your livestock, and not be bothering strangers?"

"Yes, uncle," the boys said together, dutifully. Holding the turtle away from them, the claws coming through the cloth like thorns, they went to turn the old mare out to grass. Jack Pulmer watched them go, saw their heads come together, their faces turn slyly back to look at him. Then they started to run, kicking up like colts.

The young rancher knew about the night construction of the extension to the soddy and the buttressing of the four corners of the house like a Southwest 'dobe church, stout and lasting. He had heard the girl shingling the new roof all this cool day and he didn't understand how she could plan and do these things, all the things of the Humbert, this spring. He remembered the time he found her planting late sweet corn across the Spurwheel road to the summer pasture. He stopped the car and went over to the girl.

"It is customary in this country to leave public highways passable," he announced, but smilingly.

"So-o?" she inquired politely, driving her spade into the sod, dropping two kernels in the crevice, stepping on it. "I was informed at the courthouse that this is not a laid-out road."

The way back to the car was a long and awkward one, but the young rancher made himself seem unhurried, flattening an uptilted sod or two with his boot, tossing a clod at a ground squirrel. And when he sneaked a look back, Arille Hombiert was far down the row, wasting no time.

It was after this that Jack Pulmer paid her as much of the back rent as he could, using what he had laid aside for the mortgage. Even if the girl had known about the debts, she could not have forgotten the face of Frenchy Hombiert the day she took him from the prison office, his eyes closed as the dark curtains of the soddy. Only his hands seemed alive at all.

So she took the money and then couldn't tell the old man, afraid he would call it a bribe to forget a great wrong, one miserable thousand dollars for each ten years in a black hole — and a lifetime in the habit of darkness.

The girl still shot target every day, but a little shamefacedly now, putting the rifle away among the flowers about the soddy if she saw the boys come plowing through the rushes, or heard the young rancher's car in the sand pass. But in the evenings old Frenchy still liked to touch his fingers to the centered bullet holes in her target. Yes, this Arille, the only one left to him now, was a true Hombiert, like those old ones who came pushing up the Mississippi two hundred years ago.

It was late in June, when the spiderwort lay blue along the slopes of the Humbert, the yellow currants in the brush sweetening to honey, that Dickup and Down reported seeing a man's foot sticking from behind a curtain at the soddy. Now the uncle discovered, too, that there was lemonade with cookies almost every day, and 'Reel, the girl, waving a dish towel to the boys when it was ready.

The uncle ordered them to stay away from people, and took to watching the Humbert from closer. Finally, one windy night, when the sound of his motor was blown behind him, his unexpected headlight shot through the north pass and cut the figure of an old man from the darkness about the reservoir. Blinded eyes closed, the man waited for the light to pass, motionless, gaunt and white as some lightning-charred tree, long standing. But by then young Jack knew that the girl in the Humbert could sing, too, and once he saw her dance on a knoll in the pale light of a summer moon, a wild, beautiful dance. And finally sink, light as cottonwood down, to the sand where he had killed a rattlesnake the summer before.

Now more and more often the old man stopped between the lush green rows to listen, to move swiftly toward his rifle. Then one Sunday an old open car piled full of ranch hands came through the Humbert. Noisily, with a loud "Whoa-o-o!" they jerked to a stop before the soddy. Hard at one another's heels they trooped up between the flower beds to pound on the old door, pretending a great thirst and wanting to borrow a dipper, please, ma'am.

The girl pointed out that the windmill, in plain sight, was running strong.

"It is quite possible to obtain a good drink from the pipe, you know, by just holding your hand against the flow," she explained carefully, as though they were visiting dudes.

The younger of the hands started to talk up to this pretty girl, but the others nudged their ribs, motioning to Frenchy's old rifle standing in the hollyhocks beside the door, ready at her hand. Silenced, the men fell back and hustled off toward the mill. Pretending to drink, they wiped their mouths and then drove away, the backs of their necks red above the clean work shirts.

When the car was gone, Frenchy began to talk from the darkness of his bunk. "Once more they come," he said slowly, painfully. "Hired men smelling out. We better carry automatics, plenty of shells."

In the dusk of the curtained soddy Arille brought pen and ink, but almost at once the old man started again, weary, defeated. "I don't know — maybe we better get out."

At this his granddaughter stopped, her hands tense. "You mean let them drive us away? No!"

So the guns came. They really sagged the pocket very little and fitted the palm as well as the little wooden statuettes.

Late one evening the Spurwheel hay crew moved into the Humbert, creeping through the pass like a long worm, the tall stacker first, then the mowers, the rakes and the sweeps. It was hard to explain their coming to the old settler, but he knew they must have money, and so he gave in to Arille. For two weeks the humming mowers swung around the meadow, the rakes rolled the new hay into windrows close-ribbed as corduroy and the groaning stacker threw it high. All these days Frenchy sat stiff and awake on his bunk, his rifle across his knees.

But no one came near the soddy, the cold stream of the windmill or the wide patch of watermelons ripening. Not even the two boys, who followed their uncle's sickle bar as he led the mowers, or rode the piles of hay he swept in from the far ends of the meadow.

When the valley was friendly once more, the rancher drew his horse up before the girl, waist deep in her moon poppies, stringing

the finest blooms for seed. He had brought the check for the
hay, with a notation of his measurements.

"I can't say anything definite about next year," he told her
regretfully, "but for this year I'm grateful — "

Without finishing he touched the sorrel into a lope, and for
once the girl from the Humbert stood to look after him, the white
slip of paper blowing in her hand.

The day of the rodeo and county fair in late August, Arille
came into town early to deliver her melons, early cabbage, wild
plums and green wild grapes for jelly to the stores. She had hoped
to be away before ten and the packing crowd, but at eight the
little town was already jammed, its one traffic light and the sweating deputy marshals lost in the honking, the shoutings and the
dust. Only the Indians, painted, feathered, in bead-and-scalp-
trimmed shirts for the dance in the square, got through the
crowd — the Indians and the few grizzled old cowmen, thick-
shouldered and heavy-hipped now, driving their cars as they once
spurred mustang cow ponies through the border towns on pay day.

When Arille came out of the last store, her errands done, Jack
Pulmer stood at her running board, waiting. The girl was in dull
blue, soft as fall asters against a far hill. The man had never seen
her so fragile and lovely, so far from anything like shingle laying,
or target shooting with a rifle that had killed a man. He had never
seen her in a dress.

"Not going home so soon?" he asked, making talk.

Yes, she was.

"But it isn't much after noon, and there's the rodeo and —
well, I was hoping you'd see it with me," he trailed off, without
confidence as the girl turned the car switch and moved her foot
toward the starter.

But she really ought to stay, he urged, have a bite at the barbecue pit, see the bronco busting, not like the show business, with
chutes and only ten seconds to ride. This was wild horses, eared
down, saddled, the blindfold jerked away and the whole world
wide open for man and horse to fight it out. He was alone, the
boys chasing off after old Pete, who'd bulldogged some mean
steers in his day. And besides, it might be hours before she could
get her car out.

As he talked the girl considered the young cowman, saw that
the sweep of his cheek had gaunted much this summer, his jaw
line leaned, his mouth thinned. But his shoulders were still
square as good oak beams, his fingers straight-boned and true. And

when she finally had to meet the grave brown of his eyes, she jerked the key from the lock.

"For an hour," she agreed.

Together they climbed over bumpers, slipped between running boards and were lost in the packed mass at the intersection. And everywhere around them mouths opened to exclaim above the noise, arms lifted to point them out. A Pulmer and a Humbert together!

"If you want to back out — " the man whispered to the girl. But Arille Hombiert looked straight before her, pushing on as though through a deep tangle of brush or rushes noisy in the wind.

Suddenly the center lane of cars began to move, making way for the high-school band in blue-and-white, marching double file, led by a red-headed girl in a towering white shako. The crowd broke from the street and the barbecue pit, following toward the fair-grounds; past pine booths selling red hamburgers, chances at pillow tops or looks at the headless woman, the petrified man or Popeye; past bingo stands and the agricultural exhibits to the weathered old grandstand. Jack Pulmer stuck a note for Pete in a crack in the Spurwheel section and took Arille away from the gawking crowd toward the grassy oval inside the race track. At the gate they passed a slim-hipped youth twirling a loop about himself, stepping daintily in and out as he sang in a tuneless monotone for the grandstand:

> "I'm a kissin', cussin' son of a gun,
> I'm the kid from Powder River."

"Face-Powder River, N. Y.," Arille laughed, inanely, and the rancher knew how deep the looks, the pointing out, the talk had gone. He tried to pretend too. Yes, the singing kid was an import all right, but with top contest money only twenty-five dollars, the riders out here in the oval were fresh off the range hereabouts.

They did look authentic, with their wind-burnt faces, their easy levis, standing around licking cigarettes and considering a blind-folded smoke roan. The wild horse was sagging groundward under the saddle leather, puffing himself against the tightening cinch, dust rolling before his stubborn nose.

Now the rider, a lanky, weather-beaten old cow hand from the Spurwheel, tucked in his plaid shirt and climbed awkwardly to the saddle. The hazers pulled in closer, the blind was jerked away and the sky opened.

"Ride 'im, Stovepipe!" somebody yelled from the crowd.

When three or four straight high bucks and stiff-legged landings showed no daylight between the rider and his saddle, the horse stopped. Then suddenly he shot ahead, bucking, swapping ends, spinning, sunfishing, bellowing out over the dusty plain.

The crowd was up. "Whoopee, listen at him bawl!"

The rider's teeth still gleamed in his dark face, his old hat pounding the dusty withers, his spurred heels raking. Finally the smoke roan quieted, hanging his head sullenly, swaying lower and lower, his sunken flanks heaving, his wide nostrils bloody.

"He's done! You got him licked, Stovepipe!" the crowd yelled. But over them all old Pete roared out a warning. "Watch 'im, cowboy, watch 'im!"

Pete was right. Already the horse was gathering himself into a knot. Then his forefeet snapped out, up. The riders stumbled back, their cigarettes slipping from their open lips. The hazers spurred forward. A moment the horse and rider teetered, then, with a whinny wild as a scream, the smoke roan went over backward, shaking the earth.

A groan swept the grandstand. Arille's hand clutched the rancher's arm. But old Stovepipe was free. Coolly he had waited to slide beyond the crushing horn until the last possible moment, ready now to fall back into the saddle as swiftly. But the smoke roan was done. The taut hide rippled a little, a hind foot straightened.

From a gateway a tractor came coughing, swinging around to drag the horse aside. But the girl from the Humbert had seen enough, was hurrying away, the young rancher beside her. On the way out the boys came running, leaving Pete behind. Little Down buried his face in the blue of the girl's dress. "Oh, 'Reel, it's dead! The poor horse is dead!" he sobbed, while Dickup stood close to his uncle's hand, white-faced and silent.

But before the next saddle was on, the boys were impatient to find Pete again, to see the bulldogging, the wild-cow milking, the Indian races. So the girl sent the rancher back with them and went to her car alone.

That night she sat late in the dim light of the new moon, watching her grandfather's bent back among the tomatoes, his head up at the slightest sound that was unusual. Later she listened to his sure hands move over his supper tray in the darkness, stop at the far rise of a little wind and move again when it was past.

The next day the rancher from the Spurwheel found the road

past the soddy posted with No TRESPASSING signs.

Now at last he had to go to the court records of the trial of Frenchy. It was not the story of a lawless invader he had heard from his father, but a story of long persecution of a lone settler, ending in a gate thrown back, a herd of Pulmer cattle eating his corn and garden. When he took them up for damages, men came creeping through the dusk to turn them out. Frenchy, watching, fired over their heads. When a bullet from the buckbrush grazed his arm, he fired point-blank into the stream of red still on his retina and got Colonel Pulmer through the chest. For this he was given ten years for manslaughter and dragged away.

Slowly Jack Pulmer closed the courthouse door and plodded across the street to his car, his boots heavy as iron in the dust.

All through the drought of August, thunderheads had piled high. Lightning flashed rose-red through the clouds; thunder shook the earth, a few drops of rain fell and the wind blew the storm away. In the meantime the prairie was browning, the swamp in the Humbert drying up. The day after the rodeo, Dickup and Down came home shouting they could walk into the very middle, where the boat was, without getting their shoes muddy, hardly. And now their uncle wouldn't let them go back, not with all their pleading that they could be finding a lot of shells for their collection, that next week it would be town and school again.

The rancher was firm until the old aunt had to be taken to the doctor for her gall bladder and he was busy culling stock for shipment. So he let the boys make one more trip to the swamp, just one more, and no going near anybody. The boys nodded and, with their lunch in their pockets, rode away into the hot, quiet morning.

Around noon a little cloud like a fluff of dandelion started at the zenith and spread white and high over the east, dark olive underneath. A bolt or two of lightning fell, thunder rolled. Then the wind came up and blew the smell of ozone away.

Half an hour later a shouting puncher spurred through the dust and bawling cattle to Jack Pulmer. His arm in the air, he pointed off into the east, toward the Humbert, where white smoke billowed up, twisted into yellow, blue and black, and rolled away over the hills.

Letting the cattle spread, the hands whirled their horses toward the Spurwheel. Under pressure of his knee, Jack's sorrel shot ahead for the Humbert, three miles away, while already dark specks moved in over the far hills — fire fighters in answer to the smoke signal of the range country.

At the line fence the rancher found three posts splintered and scorched, the grass blackened, and from it a widening tongue of burnt prairie spreading away toward the meadow. He spurred his winded horse on, to see that the farther swamp was a towering mass of smoke, cut by flames leaping high from the piles of dead rushes, the near end only gray ashes, reddening in the wind. The whole meadow was black, the stackyards smoldering piles, the gardens of Frenchy Hombiert cooked dark as by frost, about the sod house and the car. Otherwise there was nothing — nothing except the old pinto tied to a hackberry far up the slope and jerking to get free.

In the dark soddy Jack found only the shadowy figure of an old man, still clutching his rifle against his enemy, but begging him to find Arille, his Arille, who had run out into the smoke and did not return.

Of the boys he knew nothing, nothing at all.

While the Spurwheel outfit drove hard toward the head fire, Pete, in the ranch car, turned off to find his boss.

"The boys?" he yelled from far off. At sight of the rancher's face he jerked a gun from the car pocket and fired three rapid shots into the air — the old, old, distress signal of the hills. Then Jack slid under the wheel and headed for the narrowest strip of rushes between the meadow and the open place in the center, still veiled in curling heat and thin blue smoke.

Here the rancher leaped from the car, began kicking a path into the swamp. Old Pete jerked him back, pounded out the fire in his clothes as two, three, half a dozen cars drew up, the men out before the wheels stopped rolling. In relays of three they shoveled glowing ashes down the wind, running back to soak their burning clothes, shoveling again, driving a path into the swamp.

Jack Pulmer was the first to break through into the little quarter-acre open space, baked hard, drifted white in wind-blown ashes. There was nothing here, nothing except the boat out in the center, turned upside down, the water-logged bottom smoldering.

And face down under it lay the two boys, Arille between them, holding them safe, her own clothing scorched, her overalls burnt off above her knees.

Carefully Jack lifted the girl, brushing the hair from her soil-streaked face. Pete yanked the boys up. They looked with awed faces at the singed, blackened, sweating men about them, over the ruins of their beloved swamp, at the girl limp in their uncle's arms. Quietly Down began to cry, while Dickup ran at the heels of his uncle. "Is 'Reel," he whispered — "is she — dead?"

Pete pulled him back, sent a hand for a telephone and a doctor by plane and got the rest to the soddy. There Jack Pulmer carried the girl away, the boys hanging to Pete, afraid of this silent, terrible man who was their uncle. Inside, old Frenchy peered from the darkness of his room, squinting as the curtains at the windows were jerked back, his tongue as helpless as his eyes. But his hands were swift and sure as he helped the rancher cut away the burnt shoes, the scorched tatters of the overalls, laying bare the flesh, seared as the girl ran through the burning grass to save the boys of the Spurwheel.

The next morning, when the doctor was gone and the girl lay quiet at last, only half awake, the boys were permitted to see her. They forgot the little wooden animals they had to show her, their uncle's careful cautioning, in their excitement to tell their news. That dust cloud 'Reel had seen had been a fire, a terrible fire. "All the swamp burned up while we were hid under the boat," they cried together. "Even the grass."

Then suddenly they saw that the girl's face was very white and drawn, sick-looking, and remembering the plane and the doctor, they were quiet, afraid again. But the old man behind them spoke. Yes, the grass was gone, but it would come again. "Already it is growing at the roots, finer, greener — "

With the boys pulling at him to show them, he started to the door. A moment he hesitated there, to look back to his Arille and this grandson of Colonel Pulmer. Then, still squinting, old Frenchy stepped out into the sunlight for the first time in thirty years, to show two small boys the grass growing new in the Humbert.

The Colt

WALLACE STEGNER

Wallace Stegner is a college professor, Wisconsin to Harvard to Stanford, and at times an academic tone tinges his work — and why should you let that bother you when he can tell a story like this? Here the touch is just right, the art shrewdly concealed behind the homely simplicity; a story and theme that almost inevitably recall John Steinbeck's "The Red Pony" but are distinct and distinctive in themselves. "The Colt" was first printed in the Southwest Review but can also be found in Mr. Stegner's The Big Rock Candy Mountain, 1943.

It was the swift coming of spring that let things happen. It was spring, and the opening of the roads, that took his father out of town. It was spring that clogged the river with floodwater and ice pans, sent the dogs racing in wild aimless packs, ripped the railroad bridge out and scattered it down the river for exuberant townspeople to fish out piecemeal. It was spring that drove the whole town to the riverbank with pike poles and coffeepots and boxes of sandwiches for an impromptu picnic, lifting their sober responsibilities out of them and making them whoop blessings on the C.P.R. for a winter's firewood. Nothing might have gone wrong except for the coming of spring. Some of the neighbors might have noticed and let them know; Bruce might not have forgotten; his mother might have remembered and sent him out again after dark.

But the spring came, and the ice went out, and that night Bruce went to bed drunk and exhausted with excitement. In the restless sleep just before waking he dreamed of wolves and wild hunts, but when he awoke finally he realized that he had not been dreaming the noise. The window, wide open for the first time in months, let in a shivery draught of fresh, damp air, and he heard the faint yelping far down in the bend of the river.

He dressed and went downstairs, crowding his bottom into the warm oven, not because he was cold but because it had been a ritual for so long that not even the sight of the sun outside could convince him it wasn't necessary. The dogs were still yapping; he heard them through the open door.

"What's the matter with all the pooches?" he said. "Where's Spot?"

"He's out with them," his mother said. "They've probably got a porcupine treed. Dogs go crazy in the spring."

"It's dog days they go crazy."

"They go crazy in the spring, too." She hummed a little as she set the table. "You'd better go feed the horses. Breakfast won't be for ten minutes. And see if Daisy is all right."

Bruce stood perfectly still in the middle of the kitchen. "Oh, my gosh!" he said. "I left Daisy picketed out all night!"

His mother's head jerked around. "Where?"

"Down in the bend."

"Where those dogs are?"

"Yes," he said, sick and afraid. "Maybe she's had her colt."

"She couldn't for two or three days," his mother said. But just looking at her he knew that it might be bad, that there was something to be afraid of. In another moment they were both out the door, both running.

But it couldn't be Daisy they were barking at, he thought as he raced around Chance's barn. He'd picketed her higher up, not clear down in the U where the dogs were. His eyes swept the brown, wet, close-cropped meadow, the edge of the brush where the river ran close under the north bench. The mare wasn't there! He opened his mouth and half turned, running, to shout at his mother coming behind him, and then sprinted for the deep curve of the bend.

As soon as he rounded the little clump of brush that fringed the cut-bank behind Chance's he saw them. The mare stood planted, a bay spot, against the grey brush, and in front of her, on the ground, was another smaller spot. Six or eight dogs were leaping around, barking, sitting. Even at that distance he recognized Spot and the Chapmans' airedale.

He shouted and pumped on. At a gravelly patch he stooped and clawed and straightened, still running, with a handful of pebbles. In one pausing, straddling, aiming motion he let fly a rock at the distant pack. It fell far short, but they turned their heads, sat on their haunches and let out defiant short barks. Their tongues lolled as if they had run far.

Bruce yelled and threw again, one eye on the dogs and the other on the chestnut colt in front of the mare's feet. The mare's ears were back, and as he ran, Bruce saw the colt's head bob up and down. It was all right then. The colt was alive. He slowed and came up quietly. Never move fast or speak loud around an animal, Pa said.

The colt struggled again, raised its head with white eyeballs rolling, spraddled its white-stockinged legs and tried to stand. "Easy, boy," Bruce said. "Take it easy, old fella." His mother arrived, getting her breath, her hair half down, and he turned to her gleefully. "It's all right, Ma. They didn't hurt anything. Isn't he a beauty, Ma?"

He stroked Daisy's nose. She was heaving, her ears pricking forward and back; her flanks were lathered, and she trembled. Patting her gently, he watched the colt, sitting now like a dog on its haunches, and his happiness that nothing had really been hurt bubbled out of him. "Lookit, Ma," he said. "He's got four white socks. Can I call him Socks, Ma? He sure is a nice colt, isn't he? Aren't you, Socks, old boy?" He reached down to touch the chestnut's forelock, and the colt struggled, pulling away.

Then Bruce saw his mother's face. It was quiet, too quiet. She hadn't answered a word to all his jabber. Instead she knelt down, about ten feet from the squatting colt, and stared at it. The boy's eyes followed hers. There was something funny about . . .

"Ma!" he said. "What's the matter with its front feet?"

He left Daisy's head and came around, staring. The colt's pasterns looked bent — were bent, so that they flattened clear to the ground under its weight. Frightened by Bruce's movement, the chestnut flopped and floundered to its feet, pressing close to its mother. As it walked, Bruce saw, flat on its fetlocks, its hooves sticking out in front like a movie comedian's too-large shoes.

Bruce's mother pressed her lips together, shaking her head. She moved so gently that she got her hand on the colt's poll, and he bobbed against the pleasant scratching. "You poor broken-legged thing," she said with tears in her eyes. "You poor little friendly ruined thing!"

Still quietly, she turned towards the dogs, and for the first time in his life Bruce heard her curse. Quietly, almost in a whisper, she cursed them as they sat with hanging tongues just out of reach. "God damn you," she said. "God damn your wild hearts, chasing a mother and a poor little colt."

To Bruce, standing with trembling lips, she said, "Go get Jim Enich. Tell him to bring a wagon. And don't cry. It's not your fault."

His mouth tightened; a sob jerked in his chest. He bit his lip and drew his face down tight to keep from crying, but his eyes filled and ran over.

"It is too my fault!" he said, and turned and ran.

Later, as they came in the wagon up along the cutbank, the colt tied down in the wagon box with his head sometimes lifting, sometimes bumping on the boards, the mare trotting after with chuckling vibrations of solicitude in her throat, Bruce leaned far over and tried to touch the colt's haunch. "Gee whiz!" he said. "Poor old Socks."

His mother's arm was around him, keeping him from leaning over too far. He didn't watch where they were until he heard his mother say in surprise and relief, "Why, there's Pa!"

Instantly he was terrified. He had forgotten and left Daisy staked out all night. It was his fault, the whole thing. He slid back into the seat and crouched between Enich and his mother, watching from that narrow space like a gopher from its hole. He saw the Ford against the barn and his father's big body leaning into it and pulling out gunny sacks and straw. There was mud all over the car, mud on his father's pants. He crouched deeper into his crevice and watched his father's face while his mother was telling what had happened.

Then Pa and Jim Enich lifted and slid the colt down to the ground, and Pa stooped to feel its fetlocks. His face was still, red from wind-burn, and his big square hands were muddy. After a long examination he straightened up.

"Would've been a nice colt," he said. "Damn a pack of mangy mongrels, anyway." He brushed his pants and looked at Bruce's mother. "How come Daisy was out?"

"I told Brucie to take her out. The barn seems so cramped for her, and I thought it would do her good to stretch her legs. And then the ice went out, and the bridge with it, and there was a lot of excitement. . . ." She spoke very fast, and in her voice Bruce heard the echo of his own fear and guilt. She was trying to protect him, but in his own mind he knew he was to blame.

"I didn't mean to leave her out, Pa," he said. His voice squeaked, and he swallowed. "I was going to bring her in before supper, only when the bridge . . ."

His father's somber eyes rested on him, and he stopped. But his father didn't fly into a rage. He just seemed tired. He looked at the colt and then at Enich. "Total loss?" he said.

Enich had a leathery, withered face, with two deep creases from beside his nose to the corner of his mouth. A brown mole hid in the left one, and it emerged and disappeared as he chewed a dry grass stem. "Hide," he said.

Bruce closed his dry mouth, swallowed. "Pa!" he said. "It won't have to be shot, will it?"

"What else can you do with it?" his father said. "A crippled horse is no good. It's just plain mercy to shoot it."

"Give it to me, Pa. I'll keep it lying down and heal it up."

"Yeah," his father said, without sarcasm and without mirth. "You could keep it lying down about one hour."

Bruce's mother came up next to him, as if the two of them were standing against the others. "Jim," she said quickly, "isn't there some kind of brace you could put on it. I remember my dad had a horse once that broke a leg below the knee, and he saved it that way."

"Not much chance," Enrich said. "Both legs, like that." He plucked a weed and stripped the dry branches from the stalk. "You can't make a horse understand he has to keep still."

"But wouldn't it be worth trying?" she said. "Children's bones heal so fast, I should think a colt's would too."

"I don't know. There's an outside chance, maybe."

"Bo," she said to her husband, "why don't we try it? It seems such a shame, a lovely colt like that."

"I know it's a shame!" he said. "I don't like shooting colts any better than you do. But I never saw a broken-legged colt get well.

It'd just be a lot of worry and trouble, and then you'd have to shoot it finally anyway."

"Please," she said. She nodded at him slightly, and then the eyes of both were on Bruce. He felt the tears coming up again, and turned to grope for the colt's ears. It tried to struggle to its feet, and Enich put his foot on its neck. The mare chuckled anxiously.

"How much this hobble brace kind of thing cost?" the father said finally. Bruce turned again, his mouth open with hope.

"Two-three dollars is all," Enich said.

"You think it's got a chance?"

"One in a thousand, maybe."

"All right. Let's go see MacDonald."

"Oh, good!" Bruce's mother said, and put her arm around him tight.

"I don't know whether it's good or not," the father said. "We might wish we never did it." To Bruce he said, "It's your responsibility. You got to take complete care of it."

"I will!" Bruce said. He took his hand out of his pocket and rubbed below his eye with his knuckles. "I'll take care of it every day."

Big with contrition and shame and gratitude and the sudden sense of immense responsibility, he watched his father and Enich start for the house to get a tape measure. When they were thirty feet away he said loudly, "Thanks, Pa. Thanks an awful lot."

His father half-turned, said something to Enich. Bruce stooped to stroke the colt, looked at his mother, started to laugh and felt it turn horribly into a sob. When he turned away so that his mother wouldn't notice he saw his dog Spot looking inquiringly around the corner of the barn. Spot took three or four tentative steps and paused, wagging his tail. Very slowly (never speak loud or move fast around an animal) the boy bent and found a good-sized stone. He straightened casually, brought his arm back, and threw with all his might. The rock caught Spot squarely in the ribs. He yiped, tucked his tail, and scuttled around the barn, and Bruce chased him, throwing clods and stones and gravel, yelling, "Get out! Go on, get out of here or I'll kick you apart. Get out! Go on!"

So all that spring, while the world dried in the sun and the willows emerged from the floodwater and the mud left by the freshet hardened and caked among their roots, and the grass of the meadow greened and the river brush grew misty with tiny leaves and the dandelions spread yellow along the flats, Bruce tended his colt. While the other boys roamed the bench hills with .22s looking for gophers or rabbits or sage hens, he anxiously superintended the colt's nursing and watched it learn to nibble the grass. While his gang built a darkly secret hideout in the deep brush beyond Hazards', he was currying and brushing and trimming the chestnut mane. When packs of boys ran hare and hounds through the town and around the river's slow bends, he perched on the front porch with his slingshot and a can full of small round stones, waiting for stray dogs to appear. He waged a holy war on the dogs until they learned to detour widely around his house, and he never did completely forgive his own dog, Spot. His whole life was wrapped up in the hobbled, leg-ironed chestnut colt with the slow-motion lunging walk and the affectionate nibbling lips.

Every week or so Enich, who was now working out of town at the Half Diamond Bar, rode in and stopped. Always, with that expressionless quiet that was terrible to the boy, he stood and looked the colt over, bent to feel pastern and fetlock, stood back to watch the plunging walk when the boy held out a handful of grass. His expression said nothing; whatever he thought was hidden back of his leathery face as the dark mole was hidden in the crease beside his mouth. Bruce found himself watching that mole sometimes, as if revelation might lie there. But when he pressed Enich to tell him, when he said, "He's getting better, isn't he? He walks better, doesn't he, Mr. Enich? His ankles don't bend so much, do they?" the wrangler gave him little encouragement.

"Let him be a while. He's growin', sure enough. Maybe give him another month."

May passed. The river was slow and clear again, and some of the boys were already swimming. School was almost over. And still Bruce paid attention to nothing but Socks. He willed so strongly that the colt should get well that he grew furious even at Daisy when she sometimes wouldn't let the colt suck as much as he wanted. He took a butcher knife and cut the long tender grass in the fence corners, where Socks could not reach, and fed it to his pet by the handful. He trained him to nuzzle for sugar-lumps in his pockets. And back in his mind was a fear: In the middle of June they would be going out to the homestead again, and if Socks weren't well by that time he might not be able to go.

"Pa," he said, a week before they planned to leave. "How much of a load are we going to have, going out to the homestead?"

"I don't know, wagonful, I suppose. Why?"

"I just wondered." He ran his fingers in a walking motion along the round edge of the dining table, and strayed into the other room. If they had a wagonload, then there was no way Socks could be loaded in and taken along. And he couldn't walk thirty miles. He'd get left behind before they got up on the bench, hobbling along like the little crippled boy in the Pied Piper, and they'd look back and see him trying to run, trying to keep up.

That picture was so painful that he cried over it in bed that night. But in the morning he dared to ask his father if they couldn't take Socks along to the farm. His father turned on him eyes as sober as Jim Enich's, and when he spoke it was with a kind of tired impatience. "How can he go? He couldn't walk it."

"But I want him to go, Pa!"

"Bruce," his mother said, "don't get your hopes up. You know we'd do it if we could, if it was possible."

"But, Ma . . ."

His father said, "What you want us to do, haul a broken-legged colt thirty miles?"

"He'd be well by the end of the summer, and he could walk back."

"Look," his father said. "Why can't you make up your mind to it? He isn't getting well. He isn't going to get well."

"He is too getting well!" Bruce shouted. He half stood up at the table, and his father looked at his mother and shrugged.

"Please, Bo," she said.

"Well, he's got to make up his mind to it sometime," he said.

Jim Enich's wagon pulled up on Saturday morning, and Bruce was out the door before his father could rise from his chair. "Hi, Mr. Enich," he said.

"Hello, Bub. How's your pony?"

"He's fine," Bruce said. "I think he's got a lot better since you saw him last."

"Uh-huh." Enrich wrapped the lines around the whipstock and climbed down. "Tell me you're leaving next week."

"Yes," Bruce said. "Socks is in the back."

When they got into the back yard Bruce's father was there with his hands behind his back, studying the colt as it hobbled around. He looked at Enich. "What do you think?" he said. "The kid here thinks his colt can walk out to the homestead."

"Uh-huh," Enich said. "Well, I wouldn't say that." He inspected the chestnut, scratched between his ears. Socks bobbed, and snuffed at his pockets. "Kid's made quite a pet of him."

Bruce's father grunted. "That's just the damned trouble."

"I didn't think he could walk out," Bruce said. "I thought we could take him in the wagon, and then he'd be well enough to walk back in the fall."

"Uh," Enich said. "Let's take his braces off for a minute."

He unbuckled the triple straps on each leg, pulled the braces off, and stood back. The colt stood almost as flat on his fetlocks as he had the morning he was born. Even Bruce, watching with his whole mind tight and apprehensive, could see that. Enich shook his head.

"You see, Bruce?" his father said. "It's too bad, but he isn't getting better. You'll have to make up your mind. . . ."

"He will get better though!" Bruce said. "It just takes a long time is all." He looked at his father's face, at Enich's, and neither one had any hope in it. But when Bruce opened his mouth to say something else his father's eyebrows drew down in sudden, uncontrollable anger, and his hand made an impatient sawing motion in the air.

"We shouldn't have tried this in the first place," he said. "It just tangles everything up." He patted his coat pockets, felt in his vest. "Run in and get me a couple cigars."

Bruce hesitated, his eyes on Enich. "Run!" his father said harshly.

Reluctantly he released the colt's halter rope and started for the house. At the door he looked back, and his father and Enich were talking together, so low that their words didn't carry to where he stood. He saw his father shake his head, and Enich bend to pluck a grass stem. They were both against him; they were both sure Socks would never get well. Well, he would! There was some way.

He found the cigars, came out, watched them both light up. Disappointment was a sickness in him, and mixed with the disappointment was a question. When he could stand their silence no more, he burst out with it. "But what are we going to do? He's got to have some place to stay."

"Look, kiddo." His father sat down on a sawhorse and took him by the arm. His face was serious and his voice gentle. "We can't take him out there. He isn't well enough to walk, and we can't haul him. So Jim here has offered to buy him. He'll give you three dollars for him, and when you come back, if you want, you might be able to buy him back. That is, if he's well. It'll be better to leave him with Jim."

"Well . . ." Bruce studied the mole on Enich's cheek. "Can you get him better by fall, Mr. Enich?"

"I wouldn't expect it," Enich said. "He ain't got much of a show."

"If anybody can get him better, Jim can," his father said. "How's that deal sound to you?"

"Maybe when I come back he'll be all off his braces and running around like a house afire," Bruce said. "Maybe next time I see him I can ride him." The mole disappeared as Enich tongued his cigar.

"Well, all right then," Bruce said, bothered by their stony-eyed silence. "But I sure hate to leave you behind, Socks, old boy."

"It's the best way all around," his father said. He talked fast, as if he were in a hurry. "Can you take him along now?"

"Oh, gee!" Bruce said. "Today?"

"Come on," his father said. "Let's get it over with."

Bruce stood by while they trussed the colt and hoisted him into the wagon box, and when Jim climbed in he cried out, "Hey, we forgot to put his hobbles back on." Jim and his father looked at each other. His father shrugged. "All right," he said, and started putting the braces back on the trussed front legs. "He might hurt himself if they weren't on," Bruce said. He leaned over the endgate, stroking the white blazed face, and as the wagon pulled away he stood with tears in his eyes and the three dollars in his hand, watching the terrified straining of the colt's neck, the bony head raised above the endgate and one white eye rolling.

Five days later, in the sun-slanting dew-wet spring morning, they stood for the last time that summer on the front porch, the loaded wagon against the front fence. The father tossed the key in his hand and kicked the doorjamb. "Well, good-bye, Old Paint," he said. "See you in the fall."

As they went to the wagon Bruce sang loudly,

> Good-bye, Old Paint, I'm leavin' Cheyenne,
> I'm leavin' Cheyenne, I'm goin' to Montana,
> Good-bye, Old Paint, I'm leavin' Cheyenne.

"Turn it off," his father said. "You want to wake up the whole town?" He boosted Bruce into the back end, where he squirmed and wiggled his way neck-deep into the luggage. His mother, turning to see how he was settled, laughed at him. "You look like a baby owl in a nest," she said.

His father turned and winked at him. "Open your mouth and I'll drop in a mouse."

It was good to be leaving; the thought of the homestead was exciting. If he could have taken Socks along it would have been perfect, but he had to admit, looking around at the jammed wagon box, that there sure wasn't any room for him. He continued to sing softly as they rocked out into the road and turned east toward MacKenna's house, where they were leaving the keys.

At the low, slough-like spot that had become the town's dump ground the road split, leaving the dump like an island in the middle. The boy sniffed at the old familiar smells of rust and tar paper and ashes and refuse. He had collected at lot of old iron and tea lead and bottles and broken machinery and clocks, and once a perfectly good amber-headed cane, in that old dump ground. His father turned up the right fork, and as they passed the central part of the dump the wind, coming in from the northeast, brought a rotten, unbearable stench across them.

"Pee-you!" his mother said, and held her nose. Bruce echoed her. "Pee-you! Pee-you-willy!" He clamped his nose shut and pretended to fall dead.

"Guess I better get to windward of that coming back," said his father.

They woke MacKenna up and left the key and started back. The things they passed were sharp and clear to the boy. He was seeing them for the last time all summer. He noticed things he had never noticed so clearly before: how the hills came down into the river from the north like three folds in a blanket, how the stovepipe on the Chinaman's shack east of town had a little conical hat on it. He chanted at the things he saw. "Good-bye, old Chinaman. Good-bye, old Frenchman River. Good-bye, old Dumpground, good-bye."

"Hold your noses," his father said. He eased the wagon into the other fork around the dump. "Somebody sure dumped something rotten."

He stared ahead, bending a little, and Bruce heard him swear. He slapped the reins on the team till they trotted. "What?"

the mother said. Bruce, half rising to see what caused the speed, saw her lips go flat over her teeth, and a look on her face like the woman he had seen in the traveling dentist's chair, when the dentist dug a living nerve out of her tooth and then got down on his knees to hunt for it, and she sat there half-raised in her seat, her face lifted.

"For gosh sakes," he said. And then he saw.

He screamed at them. "Ma, it's Socks! Stop, Pa! It's Socks!"

His father drove grimly ahead, not turning, not speaking, and his mother shook her head without looking around. He screamed again, but neither of them turned. And when he dug down into the load, burrowing in and shaking with long smothered sobs, they still said nothing.

So they left town, and as they wound up the dugway to the south bench there was not a word among them except his father's low, "For Christ sakes, I thought he was going to take it out of town." None of them looked back at the view they had always admired, the flat river bottom green with spring, its village snuggled in the loops of river. Bruce's eyes, pressed against the coats and blankets under him until his sight was a red haze, could still see through it the bloated, skinned body of the colt, the chestnut hair left a little way above the hooves, the iron braces still on the broken front legs.

The Honk-Honk Breed

STEWART EDWARD WHITE

*H*is first was The Westerners in 1901. In Speaking for Myself, 1945, is a page which starts: "Other Books by Stewart Edward White" and proceeds to list them, fifty-three of them, under such headings as: Of the Far West, Of the Far North, Of the Lumber Woods, Of California, Of Africa, and so forth. Inevitably, with such output and such range, the work is uneven. But Stewart Edward White has covered American pioneering, and particularly western phases of it, in fiction and non-fiction, more thoroughly than almost any other writer.

He is not long on short stories. Most of his fiction is in novel or novelette form. For short stories Arizona Nights, 1907, which includes A Corner in Horses and The Two-Gun Man, two stalwart anthology perennials, is a good starting point. The present choice is from the same book. Perhaps offering it here is unfair to Mr. White. His work as a whole tends to be sober and informative. The Honk-Honk Breed may be informative in a surprising sort of way, but it is not sober.

I*T* WAS SUNDAY at the ranch. For a wonder the weather had been favourable; the windmills were all working, the bogs had dried up, the beef had lasted over, the remuda had not strayed — in short, there was nothing to do. Sang had given us a baked bread-pudding with raisins in it. We filled it in — a wash basin full of it — on top of a few incidental pounds of *chile con*, baked beans, soda biscuits, "air tights," and other delicacies. Then we adjourned with our pipes to the shady side of the blacksmith's shop where we could watch the ravens on top the adobe wall of the corral. Somebody told a story about ravens. They led to road-runners. This suggested rattlesnakes. They started Windy Bill.

"Speakin' of snakes," said Windy, "I mind when they catched the great-granddaddy of all the bullsnakes up at Lead in the Black Hills. I was only a kid then. This wasn't no such tur'ble long a snake, but he was more'n a foot thick. Looked just like a sahuaro stalk. Man name of Terwilliger Smith catched it. He named this yere bullsnake Clarence, and got it so plumb gentle it followed him everywhere. One day old P. T. Barnum come along and wanted to buy this Clarence snake — offered Terwilliger a thousand cold — but Smith wouldn't part with the snake nohow. So finally they fixed up a deal so Smith could go along with the show. They shoved Clarence in a box in the baggage car, but after a while Mr. Snake gets so lonesome he gnaws out and starts to crawl back to find his master. Just as he is half-way between the baggage car and the smoker, the couplin' give way — right on that heavy grade between Custer and Rocky Point. Well, sir, Clarence wound his head 'round one brake wheel and his tail around the other, and held that train together to the bottom of the grade. But it stretched him twenty-eight feet and they had to advertise him as a boa-constrictor."

Windy Bill's history of the faithful bullsnake aroused to reminiscence the grizzled stranger, who thereupon held forth as follows:

Well, I've see things and I've heard things, some of them ornery and some you'd love to believe, they was that gorgeous and improbable. Nat'ral history was always my hobby and sportin' events my special pleasure — and this yarn of Windy's reminds me of the only chanst I ever had to ring in business and pleasure and hobby all in one grand merry-go-around of joy. It came about like this:

One day, a few years back, I was sittin' on the beach at Santa Barbara watchin' the sky stay up, and wonderin' what to do with my year's wages, when a little squinch-eye round-face with big bow spectacles came and plumped down beside me.

"Did you ever stop to think," says he, shovin' back his hat, "that if the horse-power delivered by them waves on this beach in one single hour could be concentrated behind washin' machines, it would be enough to wash all the shirts for a city of four hundred and fifty-one thousand one hundred and thirty-six people?"

"Can't say I ever did," says I, squintin' at him sideways.

"Fact," says he, "and did it ever occur to you that if all the food a man eats in the course of a natural life could be gathered together at one time, it would fill a wagon-train twelve miles long?"

"You make me hungry," says I.

"And ain't it interestin' to reflect," he goes on, "that if all the finger-nail parin's of the human race for one year was to be collected and subjected to hydraulic pressure it would equal in size the pyramid of Cheops?"

"Look yere," says I, sittin' up, "did you ever pause to excogitate that if all the hot air you is dispensin' was to be collected together it would fill a balloon big enough to waft you and me over that Bullyvard of Palms to yonder gin mill on the corner?"

He didn't say nothin' to that — just yanked me to my feet, faced me towards the gin mill above mentioned, and exerted considerable pressure on my arm in urgin' me forward.

"You ain't so much of a dreamer, after all," thinks I. "In important matters you are plumb decisive."

We sat down at little tables, and my friend ordered a beer and a chicken sandwich.

"Chickens," says he, gazin' at the sandwich, "is a dollar apiece in this country, and plumb scarce. Did you ever pause to ponder over the returns chickens would give on a small investment? Say you start with ten hens. Each hatches out thirteen aigs, of which allow a loss of say six for childish accidents. At the end of the year you has eighty chickens. At the end of two years that flock has increased to six hundred and twenty. At the end of the third year — "

He had the medicine tongue! Ten days later him and me was occupyin' of an old ranch fifty miles from anywhere. When they run stage-coaches this joint used to be a road-house. The outlook was on about a thousand little brown foothills. A road two miles four rods two foot eleven inches in sight run by in front of us. It come over one foothill and disappeared over another. I know just how long it was, for later in the game I measured it.

Out back was about a hundred little wire chicken corrals filled with chickens. We had two kinds. That was the doin's of Tuscarora. My pardner called himself Tuscarora Maxillary. I asked him once if that was his real name.

"It's the realest little old name you ever heard tell of," says he. "I know, for I made it myself — liked the sound of her. Parents ain't got no rights to name their children. Parents don't have to be called them names."

Well, these chickens, as I said, was of two kinds. The first was these low-set, heavy-weight propositions with feathers on their laigs, and not much laigs at that, called Cochin Chinys. The other was a tall ridiculous outfit made up entire of bulgin' breast and gangle laigs. They stood about two foot and a half tall, and when they went to peck the ground their tail feathers stuck straight up to the sky. Tusky called 'em Japanese Games.

"Which the chief advantage of them chickens is," says he, "that in weight about ninety per cent of 'em is breast meat. Now my idee is, that if we can cross 'em with these Cochin Chiny fowls we'll have a low-hung, heavy-weight chicken runnin' strong on breast meat. These Jap Games is too small, but if we can bring 'em up in size and shorten their laigs, we'll shore have a winner."

That looked good to me, so we started in on that idee. The theery was bully, but she didn't work out. The first broods we hatched growed up with big husky Cochin Chiny bodies and little short necks, perched up on laigs three foot long. Them chickens couldn't reach ground nohow. We had to build a table for 'em to eat off, and when they went out rustlin' for themselves they had to confine themselves to sidehills or flyin' insects. Their breasts was all right, though — "And think of them drumsticks for the boardin' house trade!" says Tusky.

So far things wasn't so bad. We had a good grubstake. Tusky and me used to feed them chickens twict a day, and then used to set around watchin' the playful critters chase grasshoppers up an' down the wire corrals, while Tusky figgered out what'd happen if somebody was dumfool enough to gather up somethin' and fix it in baskets or wagons or such. That was where we showed our ignorance of chickens.

One day in the spring I hitched up, rustled a dozen of the youngsters into coops, and druv over to the railroad to make our first sale. I couldn't fold them chickens up into them coops at first, but then I stuck the coops up on aidge and they worked all right, though I will admit they was a comical sight. At the railroad one of them towerist trains had just slowed down to a halt as I come up, and the towerists was paradin' up and down allowin' they was particular enjoyin' of the warm Californy sunshine. One old terrapin, with grey chin whiskers, projected over, with his wife, and took a peek through the slats of my coop. He straightened up like someone had touched him off with a red-hot poker.

"Stranger," said he, in a scared kind of whisper, "what's them?"

"Them's chickens," says I.

He took another long look.

"Marthy," says he to the old woman, "this will be about all! We come out from Ioway to see the Wonders of Californy, but I can't go nothin' stronger than this. If these is chickens, I don't want to see no Big Trees."

Well, I sold them chickens all right for a dollar and two bits, which was better than I expected, and got an order for more. About ten days later I got a letter from the commission house.

"We are returnin' a sample of your Arts and Crafts chickens with the lovin' marks of the teeth still onto him," says they. "Don't send any more till they stops pursuin' of the nimble grasshopper. Dentist bill will foller."

With the letter came the remains of one of the chickens. Tusky and I, very indignant, cooked her for supper. She was tough, all right. We thought she might do better biled, so we put her in the pot over night. Nary bit. Well, then we got interested. Tusky kep' the fire goin' and I rustled greasewood. We cooked her three days and three nights. At the end of that time she was sort of pale and frazzled, but still givin' points to three-year-old jerky on cohesion and other uncompromisin' forces of Nature. We buried her then, and went out back to recuperate.

There we could gaze on the smilin' landscape, dotted by about four hundred long-laigged chickens swoopin' here and there after grasshoppers.

"We got to stop that," says I.

"We can't," murmured Tusky, inspired. "We can't. It's born in 'em; it's a primal instinct, like the love of a mother for her young, and it can't be eradicated! Them chickens is constructed by a divine province for the express purpose of chasin' grasshoppers, jest as the beaver is made for buildin' dams, and the cowpuncher is made for whisky and faro-games. We can't keep 'em from it. If we was to shut 'em in a dark cellar, they'd flop after imaginary grasshoppers in their dreams, and die emaciated in the midst of plenty. Jimmy, we're up agin the Cosmos, the oversoul —" Oh, he had the medicine tongue, Tusky had, and risin' on the wings of eloquence that way, he had me faded in ten minutes. In fifteen I was wedded solid to the notion that the bottom had dropped out of the chicken business. I think now that if we'd shut them hens up, we might have — still, I don't know; they was a good deal in what Tusky said.

"Tuscarora Maxillary," says I, "did you ever stop to entertain that beautiful thought that if all the dumfoolishness possessed now by the human race could be gathered together, and lined up alongside of us, the first feller to come along would say to it 'Why, hello, Solomon!' "

We quit the notion of chickens for profit right then and there, but we couldn't quit the place. We hadn't much money, for one thing, and then we kind of liked loafin' around and raisin' a little garden truck, and — oh, well, I might as well say so, we had a notion about placers in the dry wash back of the house — you know how it is. So we stayed on, and kept a-raisin' these long-laigs for the fun of it. I used to like to watch 'em projectin' around, and I fed 'em twic't a day about as usual.

So Tusky and I lived alone there together, happy as ducks in Arizona. About onc't in a month somebody'd pike along the road. She wasn't much of a road, generally more chuck-holes than bumps, though sometimes it was the other way around. Unless it happened to be a man horseback or maybe a freighter without the fear of God in his soul, we didn't have no words with them; they was too busy cussin' the highways and generally too mad for social discourses.

One day early in the year, when the 'dobe mud made ruts to add to the bumps, one of these automobeels went past. It was the first Tusky and me had seen in them parts, so we run out to view her. Owin' to the high spots on the road, she looked like one of these movin' picters, as to blur and wobble; sounded like a cyclone mingled with cuss-words, and smelt like hell on housecleanin' day.

"Which them folks don't seem to be enjoyin' of the scenery," says I to Tusky. "Do you reckon that there blue trail is smoke from the machine or remarks from the inhabitants thereof?"

Tusky raised his head and sniffed long and inquirin'.

"It's langwidge," says he. "Did you ever stop to think that all the words in the dictionary hitched end to end would reach — "

But at that minute I catched sight of somethin' brass lyin' in the road. It proved to be a curled-up sort of horn with a rubber bulb on the end. I squoze the bulb and jumped twenty foot over the remark she made.

"Jarred off the machine," says Tusky.

"Oh, did it?" says I, my nerves still wrong. "I thought maybe it had growed up from the soil like a toadstool."

About this time we abolished the wire chicken corrals, because we needed some of the wire. Them long-laigs thereupon scattered all over the flat searchin' out their prey. When feed time come I had to screech my lungs out gettin' of 'em in, and then sometimes they didn't all hear. It was plumb discouragin', and I mighty nigh made up my mind to quit 'em, but they had come to be sort of pets, and I hated to turn 'em down. It used to tickle Tusky almost to death to see me out there hollerin' away like an old bull-frog. He used to come out reg'lar, with his pipe lit, just to enjoy me. Finally I got mad and opened up on him.

"Oh," he explains, "it just plumb amuses me to see the dumfool at his childish work. Why don't you teach 'em to come to that brass horn, and save your voice?"

"Tusky," says I, with feelin', "sometimes you do seem to get a glimmer of real sense."

Well, first off them chickens used to throw back-sommersets over that horn. You have no idea how slow chickens is to learn things. I could tell you things about chickens — say, this yere bluff about roosters bein' gallant is all wrong. I've watched 'em. When one finds a nice feed he gobbles it so fast that the pieces foller down his throat like yearlin's through a hole in the fence. It's only when he scratches up a measly one-grain quick-lunch that he calls up the hens and stands noble and self-sacrificin' to one side. That ain't the point, which is, that after two months I had them long-laigs so they'd drop everythin' and come kitin' at the honk-honk of that horn. It was a purty sight to see 'em, sailin' in from all directions twenty foot at a stride. I was proud of em, and named 'em the Honk-honk Breed. We didn't have no others, for by now the coyotes and bob-cats had nailed the straight-breds. There wasn't no wild cat or coyote could catch one of my Honk-honks, no, sir!

We made a little on our placer — just enough to keep interested. Then the supervisors decided to fix our road, and what's more, *they done it!* That's the only part in this yarn that's hard to believe, but, boys, you'll have to take it on faith. They ploughed her, and crowned her, and scraped her and rolled her, and when they moved on we had the fanciest highway in the State of Californy.

That noon — the day they called her a job — Tusky and I sat smokin' our pipes as per usual, when way over the foothills we seen a cloud of dust and faint to our ears was bore a whizzin' sound. The chickens was gathered under the cottonwood for the heat of the day, but they didn't pay no attention. Then faint, but clear, we heard another of them brass horns:

"Honk! honk!" it says, and every one of them chickens woke up, and stood at attention.

"Honk! honk!" it hollered clearer and nearer. Then over the hill come an automobeel, blowin' vigorous at every jump.

"My God!" I yells to Tusky, kickin' over my chair, as I springs to my feet. "Stop 'em! Stop 'em!"

But it was too late. Out the gate sprinted them poor devoted chickens, and up the road they trailed in vain pursuit. The last we seen of 'em was a minglin' of dust and dim figgers goin' thirty mile an hour after a disappearin' automobeel.

That was all we seen for the moment. About three o'clock the first straggler came limpin' in, his wings hangin', his mouth open, his eyes glazed with the heat. By sundown fourteen had returned. All the rest had disappeared utter; we never seen 'em again. I reckon they just naturally run themselves into a sunstroke and died on the road.

It takes a long time to learn a chicken a thing, but a heap longer to unlearn him. After that two or three of these yere automobeeles went by every day, all a-blowin' of their horns, all kickin' up a hell of a dust. And every time them fourteen Honk-honks of mine took along after 'em, just as I'd taught 'em to do, layin' to get to their corn when they caught up. No more of 'em died, but that fourteen did get into elegant trainin'. After a while they got plumb to enjoyin' it. When you come right down to it, a chicken don't have many amusements and relaxations in this life. Searchin' for worms, chasin' grasshoppers, and wallerin' in the dust is about the limits of joys for chickens.

It was sure a fine sight to see 'em after they got well into the game. About nine o'clock every mornin' they would saunter down to the rise of the road where they would wait patient until a machine came along. Then it would warm your heart to see the enthusiasm of them. With exultant cackles of joy they'd trail in, reachin' out like quarter-horses, their wings half spread out, their eyes beamin' with delight. At the lower turn they'd quit. Then, after talkin' it over excited-like for a few minutes, they'd calm down and wait for another.

After a few months of this sort of trainin' they got purty good at it. I had one two-year-old rooster that made fifty-four mile an hour behind one of these sixty-horsepower Panhandles. When cars didn't come along often enough, they'd all turn out and chase jack-rabbits. They wasn't much fun at that. After a short, brief sprint the rabbit would crouch down plumb terrified, while the Honk-honks pulled off triumphal dances around his shrinkin' form.

Our ranch got to be purty well known them days among automobeelists. The strength of their cars was horse-power, of course, but the speed of them they got to ratin' by chicken-power. Some of them used to come way up from Los Angeles just to try out a new car along our road with the Honk-honks for pace-makers. We charged them a little somethin', and then, too, we opened up the road-house and the bar, so we did purty well. It wasn't necessary to work any longer at the bogus placer. Evenin's we sat around outside and swapped yarns, and I bragged on my chickens. The chickens would gather round close to listen. They liked to hear their praises sung, all right. You bet they sabe! The only reason a chicken, or any other critter, isn't intelligent is because he hasn't no chance to expand.

Why, we used to run races with 'em. Some of us would hold two or more chickens back of a chalk line, and the starter'd blow the horn from a hundred yards to a mile away, dependin' on whether it was a sprint or for distance. We had pools on the results, gave odds, made books, and kept records. After the thing got knowed we made money hand over fist.

The stranger broke off abruptly and began to roll a cigarette.

"What did you quit it for, then?" ventured Charley, out of the hushed silence.

"Pride," replied the stranger solemnly. "Haughtiness of spirit."

"How so?" urged Charley, after a pause.

"Them chickens," continued the stranger, after a moment, "stood around listenin' to me a-braggin' of what superior fowls they was until they got all puffed up. They wouldn't have nothin' whatever to do with the ordinary chickens we brought in for eatin' purposes, but stood around lookin' bored when there wasn't no sport doin'. They got to be just like that Four Hundred you read

about in the papers. It was one continual round of grasshopper
balls, race meets, and afternoon hen-parties. They got idle and
haughty, just like folks. Then come race suicide. They got to
feelin' so aristocratic the hens wouldn't have no eggs."

Nobody dared say a word.

"Windy Bill's snake — " began the narrator genially.

"Stranger," broke in Windy Bill, with great emphasis, "as to that
snake, I want you to understand this: yereafter in my estimation
that snake is nothin' but an ornery angle-worm!"

At the Sign of the Last Chance

OWEN WISTER

*T*he Virginian first came off the presses in April of 1902 and by January of 1903 it had already been reprinted sixteen times — and for more than half a century now hundreds of people have been regularly rewriting it. They have been working a rich vein, so rich that usually they have taken nothing more than single incidents or episodes and blown them into full-length novels. The material, fresh and clean when Wister used it, is shopworn now and the taint of the shoddy imitations clings to it. No matter. The Virginian's place is secure. For ever-recruited faithful, it is the western novel. And, after all, it is not the best Owen Wister.

Lin McLean is the best — as Wister created him and as Remington pictured him. Is Lin a novel or simply a series of connected stories? Again no matter. It is a book to delight the judicious — the West of the western story, at once rollicking and grim, caught by an able easterner, a Harvard man and a trained writer, who went west with wide-open eyes and mind and realized that then, and there, his education was really just beginning.

The short stories come close behind, those of Red Men and White, 1896, Members of the Family, 1911, and When West Was West, 1928. They withstand the years with a timeless vitality. One pleasant thing about them is that the same characters sometimes wander from one story to another, characters like the unquenchable Scipio le Moyne and the unforgettable Specimen Jones and the undefeatable Colonel Steptoe McDee, characters who become old friends, truly members of the family. The finest stories are probably those about the Army and Indian agencies, but they are too long for reprinting here. This one will do for a start on the real Wister trail.

And it is a start that is also an appropriate ending for this book. It is the last story in Wister's last collection of stories, When West Was West. And it compresses into one quietly moving evening "At the Sign of the Last Chance" the full authentic flavor of one typical section of the old West and is the perfect epitaph of its passing.

MORE FAMILIAR FACES than I had hoped to see were there when I came in after leaving my horse at the stable. Would I eat anything? Henry asked. Not until breakfast, I said. I had supped at Lost Soldier. Would I join the game? Not tonight; but would they mind if I sat and watched them till I felt sleepy? It was too early to go to bed. And sitting here again seemed very natural.

"Does it, now?" said Stirling. "You look kind of natural yourself."

"Glad I do. It must be five years since last time."

"Six," said James Work. "But I would have known you anywhere."

"What sort of a meal did he set for you?" Marshal inquired.

"At Lost Soldier? Fried beef, biscuits, coffee, and excellent onions."

"Old onions of course?" said Henry. "Cooked?"

"No. Fresh from his garden. Young ones."

"So he's got a garden still!" mused Henry.

"Who's running Lost Soldier these days?" inquired Stirling.

"That oldest half-breed son of Toothpick Kid," said Marshal. "Any folks to supper with you?"

"Why, yes. Six or seven. Bound for the new oil-fields on Red Spider."

"Travel is brisk down in that valley," said Work.

"I didn't know the stage had stopped running through here," said I.

"Didn't you? Why, that's a matter of years now. There's no oil up this way. In fact, there's nothing up this way any more."

They had made room for me, they had included me in their

company. Only two others were not in the game. One sat in the back of the room, leaning over something that he was reading, never looking up from it. He was the only one I had not seen before, but he was at home quite evidently. Except when he turned a page, which might have been once every five minutes, he hardly made a movement. He was a rough fellow, wearing the beard of another day; and if reading was a habit with him it was a slow process, and his lips moved in silent pronunciation of each syllable as it came.

Jed Goodland sat off by the kitchen door with his fiddle. Now and then he lightly picked or bowed some fragment of tune, like a man whispering memories to himself.

The others, save one or two that were clean-shaven, also wore the mustaches or the beards of a day that was done.

I had begun to see those beards long before they were gray; when no wire fence mutilated the freedom of the range; when fourteen mess-wagons would be at the spring round-up; when cattle wandered and pastured, dotting the endless wilderness; when roping them brought the college graduate and the boy who had never learned to read into a lusty equality of youth and skill; when songs rose by the camp-fire; and the dim form of the night herder leaned on his saddle horn as under the stars he circled slowly around the recumbent thousands; when two hundred miles stretched between all this and the whistle of the nearest locomotive.

And all this was over. It had begun to end a long while ago. It had ebbed away slowly from these now playing their nightly game as they had once played it at flood-tide. The turn of the tide had come even when the beards were still brown, or red, or golden.

The decline of their day began possibly with the first wire fence; the great ranch life was hastened to its death by the winter snows of 1886; received its mortal stroke in the rustler war of 1892; breathed its last — no, it was still breathing, it had not wholly given up the ghost. Cattlemen and sheepmen, the newcomers, were at deeds of violence with each other. And here in this place, at the poker table, the ghost still clung to the world of the sagebrush, where it had lived its headlong joys.

I watched the graybeards going on with this game that had outlived many a player, had often paused during bloodshed, and resumed as often, no matter who had been carried out. They played without zest, winning or losing little, with now and then a friendly word to me.

They had learned to tolerate me when I had come among them first; not because I ever grew skilled in what they did, either in the saddle or with a gun, but because they knew that I liked them and the life they led, and always had come back to lead it with them, in my tenderfoot way.

Did they often think of their vanished prosperity? Or did they try to forget that, and had they succeeded? Something in them seemed quenched — but they were all in their fifties now; they had been in their twenties when I knew them first.

My first sight of James Work was on a night at the Cheyenne Club. He sat at the head of a dinner-table with some twenty men as his guests. They drank champagne and they sang. Work's cattle in those days earned him twenty per cent. Had he not overstayed his market in the fatal years, he could be giving dinners still. As with him, so with the others in that mild poker game.

Fortune, after romping with them, had romped off somewhere else. What filled their hours, what filled their minds, in these days of emptiness?

So I sat and watched them. How many times had I arrived for the night and done so? They drank very little. They spoke very little. They had been so used to each other for so long! I had seen that pile of newspapers and magazines where the man was reading grow and spread and litter the back of the room since I was twenty.

It was a joke that Henry never could bring himself to throw anything away.

"I suppose," I said to him now, as I pointed to the dusty accumulation, "that would be up to the ceiling if you didn't light your stove every winter with some of it."

Henry nodded and chuckled as he picked up his hand.

The man reading at the back of the room lifted his magazine. "This is October, 1885," he said, holding the shabby cover towards us.

"Find any startling news, Gilbert?"

"Why, there's a pretty good thing," said the man. "Did you know sign-boards have been used hundreds and hundreds of years? 'Way back of Columbus."

"I don't think I have ever thought about them," said Henry.

"Come to think about it," said James Work, "sign-boards must have started whenever hotels and saloons started, or whatever they called such places at first."

"It goes away back," said the reader. "It's a good piece."

"Come to think about it," said James Work, "men must have traveled before they had houses; and after they had houses travel must have started public houses, and that would start sign-boards."

"That's so," said Henry.

A third player spoke to the reader. "Travel must have started red-light houses. Does he mention them, Gilbert?"

"He wouldn't do that, Marshal, not in a magazine he wouldn't," said James Work.

"He oughtn't," said Henry. "Such things should not be printed."

"Well, I guess it was cities started them, not travel," surmised Marshal. "I wonder whose idea the red light was."

"They had sign-boards in Ancient Rome," answered the man at the back of the room.

"Think of that!" said Henry.

"Might have been one of them emperors started the red light," said Marshal, "same as gladiators."

The game went on, always listless. Habit was strong, and what else was there to do?

"October, 1885," said Marshal. "That was when Toothpick Kid pulled his gun on Doc Barker and persuaded him to be a dentist."

"Not 1885," said James Work. "That was 1886."

"October, 1885," insisted Marshal. "That railroad came to Douglas the next year."

"He's got it correct, Jim," said Henry.

"Where is Toothpick Kid nowadays?" I inquired.

"Pulled his freight for Alaska. Not heard from since 1905. She's taken up with Duke Gardiner's brother, the Kid's woman has," said Henry.

"The Kid wanted Barker to fix his teeth same as Duke Gardiner had his," said Work.

"I don't think I've seen Duke Gardiner since '91," said I.

"When last heard from," said Henry, "Duke was running a joint in El Paso."

"There's a name for you!" exclaimed the man at the back of the room. " 'Goat and Compasses'! They had that on a sign-board in England. Well, and would you ever guess what it started from! 'God encompasseth us'!"

"Think of that!" said Henry.

"Does it say," asked Work, "if they had any double signs like Henry's here?"

"Not so far, it doesn't. If I strike any, I'll tell you."

That double sign of Henry's, hanging outside now in the dark of the silent town, told its own tale of the old life in its brief way. From Montana to Texas, I had seen them. Does anybody know when the first one was imagined and painted?

A great deal of frontier life is told by the four laconic words. They were to be found at the edges of those towns which rose overnight in the midst of nowhere, sang and danced and shot for a while, and then sank into silence. As the rider from his round-up or his mine rode into town with full pockets, he read "First Chance"; in the morning as he rode out with pockets empty, he read "Last Chance." More of the frontier life could hardly be told in four words. They were quite as revealing of the spirit of an age and people as Goat and Compasses.

That is what I thought as I sat there looking on at my old acquaintances over their listless game. It was still too early to go to bed, and what else was there to do? What a lot of old tunes Jed Goodland remembered!

"Why, where's your clock, Henry?" I asked.

Henry scratched his head. "Why," he meditated — "why, I guess it was last January."

"Did she get shot up again?"

Henry slowly shook his head. "This town is not what it was. I guess you saw the last shootin-up she got. She just quit on me one day. Yes; January. Winding of her up didn't do nothing to her. It was Lee noticed she had quit. So I didn't get a new one. Any more than I have fresh onions. Too much trouble to mend the ditch."

"Where's your Chink tonight?" I inquired. Lee was another old acquaintance; he had cooked many meals and made my bed often, season after season, when I had lodged here for the night.

"I let Lee go — let's see — I guess that must have been last April. Business is not what it used to be."

"Then you do everything yourself, now?"

"Why, yes; when there's anything to do."

"Boys don't seem as lively as they used to be," said Work.

"There are no boys," said Henry. "Just people."

This is what Henry had to say. It was said by the bullet holes in the wall, landmarks patterning the shape of the clock which had hung there till it stopped going last January. It was said by the empty shelves beneath the clock and behind the bar. It was said by the empty bottles which Henry had not yet thrown out. These occupied half one shelf. Two or three full bottles stood in the middle of the lowest shelf, looking lonely. In one of them the cork had been drawn, and could be pulled out by the fingers again, should anyone call for a drink.

"It was Buck Seabrook shot up your clock last time, wasn't it, Henry?" asked Marshal. "You knew Buck?" he said to me; and I nodded.

"Same night as that young puncher got the letter he'd been asking for every mail day," said Work.

"Opened it in the stage office," continued Marshal, "drew his gun and blew out his brains right there. I guess you heard about him?" he said to me again, and I nodded.

"No," Henry corrected. "Not there." He pointed at the ceiling. "Upstairs. He was sleeping in number four. He left no directions."

"I liked that kid," said Stirling, who had been silent. "Nice, quiet, well-behaved kid. A good roper."

"Anybody know what was in the letter?" asked Work.

"It was from a girl," said Henry. "I thought maybe there would be something in it demanding action. There was nothing beyond the action he had taken. I put it inside his shirt with him. Nobody saw it but me."

"What would you call that for a name?" said the reader at the back of the room. " 'Goose and Gridiron.' "

"I'd call that good," said Work.

"It would sound good to a hungry traveler," said Stirling.

"Any more of them?" asked Henry.

"Rafts of them. I'll tell you the next good one."

"Yes, tell us. And tell us when and where they all started, if it says." In the silence of the cards, a door shut somewhere along the dark street.

"That's Old Man Clarke," said Henry.

"First time I ever heard of him in town," said I.

"We made him come in. Old Man Clarke is getting turrible shaky. He wouldn't accept a room. So he sleeps in the old stage office and cooks for himself. If you put him in New York he'd stay a hermit all the same."

"How old is he?"

"Nobody knows. He looked about as old as he does now when

I took this hotel. That was 1887. But we don't want him to live alone up that canyon any more. He rides up to his mine now and then. Won't let anybody go along. Says the secret will die with him. Hello, Jed. Let's have the whole of 'Buffalo Girls.'" And Jed Goodland played the old quadrille music through.

"You used to hear that pretty often, I guess," said Henry to me; and I nodded.

Scraping steps shambled slowly by in the sand. We listened.

"He doesn't seem to be coming in," I said.

"He may. He will if he feels like it, and he won't if he feels like not."

"He had to let me help him onto his horse the other day," said Marshal. "But he's more limber some days than others."

Presently the scraping steps came again, passed the door, and grew distant.

"Yes," said Work. "Old Man Clarke is sure getting feeble."

"Did you say it was Buck Seabrook shot your clock the last time?"

"Yes. Buck."

"If I remember correct," pursued Stirling, "it wasn't Buck did it, it was that joker his horse bucked off that same afternoon down by the corral."

"That Hat Six wrangler?"

"Yes. Horse bucked him off. He went up so high the fashions had changed when he came down."

"So it was, George." And he chuckled over the memory.

"Where does Old Man Clarke walk to?" I asked; for the steps came scraping along again.

"Just around and around," said Henry. "He always would do things his own way. You can't change him. He has taken to talking to himself this year."

The door opened, and he looked in. "Hello, boys," said he.

"Hello yourself, Uncle Jerry," said Work. "Have a chair. Have a drink."

"Well, maybe I'll think it over." He shut the door, and the steps went shambling away.

"His voice sounds awful old," said Marshal. "Does he know the way his hair and beard look?"

"Buck Seabrook," mused Stirling. "I've not seen him for quite a while. Is he in the country now?"

Henry shook his head. "Buck is in no country any more."

"Well, now, I hadn't heard of it. Well, well."

"Any of you remember Chet Sharston?" asked Marshal.

"Sure," said Stirling. "Did him and Buck have any trouble?"

"No, they never had any trouble," said Henry. "Not they."

"What was that Hat Six wrangler's name?" asked Work.

"He said it was Johnson," replied Henry.

Again the shambling steps approached. This time Old Man Clarke came in, and Henry invited him to join the game.

"No, boys," he said. "Thank you just the same. I'll sit over here for a while." He took a chair. "You boys just go on. Don't mind me." His pale, ancient eyes seemed to notice us less than they did the shifting pictures in his brain.

"Why don't you see the barber, Uncle Jerry?" asked Marshal.

"Nearest barber is in Casper. Maybe I'll think it over."

" 'Swan and Harp,' " said the man at the back of the room. "That's another."

"Not equal to Goat and Compasses," said Work.

"It don't make you expect a good meal like Goose and Gridiron," said Henry. "I'll trim your hair tomorrow, Uncle Jerry, if you say so."

"Boys, none that tasted her flapjacks ever wanted another cook," said Old Man Clarke.

"Well, what do you think of 'Hoop and Grapes'?"

"Nothing at all," said Henry. "Hoop and Grapes makes no appeal to me."

"You boys never knowed my wife," said Old Man Clarke in his corner. "Flapjacks. Biscuits. She was a buck-skinned son-of-a-bitch." His vague eyes swam, but the next moment his inconsequent cheerfulness returned. "Dance night, and all the girls late," he said.

"A sign-board outside a hotel or saloon," said Marshal, "should have something to do with what's done inside."

"That's so," said Henry.

"Take Last Chance and First Chance," Marshal continued. "Has England anything to beat that, I'd like to know? Did you see any to beat it?" he asked me.

"No, I never did."

"You come for fishing?" asked Old Man Clarke.

"I've brought my rod," I answered.

"No trout in this country any more," said he.

"My creek is fished out. And the elk are gone. I've not jumped a blacktail deer these three years. Where are the antelope?" He frowned; his eyes seemed to be asking questions. "But I'll get ye some meat tomorro', boys," he declared in his threadbare, cheerful voice; and then it trailed off. "All at the bottom of Lake' Champlain," he said.

"Have a drink, Uncle Jerry?" said Henry.

"Not now, and thank you just the same. Maybe I'll think it over."

"Buck Seabrook was fine to travel with," said Stirling.

"A fine upstanding cow-puncher," added Work. "Honest clean through. Never knew him to go back on his word or do a crooked action."

"Him and Chet Sharston traveled together pretty much," said Henry.

Stirling chuckled over a memory. "Chet he used to try and beat Buck's flow of conversation. Wanted to converse some himself."

"Well, Chet could."

"Oh, he could some. But never equal to Buck."

"Here's a good one," said the man at the back of the room " 'Bolt-in-Tun.' "

"How do they spell a thing like that?" demanded Marshal.

It was spelled for him.

"Well, that may make sense to an Englishman," said Henry.

"Doesn't it say where sign-boards started?" asked Work.

"Not yet." And the reader continued to pore over the syllables, which he followed slowly with moving lips.

"Buck was telling Chet," said Stirling, "of a mistake he made one night at the Southern Hotel in San Antone. Buck was going to his room fair late at night, when a man came around the corner on his floor, and quick as he seen Buck, he put his hand back to his hip pocket. Well, Buck never lost any time. So when the man took a whirl and fell in a heap Buck waited to see what he would do next. But the man didn't do anything more.

"So Buck goes to him and turns him over; and it isn't any stranger, it is a prospector Buck had met up with in Nevada; and the prospector had nothing worse than a flask in his pocket. He'd been aiming to offer Buck a drink. Buck sure felt sorry about making such a mistake, he said. And Chet, he waited, for he knowed very well that Buck hoped he would ask him what he did when he discovered the truth.

"After a while Buck couldn't wait; and so in disappointment

he says to Chet very solemn, 'I carried out the wishes of the deceased.'

" 'I was lookin' over the transom when you drank his whiskey,' says Chet.

" 'Where's your memory? You were the man,' says Buck. Well, well, weren't they a nonsensical pair!"

"I remember," said Henry. "They were sitting right there." And he pointed to a table.

"They were playing cooncan," said Marshal. "I remember that night well. Buck was always Buck. Well, well! Why, didn't Buck learn you cooncan?"

"Yes, he did," said I. "It was that same night."

"Boys," said Old Man Clarke over in the corner, "I'll get ye some fresh meat tomorro'."

"That's you, Uncle Jerry!" said Henry heartily. "You get us a nice elk, or a blacktail, and I'll grubstake you for the winter."

"She's coming," said Old Man Clarke. "Winter's coming. I'll shoot any of ye a match with my new .45-90 at a hundred yards. Hit the ace of spades, five out of five."

"Sure you can, Uncle Jerry."

"Flapjacks. Biscuits. And she could look as pretty as a bride," said Old Man Clarke.

"Wasn't it Chet," said Work, "that told Toothpick Kid Doc Barker had fixed up Duke Gardiner's teeth for him?"

"Not Chet. It was Buck told him that."

Henry appealed to me. "What's your remembrance of it?"

"Why, I always thought it was Buck," I answered.

"Buck was always Buck," said Marshal. "Well, well!"

"Who did fix Duke's teeth?"

"It was a travelling dentist. He done a good job, too, on Duke. All gold. Hit Drybone when Duke was in the hospital, but he went North in two or three days on the stage for Buffalo. That's how the play come up."

"Chet could yarn as well as Buck now and then," said Stirling.

"Not often," said Henry. "Not very often."

"Well, but he could. There was that experience Chet claimed he had down in the tornado belt."

"I remember," said Henry. "Down in Texas."

"Chet mentioned it was in Kansas."

"San Saba, Texas," said Henry.

"You're right. San Saba. So it was. Chet worked for a gambler there who wanted to be owner of a house that you could go up-stairs in."

"I didn't know Chet could deal a deck," said Marshal.

"He couldn't. Never could. He hired as a carpenter to the gambler."

"Chet was handy with tools," said Henry.

"A very neat worker. So the house was to be two stories. So Chet he said he'd help. Said he built the whole thing. Said it took him four months. Said he kep' asking the gambler for some money. The day he could open the front door of his house and walk in and sit down, the gambler told Chet, he'd pay him the total. So they walk out to it the day the job's complete and chairs ready for sitting in, and the gambler he takes hold of the door-knob and whang! a cyclone hits the house.

"The gambler saved the door-knob — didn't let go of it. Chet claimed he had fulfilled his part of the contract, but the gambler said a door-knob was not sufficient evidence that any house had been there. Wouldn't pay Chet a cent."

"They used to be a mean bunch in Texas," said Stirling.

"I was in this country before any of you boys were born," said Old Man Clarke.

"Sure you were, Uncle Jerry," said Henry. "Sure you were."

"I used to be hell and repeat."

"Sure thing, Uncle Jerry."

For a while there was little sound in the Last Chance Saloon save the light notes which Jed Goodland struck on his fiddle from time to time.

"How did that play come up, Henry?" asked Work.

"Which play?"

"Why, Doc Barker and Toothpick Kid."

"Why, wasn't you right there that day?"

"I was, but I don't seem to remember exactly how it started."

"Well," said Henry, "the Kid had to admit that Doc Barker put the kibosh on him after all. You're wrong about Buck. He didn't come into that." Henry's voice seemed to be waking up, his eyes were waking up.

"Sure he put the kibosh on him," Work agreed energetically.

"Wasn't it the day after they'd corralled that fello' up on the Dry Cheyenne?" asked Stirling.

"So it was!" said Marshal. He too was waking up. Life was coming into the talk of all. "That's where the boys corralled him."

"Well," said Stirling, "you couldn't leave a man as slick as he was, foot-loose, to go around and play such a game on the whole country."

"It was at the ranch gate Toothpick Kid saw those new gold teeth of Duke's," said Marshal.

"It wasn't a mile from the gate," said Stirling. "Not a mile. And Toothpick didn't wait to ask Duke the facts, or he'd have saved his money. Duke had happened to trail his rope over the carcasses of some stock. When he was roping a steer after that, his hand was caught between a twist of the rope and his saddle horn. So his hand got burned."

"Didn't Buck tell him he'd ought to get Doc Barker to put some stuff on it?"

"Buck did warn him, but Duke wouldn't listen. So Buck had to bring him into the Drybone hospital with an arm that they had to cut his shirt-sleeve for."

"I remember," said Henry. "Duke told me that Buck never said 'I told you so' to him."

"Buck wouldn't. If ever there was a gentleman, it was Buck Seabrook. Doc Barker slashed his arm open from shoulder to elbow. And in twenty-four hours the arm wasn't so big. But it was still pretty big, and it looked like nothing at all, and Duke's brother saw it. They had sent for him. He rode into town, and when he saw the arm and the way it had been cut by Doc Barker he figured he'd lay for Doc and kill him. Doc happened to be out at the C-Y on a case.

"The boys met him as he came back, and warned him to keep out of the way till Duke's brother got sober, so Doc kep' out of the way. No use having trouble with a drunken man. Doc would have had to shoot Duke's brother or take the consequences. Well, next day the brother sobered up, and the boys persuaded him that Doc had saved Duke's life, and he was satisfied and changed his mind and there was no further hard feelings. And he got interested in the traveling dentist who had come into town to pick up business from the boys. He did good work. The brother got a couple of teeth plugged. They kept the dentist quite busy."

"I remember," said Marshal. "Chet and Buck both had work done."

"Do you remember the grass cook-fire Buck and Chet claimed they had to cook their supper with?" asked Work, with animation. Animation was warming each one, more and more. Their faces actually seemed to be growing younger.

"Out beyond Meteetsee you mean?"

"That was it."

"What was it?" asked Marshal.

"Did they never tell you that? Buck went around telling everybody."

"Grass cook-fire?" said Old Man Clarke in his withered voice. "Nobody ever cooked with grass. Grass don't burn half a minute. Rutherford B. Hayes was President when I came into this country. But Samuel J. Tilden was elected. Yes, sir."

"Sure he was, Uncle Jerry," said Henry.

"Well, Buck and Chet had to camp one night where they found a water-hole, but no wood. No sage-brush, no buffalo-chips, nothing except the grass, which was long. So Buck he filled the coffee-pot and lighted the grass. The little flames were hot, but they burned out quick and ran on to the next grass. So Buck he ran after them holding his coffee-pot over the flames as they traveled. So he said Chet lighted some more grass and held his frying-pan over those flames and kep' a-following their trail like he was doing with the coffee-pot. He said that his coffee-pot boiled after a while and Chet's meat was fried after a while, but by that time they were ten miles apart. Walked around hunting for each other till sunrise, and ate their supper for breakfast."

"What's that toon you're playing, Jed?" inquired Stirling.

"That's 'Sandy Land'," replied the fiddler.

"Play it some more, Jed. Sounds plumb natural. Like old times."

"Yes, it does so," said Henry. "Like when the boys used to dance here."

"Dance!" said Old Man Clarke. "None of you never seen me dance."

"Better have a drink, Uncle Jerry."

"Thank you kindly. Just one. Put some water in. None of you never did, I guess."

"I'll bet you shook a fancy heel, Uncle."

"I always started with the earliest and kept going with the latest. I used to call for 'em too. Salute your partners! Opposite the same! Swing your honey! That's the style I used to be. All at the bottom of Lake Champlain. None of you ever knowed her."

"Have another, Uncle Jerry. The nights are getting cold."

"Thank you kindly. I'll have one more. Winter's coming."

"Any of you see that Wolf Dance where Toothpick wore the buckskin pants?" asked Work. "Wasn't any of you to that?"

"Somebody played it on Toothpick, didn't they?" said Stirling.

"Buck did. Buck wasn't dancing. He was just looking on. Toothpick always said Buck was mad because the Indians adopted him into the tribe and wouldn't take Buck. They gave him a squaw, y'know. He lived with her on the reservation till he left for Alaska. He got her allotment of land with her, y'know. I saw him and her and their kids when I was there. I guess there were twelve kids. Probably twenty by the time he went to Alaska. She'd most always have twins."

"Here's a name for you," said the man at the back of the room. "What have you got to say about 'Whistling Oyster'?"

"Whistling Oyster?" said Henry. "Well, if I had ever the misfortune to think of such a name I'd not have mentioned it to anybody, and I'd have tried to forget it."

"Just like them English," said Marshal.

"Did Toothpick have any novelties in the way of teeth?" asked Stirling.

"If he did, he concealed them," said Work.

"But him and Doc Barker had no hard feelings," said Henry. "They both put the mistake on Duke Gardiner and Duke said, well, they could leave it there if that made them feel happier."

"Doc was happy as he could be already."

"Well, a man would be after what came so near happening to him, and what actually did happen."

"Did you say Buck was dead?" asked Marshal.

"Dead these fifteen years," said Henry. "Didn't you hear about it? Some skunk in Texas caught Buck with his wife. Buck had no time to jump for his gun."

"Well, there are worse ways to die. Poor Buck! D'you remember how he laid right down flat on his back when they told him about Doc and the Kid's teeth? The more the Kid said any man in his place would have acted the same, the flatter Buck laid in the sage-brush."

"I remember," said Stirling. "I was cutting calves by the corral."

"Duke was able to sit up in the hospital and have the dentist work on his cavities. And the dentist edged the spaces with gold, and he cleaned all the teeth till you could notice them whenever Duke laughed. So he got well and rode out to camp and praised Doc Barker for a sure good doctor. He meant his arm of course that Doc had slashed open when they expected he was dying and sent for his brother.

"Duke never thought to speak about the dentist that had come into Drybone and gone on to Buffalo, and the Kid naturally thought it was Doc Barker who had done the job on Duke's teeth. And Buck he said nothing. So Kid drops in to the hospital next time he's in town for a spree at the hog ranch, and invites the Doc to put a gold edging on his teeth for him.

" 'Not in my line,' says Doc. 'I'm a surgeon. And I've got no instruments for such a job.'

" 'You had 'em for Duke Gardiner,' says the Kid. 'Why not for me?'

" 'That was a dentist,' says Doc, 'while I was getting Duke's arm into shape.'

"So Toothpick he goes out. He feels offended at a difference being made between him and Duke, and he sits in the hog ranch thinking it over and comforting himself with some whisky. He doesn't believe in any dentist, and about four o'clock in the afternoon he returns to Doc's office and says he insists on having the job done. And Doc he gets hot and says he's not a dentist and he orders Toothpick out of the office. And Toothpick he goes back to the hog ranch feeling awful sore at the discrimination between him and the Duke.

"Well, about two o'clock a.m. Doc wakes up with a jump, and there's Toothpick. Toothpick thumps a big wad of bills down on the bureau — he'd been saving his time for a big spree, and he had the best part of four or five months' pay in his wad — and Doc saw right away Toothpick was drunk clear through. And Toothpick jams his gun against the Doc's stomach. 'You'll fix my teeth,' he says. 'You'll fix 'em right now. I'm just as good as Duke Gardiner or any other blankety-blank hobo in this country, and my money's just as good as Duke's, and I've just as much of it, and you'll do it now.' "

"I remember, I remember," said Marshal. "That's what the Kid told Doc." He beat his fist on the table and shook with enjoyment.

"Well, of course Doc Barker put on his pants at once. Doc could always make a quick decision. He takes the Kid out where he keeps his instruments and he lights his lamp; and he brings another lamp, and he lights two candles and explains that daylight would be better, but that he'll do the best he can. And he begins rummaging among his knives and scissors which make a jingling, and Toothpick sits watching him with deeper and deeper interest. And Doc Barker he keeps rummaging, and Toothpick keeps sitting

and watching, and Doc he brings out a horrible-looking saw and
gives it a sort of a swing in the air.

"'Are you going to use that thing on me?' inquires Toothpick.

"'Open your mouth,' says Doc.

"Toothpick opens his mouth but he shuts it again. 'Duke
didn't mention it hurt him,' says he.

"'It didn't, not to speak of,' says Doc. 'How can I know how
much it will hurt you, if you don't let me see your teeth?' So
the Kid's mouth goes open and Doc takes a little microscope and
sticks it in and looks right and looks left and up and down very
slow and takes out the miscroscope. 'My, my, my,' he says, very
serious.

"'Is it going to hurt bad?' inquires Toothpick.

"'I can do it,' says Doc, 'I can do it. But I'll have to charge
for emergency and operating at night.'

"'Will it take long?' says the Kid.

"'I must have an hour, or I decline to be responsible,' says the
Doc; 'the condition is complicated. Your friend Mr. Gardiner's
teeth offered no such difficulties.' And Doc collects every instru-
ment he can lay his hands on that comes anywhere near looking
like what dentists have. 'My fee is usually two hundred dollars
for emergency night operations,' says he, 'but that is for folks in
town.'

"Toothpick brings out his wad and shoves it at Doc, and Doc he
counts it and hands back twenty dollars. 'I'll accept a hundred
and fifty,' he says, 'and I'll do my best for you.'

"By this time Toothpick's eyes are bulging away out of his
head, but he had put up too much of a play to back down from
it. 'Duke didn't mention a thing about its hurting him,' he repeats.

"'I think I can manage,' says Doc. 'You tell me right off if
the pain is too much for you. Where's my sponge?' So he gets
the sponge, and he pours some ether on it and starts sponging the
Kid's teeth.

"The Kid he's grabbing the chair till his knuckles are all white.
Doc lets the sponge come near the candle, and puff! up it flares
and Toothpick gives a jump.

"'It's nothing,' says Doc. 'But a little more, and you and I and
this room would have been blown up. That's why I am obliged
to charge double for these night emergency operations. It's the
gold edging that's the risk.'

"'I'd hate to have you take any risk,' says Toothpick. 'Will it be risky to scrape my teeth, just to give them a little scrape, y'know, like you done for Duke?'

" 'Oh, no,' says Doc, 'that will not be risky.' So Doc Barker he takes an ear cleaner and he scrapes, while Toothpick holds his mouth open and grabs the chair. 'There,' says Doc. 'Come again.' And out flies Toothpick like Indians were after him. Forgets the hog ranch and his night of joy waiting for him there, jumps on his horse and makes camp shortly after sunrise. It was that same morning Buck heard about Toothpick and Doc Barker, and laid flat down in the sage-brush."

"Buck sure played it on the Kid at that Wolf Dance," said Work. "Toothpick thought the ladies had stayed after the storm."

Again Marshal beat his fist on the table. We had become a lively company.

"On the Crow reservation, wasn't it?" said Henry.

"Right on that flat between the Agency and Fort Custer, along the river. The ladies were all there."

"She always stayed as pretty as a bride," said Old Man Clarke.

"Have another drink, Uncle Jerry."

"No more, no more, thank you just the same. I'm just a-sittin' here for a while."

"The Kid had on his buckskin and admired himself to death. Admired his own dancing. You remembered how it started to pour. Of course the Kid's buckskin pants started to shrink on him. They got up to his knees. About that same time the ladies started to go home, not having brought umbrellas, and out runs Buck into the ring. He whispers to Kid: 'Your bare legs are scandalous. Look at the ladies. Go hide yourself. I'll let you know when you can come out.'

"Away runs Kid till he finds a big wet sage brush and crawls into it deep. The sun came out pretty soon. But Toothpick sat in his wet sage brush, waiting to be told the ladies had gone. Us boys stayed till the dance was over and away runs Buck to the sage brush.

" 'My,' says he, 'I'm sorry, Kid. The ladies went two hours ago. I'll have to get Doc Barker to fix up my memory.' "

"I used to be hell and repeat," said Old Man Clarke from his chair. "Play that again. Play that quadrille," he ordered peremptorily.

The fiddler smiled and humored him. We listened. There was silence for a while.

" 'Elephant and Castle,' " said the man at the back of the room. "Near London."

"That is senseless, too," said Henry. "We have more sensible signs in this country."

Jed Goodland played the quadrille quietly, like a memory, and as they made their bets, their boots tapped the floor to its rhythm.

"Swing your duckies," said Old Man Clarke. "Cage the queen. All shake your feet. Doe se doe and a doe doe doe. Sashay back. Git away, girls, git away fast. Gents in the center and four hands around. There you go to your seats."

"Give us 'Sandy Land' again," said Stirling. And Jed played "Sandy Land."

"Doc Barker became Governor of Wyoming," said Work, "about 1890."

"What year did they abandon the stage route?" I asked.

"Later," said Henry. "We had the mail here till the Burlington road got to Sheridan."

"See here," said the man at the back of the room. "Here's something."

"Well, I hope it beats Elephant and Castle," said Henry.

"It's not a sign-board, it's an old custom," said the man.

"Well, let's have your old custom."

The man referred to his magazine. "It says," he continued, "that many a flourishing inn which had been prosperous for two or three hundred years would go down for one reason or another, till no travelers patronized it any more. It says this happened to the old places where the coaches changed horses or stopped for meals going north and south every day, and along other important routes as well. Those routes were given up after the railroads began to spread.

"The railroad finally killed the coaches. So unless an inn was in some place that continued to be important, like a town where the railroads brought strangers same as the coaches used to, why, the inn's business would dry up. And that's where the custom comes in. When some inn had outlived its time and it was known that trade had left it for good, they would take down the sign of that inn and bury it. It says that right here." He touched the page.

The quiet music of Jed Goodland ceased. He laid his fiddle in his lap. One by one, each player laid down his cards. Henry from habit turned to see the clock. The bullet holes were there, and the empty shelves. Henry looked at his watch.

"Quittin' so early?" asked Old Man Clarke. "What's your hurry?"

"Five minutes of twelve," said Henry. He went to the door and looked up at the sky.

"Cold," said Old Man Clarke. "Stars small and bright. Winter's a'coming, I tell you."

Standing at the open door, Henry looked out at the night for a while and then turned and faced his friends in their chairs round the table.

"What do you say, boys?"

Without a word they rose. The man at the back of the room had risen. Jed Goodland was standing. Still in his chair, remote and busy with his own half-dim thoughts, Old Man Clarke sat watching us almost without interest.

"Gilbert," said Henry to the man at the back of the room, "there's a ladder in the corner by the stairs. Jed, you'll find a spade in the shed outside the kitchen door."

"What's your hurry, boys?" asked Old Man Clarke. "Tomorro' I'll get ye a big elk."

But as they all passed him in silence he rose and joined them without curiosity, and followed without understanding.

The ladder was set up, and Henry mounted it and laid his hands upon the sign-board. Presently it came loose, and he handed it down to James Work who stood ready for it. It was a little large for one man to carry without awkwardness, and Marshal stepped forward and took two corners of it while Work held the others.

"You boys go first with it," said Henry. "Over there by the side of the creek. I'll walk next. Stirling, you take the spade."

Their conjured youth had fled from their faces, vanished from their voices.

"I've got the spade, Henry."

"Give it to Stirling, Jed. I'll want your fiddle along."

Moving very quietly, we followed Henry in silence, Old Man Clarke last of us, Work and Marshal leading with the sign-board between them. And presently we reached the banks of Willow Creek.

"About here," said Henry.

They laid the sign-board down, and we stood round it, while Stirling struck his spade into the earth. It did not take long.

"Jed," said Henry, "you might play now. Nothing will be said. Give us 'Sound the dead march as ye bear me along.'"

In the night, the strains of that somber melody rose and fell, always quietly, as if Jed were whispering memories with his bow.

How they must have thanked the darkness that hid their faces from each other! But the darkness could not hide sound. None of us had been prepared for what the music would instantly do to us.

Somewhere near me I heard a man struggling to keep command of himself; then he walked away with his grief alone. A neighbor followed him, shaken with emotions out of control. And so, within a brief time, before the melody had reached its first cadence, none was left by the grave except Stirling with his spade and Jed with his fiddle, each now and again sweeping a hand over his eyes quickly, in furtive shame at himself. Only one of us withstood it. Old Man Clarke, puzzled, went wandering from one neighbor to the next, saying, "Boys, what's up with ye? Who's dead?"

Although it was to the days of their youth, not mine, that they were bidding this farewell, and I had only looked on when the beards were golden and the betting was high, they counted me as one of them tonight. I felt it — and I knew it when Henry moved nearer to me and touched me lightly with his elbow.

So the sign of the Last Chance was laid in its last place, and Stirling covered it and smoothed the earth while we got hold of ourselves, and Jed Goodland played the melody more and more quietly until it sank to the lightest breath and died away.

"That's all, I guess," said Henry. "Thank you, Jed. Thank you, boys. I guess we can go home now."

Yes, now we could go home. The requiem of the golden beards, their romance, their departed West, too good to live for ever, was finished.

As we returned slowly in the stillness of the cold starlight, the voice of Old Man Clarke, shrill and withered, disembodied as an echo, startled me by its sudden outbreak.

"None of you knowed her, boys. She was a buckskin son-of-a-bitch. All at the bottom of Lake Champlain!"

"Take him, boys," said Henry. "Take Uncle Jerry to bed, please. I guess I'll stroll around for a while out here by myself. Good night, boys."

I found that I could not bid him good night, and the others seemed as little able to speak as I was. Old Man Clarke said nothing more. He followed along with us as he had come, more like some old dog, not aware of our errand nor seeming to care to know, merely contented, his dim understanding remote within himself. He needed no attention when we came to the deserted stage office where he slept. He sat down on the bed and began to pull off his boots cheerfully. As we were shutting his door, he said:

"Boys, tomorro' I'll get ye a fat bull elk."

"Good night, Jed," said Marshal.

"Good night, Gilbert," said Stirling.

"Good night, all." The company dispersed along the silent street.

As we re-entered the saloon — Work and I, who were both sleeping in the hotel — the deserted room seemed to be speaking to us, it halted us on the threshold. The cards lay on the table, the vacant chairs around it. There stood the empty bottles on the shelf. Above them were the bullet holes in the wall where the clock used to be. In the back of the room the magazine lay open on the table with a lamp burning. The other lamp stood on the bar, and one lamp hung over the card-table. Work extinguished this one, the lamp by the magazine he brought to light us to our rooms where we could see to light our bedroom lamps. We left the one on the bar for Henry.

"Jed was always handy with his fiddle," said Work at the top of the stairs. "And his skill stays by him. Well, good night."

A long while afterwards I heard a door closing below and knew that Henry had come in from his stroll.